Praise for *I Got His*

'The present and the past are allowed to inhabit the same frame, whether it's the ghost of Maud Pember Reeves pestering a council clerk or a musket-wielding time-traveller appearing on the side of State Highway 1. Our past has never felt so exciting or accessible.' —Craig Cliff, *Dominion Post*

'It has the virtues of a damned good yarn as much as of a sophisticated and finished work of literature.' —Nicholas Reid, *New Zealand Books*

'Not since Nigel Cox's *The Cowboy Dog* have I found the landscape of my own country, both the people and the physical, reflected back at me through such a strange yet recognisable lens.' —Sarah Bainbridge

'*I Got His Blood on Me* underscores the way fiction can, when infused with local history and the strangeness of thinking back across time, enable us to examine our habits of seeing, thinking and dreaming. It's the kind of time travel that keeps pace with us as readers. The only thing we risk leaving behind is who we thought we were. A fantastic read.' —Rachel O'Neill

'There's a Cormac McCarthy-esque concision to the language, and Patchett's heroes share a similar outback fortitude and silence, and a respect for the momentousness of the landscape. Economy of movement and of speech lends weight to the slightest shift in position, the quietest utterance.' —Michael Larsen, *New Zealand Herald*

'You'll go a long way before you find a collection of stories that so engage, tease, taunt, and thrill your imagination as these.' —John McCrystal, *New Zealand Listener*

'The book restores my faith in the value of the short story form.' —Mike Crowl, *Otago Daily Times*

The Burning River

Lawrence Patchett

Victoria University Press

TE WHARE WĀNANGA O TE ŪPOKO O TE IKA A MĀUI

VICTORIA
UNIVERSITY OF WELLINGTON

VICTORIA UNIVERSITY PRESS
Victoria University of Wellington
PO Box 600 Wellington
Aotearoa New Zealand
vup.victoria.ac.nz

ISBN 9781776562237

A catalogue record for this book is available from the
National Library of New Zealand.

Published with the support of a grant from

creative
nz
ARTS COUNCIL OF NEW ZEALAND *TOI AOTEAROA*

Printed in China by 1010 Printing International

for Tina
Nāu anō tēnei mea i whakaputa

One

Someone had been there. Someone strange. In the centre of his camp, a new circle of sooted rocks. A campfire, with the bones of a possum or bird, heaped up. Some intruder's late-night feast. The leavings of a sloppy thief, careless of the sign they left. Or deliberate, wanting Van to see their mess. To send a signal of some sort, a threat.

Crouching in tī kōuka and undergrowth at the edge of the clearing, Van scanned his camp for signs of ambush.

But there was no movement. Nothing at his hut or the mine face. Just gluggy waves of heat. Cicadas the only sound, and a pīwaiwaka that bounced and chirped on the afternoon air, snapping insects.

Sweating inside his headwrap, Van watched the camp a moment more, and then crept on round the clearing's edge. He was careful with his load of plastic trades, holding it clear of his body. He'd fetched back a bundle of holed canisters to repair, and they were tied together with plait and liable to clonk. As he came close to his hut he saw through the mānuka that his patching fire was untouched. His piles of donor plastic and kindling still neat, not ransacked.

Then he saw it. His hut's insect lock. It had been tampered with. Before he left each day Van hitched a sheet of skins across the door flap, then locked it in place by hooking two mānuka sticks behind the door posts with knots of plait. It wasn't a perfect protection, since there were still gaps in his walls and the roof thatch that night-biters could easily come through after dark. But it stopped them from invading through the door in clouds, at least, and gave him a chance against them— another line of defence to go with his bug oils, his scarf and headwrap, his clothing ties at ankle and wrist. But this intruder hadn't reattached it, and the door flap hung slack, showing a broken rectangle of dark inside the hut.

Still in undergrowth, he watched the ruptured door for a long time, trying to work it out. Like the campfire they'd left, it didn't make sense. If they were waiting inside, or in the surrounding scrub, to ambush him, the element of surprise was gone. And if they'd meant it as a threat, there wasn't enough to it. No violence to his hut, no accompanying picture of rough fucking or death scratched into the dirt. Perhaps they were too confident to bother with that.

His heart beating harder now—he was alone and weak from days of grief—Van eased off his bags and arranged them at his feet. Scanned again across the whole camp.

No sign. The sun pouring autumn heat.

He went further back in the trees and climbed up over the mine face and down to thinner scrub, circling his camp. A narrow pond fringed his home here, stretching away towards the Dry Way and the Scarp. This had probably been the way out for his intruders, if they'd left. Sneaking back at night to rejoin the route south, restored by that meal of possum or bird and, probably, fresh water stolen from Van's hut. Yet as he came round he discovered no scattered or broken undergrowth. No footprints he could distinguish from his own of a few days back, when he'd come this way to check his possum and slopfish traps. So they were still around, it seemed, still waiting somewhere in this scrub to leap out and oblige him to reveal the secret riches of his camp at knifepoint.

Van was thirsty and sticky with sweat but he forced himself to wait. Let them show themselves. He crouched there until the sun had dropped a finger's width down the sky and any last breeze died, and sweat ran freely inside his clothes and headwrap. Then his legs began to cramp and he wished Rau was with him. He'd be very willing to search the scrub and surrounding swamp for the intruder while Van checked the hut. Right now, Van knew, Rau was yearning for the chance to wield a blade in earnest, to work out his grief on someone else.

When the sun had dropped another half-finger's width and there was still no sign of ambush, he readied his weapons. Blade in his left hand, hardened plastic bar in his right. He counted five more breaths, then ran out into the clearing. Circled on the spot with his weapons up. 'Come on,' he said. 'Come on out.'

No sound from the scrub, no flicker of branches.

He would have to switch languages. Immediately, he felt the disadvantage—he was not strong in it. 'Haere mai,' he said, twirling the blade. 'Kei konei au.'

But still the attack didn't come. Nothing but another pīwaiwaka that flitted on the air and bounced.

Van went to the fire and toed the remnants. The ashes were clumped together; not a single ember sparkled. A well-resourced thief, this one, willing to waste a water bag by dousing a fire like that.

He went on towards the hut. Stopped five paces short and waited, his ear cocked for sounds from inside. Nothing came. He stepped up to the door and pulled the sagging insect lock all the way across.

'Come on out,' he said, to the darkness. 'Haere mai ki waho.'

Nothing.

He stepped into the trapped heat. Waited while his eyes adjusted to the sunlight that filtered through the wall chinks and thatch. A light pattern of footprints dusted the floor; otherwise the hut was undisturbed. His patched canisters were in place on the workbench. His patching tool. The bed and floor mat. Even his water stores seemed to be intact.

A thief who took no water—odd.

One eye on the doorway, Van bent to the floor and examined the footprints. A single intruder, definitely, and not a large one. Someone light and spooked, in a rush. They hadn't knelt or investigated beneath their feet where the real riches were, hadn't thought to dig anything up. Or they were an expert, supremely practised at covering their thefts. The only sign they'd been there was this scattering of dust and a tiny pūkeko tail-feather that wisped about as he moved and must have blown in behind them, or come unstuck from a rag boot.

He knelt and peeled up the floor mat, then the smoothed cross-hatch of poles beneath it, then a further harakeke mat. His tub of welding tools was where it should be. He lifted it out and set it beside him, then peered into the hole again. A second dark wrap in its depths. He lowered his entire arm down to it, then froze at a swooping upwards rush outside—here it was at last, the attack—but then a bird screeched in panic, and he realised it was just a pair of tūī chasing each other.

He wiped his face of sweat. With slow care he untied the wrap.

'Oh thank god,' he said, and sank back.

His precious pieces were all still there. Ranged in size and plaited into the harakeke wrap, his finest ornaments of plastic. A life's work. A teardrop necklace on plait, pure black. Rings and reinforced needle shapes, and the white hair-pieces that

Matewai valued. Hours of squinting and sweat behind the mask at the patching fire were represented here. Plastic treasures he'd shaped and reinforced himself. Black and deep blue and red. Pure colours, these—none of the smeary yellows and whites of the canisters and drinking tubs he traded every few days, no puddles or whirls. Each piece had started from some rich discovery in his mine, some rare plastic source he'd dug out of that cliff of stinking mud and set aside, then shaped and strengthened over his patching fire, then further strengthened with fire and wet, fire and wet, and then rubbed on his shaping stone.

He ran a finger over them all to savour them and the prospect of the nights and days of work that were ahead of him, now that Ava had been sunk into the swamp mud and Rau had been left, glowering, to his grief. Van would be free now to do his own work in his own camp. Sleep in his own bed. There was a routine trade to make in the morning, a short walk with a load and then back with supplies, and then the quiet of firing and shaping and patching again before this last autumn heat died and the winter storms started up.

It was too hot, though, to kneel there for long. He stood and considered once more the light-dusted legacy of his intruder. They'd been too dumb or green to search beneath a floor mat for the richest trade, the finest work. Or too genteel, perhaps, trained to shrink back from plastic, to never touch the stuff. Especially plastic of the hut's most visible sort: the benchtop's array of canisters and pots that Van had patched, all of them alloyed and puddled with donor plastic, impurity heaped on impurity. Not someone to fear, in other words, and unlikely to come back. They hadn't even scattered the fire outside. It was nothing to worry about. If it had been supposed to signal something, that hadn't been a success. And still he'd seen nothing direct. No drawing in the dirt of figures with knives in their guts. All they'd shown was that they worked alone.

Besides, the entire amateurish incursion would have been seen by the watchers on the Scarp, who would have come down their slopes and taxed the intruder on their re-entry to the Dry Way or, if they'd been unable to pay, roughed them up and relieved them of their remaining wealth, and thrown them back into the swamp.

More relaxed now, he rewrapped the precious pieces and hid them in the hole, then went outside with his tub of tools and the mining spade. Rounding the hut, he made for the mine face. Out to the south-west the sun was now poised above the island, wavy through the columns of smoke the Burners sent up. Not much of the day left.

At the mine face, no new scrapes or footprints. Only a pūkeko chick that squawked at his approach, bringing its parents in range to flick their tails and herd the infant into stalks of raupō. Van laughed and kicked a scatter of dust after them, then traced along the cliff a seam of white and blue that had yielded recently good donor plastic. It was some days since he'd mined, and the spade felt oddly unfamiliar in his hands, its patched handle lumpen and thick as it slid through his palms. He dug out an armful of ancient, creviced bottles and uncreased them, gouging out the mud, then carried them back to the fire. This was all the mahi he had left, along with those he'd brought home on his back for patching. They could all be washed and patched before it got dark. Two large bags of canisters of varying shapes were due to be traded at Matewai's camp tomorrow, but he always took a few extra to leave with her, for her own profit.

At the patching fire he struck sparks and loaded the fire up, then poked the metal end of the patching tool into the heart of the flames. Sat back then, and fell into a trance of fire-watching and heat. The fatigue of the last few days claimed him at last. It had been a draining time. Ava's death and sinking. The noise of Rau's grief: blood-soaked, enraged.

He could have a decent rest first, he decided. Then he'd do his patching work. He flicked a guarding eye over the camp one more time, then slumped down further on his sitting log. Watched the fire. Grew drowsy. Reached into his bags and dragged out his water canister and a last twist of dried slopfish. Ate and drank and stared into the heat and grew still more lethargic, till a day-biter whined up round his face and he sat bolt upright and clapped it dead. Dug in his bags for oil. Doused afresh his hands and face and headwrap, the repellent's tangy stink searing out. Retied the plaits at his ankles and wrists, and knotted his headwrap tight. Then he went to the wood pile and threw great armloads of mānuka foliage on the fire as a further deterrent to biters.

Returning to his sitting log, he laid the oil and his weapons within easy reach, then leaned back again. Ate languorously and drank. The fire burnt fiercely and then down to embers, crumbling to the steady heat he needed to work on his plastic repairs. But still he didn't rise. He didn't want to work yet. Nor did he want to go round his traps. The sun was losing its intensity now and he was at a comfortable distance from the patching fire, and for just a few moments more Van wanted only this vacant submission to rest. To not think of Rau, or of Ava. Her wrapped and oiled form. His own hand aiding Rau's as he pushed her down into the ooze and stench. Bubbles of liquid mud coming up while Rau cut his own arm and held it over the sinking place so his blood dripped over her and his grief howled out.

He closed his eyes and forced himself to think of nothing

13

instead. Nothing but the draining of fatigue from his arms and legs into the warm and hardened mud beneath. And of Hana. Her shelter at Summer's Day, and the colours that draped down from its centre post. Her movements above him on the bed, the aroma of herbs she released as she moved.

He drowsed, and that same pūkeko chick squawked, and he hauled up on an elbow to check with woozy energy the camp clearing, then peered again over the mine face to the sliver of Whaea territory that he could just make out. Hana's place. The exalted slopes.

Even to look that way gave him a twitch in his groin. It was a full day's run from here, inland. From this distance the great fence looked to be just a line in the trees and a scarf of cleared earth that someone had cut down to be a fire break. There was no sign from here of its potency.

He'd stood beneath that fence. He'd felt its towering force. It was as high as two men up close, the posts and side poles plaited into the trees themselves, so the trunks were part of the fence. Impossible to shift or penetrate. A fence to hold them all safely, the precious things that lived inside it—the green upthrust of forest, the women and their families and their vast statue of their Whaea, and the protected birds that rose and sank. And it was a fence to keep people like him out. Those with something to run from, or something to hawk. Travellers on the Dry Way, plastic men. Te Repo people. Swamp folk.

Van jolted awake. Something from outside—a sound. He lay still, straining to hear it. No breeze out there. A calm night, the autumn moon poised at the west of the hut and filtering through the thatch. Not quite morning yet.

A ruru call. Not twenty paces off. A human fake.

14

His hand went to the floor beside his blanket and closed round his blade. Watching the filtered light for shadows, he saw nothing, no shapes flitting outside or round his hut.

The sound came again, closer this time.

Very slow, he stood from his blankets. Pulled on his coat. Blade in one hand, he went to the door and peered through the flap. Strong moonlight out there, his patching fire ashed over. He waited for movement, for a further call, then ran out and round the side of his hut. No one in the clearing. He stood still, his pulse hammering in his hands and throat. He displayed his blade; circled it at the side. Looked into the scrub at the clearing's perimeter, the moonlight bright enough to show the shades of mānuka, the browns and blacks.

'What do you want?' he said.

No movement out there, no answer.

'Show yourself,' he said. 'If you mean peace, come out.'

No response. Far off, a possum coughed.

He would have to switch languages again. He searched for a phrase that would make sense, not confident it was correct. 'Whākina mai tōu—show your . . . show your kanohi.'

He caught a noise and swung round. Left of the clearing's northern point, beneath a stand of tī kōuka, the kawakawa moved. A figure stepped out. The moonlight was strong, but he couldn't see whether the intruder's head was covered. No weapons visible as they walked into the clearing several paces.

'Āta haere,' said Van. 'Slowly now.'

The figure went with deliberate steps to the scattered fire, and stopped. Turned towards Van with both palms open. Impossible to see the face clearly.

'How many are you?' he said. 'What do you want?'

The figure lifted a hand. Slowly it went towards the throat. Paused a moment, then lifted something from around the neck. Held it out to the right.

'I can't see what that is.'

'Colours of the Whaea. I come from inside the fence.'

Van stared. It was a female voice—a young one, not adult, not yet. Perhaps a child. There had to be others with her, in protection. He looked again into the scrub, up towards the Whaea fence and forest. A glow of torchlight along its perimeter, where the guards and tamāhine toa worked. More lights where the distant statue stood.

'Who's with you?' he said.

The figure watched him for a time, very still, the coloured feathers held out. Then she lowered them slowly, so they showed as a dull speckled white, barely perceptible on her chest. 'I'm to fetch you,' she said. It seemed she might say more, but somewhere out in the night a pūkeko shrieked, wrenched from sleep, and Van tensed.

'Who's that?' he said. 'Who's out there with you?'

'No one. That wasn't us.'

'Who's us?'

'The Whaea settlement,' she said. 'But I'm alone, I promise. I'm for trade. I've been sent as a fetch.'

Van scanned again the clearing's perimeter, the night shapes of scrub. 'It's Rau you want. He trades for us on big stuff.' Watching her outline, he added, 'Strange time to call, by the way. Middle of the night. And he's paid his debts to you, if that's what you want.'

She paused, watching him. 'You're Van. It's you I've come to fetch.'

That same grab at him, icy and low. Fear. The girl was speaking Pākehā, but she had the accent of the Whaea people. Connected to Hana, surely. Come to fetch him for punishment. 'What for? You don't trade with me. You don't take plastic.'

'It's not that sort of trade,' she said.

'So what sort of trade is it?'

'I can't tell you until you're behind the fence.'

He laughed, moving his blade hand out at the side. 'This is ridiculous. How old are you? You sound like a kid.'

'I'm bartered,' she said. 'My people bartered a gap.'

She was someone important—someone high up. Had to be. A gap bartered with the Scarp for passage across the Dry Way would have cost the Whaea people a fortune. The two groups were not friends. There was a fence as high as two men between them to prove it. Only at Summer's Day did they pause for a fleeting peace—for old rituals of the Whaea people, for one day's trade and sex. Sometimes the Scarp were allowed to be part of it, along with other strangers. Like Van, last time.

He braced again while the sick knowing of what this must be about went through him. This fetch wasn't an invitation. It was a punishment.

'It's about Summer's Day, isn't it,' he said. 'About what we did.'

The figure didn't reply.

'Hana,' he said. 'It's Hana I'm talking about.' His hand went up, explaining. 'She knew where I came from. I didn't lie about it. She knew I was swamp.'

Still she didn't speak.

'If I gave her some illness, I didn't know I was carrying it. I didn't lie about any of it.'

'I don't know about any of that. I'm just the fetch.'

'Kei te hapū ia?' said Van. 'Hana—is she hapū?'

No response.

His eye caught on the dull flash of speckled white on her chest. 'You left the feather,' he said. 'You left the feather on the floor in my hut.'

17

This time she paused before she replied, as if to gauge his reaction from his voice—how angry the invasion had made him. 'He tohu,' she said. 'I had to leave some sign I wasn't just a traveller or thief.'

Van backed towards the patching fire. Still keeping her in sight, he leaned behind and raked the coals with his blade so a line of red and white sparkled. 'Come into the light,' he said. 'Slowly and with your hands held up.'

As the girl advanced he strode to the fuel pile, flung on some foliage, and blew on the embers till flames started up, then returned to the front of the fire to ensure he was backlit. Slowly she came on, her hands up and weaponless. No sound in the night but the fire and the shush of her feet on the clearing's dust and dry mud. A puff of breeze caught her twist of feathers and they turned on the string that looped them to her neck.

'That's enough,' he said.

She was six paces off. Her small face visible now, blanched by firelight but seeming unscarred by disease or bites. Her clothes unpatched, unripped. One of the Whaea people, all right. Even the waft of her insect oil was subtler than the tangy blast he was used to—Matewai's unsubtle mix of herbs that could be sourced in the swamp.

'Take out your blades,' he said.

'I have only one.'

'Take it out.'

Her hand went to an opening in her coat. The blade glinted as it came out. A metal knife.

'On the ground,' he said.

She tossed it towards him—and overthrew it, gasping an apology as soon as it left her hand and flew towards his legs. He stepped back and tripped on the fire stones behind. He swung out for balance, his blade arm going up in a wild arc.

'Fuck,' he said. 'Be careful.'

'Sorry. It stuck in my hand.'

Out of the corner of his eye he caught the great moving shadow his movements made on the scrub beyond the hut. The Scarp's watchers would have an eye on all of this, wondering what it was about. Or knowing already, from the sound of it, since a gap had been bartered to get the girl through.

But now the stranger seemed to misread his silence. 'I'm sorry. It stuck in my hand because I'm nervous. I couldn't help it.'

'You should be more careful,' he said. 'That's how fights start.'

She dropped her head. He heard the whine of a night-biter and waved at it, pulling his coat tight round his neck. He considered the risk of returning to his hut to renew his oil while she remained outside, or just telling her to piss off, shutting the door flap to his hut and getting rid of her and whatever awful responsibility was travelling in her wake.

She lifted her face towards the Whaea territories. 'The gap closes at first light.'

'Oh, for fuck's sake,' he said. 'I can't make that. I have a trade just after first light.'

'Is it at Matewai's?'

Van laughed. 'I'm not telling you where my trade is.'

She didn't drop her head or apologise. Instead she waited to be sure he was finished, then moved a hand in the direction of Matewai's camp. 'If it's at Matewai's, we could still make it. I'll come with you and then, when your trade's done, we'll go straight across the Dry Way. The Scarp might hold the gap open, if it's not too late after first light.'

He studied her. 'You want this pretty bad.'

'My people do, yes.'

19

'So why did they send a kid? If it's worth a gap.'

'I've done my training. I'm old enough.'

His eyes went to her knife on the ground. He lifted it with his free hand, careful to keep his fingers well clear of the blade. In the firelight he saw the handle of burnished wood had etchings in it, the grooved patterns hidden in shadow and difficult to make out.

'Rau can come too,' she said. 'If he wants.'

Van laughed. '*If he wants.* Have you met Rau? And you should call him Raureti, by the way. Raureti Ngahere.'

Again her response to the rebuke was silence. But he was right. Rau wouldn't be running with open arms towards whatever trade this kid was promising. Rau had run the Dry Way to the Whaea territories many times last winter, on late-night trips when Ava was still alive and needed potions for a female illness that, for reasons Van had never been told about, Matewai couldn't treat with her own oils and healing crops. But on those trips Rau had met only healers and traders, he'd said; never anyone high up. And they'd never given him a humane trade, always exacting full price.

'And you must know that he's pōuri. We just sank his wife.'

'I'm only the fetch. I just have instructions.'

He watched her a moment more, then traced with his thumb the etching in the knife's wood. It was a bird shape, finely crafted. 'Can you just tell me straight? Before we go to all this trouble. Just tell me if I'm in the shit. Are you fetching me so I can get punished by your people? For spreading swamp and infecting Hana. All that.'

'The only other thing I'm allowed to say is this. We'll teach you.'

'Eh? Teach what?'

She paused, as if giving him time to figure it out. 'We'll

20

teach,' she said. 'I mean, *they'll* teach—the people who sent me. The old waters. The joining of the rivers. They'll teach you some of that stuff.'

Van stared. 'Teach *me*?'

The girl shrugged and looked away, as if she didn't share his sense of the enormity of it. The old waters—the joining of the families and old ones, going back and back, like a river. The Whaea people were famous for holding that knowledge, but they didn't share it with strangers. Everyone knew that. And Van had no waters anyway, to speak of. He was an orphan. His waters were those of the Te Repo people who'd taken him in. They were Matewai's waters. Rau's.

She sighed. 'Are you coming? I have to get back by first light.'

He nodded, but distantly, still trying to work it out.

'Kia tere, then,' she said. 'Please.'

'If you're in such a rush, why did you leave it till tonight to fetch me? Why didn't you come earlier?'

'You were tired. I could see it. You would never have agreed to come without sleep. You're more likely to agree to come now that you've had some rest.'

'Huh. That's probably right.'

'Kia tere,' she said again, pointing to his hut. 'Get your travelling stuff, and give my knife back, and let's go.'

He nodded, coming out of his trance. He put her blade on the ground and moved towards his hut. Then, halfway to the door flap, he came back to confiscate her knife. There was fear in her instructions, fear of being caught outside the fence after the gap had closed, but he didn't want to trust her completely yet.

A thought occurred to him. 'Have you got enough water for the trip back?'

'Āe. But you should bring enough for yourself.'

21

He went into his hut, found his travelling bag and filled it with some fresh water canisters, bug oil, some wraps of food. At the last moment he lifted his wrap of precious pieces and put it in the bag too, keeping it as separate as he could from the food. Then he lifted the two bags of trades for Matewai he'd finished and packed earlier that night.

When he came back outside she was facing the scrub at the clearing's edge—keeping watch. She was vigilant but so small, so young. Too young for this sort of work, out in the moonlit swamp among its biters and ponds, its treacherous mud. Disturbing a plastic trader from his own camp, and prey to whoever else was roaming the swamp at night. No one else to help her. And not more than fourteen summers, surely—she couldn't be older than that. She was no taller than his armpit.

Two

Hana lay on her back beside Van in the skin shelter, one arm lifted above. They both watched her finger as it traced the design that snaked down her arm. It was a tan-coloured painting of koru and wing shapes. A body painting—another mark of luxury. Nobody at Te Repo wore body paintings like that.

'Don't stop,' she said. 'I like hearing you talk.'

He'd lost track of their conversation, dazed from the heat and the sex they'd had. Hypnotised, too, by the movements of her finger over the painted shapes.

'Little orphan boy,' she said. 'You were talking about when you were a tiny orphan, and when you were rescued by Rau, and all that sad and moany stuff. And you were explaining why your reo's so shit.'

She saw his look, and shoved him. 'I'm teasing you. It is shit, though, isn't it.'

He laughed. 'I'm not denying it.' He looked again into the roof of the shelter, the coloured plaits that hung down from the centre pole. It felt strange to be talking this way in this place. Disloyal somehow. Of course his version of her language was bad. He relied on the Dry Way trades, like everyone at Te

Repo did, sucking sustenance from the flow of travellers that came down endlessly from the north. Most of those exhausted people could speak Pākehā or some pidgin form of it, mixed with whatever had once been their own tongue. So that's what Van spoke, and most other swamp traders did too. Matewai and Rau needed to speak both languages, but used Pākehā most of the time with Van and Ava and many of their trading connections. From them Van had learnt enough to follow the basic thread of talk when the language switched, but not enough to reply easily.

But it was different here. He could hear that. He'd heard Hana's language several times already, inside the fence of this settlement. The female guards who'd brought Van and the others in through the south gate had talked their own reo to each other, and since coming into this shelter he'd heard it in plenty of the other shelters across the festival flats. No doubt there were other places higher up, nearer the statue, where it was the only language people spoke.

'So that's why I don't speak your reo properly,' he said. 'And why it's full of hapa. I haven't really been taught it. And I haven't heard it enough.'

'Oh, so it's because you're lazy. And you don't like us.'

'Āe, that must be it.' He watched her fingers, again tracing the design on her arm. 'But if I'd known I was going to meet you, I would have put in some effort.'

'Oh, wow,' she said. 'Smooth.' Then, before he had time to react, she said, 'Māku koe e whakaako.'

He got up to his elbow. There was always this moment of catching up, when he had to check he'd caught the correct meaning.

'I will,' she said. 'I'll teach you, if you want to learn.'

'Am I allowed to? Wait, are you allowed to teach me?'

She laughed. 'Why not?'

'I don't know. I just—'

'Well, I'd like you to talk to me in my own language. So, yes, I'm allowed to.'

'So when would you teach me? How could that ever work, considering where I live and what I do for trade?'

She dropped her arm and said nothing, but her eyes still roved the roof, as if the answer was up there. 'Kāore au i te mōhio,' she said, at last.

In the different silence that settled between them, the noises of the other shelters came across. A woman singing somewhere far off. Another woman, much closer, talking fast in her language, too rapid for Van to understand it.

When Hana next spoke, there was less of that blithe confidence in her voice. 'It's been a good festival, though, hasn't it? You've enjoyed it.'

'It's been all right,' he said. 'Some of it.'

She turned, then understood he'd meant it as a joke, and another spray of her laughter went up.

He watched her, enjoying her reaction. It was a long time since he'd heard anyone laugh like that. She laughed like a lucky person, he thought.

Van and the girl were halfway to Matewai's camp when the moon went down, plunging them into deeper darkness. He was eager to reach Matewai and Rau, to pass the problem of the girl on to them, but there was a rotten lake close on both sides of the track here. In the sudden dark it would be easy to wander off the track and pitch into that bad swamp. He also preferred to stop in extreme dark, in case of ambush.

'We'll rest here a moment,' he said. 'Wait for better light.'

25

But she didn't stop. Instead she pressed on down the track, into the dark.

'Hey! Girl! Hoki mai!'

She didn't return.

Swearing, he went after her, his plastic trades sounding on his back. It was so dark he had to keep his hands in front, groping out for trunks to guide him. It was some distance before he could make out her shape, then pull on her shoulder. 'What the fuck are you doing? I told you to stop.'

'Me haere tāua. I don't want to miss the gap.'

'Well, you need to wait for more light. It's too dangerous.'

Her shape shifted as she looked away through the vegetation. The rotten lake was just a dark body through there.

'If you fall in the water here, trust me, that's it,' said Van. 'You'll just be a mass of bites. Or diseased by the water, and dead by this time tomorrow. Gap or no gap.'

She hunched into her coat, and hunkered there without sound. After a time Van felt the weight of her rebuke. He tried to ignore it, to think only of the sections of trail they still had to walk, to rehearse the dangerous places and anticipate the sites of ambush. But the quiet shape pressed on him, needling him with guilt. At last he said, 'Would you like some water? It's treated—safe.'

She didn't take the canister he offered, the shake of her head the barest shifting of air in the dark.

He adjusted his trades on his back. They clonked and rubbed against each other. Then birds began in the trees overhead.

After a time he heard her swing down her bag and rummage for something, and then the uncorking of a vessel and the slop of liquid. Her own canister. She hadn't taken his water because she couldn't trust it, even if it had been treated with Matewai's herbs. In her mind, he supposed, it still came from the swamp.

26

Then there was just the sound of their separate drinking as light lifted out of the earth and the trees around them slowly gained shape.

'Look, don't take it too hard that I told you off,' he said. 'It's just that the water's deadly here, at this precise part of the track, and it's easy to fall into it in the dark. I'd hate to send you back covered in bites.'

She said something quiet, something that sounded like assent. Then again there was just the slop of water as she lifted her canister and drank. Then a tūī broke the silence directly above them and she gasped. It was the tūī's pre-dawn call, a two-tone drop that was ghostly and uncertain, so different from the bird's usual daytime boasts. That call woke Van most mornings before dawn in his hut, but this girl seemed unused to it. It was the horrid proximity, probably, that spooked her, unfiltered by the draped walls and thatch of the luxurious hut he supposed she slept in behind the fence.

'Won't be long,' said Van. 'We'll just wait for a bit more light.'

Taken by his change of tone, she looked up and murmured.

'Speak up,' he said. 'I can't hear that.'

'Kahurangi. My name. It's Kahurangi. Kahu for short.' She paused. 'I was supposed to say it when we met. I forgot.'

'That was in your instructions? Huh.'

Above them, the tūī bonged and glocked. Then another bird responded from further off, then another, a network forming through the canopy.

He could see her better now, small and worn-looking.

'You must be tired,' he said. 'How long have you been out?'

'I'm all right.' Then, as if remembering a need to be polite, she added, 'I'm fine, thanks.'

'Why did they send someone so young?'

'I'm not that young. I can handle it.'

He grinned. 'I didn't say *too* young.'

She scuffed with her foot at something on the mud of the track. As the pre-dawn light slowly came up, he could see more of the dyed slash that ran up the middle of her headwrap. It was purple, like fuchsia flower, wide at the forehead and narrowing towards the crown of her head. It wasn't cheap, that sort of headwrap. He'd seen them only on Whaea people, never on travelling folk or runners, though occasionally Matewai's trade brought fabrics like that into her camp and out again.

Now the girl lifted her face. 'I was the only one who could do this, I guess. The only one with the closest waters.'

'Closest to what? To who?'

She started to reply but then caught herself, ducking her head.

It was his turn to be nervous now, nervous of what might come next. But she said nothing, perhaps holding to some instruction.

'You're high up, I suppose,' he said. 'In the Whaea people.'

She looked straight at him. 'My whānau's hut is fifty paces from the statue.'

'Oh shit,' he said.

She gave no sign of having heard him, of knowing he was intimidated. Instead she just looked through the trees ahead. 'Can we go now? I don't want to miss the gap.'

He took in again her unpatched and expensive coat. Tried to picture the place she lived, so close to the statue of the Whaea, that vast and revered guardian and aunt. 'I suppose you know Hana.'

'She's—' She paused, and he sensed she was groping for the right way to phrase it carefully in Pākehā. 'She's related to me.'

'Related,' said Van. 'I see.'

She searched his face, and for a moment it seemed she was

28

waiting for him to show something more, something to trust. Then she dropped her eyes again. 'That's what I'm allowed to say about that.'

Van swallowed. Hana hadn't spoken of any children she might have had—of any family relation, in fact—on that Summer's Day and night and morning they'd shared. She wasn't allowed to, for her own protection, and Van had been told by the guards not to ask. None of the Whaea people who chose to participate in the festival would discuss their private lives, in case the partners they'd chosen for the night turned out bad, turned out to be violent. He'd been told to expect punishment if something went wrong. The fact this girl was fetching him should have scared him—it did scare him—but just to think again of that time with Hana in that skin shelter thrilled him too, sending a twitch up from his groin.

The girl interjected. 'Can we go, please? We're getting late.'

Van blushed, caught in the memory. He made a show of looking through the trees, checking the light. 'Āe, it's light enough now. But stay close.' He retightened the straps on his bags, and took a few paces down the track. Then he added, with that same scolding sound in his voice, 'Turituri now. Quiet till we hit Matewai's camp.'

Van stood at the entrance to Te Repo, kawakawa to his waist. The healing crops that flanked the famous mound were in front of him, then the mound itself, a conical hill that poked from the swamp and gave views in every direction. The huts of Matewai's people huddled round its base and up its flanks. Smoke rose from the cooking fires and from Matewai's oiling hut. Van dropped his hand in the kawakawa crop to feel the leaves' cool flutter against his wrist. It was a good sensation. Here at this camp would be some relief from the girl's crowding presence. He walked further into the green coolness. Kawakawa grew densely in the places protected from frost, then other crops. No one was working in the plants or harakeke, though, or in the boggy stretch where the campers sourced their fresh water. Too early for that.

He sent forward his pūkeko call, then repeated it.

Matewai pulled back the door flap of her oiling hut and peered. Her outline rose and fell as she eased her hip and gauged the bags on his back—assessing what he'd brought— and then the girl beyond him. After a pause, she waved him on.

He turned, summoning Kahu to come forward.

She seemed diminished, her hands held together in her lap.

'Come on. Just remember you can't touch the plants.'

She nodded quickly, as if she didn't need to be told that.

'E hine, kei te pai koe?'

No reply from the girl, no movement. At that moment Matewai bent through the door and threw dirty liquid out, and Van saw that Kahu was intimidated. It was the reputation of this place that pushed her back. Matewai Ngahere. The great trader of the swamps. Oil merchant, and boss of the network of traders and runners and other ferals who worked this boggy, less profitable side of the Dry Way.

'You'll find us pōuri,' he said. 'We've had a loss.'

Kahu said something indistinct. She murmured like this, he realised, when she was nervous.

'Pardon?' said Van. 'You need to speak up.'

But her eyes were closed. She was talking to the Whaea, not to him. A karakia of some sort.

He waited for her to finish, letting his gaze rest on the crops and huts. Lifted his hand to acknowledge an older man who went across the camp for water. Too old to be sent out on trade, that man, no running duties left for him. Watching his stooped progress, Van felt the same old grab of feeling whenever he faced these empty buildings, their unoccupied air. They'd been emptied by sickness, by the promise of children who might once have come from unions like Rau's with Ava, but because of sickness and the general impossibility of children these days had never arrived.

Kahu finished her prayer at last and he took her through the crops, holding back the protruding branches so she wouldn't have to touch them. As she walked she shrank into herself, arms held in tight at her sides.

At the cooking fires he swung down his bags of trades. Sniffed at the ancient cooking pots. 'Stand there,' he said. 'Don't move.'

Her eyes darted beyond him to Matewai's hut.

'Don't look at anything. Don't touch anything. Just watch the fire till I come back.'

Van went with his trades round the side of Matewai's hut. Removed the vessels from his bags and ranged them in a neat line against the wall: the smaller bottles first, then the smeary white water tanks, squat and almost as large as his head. He glanced towards the girl to be sure she wasn't watching, and found her still turned towards the fire as commanded, the coloured wrap smooth over her head. As he laid out each trade he checked their plugs and ran his fingers one more time over the patched places, feeling for imperfections and lumps. There was a prickled area on one of the water tanks where the plastic had stippled as it cooled and he, distracted by something, hadn't returned with his shaping tool and smoothed it flat. Matewai would notice that. But she would forgive him, given the distraction of Ava's death and sinking, the interruption to the flow of his patching craft. Besides, it wouldn't matter at the Dry Way entrance. No imperfection short of a gaping hole would deter the travellers who bought his trades. They always paid a good price.

Every few days Matewai sent runners to hawk Van's water tanks at the entrance to the Dry Way, where the exhausted travellers first climbed onto the high and ramparted path that ran through the swamps and saw for the first time the South Strait in the distance, its wavering blueness and island shapes. It was there, at the entrance to the Dry Way, from where they could see their destination in the distance at last, that those broken folk began to imagine they'd made it, and that soon they would board the boats and cross to the less violent, less storm-ravaged, less bug-infested island, and began therefore to imagine they'd soon need new and larger water tanks to sustain them once they arrived at the waiting camps and prepared for their last boat trip. They'd trade handsomely for such a tank; surging with renewed hope and urgency, they'd give over some last, long-guarded treasure—a blade or metal pot or ancient cloth. A trade they'd never make if only they could know what would come next, only five hundred paces further down the Dry Way, where it dipped to its lowest point and was lapped by brown and stinking ponds on each side; where the road agents of the Scarp would melt down from the slopes and demand a fresh tax for the passage of travellers through the swamps on that only viable path. And so it would be relieved of them, so soon after seeing the South Strait for the first time, the soaring hope of those ragged travellers and their families. Their last treasures ripped away as road tax by the Scarp, or their most useful clothes if they didn't have treasures, and their fresh-bought plastic water tanks if they didn't have anything else left that was precious, and, if they had none of these, punished with sticks or sliced with blades, and thrown off the Dry Way into the disease-ridden water, where biters and then Matewai's runners would again catch up with them and trade afresh for the insect and healing oils the despairing and sometimes bleeding travellers would need to survive a night in the swamps.

It wasn't a fair system, if you thought about it, but Van didn't think about it, because he had no power over it, and neither, as he understood it, did Matewai or Ava or Rau—it was the Scarp who controlled it, someone among that elite group of Raka's people who controlled the long escarpment slopes and the Way beneath them, and who kept the whole circle of trade and predation on the travellers in motion. And whatever violence and storms and land-robbing seep was happening in the north that sent all those travellers south, Van was just a tiny piece in it, and he didn't have much choice. He simply made his tanks and canisters to Matewai's request, and some other canisters and plastic pieces on spec, which he traded himself or with Matewai's runners, and beyond that he kept his own camp and ran to Rau's side when summoned. That was the extent of his duty, and it was good in its containment, its culmination in a nice line of canisters and tanks like the one he now stacked against the back of Matewai's hut.

The door flap sounded and he looked up. It was Matewai herself, easing down from the hut and towards him, careful on her bad hip. A coat was drawn about her and held closed at the front by a fist, the knuckles stained with oil. It was not a working coat; if there were stains and patches on it, she'd hidden them round the back. A concession to the visitor, or to the time of grief. As she came closer, he saw her forehead was creased and her eyes wet. Without speaking, she opened her arms and took him into an embrace.

'Vannie,' she said.

He couldn't find his voice. His throat was blocked and his

33

own eyes were wet, and then they were streaming. It was the first time he'd seen her since Ava had passed, since Matewai had wrapped and prepared the body for the sinking, and all the Te Repo people had said or shouted their angry or happy stories over her, saying goodbye that way, before he and Rau had gone to sink it in mud, and now he felt it properly, his own grief. For a long time he could only sob and be held against Matewai, mushed against her vast body and its smells of the oils she'd been cooking up.

'Was it all right?' she said.

When he still couldn't answer her questions, and couldn't speak, her voice changed, and she put her hand against the back of his head, holding it until he was calmer. 'It was all right, I bet. You did well by Ava, I bet.'

His face and beard were wet. He smeared the tears and snot with his fist. 'Oh, fuck.'

She held on to him still. 'We have our griefs, don't we, tama.'

He didn't say anything, not wanting to pull away yet, to show his face.

At last she released him, and wiped her own eyes. 'And you've brought someone with you.'

He turned that way and saw the girl standing there, still staring at the fire. She was not much taller than the green pattern of crops behind her. 'The Whaea people want to talk. This one is the fetch. They traded a gap to get her across.'

She raised an eyebrow. 'Someone's in the shit, then.'

He wiped his eyes and nose again. 'That's what I thought. But she says it's not a punishment.'

Matewai shifted to look towards the escarpment. 'How long is the gap?'

'It closed at first light, but she thinks it will hold for a bit. Wants Rau as well.'

'Huh,' she said. 'They don't want much.' She continued to watch the girl, who still stood twenty paces back with her head lowered. At last Matewai lifted her hand to her. 'Welcome. I acknowledge our ancient waters.' She was speaking in Pākehā, and it sounded strange in that tongue, the ceremonial phrasing. Perhaps she was doing it to reinforce that the intruder was not on her home turf, or perhaps it was because Matewai didn't feel confident trading reo with a Whaea speaker, even a young one. 'I acknowledge your Whaea, and your whānau, and your rivers. And I greet your sacred self.'

Kahu bent her arm at the elbow and held her hand up. The Whaea sign, mimicking the way their statue stood.

Matewai didn't respond to that, didn't beckon her across. Instead she looked over her crops and the inland sky, the clouds that had begun to mass further south. It wasn't rude, exactly, but Matewai was letting the visitor feel, it seemed, the weight of the plants around her and the camp, the reputation of the place the girl had entered. 'I can't welcome you the way I'd like,' she said. 'It's the season for my work—when I do my cooking up. And, for other reasons, your timing isn't good.'

Kahu looked towards her. At last she cleared her throat, and spoke in Pākehā. 'I acknowledge your dead. I acknowledge your hurts.'

'Oh, I'll bet,' muttered Matewai, so only Van could hear it. Then she lifted a hand again. 'All right, girl—I acknowledge it right back. Have a kai. Something from these pots. Van will help you.' Then she turned away and indicated the stacks of patched and re-formed canisters Van had lined up against the hut. 'These look all right.'

Van glanced towards Kahu. It made him nervous, how cursory Matewai's welcome had been.

'E tama, your trades. Tell me about them.'

Van shook his head to clear his surprise. 'Kahurangi,' he said. 'That's her name—Kahurangi. Kahu for short.'

Matewai just nodded.

'Right,' he said, 'four tubs and six canisters, as requested. Plus another six for you—for bonus. Did Rau stay here last night?'

She sighed, waving at the huts on the mound. 'Woke me up before first light. Not in the best shape.'

'I tried to tell him not to camp out, not with the cut on his arm, and his chest like that. But he was determined. He stayed at that place he and Ava liked.'

'Āe. But it was a bad night, I think. Bites, bad chest, the lot.'

Before he could stop himself, Van glanced at Matewai's own arms for signs of slicing with a blade or whatever grief had been cut into them, but she'd plaited both sleeves of her coat tight at the wrists.

'I should finish up.' She lifted her voice to Kahu. 'E kai. There's slopfish in the pot. Fresh water—it won't be like you're used to, but it's safe. And sit down now.'

Kahu looked forlornly towards the cooking fires.

Then Matewai made towards her hut, and Kahu sat on one of the great sitting logs, silent.

Van turned away to restraighten his scarf and headwrap, and to wipe his face of any lingering tears and snot. He wished Kahu hadn't seen his signs of grief, not only for his sake. She looked fragile herself.

'So it looks like we'll have to wait a bit longer,' he said. 'You should eat while we wait.'

Free to look anywhere now, she sent her gaze beyond him to the slopes where the Whaea people lived. The sun was well up, and her gaze seemed to implore it to reverse its trajectory and dip below the horizon, returning the world to night.

Van made an effort to use her name, thinking it might help. 'As I said, Kahu, there is grief. The timing of your visit isn't the best.'

She gave that same bleak nod, and he saw it claiming her at last—the realisation of how naive they'd been, whoever had sent her across, to think she could do it all before first light. Cross the Dry Way and penetrate the swamps, and drag two traders out of their camps with less than half a day's notice, and all for the sake of an undisclosed trade with unspecified profits and risks. Only the Whaea people could have thought it possible. Only someone with no real knowledge of how it worked out here, beyond the reaches of their fence. The thought took him to Hana, that sharing of waters Kahu had hinted at. Related. She'd said they were related.

He went to the pots and peered into the steam and, with a stick from the side, stirred the mixture until flakes of slopfish circled up. 'Kahu, can you eat out of plastic?'

Her eye went to the vessel he held up, its yellow and malformed shape.

'Āe.'

He grinned. 'Don't force yourself. I'm sure Matewai's got some wood bowls in the hut.'

She shook her head with quick force. 'I want the plastic one. I've done it before—I can eat from it.' She slid her coat over her knees, preparing for him to lay the bowl on the top. When he brought it to her, she took in the grey surface of the soup and her face tightened, visibly steeling herself to consume it. Catching his eye, she said, 'I'll just let it settle first.'

A pīwaiwaka flew into the crops from the surrounding trees and chirped, bouncing on the air while its tail fanned and flicked.

The girl looked up but didn't smile at the bird's comic air-bounces. The bowl of soup was on her knees, balanced by a fingertip on its rim.

'Do you need to say something first? A karakia kai or something?'

'It's fine. I'll take care of it.'

He dithered, unwilling to leave her like this—burdened with food she seemed to find strange, running late on her fetch and clearly unhappy about it.

'I see the island's burning again,' he said, looking out there. 'The Burners like a fire. They love it, in fact.'

'We call them something different,' she said.

'Oh yeah?' said Van, pleased at this opening. 'What's that?'

But this seemed difficult for her too. 'In your language . . . the People in Smoke.'

'That makes sense,' he said, not really sure he understood.

But nothing more came from her.

'At least they're still just burning the island, though. Haven't troubled the mainland since spring, and even then it was just the beaches. No problems for us in the bogs.'

It was the one guaranteed topic of talk between most traders these days—the fires and strange unpredictability of those people out there, the speculating on where they'd go next—but now it brought only a deeper silence from Kahu, who hunched further into herself.

'You want some water? Matewai's treated it. It's herbed and boiled. You can trust it. Better than my stuff.'

Without warning she put the soup down and turned her face away, and a hand went to her eyes. He saw with a shock that she was crying.

'Oh, fuck.' He sent a panicked look towards Matewai's hut. But she was cooking up in there. She was unlikely to come and help. And Rau still wasn't up. He eased down beside Kahu and, as soon as he was sitting, found her turning into him, her shoulder hitting his chest, so his arms had to go round to catch her and stop her falling to the mud. A sob shook out, her tiny form racked by it.

As Van held the girl his eye roved beyond for help. Where were the old ones? Most mornings they'd be hovering about the pots by now, muttering about the lack of kawakawa in the soup, or over-reliance on it, the absence of decent meat, before shambling off to the latrine crops, still groaning to themselves and each other as they squatted and shat.

The girl's headwrap was pressed against his chin, scratching at his beard as she sobbed. She eased back at last, and dried her face with quick swipes.

He pitched his voice to be quiet. 'So what's this all about?'

'We were supposed to cross at first light,' she said. 'By the time we get to the Dry Way, even the grace time will be used up.'

He nodded, looking for sign of Rau. He was going to have to wake him up.

'Why do we have to wait?' she said, wiping her face again. 'Why can't we just go?'

He sat back from her, and frowned. 'You asked for Rau. I had to come here to get him.'

'I didn't ask for him. I said he could come too, if he likes.' She kept her eyes averted as she said this, as if she didn't want to correct him. 'That's all I said. His help wasn't part of our request.'

'But I had to ask him. I couldn't just take off without checking first.'

'Why not?'

Van stared. 'Well, he's my tuakana, and he's grieving. I can't just take off.' He looked about the camp, and had the sense of

39

losing his grip on his reasons. 'And there's Matewai. My trades.'

Her head was down. The only sound was the pīwaiwaka's chirp, and the wind-rustle of crops.

'We're busy people, you know. We've got trades. Work.'

He heard his own sharp tone, and saw her head duck away from him, and he regretted the rebuke. She was tired and upset, and Matewai had been harsh to her.

'Look, please eat your soup. It will help, trust me. You're going to need your strength.'

Three

He was still ten paces from Rau's hut, turning up the zigzag track, when the door flap sounded and Rau poked his head out. His face was bleary, his head not yet covered. His eye went to Van, then down to the camp below—and then he saw the stranger, and tensed.

'It's all right. I brought her. She's alone.'

Rau said nothing, eyeing the girl.

'She's from the Whaea people. She came to my camp last night.'

Van's eye strayed to Rau's forearm. A blade of harakeke was wrapped round a rag as a bandage, the whole mess of wound muddied with dust and blood.

'Hey,' said Rau, dragging Van's attention up from his arm. 'What does she want?'

'Not sure. But she's doing what we tell her. Matewai scared her shitless.'

Rau surveyed Kahu again. Then he turned, shouldering back to his hut and through the door flap. The floor logs creaked as he moved around in there. Then came the tang of breathing oil, penetrating even the walls of the hut. As the son of Matewai, Rau was able to get oils for his breathing illness that were many times stronger than those she traded with others.

'She's kind of in a rush,' said Van, speaking to the hut.

Rau's movements inside stopped.

'But I told her we're not—not especially.'

Rau's noises resumed and Van came closer to the hut, keeping a few paces back. The atmosphere of Ava's sickness still hung over the building. It surprised Van that Rau was still allowed to sleep inside it, now that Ava had passed. Normally, as he understood it, a hut where someone had died was cleared with water and rituals he wasn't privy to, so that it could be filled again with a new family and kids. Perhaps that was why Rau had been allowed to keep it—there were no children to fill up his hut, or any of the other empty huts on the mound.

Rau emerged from the door flap and straightened, mostly clothed but not belted up yet, the same coat he'd worn yesterday hanging free, still reeking of swamp mud from Ava's sinking. The bandage on the arm was just as bloody and stained and neglected as before. Bites showed all round it, some of them already swollen to welts. More bites on his forehead, another engorged on his knuckle. Coming towards Van, he took his hand, then his elbow. They hit shoulders and stepped apart.

'So,' said Van, 'you look brilliant.'

For answer Rau just brought a canister to his nose, and wheezed the healing fumes back. Then he jerked his head down in the direction of the girl. 'Does Ma know about this?'

'Āe. Her name's Kahu. She turned up at my camp last night. Says she's a fetch.'

Rau's eyebrow went up. 'How'd she get across?'

'A gap, apparently. They paid for it.'

'Huh,' said Rau. Van saw him take in the fuchsia blaze on Kahu's headwrap, the unpatched coat and fine scarf. Impressed, despite himself. Then he hunched again over his canister.

Matewai's door flap sounded, and they both watched as

she eased from the hut. With painful steps she went towards the cooking fires and the girl who sat on the log. Bending to Kahu, Matewai held something towards her—some better drink or snack—and spoke as she did so. It relieved Van to see it. Matewai was relenting while her sons were absent, while she didn't need to keep up her display of affront.

'It's about what's-her-name, isn't it?' said Rau, watching the exchange. 'The one you fucked. I bet she's hapū.'

Van winced. There was no teasing in Rau's voice, no excitement. Just a certainty about the way the world worked. His own wife dead now, and no children coming from their union. No one left for Matewai to pass her oiling trade on to. Ava's death itself a relief from many summers of cramping female agony. And now Van a likely father, in Rau's mind, after one ceremonial shot at Summer's Day with someone he'd met only once.

'I'm worried she might be sick,' said Van. 'Hana. I think maybe I gave her something, and now she's sick. And they're getting me up there to punish me for it.'

Rau snorted. 'You'd actually have to fuck someone else first, Van, to carry something on your dick.'

'Oh,' said Van. 'Nice.'

For a moment Rau squared up at him, as if hoping he'd start something, provide him with a face to punch. But then he just shook his head and shouldered away, returning to his darkened hut and its atmosphere of sick. But before reaching it, he turned. 'So are you going with her, or what?'

'Going where?'

'With that girl. To Hana. That's what it's about, right? This fetch.'

'Well, that's what I came here to ask. Kahurangi says you can come too, if you want.'

Rau frowned. 'Why?'

'Escort, I think.'

Rau surveyed the cooking fires below, the swamp, and the island with its waving smoke. 'Well, I'm up now. If you want me to come, and you've decided to go, I'll come across.'

'So you think we should go with her?'

Rau brought the oil canister up, and massaged his chest while he huffed the fumes back. '*I'm* not saying that. I'm just asking what you want me to do.'

'Well, that's what I'm asking for. I'm trying to get some advice.'

'Van, I've just sunk my wife. And Ma's busy cooking up. Help us out. Don't make us decide what you want.'

'I wasn't asking you to decide.'

'Yes, you were,' said Rau. 'You always do that.'

'What? That's bullshit.'

'Just tell me what you want.'

Van shook his head, amazed. 'Well, it's the timing, for one thing. Ava's just been sunk. You're bitten all over, and your arm's fucked, and you can hardly breathe by the sounds of it. You can't run the Dry Way with your chest like that. And Matewai's got the trade at noon. We should be here to flank her.'

'She can get someone else to take care of that. And I'm fit enough.'

Van couldn't follow Rau's thinking. They always flanked Matewai when a trade was taking place. The runners were generally reliable—those Matewai worked with at least—but a runner's existence was perilous. It had been known to make them desperate. There was always the chance one of them would pull a blade, turn over a camp and grab whatever they could to trade a safe way south.

'If there's a gap, we'll be fine,' said Rau. 'A gap means we won't have to go too fast, and I'll be able to keep up. And I'll get Ma to fix my chest before we head out.'

'Well, the gap closed at first light,' said Van.

'They'll keep it open for that kid,' said Rau. 'Look at her. You can tell she's worth heaps.'

'But there's no guarantee the Scarp will keep others off the Way. There'll be travellers. Ferals. All sorts. And you're completely sick. So if anything happens, that leaves just me and a kid to do the fighting. It's too big a risk.'

Rau sighed. 'Get a grip, Van. We're taking this trade. Of course we are.'

'What do you mean, of course?'

Rau threw an arm over the camp below them. 'Look at this place, Van. Look at it. Help us out.'

'I know,' said Van, more quietly. 'I know all that.'

'What?' said Rau, squaring up again. 'You know what? No kids? No one in these huts? Disease all round?' He seemed ready to say more but the outburst brought on his cough, and then he was bent over, hitting his chest and wheezing in breath. 'Fuck this,' he said. 'Fuck's sake.'

'I'm sorry,' said Van. 'I want to help out.'

Rau was still bent over. 'So what's the problem?'

'Well, all those things I just said. There's Matewai's trade. And we don't even know what it's about—they haven't said. It could be a punishment. And you're sick. And it's bloody rude of them to send a fetch when we've just sunk one of our own—a wife in your case. It's not right.'

Rau straightened at last. His chest rasped and caught. When his voice came again, it was in a different tone. 'Kāore ōu wai,' he said. 'He pōhara hoki. That's it, eh. That's what you're really worried about. She's posh and high-born and all that. She's got the good waters, and the flash reo. And you haven't.'

Van dropped his head.

'Oh, mate,' said Rau. 'I'm sure she doesn't care about that. Did they say anything about it in the wording of the fetch?'

Van said nothing. His eyes on his own rag boots.

'And was it a problem at Summer's Day? When you were getting some?' He paused. 'Some sweet—sweet—'

Van didn't look up. He knew Rau was making some grinding manoeuvre with his crotch, but he didn't want to acknowledge it, not while Kahu was watching.

Rau sighed. 'Look, just forget all that. She wants to see you. I'd say she's got someone's ear, someone important, and they've sent you a fetch. It's brilliant. My bet is she's hapū. And they sent a kid, so obviously the Whaeas aren't planning to punish you for it. If it was a punishment, they wouldn't have sent some posh kid through all that danger. They would have just sent across some patrol of tamāhine toa at night to slit your throat and cut your guts out. You know that.'

He paused to work on his breath, the canister right beneath his nose. It amazed Van that he could stand the fumes like that. But then Rau lowered the canister to indicate the crops below them, the huts. 'Look around you, man. Ma's, like, a hundred. There's no kids. And Ava's—' He coughed. Unprepared for his own grief—the same rage he'd cut into his arm with a knife and stayed out all night to honour, and taken multiple bites for. As if to blast it away, he flicked oil with his fingers towards his eyes, blinking at its sting. 'Look, this is a great chance, Van. It's exactly why Ava sent you across there, why she traded for a Summer's Day invite for you. She hoped something like this would happen. For her sake, you have to take it.'

Van's eye went down towards Kahu, and she dropped her

46

face; even though she couldn't hear them, she'd been watching their distant talk. Under his attention she shifted the plastic bowl of soup and looked intently at it, as if willing it to be eaten without involving her own mouth. Then she lifted the bowl to her face, sculling back the soup. When she'd finished, she dropped the plastic bowl to the mud and, even from that distance, Van saw her shudder.

'You do like her, don't you,' said Rau. 'The one we're talking about.'

'Hana,' said Van.

'That's right. Hana. You do like her.'

'Āe,' he said. 'She's stuck in my head. I think about her all the time.'

'She's stuck in your head,' said Rau. 'You like her that much.'

Van met his eye, and nodded.

Rau's hand went up; he pulled Van into his aroma of mud and oil, and they knocked shoulders. 'In that case, I'll get my stuff.'

'They said something else.'

Rau turned.

'They said they'd teach me.'

'Teach you what?'

'About the old waters. That's what Kahu said. This is what I don't get. I can't believe they'd do that—teach a stranger about their old waters.'

Rau grinned. 'Not about theirs, stupid. They're not going to teach you about their waters.' He pointed. 'Yours.'

Van stared. 'But I don't have any, besides yours. Mine are all dead, remember?' He swept a hand over the camp, the sprawling swamp he lived in. 'Orphan—swamp. That's why I live where I do. The only waters I've got are yours. That's the whole point.'

Rau shook his head. 'They must know something else. They must know something different.'

Oil fumes came from Matewai's hut. Behind her, hanging in the building's interior, Van glimpsed branches of mānuka and kawakawa, along with bunches of lavender and what he thought could be rosemary. But then she pulled the door flap tight behind her, blocking her work from sight.

Standing on her stoop, she regarded the two men. 'You've decided.'

'*He* has,' said Rau.

She looked in Van's face, reading it, then at the girl beyond. 'Ka pai. Neke atu, boy. I'm coming down.'

Van stepped aside and she eased to the ground, her movements heavy on her bad hip. The two men followed her around the side of the hut; as usual when strangers were in camp, they would plan their trade talk out of sight.

Once in their places, Matewai looked pointedly at Rau's noisy chest.

'I'm all right,' he said, anticipating her.

'Because Van can go without you, you know. No need to babysit him.'

Rau scowled. 'I never said I was babysitting him.'

Matewai looked in the direction of the Whaea slopes. 'And we don't owe them anything. They're bold to ask us in our time of grief.' She looked more directly at her son. 'And you don't have to cut your grief short. You should have your marama pōuri.'

'Could people please stop telling me about my grief? I can make up my own mind about that.' The outburst made him cough. He hit his chest and spat a string of green phlegm onto the mud. 'Fuck's sake.'

After a time Van said, 'That southerly's getting up. We should get started.'

Matewai pointed at Rau's bandaged arm. 'Before you go, I'm going to re-treat those bites, and that bloody paru bandage, and your chest. You won't be much use to him with breath like that.' She paused, as if considering what to say next. 'You shouldn't have camped out last night. Not the best choice, kid.'

For answer, Rau barged away. Once far enough off, facing the clear sky to the north, he opened his clothes and pissed into the shelter crops.

Matewai sighed.

The sun was still climbing, as if to refute the clouds that were brewing up further south.

'How's your wai?'

'I brought enough to get us across,' said Van. He dropped his voice so Rau wouldn't hear. 'A gap was promised. It's expired apparently, so we'll have to run the Way like normal, but hopefully they'll keep it open and we won't have to fight our way across. It shouldn't be too hard on his breath.'

Matewai swivelled to look at Kahu. 'All right. Let's get her told.'

Tucking himself back together, Rau spoke over his shoulder. 'Don't make shit with her, Ma. Don't drag up all that old shit.'

'I'm not going to make shit. I'm just going to say what needs to be said.'

'It's a good chance for Van—for all of us. Don't mess up his root.'

She put a hand up. 'I'm not going to mess up Van's root. I'm just saying that if this girl is fetching you two, then she can fetch a message back to her aunties too. They're due to hear it.'

'Please stop calling her my root,' said Van. 'Her name is Hana.'

Matewai cocked an eye at him.

'You see?' said Rau. 'That's why I say don't make shit.'

Matewai lifted her hand again. 'Son, I heard you the first time.'

They took their flanking positions: Rau on the right-hand side of Matewai, Van on the left. As Kahu stood up to face them, Van saw her gauge Matewai for what attitude she would bring this time.

Matewai indicated the bowl, the liquid the girl had forced down. 'Not quite what you're used to, probably, that soup.'

Kahu's eye darted to Van. 'He reka te kai. I liked it.'

Matewai nodded, and looked beyond the girl as another puff of breeze came into the crops, making the blades of harakeke shift and scrape. 'The boys told me your request.'

Kahu did a pace, wet her lips. 'Kei te māuiui tōku kuia. She's really sick. We need some help.'

Immediately, Matewai and Rau turned to Van.

'You didn't say that to me,' he said. 'Why didn't you tell me that?'

'I wasn't allowed to. Not until ... not until I met ...' The girl's voice failed her. She couldn't look Matewai in the face, let alone say her name.

Van, his face burning, felt all their eyes on him. It was a standard trading trick—the trader giving layers of reasons to obscure the real purpose of the trade, to keep real motivations hidden and people safe—and he'd fallen straight into it.

'Ka pai, girl,' said Rau. 'Well played. Is she really sick, though? Your Nan?'

'That's part of it, I'd imagine.' This was from Matewai, under her breath.

Kahu just nodded, and Van found it hard to maintain his reproach. She looked sick herself; her feet drawn together, her head bowed at being caught in the mistruth she must have been instructed to give.

'Not Van's lady, though,' said Rau. 'She's not sick, is she? You're not dragging him to some punishment because she's fallen sick.'

'Kāo.'

For a time there was just the noise of Rau's wheezing chest and the leaves of the crops as they moved in the rising wind.

'All the same,' said Matewai, at last, 'there's no reason why our whānau should help you out. We've never been invited up to your place in all the many summers since your people walked out. Not to a sinking up at your place, and not for a feast. We've never had the honour, before this. Despite the joining of our old waters, way back.'

'That's not quite true,' said Van.

Matewai turned, an eyebrow up.

'Well, I went to Summer's Day.'

'Āe, and that's because we spent a fortune on fancy Whaea oils for Ava,' said Matewai. 'And because they owed her already, from before, and that was our payback.'

Kahu stepped forward, that same half-pace brought on by nerves. 'They might ask Van and Raureti to bring my Nan across,' she said. 'I think that's part of what it's about. And they want to teach Van some things—things I don't know about.'

Matewai said nothing to this—didn't even nod. She let her eyes weigh on Kahu, then looked away into the forest that bordered her crops, and the dark trunks that stood there in silence. She seemed irritated with everyone at the moment: with Van, with Rau, with the girl facing her across the mud.

51

'Nan is very old. Her tūpuna came from here—from the swamp.'

'Really,' said Matewai.

Her tone made Kahu flinch, and again Van had the sense that Kahu was trying to say something she didn't want to, some message she'd been instructed to impart. 'There's a story that one of her tūpuna was carried out of the swamp, during their heke out of here, in her Māmā's kōpū.' She scanned their faces for sign they knew what she meant. Then a hand went over her own belly. 'Te whare tangata, we call it.'

'Yeah, we know the expression, darling. Thanks.'

Kahu's hand went up. 'She told me to say why,' she said to Van. 'Why we're fetching you.'

'It's okay,' said Van. 'It's all right.'

She cast another look at Matewai, her face hurt. 'That's why my Nan has to come back here. Because of that kōrero. That's why I said that.'

Matewai sighed. 'We're aware of your tradition. We know what you're saying.' She adjusted her weight again, and gazed in the direction of the Whaea territories, the enclosure of forest up there. 'This is it, though, isn't it? Your lot's hīkoi out of here. Coming back. All that.'

Kahu darted a look towards her, wary, and Matewai made a gesture to encompass her own camp and the trees and swamp beyond—the whole coast perhaps. 'Your tradition would have been fine,' she said. 'But your people didn't just walk out of here, did they? As soon as they got up there, they dug a lake. Put a dam across. And then that bloody fence. And that just turned our stream to crap, so there was no flow anymore and it got all paru'd up. But you wouldn't know that, because it's all below your precious freshwater lake, so you don't have to care about it.' She put her hand on her hip and frowned, as if it increased her pain to be angry all over again. 'It was our creek too, girl. And you put a bloody great dam across it, and a fence, and now it tastes like shit.'

'Not her exactly,' said Van.

Matewai whirled on him.

'Well, she's just a kid, and you're talking about what happened so many summers back. It was her tūpuna who did that. That's all I'm saying.'

'Well, she's the fetch—' She lifted her voice. 'You're the fetch, girl, and we get no chances to say this, down here. Look how old I am, and I've never been able to say it. And my Māmā didn't either, may she rest. You just never come down here to ask us what we thought.'

'And never once brought medicines across,' said Rau. 'Made me run the Dry Way every time, no matter how sick Ava was, and no matter how many times she'd helped your healers out, way back.'

Matewai moved her hand, as if not wanting Rau to contaminate her message. 'I'm not saying your Nan's sickness isn't important, girl. I'm not saying that. And if they'd sent you at a better time, when I'm not cooking up, and when someone's not just been sunk, then I would have hosted you properly. But we've had a grief, and I'm working, because we have to keep trading down here, even through a sad time, and anyway your aunties have never thought about what's best for us, have they.'

At the mention of the death, Kahu made to lift her forearm in the Whaea sign, but it was stopped by a rough swipe of Matewai's own hand. 'That doesn't change a thing, kid. I'm sorry, but it doesn't.'

'Hey, be gentle,' said Van. 'She's trying. And they wrecked the stream ages back. Not her fault.'

'Well, we've still got the taint.' Matewai indicated the bowl and cup at the girl's feet. 'You tasted our water. What did you think of it?'

Kahu's voice was just a murmur. 'Thank you for the food and drink.'

'Mud and down-flowed pūkeko shit. That's what it tastes like. And that's after we've boiled it, and herbed it, and god knows what else. 'Cause that's all that comes from your lake— comes down past your dam. When you see fit to release any water at all, that is.' She adjusted her stance again, and sighed. 'Oh, whatever.' A few first spits of rain pattered into the leaves. 'Go on, then. Get your stuff, you two. Get her home safe.'

'Is that—' Van knew he risked a further rebuke from Matewai, but her treatment of Kahu worried him. 'Is that all you want to say to her?'

Matewai shook her head, but it was in that heavy way of before, as if her whole anger was too complicated and too old—far too old—for a girl and two men, messed up by grief, to make sense of. 'This won't be my only chance. I'll be seeing that kid again, is my guess.' But then, as if hearing something in her own words, she sighed. 'Oh, bugger it. Haere mai then, girl.'

Kahu looked up, and Matewai waved her on.

'Kia tere. It hurts me to stand still in one place.'

Glancing again at Van, as if to check she'd heard the instruction right, she came towards the older woman. 'Tēnā koe, e hine,' said Matewai. 'Kia tau te rangimārie ki runga i a koe.' She squeezed the girl against her. Then she held Kahu back, her vast and work-stained hand spanning the younger woman's shoulder. 'And they don't even feed you enough. Bad enough that they send you out alone to places like this, but they don't even give you a decent kai, either. For goodness' sake.'

Kahu's eyes were wide, her face all awe at the contact.

'Kei te pai, girl,' said Matewai. 'You just take my message

back, and look after this Pākehā here, and you and I will get along all right.'

She grunted, and reached out to rub the girl's arm. Then she pushed her away, and hoisted her own weight round for the painful walk back towards her hut. Before reaching it she turned, knowing that none of them would have moved. With a rough hand, she motioned Van inland. 'Go on then, if you're going,' she said. 'Get your stuff, boy. Get.'

Four

Wind thrashed the branches, blocking the view of the risk ahead. They were huddled in the last of the covering scrub, Kahu kneeling to part the taupata so that Van and Rau could see the earth and swamp they'd have to cross. First, a run over no man's land, where Raka's workers of the Scarp had cut down all trees and gorse so that any attempt to reach the Dry Way would be clearly visible. Then the Runalong Ponds. Finally, the banks of the Dry Way, high on its own ramparts, banked up with stones to be clear of the surrounding ponds.

The wind blasted again, blowing the branches back. So far the storm had brought only wind, no rain yet.

'What a perfect day,' said Van.

'It looks good, though, right? There's no one out.' Kahu's eyes were bright, her tension obvious.

Van kept his voice slow to stop her nerves from infecting him. 'That wind's a problem, Rau. Do you think you can make it?'

Rau nodded. 'Never done the north gate before, but otherwise, āe. What's our formation?' He was doing it again, relinquishing his usual role as boss.

'Well, you should take the middle, in case your breath gets worse and we have to stop. I'll be at the back. Which leaves

Kahurangi at the front.'

The use of the girl's full name seemed to interest Rau in her again. He studied her crouching form, even as he brought out his breathing canister and unstoppered it.

'Can we go now?' she said.

'Not too fast, Kahu,' said Van. 'Don't get ahead.'

She nodded. 'You'll see the gate once we're up on the way itself.'

'Keep with us,' said Van. 'We stay together, in a clump.'

She watched his mouth move as he spoke, her eyes again very bright. Her hand closed round a branch of taupata, as if holding herself safe in cover for one more moment. Then she spurted out at full speed, her colours released and flying back from her neck.

'Brilliant,' said Rau. 'Sprint ahead on your own. Just like we said.' He took one more snort from the canister and stoppered it, then shouldered out into the gust. It pierced Van to see that lumbering run, made more difficult by this wind and the worsening of Rau's breath. Rau was breaking his days of grief for Van's sake, and all at such risk to his health.

Not leaving cover yet, Van traced the girl's course ahead. She was much too far in front of Rau—was already getting isolated—but she'd chosen a good route along the bank of an outlying finger of pond. Further out the grass was littered with the stumps of trees the Scarp workers had hacked down, clearing cover so no one could hide in it. They were scrupulous in their work to make the Dry Way the only—and the most frightening—way through, flanked on one side by waist-high ponds, and by the guarded steeps of the Scarp on the other. The alternative route down the beach, out to the west beyond the swamp, was no longer safe since the Burners had taken the island and burnt out the last of the coastal villages.

Van stepped out, and the wind hit him. He picked up speed, and felt the exposure of it: sprinting in full view of anyone up on the Way or the Scarp, his bags flailing.

As he closed on Rau he heard the noise of his chest.

'Do you need to stop?'

Rau shook his head but his face was screwed up with the effort of wheezing in breath.

Van looked for Kahu and swore. They were getting too separated. 'Fucking hell. I'm going to have to catch her.'

Rau just waved him forward.

Van sprinted down the bank and onto the broken ground. A pūkeko squawked up, wings and legs beating hard. Kahu was making for an old stand of gorse that hadn't been cut down; she would corner it and run into the ponds. She'd lost all caution. He waved his hand wildly, shouted. Somehow she heard him in the wind and turned.

He waved for her to get down, to stop.

She dived backwards, crawling under the gorse.

As Van sprinted towards the cover he scanned the Way and the Scarp beyond and saw no sign just yet. Reaching the gorse he slid in, thorns stabbing his hands and neck. Then his hands were on the girl. 'What the fuck are you doing?'

Panting, she stared.

'I said slow,' said Van. 'I said fucking stay together.'

Then Rau was coming. Van shoved Kahu to the side to make room, and Rau barged in, showering old twigs and thorns from above. They untangled from each other, and Rau coughed and coughed and hit his chest and spat phlegm.

Overhead the wind thrashed.

Van peered out. No one was running down the Wayside rocks. He put his hands again on the girl, and felt her coiled fright. It seemed he had to hold her down, like a rabbit that would bolt. 'Slow down, for fuck's sake. I said to stay together. You'll get killed.'

Her eyes followed his mouth.

'Kei te mārama koe? We can't protect you if you're out in front.'

Another gust flailed the gorse above them, and Kahu wiped her face of flecks of bark. Then her eyes went to Rau. He had a canister at his nostril to huff vapours while his other hand massaged his chest.

'Can you make the Way?' said Van.

Rau nodded, but it was some time before he could gather enough breath to speak. 'Any sign?'

Van peered out. Only ten or fifteen paces on, the joining-place of ponds. Wind stippled the brown water there; they would have to wade almost as soon as they left this hiding place. On the far banks, the broken rock that led up to the Dry Way was snarled with blackberry and gorse. 'Kāo. We're good for now.'

Rau took one more long inhale, then stoppered the canister. Hit his chest twice with his free hand and coughed. 'Right.'

Immediately, Kahu made to stand up.

'Taihoa,' said Van. 'What's the depth in the pond there? I think we should link arms.'

'It was only up to my knees when I came over,' said Kahu. 'I was fine on my own.'

'But there might be sink-holes underfoot,' said Van. 'We'll look stronger too, if we link up, to people who can see us from the Way.'

Something in Kahu's reaction made Rau laugh. 'Do what he says, girl. You don't know shit.'

She blinked, shocked but trying not to show it.

Rau's laughter brought on a cough, and she looked away

59

from the phlegm he spat on the mud. When he'd recovered, Rau reached through his coat and brought out a second, larger canister and, before she could protest, gripped Kahu by the wrist and flicked oil at her headwrap and hands and wrists. The tang of the treatment was fierce—mānuka and horopito and other crops, at serious strengths—and she squirmed away from it, burrowing back into the hoary gorse before recoiling from its spikes. Again she reminded Van of an animal trying to hide itself.

'Kahu, hold still,' said Van. 'He's dosing you.'

She looked at him, surprised at the use of her name, then winced them shut against the fumes. Rau held her by the wrist to splash her further. It was an uncomfortable picture: all of them crouching under the gorse, the girl in the grip of Rau's huge fist, her face and hands unblemished by bites; Rau's coat of possum and rabbit skins ripped, and, showing through the gaps, his skin patterned with fresh, angry-looking bites.

'All right,' said Rau, treating himself next, smearing it on his face and wrist and neck. 'Van goes into the water first. He sets the pace.'

It went against all instinct, to offer yourself into swamp water like this. The murk was warm; it seeped into Van's rag boots, then round his calves and up the back of his knees. Kahu strained at the arms that held her back—wanting to run, he sensed, to surge through the pond and sprint up the bank, then down the remaining distance to her people and safety.

'Careful,' said Rau. 'Not too fast.'

For what seemed a long time they were slogging through the water, with nowhere to hide, their feet hidden below and sludged in mud. Van noticed Rau was holding his arm, freshly washed and wrapped by Matewai, above the water's surface. Protecting it from the paru.

Then Van's foot came down on something. Whatever it was had a spongy give; as his weight went down, it snapped. Long sunk in mud, it felt like the ribcage of some traveller pushed into the pond at knifepoint. He told himself it wasn't; it was probably just a branch of some sunken tree, but all the same he skirted it, pushing the others wide.

'Keep steady,' said Rau.

Then Kahu snagged her foot and gasped too, pitching towards the water. Her arms were linked with Van's and Rau's, and they both strained, pulling her up.

'Kia tūpato, for fuck's sake,' said Rau. 'You're as bad as each other, you two.'

Van's eye searched along the Way, but there was still no sign of running Scarp.

They slogged further into the wind and mud.

At last they found shallower footing. They broke arms and surged up out of the last part. Water streamed from them and sagged their clothes round their belts.

Van scrambled onto the incline of the Way and immediately spiked his hand on blackberry. 'Fuck.' Kahu was above him, dislodging rocks. He saw the undersoles of her boots—thick and doubled possum skins. Pricey.

He slogged further up. Rau already stood there on the Way. The trails of his headwrap whipped in the wind as he scanned north and south.

Van reached the barrier of gorse branches and brambles that made the Wayside fence. The lower part of his coat caught on blackberry vine; he pulled against it and got further spiked.

'Hurry up, Van,' said Rau.

Van saw that Kahu had joined Rau and was looking south.

He tried again to release his coat, and swore, then gripped it with his hands and ripped a gap below his crotch. Cold air rushed in and flapped. He lurched over the barrier; he was in the Way.

'Clear to the north and south,' said Rau.

Van scanned all ways himself. The wind was much stronger up here. He had to shout to make himself heard. 'How's your breath?'

Rau showed the canister in his fist. 'Working on it.' Then he eyed Van's ripped coat and the gaping rip on his inside leg, and grinned. 'I know you don't do much woman-chasing, Van, but you know it's normal to get there first, then get naked.'

Van shook his head. Rau found his enjoyment in the grimmest of places.

'Kahu, you all right?'

She nodded, her face tight. Not so brave now.

'Stay in close by me.'

They ran again, into the wind that blasted dust. Van took care with his footing. The Way's surface was a rubble of stones and dirt and root-holes where plants had been ripped out and thrown aside. Kahu spurted along at Van's shoulder, a light-stepping shadow at his right.

No one in the Way so far.

It was strange to be up so high, so exposed. On both sides the stretching swamp, then the vast island smoking off the coast. Here and there along the Way, baskets and bags lay where they'd been ripped off travellers and scattered, the flax and skins left to rot.

Rau was noisy beside him, already slowing down.

'You all right?'

He didn't respond; too much effort.

Fifty paces on, a clot of mānuka had been left standing in

the centre of the Way; a pair of old harakeke bags were tied into it, rotted and flying about in the wind. But there was something else in there too. It moved.

'Rau,' said Van. 'Rau.'

The shape stepped from the mānuka. A long, downways weapon at its right.

'Scarper!' said Van. 'Scarp!'

Instead of stopping, Kahu spurted ahead, her headwrap and colours flying back. In her fear she was running for home, for the safety of the Whaea place. It was suicide, though; to get there she'd have to run right through this man and his weapon. Van sprinted after her. In his panic he forgot her name. 'Hey, girl! Girl! Stop!'

He reached her shoulder and yanked her back. She overbalanced, and he put his arm right over her, dragging her in against him. At the same time, his free hand went beneath his coat for his plastic bar. His mind racing to his precious pieces. He'd stowed a dozen in his bag, and now he feared for them.

Kahu had her balance now and she tried to stand free of Van, but he held her back. 'Stay right here!'

The man was too far away for Van to see his face. Shorter than him, though. His head covered with a simple grey. As they watched, he leaned back into the scrub and bags that thrashed in the storm-wind, and then a second figure melted out from it. Bigger.

'Fuck,' said Rau. He wheezed heavily, but he'd brought his own blade out—metal, made generations back, impossible to trade for—and now he swung the vast chopper at his side.

The two figures stood motionless down the Way.

'How are you two, Van?' said Rau, circling his blade. 'Ready for this?'

63

Van shoved Kahu behind himself, hiding her from the Scarpers. He held his bar out from his leg, showing its plastic length and weight. He'd dug it from his mine many summers back. It was a brutal instrument, as thick as a man's forearm and hardened by some ancient technique. He swung it now and glanced at Kahu. She was blank with fright. Then she dropped her head. Muttered fast in a string of words he couldn't catch. Another prayer, from the sound of it.

'I don't like this, Rau.'

Neither man took his eye from the pair ahead. It frightened Van that Rau made no joke, sent no 'fuck you' gesture in their direction. Not confident enough.

'Yeah, I don't like the look of that big one,' said Rau. 'But I can't run faster than either of those people right now, with this chest. Plus they've got all those arseholes up on the slopes to help them. So it's either a trade or a fight.'

Van felt the pissy squirt of fear in his groin.

'Let's step up, then,' said Rau. 'Keep the girl close.'

Van reached behind and, with the hand that held the bar, brought her right alongside. 'Stay right in by me.'

Another forty paces to the two figures.

Rau was slightly forward now, still on the inland side. He checked to the left for runners that might come down from the Scarp to support these two. Van glanced that way as well, his hand still wrapped round the girl's wrist, the bar like a splint on her forearm.

'Should I keep my colours out?'

She had the feathers in her fist in front of her chest, held there in protection, it seemed.

'Put them away,' he said. 'And stay right in here beside me.'

'Eyes up,' said Rau. 'Here they come.'

The original man came first, the much larger figure behind,

heavy-shouldered and toting the handle of some broken weapon. The clothes of the advancing pair were sufficiently heavy not to swing round in the gale. They looked to be made of possum skins, the coats cinched tight at the waist with serious belts.

'Rau, it would be good to know our strategy.'

'Yep. Working on it.' His breath rasping, Rau peered through the streaking wind.

Kahu's voice came again, murmuring karakia.

The strangers were close now. Van saw Rau thinking hard, straining at something. His free hand moved in little circles. Something was coming to him.

'Kahu, get your blade out.' Van motioned her to be quick. 'Show your blade.'

They came on. Van found his own bar up at chest height of its own accord, the handle clenched tight in his fist.

Rau's eyes were closed.

'Rau!' he said. 'What's our fucking plan?'

The pair were a dozen paces off.

Just a stream of prayer now from Kahu, her voice catching on itself in fright.

'Fuck this,' said Van. He stepped well clear and swung the bar.

The pair slowed.

'Squat,' said Rau.

'What?' A further gust; Van had to turn and shout through it. 'What are you saying?'

'It's Squat,' said Rau. 'Yeah, that's Squat, and that's his wife.'

'You know these people?' said Van.

'It's Squat. Āe, I know him—kind of.'

Van jerked his head towards Kahu. 'Will they be all right with her?'

As he lifted a high palm towards the couple, Rau looked at Kahu. 'Dunno. Your people owe him anything?'

Kahu just stared.

'Stay close to Van,' said Rau, seeing she was too frightened to speak. 'He's a shady fucker, this one.'

Van signalled Kahu in behind him. The weapons the pair held were lengths of hardwood with some kind of fire-moulded spikes at their ends.

'Easy now, Squat,' said Rau, lifting his voice. 'We're on a trade.'

The man stayed still to hear Rau's announcement, then slung himself forward again, leading from the hips.

Rau let out a mirthless laugh. 'God, he's dirty. That's close enough, Squat. No offence.'

The man's face was visible now, notched below the eyes, in the way of the Scarp. His squint fixed on Rau and Van, and then on the girl behind.

'That must be your wife with you, Squat,' said Rau. 'Our regards to your lady.'

Squat nodded. 'You can call her Hine.'

Barely moving, Rau acknowledged the woman. She was notched under the eyes like Squat, but taller, and much stronger through the shoulders. Her wide face was impassive.

Van cleared his throat, and edged further in front of Kahu. The whole time, Squat had not taken his eyes off her.

'Who've you got with you?'

'She's a trade,' said Rau. 'Coming through a gap your people made with the Whaeas. We're walking through that gap today.'

Squat said nothing.

'You heard about it, I reckon,' said Rau.

Squat let his eye go again from Rau to Van and then to Kahu. 'Didn't hear about a gap. No mention.'

'Well, it's a gap,' said Rau. 'Fair and square.'

'Kāo,' said Squat. 'No mention.'

Whereas Rau raised his voice into the mess of wind and dust, almost shouting, Squat seemed to need only to murmur for his voice to carry. It was unnerving. Wind blasted once more, and they all turned against it and Van used the chance to check on Kahu. She had her colours in her fist, holding them against her chest again. Van saw the small fist shake, the hand that held her blade shivering too. Strange to see her so terrified. The young Whaea women were supposed to be famous for fighting, trained to deal with Scarpers just like this. Perhaps it was because she'd missed the deadline of the gap, or perhaps it was just that this Way worker seemed particularly feral.

'It's all right,' he told her. 'We can take them out, if we have to.'

It was a moment before she understood, staring at his mouth as it moved. Then she nodded quickly.

Now Squat was in conference with his wife, the big woman's head leaning down to him. Squat scowled as he listened, as if reluctant to concede anything, to show he was the mouthpiece only and really his wife lay down their strategy. At length he turned to face them, and squared his shoulders back. He indicated the harakeke bandage on Rau's arm. 'Sorry about Ava,' he said. 'We saw your walk with her. Saw the sinking.'

Rau stiffened.

Again Van checked the slope for reinforcements coming down to help Squat.

'He mihi aroha ki a koe, e Rau.'

Still Rau gave no response.

'I'm trying to acknowledge your hurts,' said Squat.

'Yeah, all right,' said Rau. 'I heard it.' He rolled his shoulders. It was unclear why Squat's comment had angered him.

Something in their history, perhaps, something that touched on Ava.

'What's this trade about, again?' said Squat. 'Run that by me one more time.'

Rau didn't answer right away. Instead he turned to look at the slope. 'You got an eye on our position, Van?'

'Āe. I got it.'

Rau hoisted a shoulder and turned to face Squat, and his face was hard, and for a moment it seemed he would spring on the smaller man and club him, then elbow the big woman's jaw, chopping his blade on her neck as she went down. Then he hit his own chest instead, and spat on the mud between them. When his voice came, Van could hear the suppressed rage in it. 'My Ma was good to your lady once, Squat, as I remember it. An oil trade, I think it was, for her health. Ma helped her with lady problems, I believe.'

Squat said nothing.

Beside him, Hine just watched Rau with that same wooden expression.

'We've come straight from Ma, in fact, on trade with the Whaea people. As per the gap agreement you also can remember. We're taking this young person over right now, just like it says in the agreement.'

Squat snorted. 'The agreement that's expired.'

Then something made Squat flinch. He turned again towards his wife. Hine—if that was her name—hadn't moved, yet there was some kind of unspoken signal coming from her, one Squat had understood but didn't want to acknowledge. As he listened to her few words, he squinted beyond Rau to the Scarp on the inland side, its slope scarred with tracks where the Scarpers ran down to the Dry Way at moments like this, assisting their Way workers when travellers got above themselves. Then he rolled his own shoulders, as if to mimic the same movement of Rau's, and better it. 'You know that when a trade expires a roadie like me has some discretion. Some discretion to take payment. I'm sure you all know that.'

Van saw the woman draw up alongside her husband. She did not turn to him, didn't talk; instead she faced down the Way towards the three of them, as if her only intention was to intimidate them better. But it changed Squat's tone once more. It went whiny. 'An' I just want to know why, if it's up to me, I would help out that bunch of fucking hoity-toities.' His head jerked in Kahu's direction. 'And especially when that one you've got there looks tasty—real tasty and pricey.'

Before he could stop himself Van stepped closer to Squat and swung the bar, making vicious circles with it. At the same time, he felt moisture in his groin—a squirt of piss in his fear.

The smaller man looked up Van's height. Then, without warning, Squat grabbed his crotch and shouted, 'Fuck you, swamp bitch.'

'Easy now, Van,' said Rau. 'Take it easy, Van.' Then he sent his voice beyond, speaking fast. 'Well, ngā mihi ki a koe, e Squat. Peace on your waters. Let us through now.'

'E hē,' said Squat. 'I am *not* finished with you.'

'Don't make a mistake here, Squat.'

'Don't fucking tell me what to do. You're not in your fucking swamp huts now, boy. You're in my Way. And if I want to cut your nancy piece of Pākehā there, I will.'

Van swung the bar, coming closer. 'Come on then, fucker.'

Squat threw his head back. 'Ha ha! I love it.' He made the same grab at his crotch, more wildly this time. He called Van a nancy Pākehā swamp bitch again too, even though Squat's own features looked Pākehā to Van, but perhaps that was just his āhua. 'And if I want some of that posh bitch behind you, same

69

goes. I'm going for it—no one to stop me.'

'I'm going to fucking club you,' shouted Van, advancing. 'I'm gonna club you down.'

Then someone pulled him. It was Rau, yanking him back.

Squat pointed with his spike weapon, laughing maniacally. His hand still on his crotch, he repeated that 'fuck you' motion. Then Hine's hand descended on him. He scowled as she spoke her few words to him.

A further blast of wind, then Van heard a renewed stream of karakia—Kahu again.

Squat wiped his face, as if clearing road dust, and his face turned even meaner. 'Rules are rules, fuckers. The price will be—'

Rau interrupted him, calling from alongside Van. 'What's it going to cost us, Hine? What's the price?'

'You're trading with me. Talk to *me*, fuckers.' Squat jabbed at his chest. 'I decide the price, and the price will be precious pieces, plastic ones.' He looked straight at Van as he repeated it. 'Six precious pieces—those big ones. And a bag of fresh water, just to wash our feet with after our trip back tonight.'

'Are you joking me?' said Van.

'Why would I joke, swamp-shit?'

'All right,' said Rau, his hands calming them both. 'If that's going to make it work, then that's the price.'

'Oh, for fuck's sake.' Van pushed away, storming to the edge of the Dry Way.

'Look at me, Van,' said Rau, following him. 'Van, look at me. Remember what this is about.'

Van threw his arm, his bar flying out with it. 'Who is this guy, Rau? I don't even know him. Why don't we just smash the little shit? We can take him, easy.'

'Don't be stupid. That'll just bring his mates down from the

Scarp. And we've got that girl. We've got to get her through, and you as well. That's the point of all this.' He paused, wheezing in breath. 'Look, I'm eating shit here. I hate this guy.'

'Yeah, why is that? What'd he do?'

Rau shook his head. 'Have you got some precious pieces on you?'

'He wants six pieces,' said Van. '*Six* of them.'

'So you've got some? On you?'

'Āe, but—'

'Then this is what you brought them for. For trade. For safety for that girl.'

'No, it's not. I brought them for—' He swore. 'They're not for scrotes like him.'

'Hana can't take plastic, Van,' said Rau, reading him. 'She can't accept it.'

'You don't know that,' said Van. 'Mine's different. She might take high-end work like my precious pieces. That's why I brought it—to show her it's not just regular paru plastic.' He indicated Kahu. 'And she's eaten out of plastic before. She told me that herself. Right before she ate Matewai's soup from my plastic bowl today. Which means it can't be that poisonous for them.'

Rau shook his head. 'We're doing this, Van. If we don't, it's not safe for that girl. Squat is fucking horrible, trust me.'

'I'm not giving him six. That's four whole summers of work.'

'Yes, you are,' said Rau. 'If you want to get through to Hana, and get that girl home, that's exactly what you're doing.'

Van looked away through the thrashes of wind to the slopes that protected Squat's friends. A rich canopy of kohekohe and other bush obscured the hides up there, all of them peopled with Scarper ferals just like Squat. All summer those cowards had watched him from their looking-out places, throughout the stifling days he'd spent at the mine face and before the fire in his patching mask, rearing back from the fumes and heat, sweating for the sake of his low-status work with patched tubs and restored canisters. And now they stole the best of his work—the truly valuable pieces—because they couldn't do it themselves, or couldn't be fucked learning how to.

'Whatever,' he said. 'Do what you want.'

'No, it's what *you* want, Van. This gets you to Hana, remember, and gets that girl home safe.'

Again Van pushed past him, back into the force of the dust-pelting wind, heading further away from Squat and from all of them. He was still shaking his head as he bent to dig through the bag, the bottom of it wet from his wade through the Runalong Ponds. He found the wrap of precious pieces, but he didn't draw it out. Instead he unwrapped it inside the bag. It seemed important to keep it obscured from any of Squat's mates who might be watching. It was unlikely they'd be able to see the contents of his bag from up there, but if Hana was ever to see the pieces that remained, he didn't want any taint of Scarp eyes lingering on them.

Rau came to his side and crouched down too, as if to assist but really to talk. 'We can make him pay another time. You know it will come back round. These things always do.'

'Just keep him away from me, Rau, or I swear I'll fucking kill him.'

'Kei te pai,' said Rau. 'I don't blame you for that.'

Van's fingers were on the largest piece now. It was a deep blue-black, and unsullied. A neckpiece that had been reinforced and hardened and finished in a way that was invisible to the eye and had cost Van many afternoons at the fire. Surely Hana would have seen the craft in this, its freedom from taint. He picked out five more—all the largest pieces. If any of his work was to impress her it would have to be the most delicate of his rings or hairpins, or something entirely new, something he hadn't made yet but could craft once he knew her better. A plastic shell, maybe, for wearing round her neck on plait. Or a kawakawa leaf, eaten into a spider-web pattern by grubs. He pictured such a piece sitting against the skin beneath her throat, and his own finger tracing round its edge. Then Rau coughed above him, and Van came back to the moment: the wind squalling over him, the distasteful trade he was making. He emptied a wrap of dried slopfish from inside his bag and filled it with half of the precious pieces. He knew he shouldn't put such taonga to be worn in a foodwrap, but they were destined now for Squat anyway so fuck him. 'Half a dozen precious pieces,' he said, handing the wrap to Rau. 'And tell them both—him and his wife—to stay the fuck away from me.'

Rau nodded. 'You just concentrate on looking after that girl while I finish this trade. Focus on that.'

Kahu's teeth were chattering as Van came across. 'I want to go home,' she said.

'Almost there,' he said. 'Just the formalities now.'

Rau had laid the wrap of pieces on the Way. Now Squat raised both palms towards the hides up on the slope, and moved them in a waving motion: the 'all clear' signal to the other Scarpers. 'Good to renew our gratitude,' he said, casting his voice so it would carry to Van. 'Sometimes it's a shame there are rules.'

'Oh, go fuck yourself.'

'What's that?' said Squat.

Van stepped up, barging past Rau and the hand he tried to stop him with. 'I said, Good days in the Way, is it? Picked off some people, have you?'

That same squint of Squat's rested on Van, then on the girl beyond. 'It is good, to be honest. The Burners, on the island

73

there, and another bunch of Northerners further up, have got a lot of people spooked. Running while they can.' His chin went up, eyes glinting at Van. 'Makes for some fun.'

They were closer now, barely five paces between them. Hine was huge and impassive behind Squat.

'Well, it's noble work,' said Van.

'Just plying my trade, man. Same as you.'

Rau was alongside Van now and he snapped his eyes at him, warning him not to leave it this way, but Van didn't care; he shrugged and turned to Kahu, with a hand on her arm to encourage her forward. 'We can go now,' he said. 'Sorry for the delay.'

But Squat raised his voice. 'Not a good time to trade up to the Whaeas, man. Even if you've managed to stick a sprog in one, like everybody says.'

Van gave no sign he'd heard him, bending to Kahu instead, as if listening to something she was saying. In fact he was trying to shield her from this talk.

Squat shouted again. 'Because they're on their way out, man.' He turned his voice sing-song. 'Here come the Burners. Here they come.'

Kahu was staring at Squat, for a moment too appalled for her body to keep up its shivers and teeth-chattering.

'Don't listen to him,' said Van.

But he was too late. Squat leapt towards her, throwing his hands and arms forward, a loud noise of flame erupting from him. 'Whoosh! *Burning*.'

'Right, fuck you.' Van ran at Squat with the bar raised high; the smaller man went into a crouch with his blade out, grinning as Van came on. There was barely a pace between them. Van would break Squat's hand with the bar and then, once the knife was gone, hit him on the temple. He swung the bar.

Then Hine rushed him. She barged him backwards, then punched his throat. Van gagged, staggering back. She came on again—she shoved him and punched him on the shoulder, the throat. He tripped backwards. Still she came at him, her fists thudding into the hands he held up, hitting him on the upper chest as well.

Squat advanced too, snarling in her wake. 'Yeah. Have some of that, you arsehole.'

Barely breaking her stride, Hine gripped her husband by the coat and threw him to the ground. Then she came at Van again, punching at the arms he held up to protect his neck and face.

Van reeled back, falling against Rau and Kahu.

At last Hine's attack stopped. She put one arm behind her, to freeze Squat in his place on the ground. At the same time, she pointed at Van, indicating where he should stand.

Van went there slowly, one hand at his ravaged throat.

Rau tried to speak, but coughed instead, his breathing thick again.

Hine just waited for them both to be ready, as if too weathered by so many seasons of this—so long working the Dry Way in the wind and heat, and pushing past inclement weather and travellers and idiot husbands—to waste further breath on this episode. With stony patience she waited for Rau to finish his coughing.

Getting to his feet behind her, Squat picked up her spike weapon. She hadn't needed it for her assault on Van, and clearly she still felt she wouldn't need it. When Squat handed it to her, she barely acknowledged him. Her eyes went to Kahu instead. After a long time surveying her, she lifted her hand. 'E te kōtiro, ngā mihi. Peace on your waters.'

Kahu stared at Hine's large and work-scarred hand, the

mighty shoulder behind it.

'Make your sign, girl,' said Hine. 'I'm letting you through.'

It was to Van that Kahu looked for help. It pained him to look in her face. Blank with fright, she was far too young for this.

His voice croaked when he tried to speak. 'It's all right, Kahu. Make your sign. We're safe now.'

She lifted her arm. The sleeve, still damp from the Runalong Ponds, sagged from the wrist plait, where she'd tied it to protect her skin from biters.

Hine held the girl's eye a moment. Then she turned to Rau. He was still hooped over, massaging his chest. 'E mōhio ana ahau ki tō pōuritanga. Ka aroha hoki, e Rau. Peace on Ava. Peace on all our old waters.'

Rau couldn't speak. He signalled his chest—it was the tension; it had wrecked his breath.

Hine stepped to the side and indicated the free Way, her eye and voice again addressing Kahu. 'Kei a koe te huarahi. The Way is yours. And may your Whaea protect you and your forest, eh girl. You're going to need it.'

Five

Kahu shouted. 'They're waiting for a break in the wind.'

Van just nodded. The gust made it impossible to do anything else.

Coloured plaits were tied into the gate that towered above, and they whipped and cracked as the wind caught them. On either side of the gate stood a vast fence of tall cut poles and live trees. They grew right through the fence, these trees, taking its weight as it bent, so the whole thing swayed gently forwards and back. Festooned with colours and foliage at its top, the fence marched away on both sides of the gate: out to the right on the Wayside, stretching right round the front of the lake, and on the left too, heading uphill and far inland.

Van's eye jagged down to below waist height. The gaps between the fence poles were stoppered with mud and, in some places, with bits of old metal that were dug into the earth. 'Fuck me,' he said, 'look what they use metal for.'

But Rau just bent over his canister, his chest still tight from the confrontation with Hine and Squat.

'Turituri, please,' said Kahu. 'They hardly ever open this gate.'

Van straightened his headwrap and clothes. He tried to obscure the rip in his coat.

At last there was a pause in the wind and the gate opened a crack. A young woman showed through the gap, then two more. Plaits were looped over their shoulders, and then round their waists and tied to the gate. Bracing against gusts, they eased the gate open by paying out their plaits. These young women were older than Kahu by a few summers, it seemed, and their coats and belts were plainer than hers too, their headcovers smeared with work.

Kahu bent her arm in the Whaea signal, speaking to the young woman who seemed to be the leader of this group. The guard grimaced and returned the signal as best she could, one-armed and off-balance with the plaits wrapped round her arm and waist. Another pair traded looks, as if amazed by the timing of Kahu's formality, the impracticality of it. Then their leader jerked her head at Van, indicating he should go first.

He ducked his head and went through, then found there was another gate to negotiate. Both gates were braced by a network of thick plaits that came down and were hitched to posts dug into the ground; he stepped carefully over the plaits, wanting not to trip or damage any of the apparatus.

Rau came behind, then Kahu. She leaned in to speak to another of the guards, and Van saw the young woman nod grimly back, focused on her task. The first gate was closed behind them, and then the second opened.

Van went through first—and into a rush of forest. It was a high green wall of nīkau. He'd never seen so many of the palms in one place. Their vast fronds held up, their ribbed trunks streaming with colours. A pair of older women knelt at one of the nearer nīkau, laying red stones in a semi-circle at its base, dunking the stones in a water bowl to wash them first. At the base of another tree a girl younger than Kahu re-knotted the colours to its trunk, then raised her forearm to the tree and spoke directly to it.

Van looked to Rau for his reaction—in a storm like this, these Whaea people didn't rush to tie down the thatch of their huts or to gather up belongings they'd left out. They tended to these shrines instead.

But Rau barely looked up. 'I wish she'd hurry up. My chest's fucked.'

Kahu came up from her conference at the fence, her eyes averted. Van sensed she'd been hurt by something the guards had said to her but didn't want to show it.

'How far is it?' said Van. 'Rau's breath isn't good.'

'There's just a slight hill through the nīkau forest, then we go inland across some flats, then the statue hill.'

'I can make it,' said Rau.

She led them into the nīkau, and immediately the storm was quietened, its violence turning to a wet-sounding shush of fronds and kererū that swooped above. Van felt the specialness of the place. The ancient trunks stretching up to the canopy. The forest floor itself a carpet of old fronds that had fallen and suppressed all undergrowth.

'Look at that.' He pointed Rau towards a possum that was spiked in a wooden trap, the mechanism suspended from the trunk with coloured plait.

At the sound of his voice, Kahu turned.

'What is it?' he said.

She hesitated, biting her lip.

'It's all right. You can tell us—whatever it is. Just tell us.'

'I know you haven't done this yet. I'm not saying you will, but please don't swear in this forest. It's a sacred place. Don't go to the toilet in here—like, don't mimi on the plants—and don't stray off the track. Please respect it.'

Van found himself working hard to keep a straight face. Her solemnity was hard to take.

'It's probably best to just be silent,' she said. 'That's what we do, most times.'

'Kei te pai,' said Rau, pausing between breaths. 'I can't hardly talk anyway.'

'You'll get good medicine up at home.'

Rau nodded, and kept his head down again, as if barely able to think that far ahead.

'Don't go too fast, please, Kahu,' said Van. 'His chest won't take it.'

All the way through the nīkau forest and up the hill of bush beyond it, then across the ridge beyond that, Kahu had scarcely stopped or even looked round. She was now more than thirty paces ahead, lost to Van and Rau for whole sections of the track. They were walking between huts and traders now, the little buildings crouching on each side under the bush. It didn't feel right to wander through these rude homes and their lines of drying wares outside—harakeke, and possum and ferret and stoat skins—without Kahu to escort them.

Twice the bush had opened out and Van caught sight of her and tried to wave her back. But she didn't seem to see him, hurrying round the next turning of the path. Finally he just cupped his hands and shouted. 'Hey! Taihoa.'

She turned and lifted both palms, her whole body indignant—but still didn't come back or even wait long. As soon as they were within ten paces, she was off again.

'It's her Nan, isn't it,' said Rau. 'That's why she's in such a rush to get back.'

'I guess,' said Van. 'But I still think she should wait.'

Saving his breath this time, Rau simply indicated the huts around them, the trees above, all of it secured by the fence. It was safe enough, he was saying; they would be all right. Then he lumbered on, leading Van into another cluster of trappers' huts. Rows of skins were stretched outside on racks, the slick pink-and-white shapes of carcasses suspended from branches. They were possums, mostly, but Van saw also the smaller shapes of what must have been stoats and rats. Alongside some huts live possums hunkered in cages of angled and bound stakes, with bits of branches and the remains of berries at their feet. Van had eaten enough paru-tasting possum meat to know this tactic: the possums, having escaped the spike traps, were being fed up on sweeter fare for the meat's sake, just in case they'd been feasting on rubbish before they'd been caught.

Van and Rau were nearing a bend in the track when a child ran out from the rows of carcasses and stopped in front of them. The boy, not higher than Van's waist, stared up. His features were like Kahu's, black hair lifting off his face in the forest-filtered wind. He opened his mouth and pointed. 'Fire man?'

Van stared. The boy had pointed straight up at his face. Van looked to Rau for help, but Rau, after a quick check for danger from the huts, just shrugged, using the rest-time to massage his breastbone with two fingers. Unwilling to show Matewai's oil in this place, he was using his alternative cure instead.

'The fire man,' said the boy.

'Kāo,' said Van. 'I'm not the fire man, kid.'

The boy's stare went to Rau but didn't linger, fixing again on Van. 'Fire man.'

A shout came from a hut set back in the bush. A man poked his head through the door flap and waved the boy back.

The boy didn't move, even as a fresh gust swept through the

canopy above, and spattered down twigs and leaves and sent the skins and corpses that hung in lines to sway and dance. The man stepped from his house and came through the carcasses. His coat and boots were patched in many places, his beard ragged. Van realised this was the first man he'd seen inside the fence, apart from the outsiders like him he'd briefly been grouped with at Summer's Day. Ignoring him and Rau, the man shouted again, losing patience with his son.

Van put his hand down to the boy. 'Go to your Dad.'

The boy wiped his fringe from his eyes and looked in the direction Van pointed. He seemed marooned by the journey he'd taken, unable to conceive of a way back.

'Hoki atu, little man,' said Van. With a careful hand he pushed the boy's tiny back.

The man called out again, and ducked under a further line of carcasses. At the same time, a woman's voice came from inside the hut, too panicked and fast for Van to understand it.

The man pulled at the boy, trying to take him. The boy pointed up at Van. 'The fire man,' he said. 'Fire.'

This time the father looked up at Van, and at Rau. His face showed immense fatigue. 'So is he right?' he said, his Pākehā strongly accented. 'Are you guys from the island?'

Puzzled, Van looked at Rau, but again Rau just eyed the boy and his father, and shrugged.

'Kāo,' said Van. 'Nō Te Repo kē.'

The man's eye roved over him, trying to guess his trade. Then he looked beyond him, and Van turned too and saw what had taken his eye. The Whaea statue was much closer here, standing on her hill above the surrounding bush and huts. Van could see the wooden latticework and old rock-type surface that made up her serene face and head, her hands held in prayer towards the north.

Looking at her must have reminded the man of his duty. He bent his elbow in a tired version of the sign Kahu habitually gave out. 'Tēnā kōrua,' he said. 'Kia pai te haere.'

'Ngā mihi,' said Van.

The man put his hand on the boy's back, and shepherded him through the lines of skins and carcasses towards the hut.

Van turned. 'What was that about?'

'Aua. How would I know?' Rau's fingers still worked on the central bone of his chest. He indicated the direction Kahu had taken. 'We should catch up with your kid. She's in a rush.'

Van nodded, but didn't move off. The fire man. It was something to do with his trade, perhaps, his patching fire. The flames of his fire could probably be seen from the highest of the Whaea places, if not from these blood-and-guts camps on the flats. But the man had mentioned the island. They'd thought he was one of them, one of the Burners who'd arrived on the island and set fire to the forest there, and then done their work on the coastal villages too.

'Hurry up, man,' said Rau. 'She'll be halfway up the statue's skirt by now.'

They finally caught Kahu at the base of the statue path. An archway of wood stood over the track that led up the hill, coloured plaits streaming down from the wood.

'Thanks for waiting for us,' said Van.

'Sorry. I just really have to get back.' She stepped from foot to foot, and Van wondered if actually she was just busting, and needed to go to the wharepaku. He looked up the hill. Kohekohe and the occasional pōhutukawa spread their branches up; long huts were anchored solidly to the hill's sheltered slope. It seemed too fine a place for wharepaku or latrine pits. Hard to imagine where such dirty facilities might be. Round the back of the hill somewhere, perhaps, where someone else had to look at the piss and shit and deal with it.

'It's all right, girl,' said Rau. 'Take us up.'

'Wait,' said Van. 'Can I just check—can men come up here onto the hill?'

'Of course.' She waved him through the archway. 'Kia tere.'

'I thought we had to ask permission.'

'Āe. You've got it. My permission.'

'All right,' said Van. But he still hesitated. It felt too soon, or too easy, to pass under this archway. 'Rau, don't you have to tuku karakia, before we go through this gate?'

Rau just took a handful of Van's coat, and shoved him up the track. 'Stop fucking about, man. Show Kahu some respect. Also, I want this medicine she's promised.'

Six

There was no insect lock. Apparently they didn't need one. And it wasn't just a door flap. It was a door of solid wood, with poles as thick as Van's wrist tied together, and criss-crossed with supports. And it was firmly shut. Kahu, unable to wait on Rau's laboured progress up the zigzag track, had run through it earlier, throwing a promise over her shoulder to send someone out.

Since then, Van had stood with Rau and waited and waited and knocked, and still no one had come out. While he stood there, he had twisted his coat about, trying without success to hide the rip at his crotch. It worried him too that his rag boots and legs were still slimed with pond water. He looked and smelt bad.

Looking at Rau just made his nerves worse. Rau was hunched over a canister and ignoring him, recovering the breath he'd lost on the trip.

To calm himself Van looked up into the branches that spread above, and made out the shapes of birds that hopped and screeched. They were as large as kererū but more agile. One of them parrot-walked down a branch towards him. Red and brown on its back and grey over its head, the bird stopped right opposite Van's face. Head on one side, it eyed him, bobbing. With a shock he realised he was looking at a kākā. He'd heard their discordant calls last time at Summer's Day, and he knew they lived inside the fence, a miracle of the people's trapping work and the forest they protected. But he'd never seen one up close. Now one of these kākā was almost close enough to touch. He thought of reaching a hand towards it, and wondered whether touching the birds was forbidden. Without warning, the bird raised its head and let out an ungodly squawk.

'Shit!' said Van.

Someone laughed.

He turned, and it was a woman in the doorway. Her grey hair was uncovered; she was dressed for the indoors in a light coat that showed no rips or patches. She looked beyond Van to the bird. 'He does that to all our visitors. It's his trick.'

'Right,' said Van. He was reluctant to turn his back on the bird. He didn't want it to creep closer and squawk again and give him the shits.

'I'm one of Kahu's aunties. Ko Rerū tōku ingoa. And you must be Van.'

'Āe. And this is Rau.'

Rau gave no sign he wanted to speak. Instead he cast his eyes somewhere between Rerū's feet and his own.

After a quick glance, the aunt paid no attention to Rau. She assessed Van for a long time instead. Then she made the Whaea sign. 'Ngā mihi. Peace on our old waters. Kuhu mai, boys. Come out of that awful gust.'

Van ducked under the door and onto a floor of mānuka trunks that adjusted under his weight. He looked for a place to put his boots. Coats and belts and outdoor things hung on a row of pegs in the wall; below them, a bench for rag boots. One small and soggy pair was there among the rest. Kahu's. For some reason seeing them there made Van remember the karakia she'd stammered out when she'd been faced with Squat.

Rau still hadn't moved. He stood outside with his head down, an immobile and wheezing block.

'Please,' said Rerū. 'Kuhu mai.'

'Kua ea,' said Rau, looking up at last. 'I don't owe you anything. I paid your healers in full.'

'I understand. And I'm sorry for your loss. We heard about Ava. Safely may she sink.'

'I'm here because you invited Van.'

Van said nothing, not wanting to detract from whatever point Rau was making.

'It pleased our healers to help Ava,' said Rerū. 'But I understand your debt to them is finished. You should come out of the storm. And you can both remove your headcovers. The height up here means only a few biters trouble us, and the huts are treated each night as well, so it's safe.'

Van peeled off his headwrap and coat and handed them across, then indicated the muddied rags at his feet. 'I'm sorry about these.'

She didn't take them, but indicated the space beside Kahu's. Then she went to the next door and stood with her back to it, blocking the way. She caught Van with his hand at his ripped crotch again, trying to hide where the skin of his upper thigh showed through the flap.

'In this next room is one of our oldest aunties. You will have heard that she's been māuiui.'

'Kahu told us of someone's sickness,' he said. 'But she said it was some kind of Nan who was sick.'

Rerū didn't react to this. Neither did she seem to notice Rau's silence. It was Van she directed her talk to, his face she watched. 'I'm saying this so you're prepared. Our custom is to keep a sick person in the front room. To prepare them for their flight out.'

'Thank you,' said Van. 'I didn't know that.'

There was a break in Rerū's hardness, and she smiled. 'Of course you didn't. This is the first time you've come to visit us. Up here on the hill, at least—Summer's Day being a bit different, of course.'

He blinked.

But she spoke as if nothing suggestive had been said. 'We've prepared a room for you. You can wash there, and there'll be fresh coats for you. I'll take you through now.'

'Through the mourners? Will they like that?'

She frowned. 'They're not mourning. They're waiting for our aunt to rest.'

'Aroha mai,' he said. 'I didn't mean that.'

'And as long as you don't interrupt them, and don't speak, they won't take offence.' She studied him afresh, as if doubting his ability to do this. She also reviewed Rau, her mouth tightening further. 'Kei te mārama?'

'Āe, āe.'

Rerū paused another moment, then went through the door. Van followed her into a much larger room. The ceiling was hung with colours, skins draped on the walls and floor for warmth. Deeper in the room there was a bed with people kneeling round it. All but two of them were women, all bent over the bed with their heads uncovered. One of their number was talking steadily in Kahu's language, too fast for Van to understand it; beneath that voice, a slow gasping came from the bed. Van made out the prone form of an old woman, her face ravaged and her mouth open. At the top end of the bed he saw the compact shape of Kahu, her hair now free of her headwrap. It was surprisingly short. Her hair spiked about, as if she'd worked it that way on purpose.

Sensing his attention, she looked up. Her eyes were red.

He tried to nod discreetly, but she kept her eyes on him—waiting, it seemed, wanting something from him. He brought his arm up in a wave, to acknowledge that he was here and he saw her, that he hoped she was all right, but Rerū hissed at him.

'Don't disturb them. This way.' She indicated the way round the foot of the bed.

Yet Kahu watched him even harder. She was the only one looking up. The others still had their attention on the old woman, their heads and backs bowed. The voice seemed to be narrating a story, but it wasn't clear to Van whether it was to the whole group or to the old woman. And as Van stood rooted in place, and Kahu's head poked up from the rest like a pūkeko from raupō, still seeming to want something from him that he couldn't work out, many of the others who were kneeling there lifted their heads too and turned, confused by the interruption.

Now nearly all of them were staring at him. Not knowing what else to do, Van lifted his hand again. 'He mihi aroha. Our best respects.'

Beside him, Rerū groaned.

A murmur went round the group, and as one they stood up. They raised their arms, bent at the elbow in the signal that mimicked their statue, the symbol of the Whaea standing up.

Panicked, Van turned to Rerū for help.

She snapped her eyes, furious.

'What?' he said. 'What am I supposed to do?'

Rerū just shook her head. Her own arm bent at the elbow, sending the same signal back.

Rau did the same, so Van attempted it too, but it felt false to make this gesture that didn't belong to him, so he dropped it and simply stood instead, grinning to show his intentions were good.

Now the last of the women turned. She removed a fine

headwrap as she stood up, and a jolt went through Van as her hair showed. It was long and dark, with tiny feathers and colours plaited into it, purple and blue and red.

Hana.

Her eyes were red from grief too, but she seemed more weighed down with the general sadness than distraught. She looked to Rerū, and something unspoken passed between them. And although she then turned to acknowledge Rau first, Van felt every single person in the room watching him. His face began to burn. In the silence, the dying woman's gasp came up from the bed, Rau's wheeze interplaying with it.

'He mihi aroha ki a koe, e Rau. I wish the purest water on what you sink.'

Rau lifted a hand. It pained Van to see Rau having to acknowledge yet another reference to Ava's death. She'd been spoken of at least five times since first light, and every single time it was because Van had been fetched and needed Rau to support him.

'Tēnā koe, e Van. I wish you could meet us all at a better moment.'

Van just blinked. She had the same effect on him as when they'd last met, but he hadn't remembered these manners, this formality.

She went on, as if his silence had meant he wanted more explanation. 'I've had to be here with Nan.'

'Oh no, it's all my fault,' he said. 'I made us late, me and Kahu, because I made her go and get Rau, and also I had to take my trades to Matewai, and I wanted to talk to her and Rau and all that, so it's me who's stuffed it all up.'

A laugh shot out of her—she dashed a hand up to stifle it.

'Oh, for goodness' sake,' said Rerū.

He could see Hana suppressing another laugh. It was the

clash of Van's giddiness, he supposed, his blurting explanation, with the solemn rituals of grief in the room. That was what shocked her into laughing.

For a time the only sounds were Rau's wheezing breath and the scraping sound the old woman made on the bed, searching up and back down for air. Then someone murmured, and all the other women who were standing there dropped their arms and turned to kneel again, the floor poles shifting with their movement. The woman who'd been narrating the story started up once more.

Hana was the only one of them still standing up. She wore no protecting scarf round her neck, and on the skin there he saw the tip of a body painting that he remembered from their first meeting. It stood more boldly from her skin this time; it must have been redone since then. Seeing its tip now on her neck, and remembering the tumble and furl of its design down her backbone stirred something in his groin, which in turn made him try again to cover the ripped crotch of his coat.

'Thanks for coming when Kahu fetched you,' said Hana, her voice lower now. 'It was my request she took. But I suppose you'd already worked that out. You've probably realised she's my daughter.'

Still sitting upright at the head of the bed, Kahu was watching them both.

'It's our honour to come,' said Van. 'But I'm sorry for your Nan's illness.'

Hana bowed her head in respect for the dying woman, and nodded. But when she lifted her face again he was sure he saw her eyes roll, very quickly, towards the group behind her, as if to acknowledge the audience, their pretence at not listening to their conversation.

Startled, Van laughed. It was a short and randy-sounding bark.

Immediately, Rau coughed and hit his chest. At first it seemed a pretend coughing fit he'd started to save Van, but then it went on much longer; he turned away to hack and fight with his breath.

Rerū lifted her voice above the racket. 'Hey, tama,' she said, snapping her fingers at Van. 'You and Hana will meet again soon, at the hākari. But now—*right now*—I'm taking you through to wash.'

Van didn't move. His eye was still on Hana, on her hair with its plaited colours, her flowing indoor coat. He saw her cock a quick eyebrow again, this time at Rerū's rebuke, but he was taken by a movement beyond. Kahu was no longer watching them but gazing distantly at the bed, her hand moving on the top blanket, not quite touching the thin wrist of the dying woman. It was an unfocused movement. Her eyes looked heavy, as if she might soon be put to sleep by the story that was being told. She was exhausted.

'Okay, Van,' said Rau, 'let's leave them to it.' He shouldered towards the door.

Hana had followed Van's gaze towards Kahu, and when Rau's voice returned her attention to the visitors, her concern for Kahu was still showing on her face. But then she fixed on Van again and smiled, and simply looked happy to see him, and he felt a great leaping up inside himself. He wanted to cross the room to her, and put his arms right round her.

But Rerū gripped his elbow and pulled him hard in the opposite direction. 'This way, Van. Ināia tonu nei.'

Hana watched him as he was taken out, and he saw it play again on her mouth, that laugh he remembered.

Seven

The food was unfamiliar and Van was careful with it. A rich sauce of herbs coated the meat and made each piece difficult to grip. Twice he dropped bits of food to his plate, splashing sauce on the fine indoor coat he'd been loaned for the night. He tried to dab away the stain, first with his fingers, and then by wetting a part of his sleeve and rubbing it. When he still wasn't successful, he gave up.

'Well, I'm stuffed,' he said, sitting back. 'That was delicious.'

'Kua mākona te hiakai?' said Rerū. 'Surely not. You should try the rabbit—it comes from the furthest corner of our territory, beyond the forest.' She was seated opposite him, right next to Hana at the table's head. She spoke in Van's own language, and it seemed she'd been appointed a kind of minder for him during his visit. She was good at it, he thought—at least, she scared him.

In an effort to divert her attention, he looked further down the table. They all seemed to be high-born people, most of them women who were older than Hana, and most speaking in their own reo, sometimes with Pākehā words weaving in and out. Down at the far corner was Kahu. Her hack of hair showed as she bent to the aunt who sat beside her, listening in respectful pose. She was being looked after down there, but while he watched she cast a desperate glance in Hana's direction, clearly wanting the dinner to be over. She was by far the youngest person present. It must have been hard for her: separated from her mother, and her Nan dying in that other room. It wasn't right, what she'd been made to endure in the last few nights.

Rerū noticed his attention on Kahu. 'Go on, Van,' she said. 'E kai.'

Van eyed the rabbit without hope. The joints were slathered in a mash of berries that looked even more likely to stain and splash his new and borrowed coat.

Not that Rau was holding back. Without lifting his head, he mowed into the meat. Grunts and clacks came from him as he broke apart the bones and sucked and dropped them in pieces to his plate. He wiped his mouth with his wrist and licked his fingers with elaborate smacks. It was an over-the-top act that seemed partly designed to needle the Whaea group—its posh wankery of high food and pointless talk—and partly to remind Van that Rau was here only for his sake.

Rerū's eye was still on Van.

'It's the water I like best of all.' Van lifted the bowl of water before him. 'It's an incredible taste.'

Rerū turned away, her lips pressed tight.

Van tried to keep smiling, but despaired inside. It was so hard to avoid causing offence. In this place, every comment he made seemed a reflection on how he and Rau had none of these fine things. He'd meant it simply enough: the water *was* delicious. Clear and cold, it had no swirling flakes or grits, no aroma of mud rising from it.

'And your mahi,' said Hana. 'How is it?'

Van turned, flooding with relief. She was rescuing him.

'All your work, I mean. How's your mahi, and Matewai's— all your people's mahi?'

94

It was then he saw the strain in her face. She was sitting at the head of the table, and clearly wasn't used to the position. Rerū and the woman next to her were supposedly talking to each other but seemed to be aware of everything Hana said, noting every movement of her head. And running down on each side of the table were what seemed to be the settlement's most prominent aunties, all of them attuned to Hana's movements. And her own daughter was in a sort of agony down there at the end.

'It's the same,' he said. 'I patch things, and people trade for them. And Matewai's cooking up—it's her season for that. For making oils, I mean. Medicines.'

Hana nodded, distracted again. Her eye went down the table, monitoring the meal's progress.

'Actually, I do have some new work. Different pieces. It's probably different from most plastic that you've seen. Much finer. I could show you, if you want.'

Rerū looked up, as if alarmed that he would produce it right then and there, plonk it on the table among the food bowls.

'Some other time, I mean. When it's safe—appropriate.'

They all stared at him—Hana and both of those monitoring aunties—and he felt his face going red.

Rerū beckoned Hana close and said something behind her hand.

Nodding, Hana looked down the table and cleared her throat, as if preparing to make an announcement.

Van saw the way Rau was hoeing into a joint of rabbit, and jabbed him with his elbow. 'You guts. You'll puke.'

'They can't eat all of this.'

Van laughed. At least Rau's breathing had improved. The feast and rest, along with the array of breathing oils he'd been gifted earlier, would help restore his strength. Three burnished canisters of oils had been stacked on a handsome wooden plank for him, a gesture that had impressed even Rau.

Now Hana knocked her knuckle on the table and stood up. 'Tēnā tātou. Koinei āku mihi maioha ki ō mātou manuhiri, otirā ki a koutou katoa kua haramai nei ki te hākari. Koinei te mihi ki ō tātou wai tawhito, huri noa. Thank you all for taking food with us, and with our guests. Today we welcome Van and Raureti, and we acknowledge our ancient waters, the waters that unite us. As you all know, Van and Rau are our lowland friends.'

Rau laughed, not even pretending to hide it.

Van kept his eyes down. It was probably that Hana was having to turn her greeting into Pākehā that made it sound so strange. No one said 'lowland' when they meant 'swamps' or Matewai's own camp at Te Repo, and no one reversed the order of their names like that. It was Rau and then Van, always: the first the direct descendant of Matewai's old waters; the second the scared kid she'd taken in as a Wayside orphan and helped to set up in the mongrel trade of plastics, a stray Pākehā without known waters or a place to stand, sheltered by Matewai because her only child had found him trapped in a pond of swamp-seep and pulled him free and brought him back to her hut.

Pretending not to notice, Hana went on. 'Peace of the Whaea on all of you as you look to the sick and to your work.' She made the Whaea sign, and all the others pushed back their sitting logs to return the gesture. One of the oldest aunties there gave a karakia Van had never heard before and couldn't follow beyond a couple of phrases, and then Hana sat back down and the rest all filed out. In the commotion of bowls and sitting logs, Van saw Hana follow Kahu's head as she left the room. The small figure was among aunties again, guided out. He shook his head, watching them both. It was stupid, separating Hana and her daughter like that, not to mention forcing a public meal at such a moment. Surely it would have been simpler if all four of them could have just sat in a room and talked—Rau, Hana, Van and Kahu—and worked out the trade that way.

Rau pushed back from the table and groaned. He gave his puku an exaggerated stroke.

'You'll get the guts ache, for sure,' said Van.

'Got one already, bro. Ka nui te puku.'

'Well, it's good someone enjoyed it.' Hana's smile at Rau was careful. She was still uncertain of him—his reputation, perhaps, or this act of simple gluttony he was performing right now. Then she leaned to Van, and made her voice low and quick. 'It won't always be like this.' She indicated the table, still cluttered with bowls and water cups. 'You know, all this la-di-da stuff.'

'Thank god,' said Van.

The door flap was swept aside again, and Hana stood as a handful of women re-entered. Rerū was among them, but it was an older woman who came towards the table's head. Her hair was long and grey and uncovered, a red feather twined into it. Blue and white pūkeko feathers were prominent on her chest. Her features looked Pākehā, but Van had learnt not to make assumptions about that.

She stood opposite Rau and Van, her arm bent in the Whaea sign.

'Tēnā kōrua. Ko Bel tōku ingoa.'

'Tēnā koe,' said Van.

Bel sat; they all sat. Bel moved her hand towards Hana. 'E hine, kei a koe.'

Hana took a deep breath. 'Ko te tīmatanga, ko te wai.'

She poured a cup and waited for the group to do the same. Seven of them—six women, and one man, all old. Kahu was not

97

among them. Again, as Hana lifted the bowl of water, Van saw her swallow a lump in her throat. He was sure she wasn't used to this sort of leadership. She began in her own language, then quickly shifted to Van's. 'We give rightful thanks to the Whaea, who brought forth the water, and who brought forth the forest, and who returns us to the forest.' They all lifted water and drank, and as they swallowed they made their faces show how good it was. Van hoped Rau was seeing that.

Hana turned to Van. 'Thank you for bringing Kahu safely across. We know it was a big request, given your recent loss.'

Van leaned back. 'Rau is our trader. On trade he speaks for us.'

'Oh.' She adjusted to this. 'As you've seen, we also have someone preparing to leave us.' Van felt the effort that speaking in his language was forcing on her, the tortured formality of it. He saw also the furtive look she sent to Bel, as if to check she was taking the right approach. 'Our aunty is old, but her sickness has been rapid. It's still a shock to us all.'

Van felt the same instinct as before to say something, to offer respects. But beside him Rau just tilted his cup on the table, watching the water's movement inside it.

'I think Kahu explained,' said Hana, 'why our aunty must go to her rest on the coast. Why she has asked for it. That's part of what we will discuss tonight.'

Again Rau said nothing, and Hana's eyes flicked towards Van, searching for help. He tried to send her some reassurance.

The silence stretched out. The only sound was the tilting of Rau's cup on the tabletop and the squeering call of kākā. It seemed the storm had quietened out there, and the birds were reclaiming their territory above the huts.

At last Rau looked up. His eyes went slowly round the group. 'E ngā wāhine o te Whaea, tēnā koutou katoa. Ngā mihi nui ki a koutou. I acknowledge you all, and especially your healers. I'll always be grateful to anyone who helped Ava. Engari, kua ea te utu. My debt to you is finished.' He motioned at Rerū. 'I said this before I crossed your door.'

Rerū acknowledged this with a nod, her lips tight.

'Ā, ka tangi te ngākau, nē. Having suffered a loss, we feel yours. I feel for you, Hana, and I feel for the wee girl who fetched us.' His voice was flat, deadened by his own grief, but there was no trace now of the violent pain of a few days back. 'But my debts have always been to your people on the flats— your healers and weavers. With respect, I've never had a debt to you high-born ones on this hill. And neither'—he indicated Van beside him—'until recently, has my teina here. And my mother doesn't have the kindest things to say about your dam and your fence.'

He looked around the group, then faced Hana again. 'Your stories may be different, but the story we know is this. You used to share our swamp. And then you walked out and left us behind. And that's fair enough too, I guess—kei a koutou. But then you locked us out of your new space. And you'—he paused, searching for a polite way to say it—'you fouled our water. Dammed it and wrecked it. And that just sped up our problems with sickness, and with having pēpi. Karekau ngā pēpi, nē.' He tilted the cup of water again, and shook his head slowly. 'But I don't suppose your stories say this. They say something else, I bet. Or perhaps nothing at all—perhaps you don't have a kōrero about that.'

Van risked a glance along the faces opposite, and found they were all concentrating on Rau and what he would say next—Hana included. She, like the others, seemed fascinated by Rau, by the controlled anger in his voice. It was just a story to them. The grief and gut-wrecking sick Rau talked about was intriguing, but they hadn't shared it. They didn't know. If only they could taste our water, Van thought; if they had to boil and herb it and treat it, and drink it for two days and two nights, and then wake with the shivering and shits that sooner or later struck anyone new to the swamp camps, the dam would come down, and the fence.

But Rau was breathing more easily, Van noticed. That array of canisters had done its work well. If it all collapsed, if this whole trade with Hana and her people fell to shit, at least the visit would have helped fix up Rau's breath, for a short time at least.

Van shifted in his seat, and Rau looked across sharply, checking for whatever signal he might have been trying to give.

'Kei te pai,' said Van. 'Just getting comfortable.'

Hana smiled, and further down the table someone gave a polite laugh.

'Āe,' sighed Rau, as if resuming a tale he didn't want to continue. 'So our water does *not* taste like this.' He nudged the cup before him. 'We have reasons why we want to help you, of course. But I'm going to be plain about it. The question for us, for me and my Māmā anyway, is this. With all due respect, what does the passing of some high-born old lady, who we don't even know—and when you haven't been all that nice to us in the past—have to do with me and Ma?'

For a time, Hana didn't speak. Her head was lowered, as if waiting for someone else to take over the talking on this topic. Van focused on his hands on the table top, then found his eye going towards Hana's hand and the tan-coloured design that trailed from her wrist and up over the back of her hand towards the tip of her smallest finger. It had been painted on by someone who was highly skilled. It showed fern fronds and wing shapes that tumbled onto and over each other. It hadn't been there at Summer's Day, Van was sure of it.

Then Bel spoke. 'Tēnā anō koe, e Rau. He pai tō kōrero, e tama. I acknowledge what your mother has said. It's been said by others downstream of us, but your mother's camp is the most directly downstream. So—' With her hands, she showed these hurts coming back towards her.

'Not just her camp,' said Rau. 'Her mahi too, and her health. The health of all of us. And my brother here. They've all been affected. It was a good few summers that Van lived at our camp.'

'As I say, I acknowledge all this.' Another slow movement of Bel's hand brought those mamae towards her. 'But Hana has new trades to make. And some of these might help—they might help . . .' She gazed at Van, then at both the visitors, seeming to search for the right way to say it. Then she just held her hands up. 'Look, I'll leave it to Hana.'

Immediately, Hana leaned forward. 'Our aunty and Nan, the one who is lying in our front room, she wants to return to the Raumu sinking place once she's passed. That's where she wants to sink into the mud.'

Van waited for Rau to protest, but Rau said nothing. He tilted and watched the water in his cup instead.

'Her people once had a place there. That's what our stories tell us. So my aunties want to send a sinking party across your lands to the Raumu sinking place. We want to cross the swamps.'

'But the Raumu is Ava's place right now,' said Van. 'That's where she rests. We just sank her there.'

Hana winced.

'Sorry,' said Van. 'It is, though. That's where we just put her down, a few days back.'

'It's all right, Van,' said Rau.

'No, it's not. It's—'

'Brother, it's all right.' Rau lifted his voice to Hana. 'And so, my new friend, is there anything else? Please be plain about it.'

Hana's eyes flicked away. 'There are other trades. But this one is first.'

'Right. So you send a burial party to the Raumu sinking place. And then what?'

'Our custom here is to let one sun rise on the person who's passed, at the place of their sinking, before she actually goes down into the mud.' She used her hands to suggest the stages of the process. 'Then my aunties will sink her and then, when that's done, when it's safe, they'll return across the Dry Way, and come back inside the fence.'

'So you're wanting to go twice across the Dry Way and deep into the swamps. And you've traded two more gaps, I take it, to allow these two crossings to take place.'

'We couldn't secure that.'

Rau sucked in through his teeth.

'Just to clarify,' Hana said, 'we're not asking you to help us cross. My aunties are only asking for access. And they will take a patrol of tamāhine toa with them, to guard the group as they cross.'

'But if you want access, you have to request my help. I'm not letting you lot cross the Dry Way and go all the way over there to that sinking lake without my escort. It's too dangerous for you. And I'm not going back across the Dry Way with a bloody burial party with a bunch of old ladies and a few kids—all due respect—unless there's a bloody good gap to go through.'

'I hope you'll reconsider,' said Hana. 'I really hope you will.'

Rau opened his hands. 'Hana, I want to help you. But there are two problems. First, you ask me to go back there, with a whole lot more problems coming with me, without securing a gap. And, second, you still haven't said what this is really about. Why we're really here. No disrespect and all that, but I asked for plain talk about this.'

Hana looked warily at Rau. 'We are asking to access the swamps because we haven't always asked. You've drawn attention to past hurts. This time we'd prefer not to trespass on your places without asking first.'

Rau snorted.

'And I heard you say our dam is a problem. We can talk about that.'

Rau's head jerked up. 'We'll talk about it? The lake, the dam—all that?'

Hana glanced at the other women. Her next breath was shaky, and it came to Van that earlier, at some time before this dinner, she'd stuck her neck out on this, and got herself into trouble with the others by negotiating hard for the right to make it a trading point. 'I'm undertaking that we'll talk about it.'

'E kī, e kī! It's certainly not too soon for that.' Rau turned to Van. 'You heard what she said. You're my witness to what she said.'

There was movement further down the table, and Van saw a pair of older women swap a look, and he was even more certain that Hana had brokered a trade that wasn't popular among some of these people.

'Look, ladies, we're not here to make strife,' he said suddenly, 'but you're asking a lot. This sinking-party work, on top of everything else. You're asking a lot.'

Everyone looked at him, the visitor sitting between Hana and Rau with the sudden opinion, and he leaned back again, his face hot.

'Sorry, Hana. That just came out.'

But Rau nodded sagely, as if Van had made a wise point. 'As I say, we're open to this trade. We want to make it work. But this is welcome, what you've said. The water at my mother's camp—at all our camps . . .' He waved a hand, as if there was no need to explain further, and he'd had enough of polite talk anyway. 'The little one who fetched us can tell you how it tastes.'

'And, as I say,' said Hana, 'we want to talk about that. And we're aware that we'll be crossing your place. We want to ask your permission before we do that.'

Rau laughed. 'We just live there. We haven't put a fence round it.'

There was a sharp intake of breath from some of the aunties, but Rau went on. If anything, there was a lift in his voice, as if he was enjoying the chance to make these digs at them. 'People cross it all the time, which doesn't always work out well for them, to be honest, but that's what they do. It's not *our* place. We don't claim it like that.'

Van lurched forward. 'But we appreciate that you're reaching out. It's good.' He blushed again; the outburst had taken him by surprise, and this time he saw Hana bite back a smile.

'I just meant that we don't kick people out of the swamps,' Rau said. 'Anyone can pass. The only place we claim is our camp at Te Repo, and that's because Ma lives there, and her crops are there, and because the slopes of the mound are good for our older ones and for my breath.'

'Yes, but that's—' Van stopped. 'Sorry, may I speak?'

This time Hana waited for Bel to give the permission.

'Of course.'

'My point is there's Ava. Sorry to bring this up, Rau, but we've only just sunk her down to rest there at Raumu, and practically in the same place to where your aunties want to put this new lady down. To be honest, I can't understand why you

104

want to do that. No one should be going there, or anywhere near that place.' His heart was beating hard. It couldn't have been Hana who had asked for this. There was someone older, some heavier authority driving it. This Bel perhaps, or some other aunties, a hidden and higher-up group who would be right now sitting in a finer room even than this one, making decisions. Whoever they were, they'd given Hana the table this time but instructed her what to say, what to request—if she wanted to make concessions with the swamp folk, then she had to secure this trade first. He felt he had to persuade these people, to talk them down somehow, even though they weren't in the room.

'And it's autumn, which is the worst time for Rau's breath. Normally we'd be keeping Rau high up on the mound at Te Repo, and close to his Ma and her treatments until the first storms have passed. Instead we ran the Dry Way in extreme wind today, and you can hear the effects. Well, I could hear them earlier—his breath. It's bad. And we did all this when Rau is still in his marama of grief.'

Rau made to speak, but Van leaned forward again. 'He'll say it's all right,' he said, 'because he's generous and because he wants—he wants . . .' He cleared his throat. 'The point is you've brought him here through a dry storm, at great risk to his breath, and now you're asking to trespass the place where his own wife has just been sunk. It's not right.'

Rau put his hand on Van's forearm. 'That'll do, mate.'

'I'm sorry, it's just—it's not right.'

Hana again had that pained expression, and he saw that he'd been correct. This hadn't been her idea, and she was against it.

Now when Rau spoke his words came more slowly, his tone more deliberate. 'My brother makes good points. But I'm not too concerned for my breath. Your oils have helped. And I'll make sure you don't get too close to Ava's sinking place, when we get there. And as for my own grief, well, coming across here has taken by mind off that.' He chuckled. 'We ran into Squat this morning. I don't know if you know him.'

There was no reply. But he and Van certainly had their attention. They all craned towards the visitors. They seemed fascinated by what Rau and Van spoke of, by the hunger and dirt that was in their faces, and their stories of all that stalked outside the big and protecting fence.

'He's a total cunt, old Squat,' said Rau. 'S'cuse my language. But he's handy to know, sometimes. Like this morning.'

Van looked up to see how the bad word had been taken, and was startled to find Bel staring at him, even as Rau talked. She was intrigued by Van's earlier resistance, it seemed, his challenge to the core concession he and Rau had been supposed to make.

'But it's good of Van to think of me and my grief,' said Rau. 'He's good like that. He's loyal. I can definitely say that.'

Still watching Van, Bel arched an eyebrow. 'Gosh. Quite a chap.'

Rau turned to her, his movement deliberate. 'Did you want to say something about that?'

Lifting her hands, Bel leaned back. 'Kāo.'

'While we're on the topic,' said Rau, 'there's been no mention of Van's role in all this. I'm guessing that he's not here just as another representative of Matewai, or of the swamp, or anything like that. Because I could have come alone for that.'

Bel was still staring straight at Van, unhindered by any embarrassment. After a long pause, she said, 'Hana?'

'It's true that I have my own request of Van,' said Hana. 'It's a private request.'

Silence.

'If anyone has any problem with that, can they say it now, please.'

Everyone looked at him, then at him and Hana together.

'It's a request of the heart,' said Hana. 'A request of what comes next.'

Taken off-guard for once, Rau stared at Hana. At last a grin spread across his face. 'I like this.'

'Such trades are best discussed in private,' said Bel. Abruptly she got up, and all the others stood, making the sitting logs roll as they were pushed back in haste. There was no Whaea signal of their arms, nothing like that. Just all of them standing.

Hana leaned towards him, whispering. 'They're waiting for us to go first.'

Van looked at all the standing people. 'Ki hea?'

Her whisper was more exaggerated this time. 'Somewhere more private.' She leaned back, laughing again at the reaction in his face. 'Kia tau. It'll be fun.'

Eight

Hana crossed the dark room and crouched. Van heard a sparking tool strike; her silhouette was thrown back. In the brief light he saw a large and low bed. Hana struck the sparking tool again, and a flame caught, and she lowered it first to one candle, then another. All that trapping, he thought, remembering the many huts he and Rau had walked through with carcasses and skins hanging outside them. That's where all the fine things in this room—the skin drapings and candles—must have come from. Fat from those animals made these flames work. And the candle fat must have been sweetened with some of the exotic herbs that grew so well here. An aroma was released as the candles burnt down, filling the hut with a pleasant spice.

Hana came back and took his hand. 'Sorry about all that talk at the hākari. I hope it wasn't too much.'

He shook his head. 'I just hope I didn't muck it up. I'm not good at fancy talk.'

'You are really. You were perfect.'

'I've never tasted food like that.' He moved his thumb over her hand, and for a moment they were both silent, watching it go over the curling shapes that were painted on the back of it.

'We have these rules,' she said. 'Procedures. We have to go through them, or there's no end of talk.' She waved her free hand to suggest the aunties and other people out there, their rules and censure. But her movement caused something in the darker part of the room to whir and flap.

Van reared, his hand going for his blade. Here it was, at last—his punishment. A guard coming with a club. A tamāhine toa, perhaps.

Then there was a squawk.

A bird—there was a bird in the room. Its shape became clearer as Hana went across to it with a candle. It was big, standing on a branch that came inside through the window, the skin drapings fitted skilfully around the wood.

'Ko Ru tēnei,' said Hana. 'Tāku hoa.'

'Thank god,' said Van. 'I thought I was going to get knifed.'

It was a kākā, a parrot like those he'd seen outside earlier that day. His head was on one side, his round eye regarding Van with supreme distaste. Ru squawked again, and Hana bent to him, murmuring low and nonsense talk. In the candlelight the bird seemed to have more grey feathers in the reddish-brown on the top of his head.

Hana aimed her forefinger below the bird's chest, then, once it had adjusted to her closeness, she knuckled the grey patch on its head. The parrot pushed and swayed against her hand, seeming to enjoy the contact, even while it sent Van that same baleful look.

Hana laughed. 'You should know that Ru is old and terribly hōhā, most of the time.'

'How old is he?'

As soon as Van spoke, the bird flapped wildly, scattering a detritus of seeds and feathers from underneath his branch.

Hana put a finger on the base of her own throat. 'Try not to speak too loud. Your voice is new to him, and it's deeper than he's used to.'

Again Ru regarded Van with an offended look.

'I'll take him somewhere else, I think,' said Hana. 'Until he gets used to you. Haere mai, e Ru, you old grump.' She clucked and coaxed Ru towards her outstretched finger, but he just puffed out his feathers and sulked. 'Oh, all right, then.' From a plaited-together box on the floor she lifted a handful of seeds and crumbled bark. Alert suddenly, the bird craned his neck towards the food, then waddled up the branch. Teasing him onto her hand, Hana went out with Ru through the door flap. Van imagined another room with open windows filled entirely with birds who'd been evicted from their perches by humans who wanted to have sex, all haughty feathers and outraged parrot talk.

Hana was gone a long time and Van spent it sitting on the edge of the bed, working spit into the stains of dirt that were deep in his knuckles and the sides of his fingers. Even with the hot wash that he and Rau had been treated to after they arrived, the ingrained mud of his mining work was still there.

The floor shifted again; Hana was back.

Van hid his hands.

'Sorry about that. I just had to make sure Kahu was all right.'

'If you need to look after her—?'

She shook her head, tying the door flap shut. 'We had a good talk. She's with my aunties now. She's upset about Nan, but exhausted as well. She'll be asleep soon, I'd say.'

'I'm not surprised she's exhausted. Why didn't she have help, fetching us?'

'It's part of her training to tackle a wero like that. A solitary one. And I didn't want it to be anyone else who fetched you.'

Reading something in Van's look, Hana lifted a hand. 'I know it might seem tough on Kahu, but she was happy to do it. Especially because it's what Nan wanted. Believe me, Nan wanted this. She wanted this from Kahu, from all of us. She wants us to be together.'

She reached to his face.

He was glad he'd trimmed his beard earlier, seizing on the fine metal blades he and Rau had been given when they washed.

'I know it's not easy to do,' said Hana, 'but we have to try to let Kahu look after herself for a while tonight, or at least let my aunties look after her.' She dropped her hand to his hip. 'It's like Bel said. Some trades are best made in private. We have to have our own time first.'

He bent down to her face and they kissed. Her mouth tasted good, free of taint. His hand was in her hair, catching in the plaits and feathers that were tied into it.

At length Hana pushed away from him. She peeled back the blankets on the bed. 'Hop in. I won't be a moment.' Then she was gone to a bench against the wall, not far from where the bird had been. Her back to him, she removed a succession of rings, bracelets, necklaces. He saw that all of her ornaments were made of wood and bone, no plastic. Sensing his attention, she stopped. 'Could you look away, please.'

He rolled over and tried to twist his coat at the same time. She hadn't said whether he should undress before getting in the bed, and now his long coat was tangled round his crotch and his erection was uncomfortably caught. He put a hand down to ease it. Then he froze, as Hana turned and spoke.

'Anō?' he said, his voice as normal as he could make it.

'My Nan will pass soon. Our healers don't think she'll make the morning. Not by a long shot.'

He grimaced, his hand still frozen down by his crotch.

She looked along the bench beside her, as if for a sign of what to say next. 'She waited till Kahu was back from the fetch—till you'd brought her back safe. So that's something. That's good.

Our healers will say that's a tohu. Now she can happily return to the forest.'

It was almost choking him, his urge to get this talk over with. For a desperate moment he imagined a long and chaste night of lying on the bed and attempting to sleep while she talked all night and his erection pulsed furiously at the restraining blanket.

But then water sounded again and she began to wash. He eased his crotch and turned to watch her, disobeying her instruction not to look. She was in a fine night-coat that came to her knees, the work of some expensive Whaea weaver, no doubt. Her hair was all out and it flowed down her back, the blue and white of two pūkeko feathers still showing in it, woven tight together and tied with very thin plait. She scooped water again and turned. 'I told you not to look.'

'I can't help it.'

'Just be patient. I don't want you to see this bit.'

He rolled away.

At last she was finished and came to the bed. She lay beside him and guided his hand to her hip, the soft incurve just above it. 'Come closer.'

He moved into her aroma, that smell of herbs he remembered.

'I'm so glad you came back.'

His voice was very thick. 'I've thought about you non-stop.'

She pulled him to her and they kissed.

'You taste like your water,' he said. 'You taste so good.'

She helped along their talk and their sex. She got up to pour more fresh water, and later, when they got hungry, she padded away through the door flap in bare feet, returning with a wood platter of food that was left over from the hākari. Mocked him as he promptly spilt it onto the bed.

At Summer's Day it had been similar—his nerves conquered by her laughter. It had been his first time at Summer's Day, his first time ever inside the fence of the Whaea people, and it had begun back in Matewai's camp, with Ava telling him she'd secured him a place, at that annual opening of the gates, for access to a shelter and a chance of sex, a chance to advantage himself at the strange Whaea festival of trade and ritual meetings in intimate shelters, though how she'd organised it all from her sickbed he couldn't guess. Matewai must have been behind it as well, or Rau. All of them would have played their part, he supposed.

'You might even meet someone you really like,' Ava had said. 'It's a good chance for that.'

'Or just a chance to get laid,' said Rau. 'Because no one else round here is.'

Ava hadn't even flinched when he'd said that. Night after night she'd lain in the hut she shared with Rau, cramped in a horrible shape by the female ache that had brought her so low and that Matewai's oils had seemed unable to fix. Even the best of the Whaea potions that Rau fetched at such cost and such risk—running the Dry Way at night—could not get rid of it.

And when Van had been brought through the south gate with the other hopefuls, and on round the back of the settlement to a skin shelter, and told to wash his face if he felt like it—it was hot, but he wasn't willing to remove his headwrap yet—and to wait for whoever was due to visit his shelter, he'd hoped only for someone who wouldn't shrink from his simple swamp coat and the reputation that he knew hung about him of plastic. And his heart had sunk when Hana stepped through the door flap in long coats of fibres he'd never seen up close before, her hair tied with red feathers as well as the white and blue of pūkeko that Rau had warned him to expect. The high-born look she carried.

But on seeing him she'd smiled diffidently, and apologised that it had been some time since her last Summer's Day, and said she didn't know how to talk to a tāne anymore, and they'd made some humour about being awkward and unpractised, and then they'd just talked for a time and eaten from the food bowls that were laid out, and she'd ridiculed the whole ritual of Summer's Day and why the Whaea people even needed it in the first place—the kind of banter that had shocked him, coming from someone who so obviously benefited from all this, from living right underneath, as she put it, the Whaea's big toe.

And then she'd let him stay on for the night in the shelter. He'd arrived with others who seemed richer than he was, and not tainted by swamp or plastic or muddied and lost waters, and confident in their own high-born waters, and they were all waiting in the next-door shelters for their chance to meet her. But it was with Van, for some reason, that she'd stayed, and then at some point she'd given the signal to someone, and those others had been dismissed and escorted back outside the fence. Leaving only Hana with Van, her baffled favourite, and the other Whaea people with their selections in other shelters— the women and men from all over, allowed in to enlarge the pleasure and prospects of the Whaea people in the hope of lasting relationships and even the possibility of children for some who took part.

It had puzzled him, her willingness to stay with him, to reach again to his body when their murmured talk and laughter came to a stop and the people in the other shelters had fallen silent and ruru calls passed over the night and finally a woman's voice had called from another shelter to shut them up.

'Oh shut up yourself,' Hana had shouted back, shocking him—such irreverence for the protocols of the night, such delight in his fear of the response.

It was like that again now. She had that same ready laugh, the same instinct to tease him. But it was different too, this time. She'd asked him to come back. Knowing where he'd come from, knowing his trade in plastic, she'd sent for him and brought him to her own room, halfway up the Whaea slope itself, the statue's great shadow darkening the trees right above them.

Now he took a piece of cold kūmara she passed him. Again he caught the outline of the painted design on her hand, and she saw him looking and lowered it to the blanket.

'It was Nan who told me to fetch you. She was quite forceful about it. "Tīkina mai tō tāne" was what she said.' Hana smiled, looking down at her hand. 'She's not one to muck about.'

When he didn't react, she shoved him so hard that he fell, spilling water to the bed.

'This is when you say you're glad that I did. Glad I fetched you.'

He laughed, taking the rag she passed him to mop up. It felt wasteful to get rid of water like this, simply sponging it half into the rag and half into the bed's thick possum blanket. But it was strangely good too. It was a feeling of luxury, of pretending to be rich even if it was only for part of a night or however long their meeting was meant to last.

'Van, you know why you're here, right?'

'Not really. I've been trying to figure it out.'

'It's because we've made a trade. A trade that will last.'

He eyed her, wary. The tone of her voice had changed, but still he was cautious of the smile that lingered on her face, the sense he was being mocked for something: his seriousness perhaps, or his slowness.

'Kei te hapū au, Van.'

'A baby? You have a baby?'

She smiled. 'She's from Summer's Day.'

'How do you know it's a girl?'

'I just do. We do—my aunties and me.'

He felt again that huge leaping inside, the force he'd felt in the front room when he'd first entered the hut and seen Hana among those others, the force that took him towards her.

'Are you sure about it?'

She nodded. 'My aunties are all sure, and my healers too. We're confident.'

'Oh,' said Van. 'Oh.'

'You *are* pleased, aren't you? Happy.'

'Āe. But it's a shock. It's . . .'

She laughed at him, and he shook his head, stunned by it.

There was movement in a nearby room; the poles of the floor creaked and adjusted.

'So what happens with this?' he said. 'With us?'

'What do you mean?'

'Well, I'm from the swamp.' He gestured at the comfort around them, its drapings of skins and mats, the colours that hung in the ceiling space. 'And you're clearly not.'

'Oh,' she said, waving a hand, 'don't worry about that.'

He found his water cup, tried to drink from it, and found his hand was shaking. He put it down again. 'Because you know I don't have any flash waters. No rivers to speak of. Except Rau's and Matewai's, as a whāngai, which is good, but probably not—'

'But that's not right, Van. It's just that you don't know them yet.' She saw his disbelief and nodded firmly, negating it. 'You understand that only people with good waters are able to come inside the fence at Summer's Day, don't you? Rivers that are useful to us? You have those.'

'But how could you know that? How could you know my waters? I don't. Even Matewai doesn't. Not my own waters, from my birth parents.'

'Our aunties do. They know that stuff.'

He looked into the dark at the limit of the candle's reach, the outline of the branch where that bird had eyed him with such distrust. 'So who are they? These people. My waters I don't know about.'

'The Donovans.'

'The Donovans? What is that—a whānau? I've never even heard of it.'

'Āe, a Pākehā whānau. Well, somewhat Pākehā, anyway—some of them. They're way inland, apparently.'

'Seriously?'

'Apparently. Up a river that connects to our own and then leads way, way back.'

'Where exactly?'

'I don't know yet. I'm finding out. Rerū looks after all that knowledge, and she's told me some of it, and she's still teaching me the rest. She can't teach it to you directly, she says. It has to come through me.'

'Why?'

She shrugged. 'Rules.'

'Huh.'

'I know. It's a bit nuts.' She thought for a moment. 'It's really complicated, actually, what she's teaching me, how your whānau works. I hope I remember it right.' She smoothed something on the bed. 'But it'll be fine. If I forget it all, we can just make something up, some river with people's names in it, and then you can blurt that out when you meet these folk.'

'Oh my god.'

She pushed him again. 'I'm joking.'

117

He couldn't laugh. It didn't seem like something to joke about. 'So is this why I'm back here, really? This is why I'm allowed inside the fence. Because of these waters you've found. This river. My long-lost and useful folks.'

'Kāo. You're here because of this—because of us. And because of the pēpi we've made.' She pulled his hand down, laying it palm-flat on her belly. He couldn't detect a presence there. Only a softness, the comfort of someone who'd never starved. But perhaps it was too soon to feel a pēpi shape. 'But it definitely helps that you have good waters. It helps all of us.'

'Because it means I'm not just swamp. Not just some plastic trader from the swamp with no waters.'

'No, it's more than that. But it certainly helps.' She eyed him. 'You're not offended, are you?'

He lifted his hands. 'It's hard to be offended. It's more—surprised. I didn't know about any of this until tonight. This pēpi. These waters.'

'Well, the pēpi is coming, like it or not. And you're going to have to learn about your waters. Because we're going to need those connections. We're going to need all your help.'

He shook his head. It seemed so unlikely that the Whaea people could need him for anything. Probably it was the help of Rau or Matewai, or the Te Repo people, they really needed.

'So what is it?' he said. 'What's the emergency?'

'Hang on,' she said, twisting in the bed to see him better. 'First, I want to get this straight. It's not the main reason you're here. The real reason is this. Us.' Her hand went out to encompass them, their rumpled bed, their night. 'We're both here because of this, Van. Because of what this feels like.' She was above him now, looking directly into his face. 'Don't you like this?'

'Of course,' he said. 'Of course I do.'

'So this is what I remember from our first time—this feeling—and this is what I like. What I want in my life. And this is the real reason why you're back here now, why you've been fetched. And it's why you're the father of this pēpi.'

'Right.' He thought for a moment, his mind going away through the rooms of this place, the other people who must already know about this. The aunties and great-aunties who'd already discussed their match. 'What about Kahu?'

'What about her?'

'Well, what does she think about it?'

She smiled. 'I'd say probably she's on the fence. Getting used to it. But when she'd finished fetching you, she said you were all right. Actually, "hūmārie" is what she said about you.'

'Huh. I don't think I was particularly hūmārie when we met. She was brave, I thought, coming into my camp like that, at night.'

'Oh, āe, Van. You're very frightening. We're all terrified.'

He laughed, a sharp bark of relief.

'It's so good to hear you laugh. God, it's been so tense.'

Only one of the candles she'd lit earlier was still burning, and he looked now into the outer reaches of the halo it cast. 'Because of this? Because of us? Have people been upset?'

'Kāo. *That* has been good. It's all the rest. All the other stuff I have to tell you about. The rest is not so good.'

'What's the rest?'

She looked down at her hands. 'I'm glad we've had this nice time tonight. I'm glad we've had it. Because we've got some hard work ahead of us.' She looked away for a time, and when her face turned to him again it was tight, tense. 'He hīkoi. You and me and Kahu. We're going to have to take a long walk inland to meet these people that your waters flow into.'

'When?'

119

'Very soon. The morning after tomorrow, perhaps.'

'But what about your Nan?'

'We'll have our own rites for her. Private rites. Just for us— the travelling group.'

He considered this. 'It's serious, this thing.'

'It's not great.'

He thought again. 'And can you do that—walking so far? With a pēpi.'

She looked down and put a hand there. 'I'm going to have to. We all have to. Look,' she said, 'I'll tell you all this in time. But, please, just not right now. It's a long talk, and it's exhausting. I know you need to hear it, but I need to have a rest first so that I can say it right—so that I can say it with hope, and with faith.'

He nodded, but then another question occurred to him. 'Is anyone else coming?'

'Three tamāhine toa.'

'Three? Do we need them?'

'Āe, kāore e kore. To keep us safe. I tried to get more, but I wasn't allowed them. With the way things are, they're needed here in our camp.'

'Shit. It sounds bad.'

'Āe.' She sighed, and looked towards the wall where her pet bird had been. 'It's not great at the moment. But we'll make it good. You and me and Kahu, and this pēpi. We'll make it good.'

Nine

Van hadn't slept long before the noise of people moving outside the room woke him. Careful not to rouse Hana, he lay still and listened to their movements out there, their murmured talk. It was impossible to know from those sounds whether the old woman had died in the night.

But there was more noise coming from beyond the hut. Overhead, a riot of birds, louder than any chorus he'd ever heard. Tūī and korimako, and then kākā doing their weird squeers and scrapes. No sign in the room of the old pet that had been evicted in the night.

And there was a commotion too of people moving up the hill. Some sang out there; he also heard kids who laughed and shrieked.

'It's the statue market,' said Hana. She stretched her arms above her head. 'We should head up there soon. Meet Rau.'

When he looked blankly at her, she said, 'Remember? We told him we would—and Bel. We told them we'd pass on to Rau the result of our trade talk.'

'Oh, right.' He looked over the bed, readjusting the night they'd just shared to a meeting on trade. It was true that they'd discussed some major trades, but still the main thing he'd taken from the night was the rumpled and blissed feeling after sex. 'Actually, would it be all right if I talk to Rau on my own?'

She looked towards the drapings of skins on the far wall, as if to gauge the morning he would face out there beyond the hut.

'I think I should be the one to tell him about the pēpi. He and Ava tried for so long. And then she got so sick—in her whare tangata.' It was not something he would normally say; they were Kahu's words from that meeting with Matewai.

'Āe, I heard about Ava's troubles. I felt for her.'

'I think it's best if I break it to him. If there's anything you need to tell him, could you do it afterwards?'

She shook her head. 'I have to talk to him. About our hīkoi. And one of our tamāhine toa needs to talk to him too—to both of you—because she doesn't agree with what's been decided. She has to be allowed her say. So we'll both come up and talk with Rau, and with you.'

'Oh. I was thinking you could catch up with Kahu while I'm gone.'

'I've already done that,' she said. 'I saw her while you were still asleep.'

'How is she?'

Hana made a face. 'Not too bad, considering all that's been going on. She was close to Nan, of course—closer than I was, really. Nan was my first tāne's mother, so there was always that between us, even though she's always been good to me.'

Van nodded, deciding not to ask more about this. It still amazed him that Kahu was to come on their journey, along with him and Hana and their three tamāhine toa protectors. He tried again to picture it, how that journey would work. Every time he thought of it he felt he would have to look after Kahu, keep her safe. He was nervous of Hana's lack of wariness; she seemed too likely to lead them into danger.

'How about this?' said Hana. 'How about you talk to Rau first, about our pēpi, and then I'll come up with the tamāhine toa to talk about our hīkoi and all that.'

'All right.' He registered the seriousness in her face. But then she visibly—deliberately—brightened. 'Kaua e māharahara, Van. We're going to be all right.'

'You really think that?'

'Well, I've got faith. I'm working on having faith.' She looked away, then thought of something. 'Bring him back for parakuihi. Rau. If he's all right with it, please bring him back for breakfast.'

Van eased out his side of the bed. Shy in the growing daylight, he turned to hide his nakedness, and she laughed.

But when he turned, she lifted her hands. 'I didn't say anything.'

Soon he was dressed and dosed with oil, and his headwrap was tied down again. Something about him—perhaps the headwrap, seldom seen up on this hill—made her smile.

'What?'

'Just be careful up there. The dawn market is a bit crazy.'

He nodded.

'Tuku karakia. For me. For us.'

'Really? I don't know your karakia. I'll muck it up.'

She watched him for a time, that same smile playing on her face. He wondered if it was a serious request, or whether she'd said it just to see him react. 'Nah. I'll do it when I come up.'

He paused at the door flap. 'Do I have to go through this room? I don't want to disturb your Nan, the people with her.'

She stood up, pulling a coat round herself. 'I'll show you another way out.'

The next room was empty of people, still quiet from the night, its only sounds those that came from outside. Hana bent up to kiss him goodbye, but in the new room he felt a difference settle on them. There was a firmer set to her mouth as she pointed him through the room to the way out.

The track was crammed, and Van couldn't get onto it. Two and three abreast, traders and their families pressed up the track. Some of the adults sang as they went up, holding their hands aloft to brush the colours that trailed down from the branches above. They sang in praise, chanting the Whaea's name.

But most were too burdened for that, weighed down with the trades they carried up the zigzag track. He saw many children carrying rolled-up mats and all kinds of vessels holding vegetables, bundles of meat and herbed water— wooden canisters and bowls, kete and mats tied up with plait. Most of the children were quiet, mutely accepting their loads, but some grumbled and sulked when their parents scolded and hurried them up the path.

These were plainer folk. Their clothes were patched and dirty with work, and there were more men than he'd seen last night. More variety than at that dinner too—more than a few with Pākehā looks. Some of them glanced sharply at Van, a stranger standing at the main track's meeting place with a pathway that led to a high-born hut.

To avoid more attention, he had to push in. After waiting a long time for a gap, a meat-trader laden down with wares came up, and Van barged into the half-gap in front of him.

'Don't shove,' the man said. 'Prick.'

There was more complaint from further back, some of it in Van's own language, some not.

He didn't stop but looked over the heads in front of him, their uphill surge of trade-noise and colours and song. He was pushed up with them, zigzagging right and then left up to the top, until everything stalled. Something blocked the track up ahead. Too many people were already up there, it seemed.

Straight away, remonstrations started. Traders swore and pushed. Some stepped off the track and went up through the bush, making their own way to the top. Others simply began setting up their stalls where they were, plonking a frame of plaited branches among the trees, and then a benchtop, and then set out their mats or meats. Shouting to be heard, they hawked. Still others had no stall; instead they hung their baskets round their necks and hollered for purchasers.

Most were ignored, as the remaining trekkers craned to see further up. They pushed at the crowd for a time before ducking up the track or quitting to peel away and shove back down the pathway towards home.

Not wanting to get yelled at again, Van didn't step off the track or try to push up. Instead he stood in his place, jostled by the others and bawled at by a hawker of coloured plaits who'd set up her trading spot two paces from him, one hand round a kohekohe tree for balance on the steep slope. She offered colours for sweethearts and kids, she told them. Whaea colours, made in praise.

Still searching for Rau among the trekkers, Van made the mistake of catching her eye. Immediately she responded, switching to his language.

'The tall honky wants one for his sweetheart. His lofty miss. A lofty colour for a high-born miss.'

He smiled and shook his head. He had no idea what such colours would cost, and he had nothing to trade with anyway, except those plastic pieces he'd smuggled in and kept in Hana's hut, and those probably had no great value inside the fence. He had no riches here, he realised, no trading status.

'He'll need more than one, though. He's aiming high, from what I've heard. This fellow from the swamp—he's shooting high.'

He shook his head again, trying to laugh her off. Other people were turning now to see the target of her attack. Their eyes lingered on his unfamiliar face and headwrap, the jibes in Pākehā language.

Now that it was clear he wasn't going to trade with her, the woman switched to simply taunting him. 'Getting a bit above yourself, aren't you, mate? Let me tell you, you'll need to trade more than a broken plastic bucket to get that lofty bitch.' She laughed in a way that sounded a bit unhinged.

More of the traders and praisers turned to stare at him. Van prayed she would shut up. But then she made to speak again, and he walked directly towards her, putting his hand beneath his coat as if to pull a blade. Her face went blank with fright. At the last moment he changed direction, and barged up the side of the track instead, shoving through people with stalls and vegetables and trades. Children scattered, and some adults shouted, but no one actively tried to stop him, and he saw the top of the track and kept pushing until he reached it.

The entire plateau was crammed with people who stood very close and hawked their wares to one another. A handful of others were at the base of the statue, singing up to the Whaea. She was a vast structure of tree poles and branches plaited together and lashed over some other, ancient surface like painted rock, which was crumbled and cracked and had been many times repaired with what looked like thoroughly worked-over mud. All of it was in the shape of a woman who stood with her hands together and her face turned serenely to the north. She was the revered aunty of these people, the guardian of their forests and settlement, and moored to the ground by plaited ropes that came off her in multiple places and were hung about, too, with colours that flicked and swayed around. Looking up her vast height, Van wondered at the work it must have taken to keep her upright through storms and wind and rain damage over lifetimes, the constant repairs she must need. Even now there were workers attending to her, crawling over a scaffolding of latticed wood that stood at her back, where two men lifted plaits and, under the instruction of a young woman, replaced frayed knots at the jointed wood of one of her elbows. And higher up an older woman dabbed mud with a delicate tool of metal at the ancient surface of her face. It had been made of that crumbled rock many lifetimes back, and then, it seemed, repaired and dyed thousands of times since then, so her face had a pied and patched look. Yet the serenity she was revered for shone through, gazing towards whatever danger was coming from the north. It took even Van's breath away to be so close and peer up at that ancient face.

He searched the crush for Rau but saw no sign. Barged again by two traders, he looked simply for some free space. He saw an opening at the far side of the plateau, where the trees had been cut away and people stood looking out towards the coast. They weren't trading or praying, but surveying the territory and the movements of the day out there. He'd be able to get a bit of space and a view of the swamps, at least, and perhaps the damage from yesterday's dry storm.

He was halfway there, pushing through the clamour, when he saw the big shoulders and tied-back hair of a shape that looked like Rau's. He was at the far edge of the clearing, looking out, his foot braced against a branch. He turned, and lifted his eyebrows and chin in greeting as Van edged through the crowd.

Then Van found his way blocked by a boy hawker of about

twelve summers. Water bags hung from his neck. He stared up at Van.

'Tēnā koe, e tama,' said Van. 'Can I get past, please?'

Still the boy stared. He lifted one of his bags. 'Half-water?'

Van looked at the water bag. It wasn't clear what qualified it as 'half-water'.

'No thanks.'

Still the boy didn't move. He wore no colours. His face looked drained of energy in the way of hungry kids.

Van had nothing to offer him, and other people were starting to look now. He put his hand on the boy's shoulder, edging past. 'Good luck, kid.'

Rau raised his eyebrows. 'Looks like some bug's eating that kid from the inside out.'

'How's your breath?' said Van.

For answer, Rau indicated the view. 'It's ridiculous how easily they can watch us from up here. Our camps stick out like crotch rot.'

Van followed Rau's hand. They certainly were obvious down there, the bloomings of green bush among scrub that gave away his own camp, and then, further south, the larger settlement at Te Repo with the crops and the mound poking up. Their access to water, their travel routes through and round the dark ponds of seep, it could all be monitored from this place.

'They just see everything from up here. They could see the warts on your cock, if they looked at the right time. Those aunties probably got a good look at yours when you took a piss. Which probably explains why they were so unimpressed with you last night.'

Van nodded, not really listening. Rau was like this sometimes, acting as crass as possible when intimidated by something. Van's own attention was taken by the bulk and smoke of the island that stood beyond the swamp and dominated the whole coast. The twin fires the Burners maintained out there seemed this morning to smoke more insistently than before, as if to reinforce Hana's warnings of the night.

'It's the bird's perch, up here,' said Rau, still indignant. 'No wonder people fight and scrap so much over these hills. You get to control a lot.' He turned to Van, searching for a matching outrage.

But Van couldn't muster it. It was hardly a secret that down there he and all the swamp people were at the bottom of everything, their camps swarming with biters, and their freshwater ponds tainted with brack.

Rau sighed. 'So, a good night?'

Van looked over his shoulder. The crowd of market traders and praisers still kept up their racket. He'd hoped to go somewhere quieter, some stretch of forest or lakeside where they could talk without being overheard. But it would take some concerted pushing to even make it back across the plateau, let alone down the zigzag track. Strange that Bel had insisted they meet here. Perhaps she'd wanted them to be right amongst the problem, to be faced with the smoking island opposite, and amongst the hawking and teeming people, who were so clearly unprepared for any sort of attack.

'Well, the first thing is,' said Van, 'you were right. Kei te hapū a Hana.'

'I knew it,' said Rau. 'Congratulations.' But he didn't clap his hand to Van's, didn't bring him in to knock shoulders. Instead he just nodded to himself a few times, then looked out over the trees to the swamp and the island, the sea that ruffled around its edge.

'I'm sorry it wasn't you and Ava. I know it's unfair.'

Rau said nothing.

129

'If things were fair, you and Ava would have made a pēpi. I know that.'

Rau shook his head but couldn't hold Van's look. 'It's not like that, brother. This is what Ava wanted. It's what we all wanted. I'm happy for you.'

They were silent in the clamour of traders and prayer.

'The second thing is,' said Van, 'Hana's coming up here to talk about this with you, and about the other trades we've made—she and I.'

Rau seemed not to hear this. Instead, as if remembering at last, he turned and took Van's hand and bumped him into a shouldery embrace. 'This is good, Van. I'm glad of it.' His voice was husky. 'It's pretty obvious she's gagging for you. By the way, did you hear about the old one? She died as the sun came up.'

'I didn't know that.'

Rau nodded, and they were quiet for a time.

Van wondered why Hana hadn't told him. She must have known about it.

'Heoi, she was an old duck, I guess.' Rau turned again to the view and nodded to himself, more pacifically this time, as if Van's news of the coming pēpi had made it easier to look at the swamps and this outlook over them, this reveal of their impoverishment.

'Do you know how their grief ritual works? Like, won't you have to wait before you take the sinking party across? I'm having a hard time understanding their rituals.'

Rau shrugged. 'We'll just follow their lead, I guess.' He looked again over the view. 'Different world up here, isn't it.'

Van cleared his throat, preparing to speak.

But Rau turned, interrupting him. 'I know what you're worrying about. But don't start. Don't overthink it, Van.'

Van made to interrupt, but Rau surged on, determined to make his point.

'She likes you,' he said. 'And you've made a pēpi. That will take care of all of that stuff—who's Pākehā and who's not, who's rich and who isn't, who's got the best waters and who hasn't.'

'Actually, I wasn't going to talk about that. I was going to tell you about something else. She says my waters join with some Inlanders'. Some folk who've got a settlement up some river somewhere. Her aunties know about it.'

Rau looked only half-surprised.

'Did you know this already?'

'Kāo, but it makes sense,' said Rau. 'It's like I told you. Nobody's got no waters. Nobody's just an orphan. We've told you that heaps of times. Plus, you've got ours, of course.'

'Yeah, but there was no proof about my own. No story. No kōrero I could recite.'

'Whatever,' said Rau. 'You've got nothing to be ashamed of. You're a good trader, and your product is worth heaps, and you're part of my family. You'll be a bloody good father. She knows that. And now it seems you've got good waters of your own, or useful waters anyway, which is the same thing. No wonder she's hot for you. She's lucky to get you, I think.'

Van watched him, the certainty that had transformed his face. He seemed to have forgotten already what he'd just been complaining about—how visibly lowly they were down there in the swamp. Or perhaps he just no longer wanted to acknowledge it.

'She'd better be worth it,' said Rau. 'I'm not looking forward to taking that dead one back across the Way. They don't half ask for much.'

'But they didn't ask you to do that,' said Van. 'All they asked for was access.'

131

Rau snorted. 'As if I'm going to let them blunder across there and end up in some mud-hole, and then have to drag them out anyway.'

Van laughed. 'You don't make any sense.'

'Hey, just because they're whānau now, it doesn't mean they're not a stupid bunch of spoilt bitches. Some of them.'

Van laughed again, and this time some of the traders nearby turned to look at them. He didn't care. It was a relief to laugh, and for a moment he wished that Rau could come with him. He would ease the journey's risk and the work of getting to know Kahu—and almost immediately he saw the impossibility of it. He saw how, without meaning to, Rau would take over the trip and dominate it, how he would bend that little family—Hana, Van and Kahu—out of shape at its very start. 'By the way,' he said, 'does it seem weird to you that the Scarp is so close? They seem nearer up here than how it looks from the swamp. Up here you can see there's just a big lake in between this place and theirs, and a fence, and some bush, and that's all.'

Rau shrugged. 'It's a pretty big lake. Plus I suppose they trade with each other.'

'What do you mean "trade"? They hate each other. That's what the fence is all about.'

'Oh come on, Van. Surely you're not fooled by that.'

Van frowned, struggling to make this idea work in his head.

But Rau went on, as if he didn't want Van to follow the thought through to its conclusion. 'There's Summer's Day, at least, isn't there. Some of the Scarpers come to that. So that's a trading link between them.'

Van looked away, still confused, and saw Hana coming through the crowd, a young woman in plainer clothes following in her wake.

Rau, seeing them too, leaned in close. 'So what's the rest of it? What's going on with these people? It can't be just that you stuck a pēpi in one of them.'

Van spoke low and fast. 'Well, basically, this place is finished. It's fucked.'

'This place? You mean this settlement?'

When Van nodded, Rau glanced at the people behind them. 'It's the Burners, isn't it?' said Rau. 'Like Squat said. They're going to raid this place.'

Van could hear the thrill in Rau's voice. It was the nearness of disaster, its pulse of fright.

Hana was close now. Van eased away from Rau, but nodded as he did so. 'They call them People in Smoke—the Whaeas do,' said Van. 'But yeah, that's basically it.'

Then Hana was at his side, and he saw that she'd been crying in the time since he'd left her. She took his hand now. He turned to check if anybody had seen, and a few of those nearby were looking, but they turned away again, pretending not to notice. The young woman who'd arrived with Hana was a few summers older than Kahu, but still very young. She flinched when Van smiled at her.

'Ata mārie,' said Hana.

'Ngā mihi,' said Rau. 'I'm sorry for your loss.'

Hana swallowed, and visibly made an effort to nod, and to continue. 'Ko Tuku tēnei,' she said, indicating the young woman beside her. 'She'll be helping Van and Kahu and me on a trade we've negotiated. She's also here to advocate for a different approach. Tuku and some other tamāhine toa, and some older ones too, I have to say, don't agree with ours. They want us to stay and fight.' She paused, realising she'd gone further than she meant to. Then she waved this off. 'Anyway, she has the right to have her say. And as our new trading partners, you have the right to hear her thoughts, as well as the decision that has been made.'

'Ka pai,' said Rau. 'Tēnā koe, e Tuku. Peace on your waters.'

Tuku darted a wary smile at them both, then resumed her stony look.

'And congratulations on the pēpi, Hana,' said Rau. 'It's the best news—the best.'

Hana blinked, as if assailed at the same time by joy and grief. Then she squeezed Van's hand with more force. 'Thank you, Rau. I know from Van that you've had your own griefs, in terms of pēpi, in the past. Ka aroha hoki.'

Rau cleared his throat, and seemed to want to get off the topic. 'I know that my Māmā will be pleased.'

Van winced. 'She will—she will.'

'So—' Rau coughed, and hit his chest. 'Van tells me you've got some trouble too. Someone who wants your place.'

Hana sighed, and edged them further away from listeners. 'The People in Smoke want to raid us. They want to push us out. Some other people—some other Northerners—are coming south, so the People in Smoke want to get off the island before those new people arrive.'

'So let me get this straight,' said Rau. 'When you say the People in Smoke, you're talking about the Burners—that lot out there.'

Hana nodded. 'It's hard to change it to another language—the name we use. But, yes, more or less.'

'Because they turn everything to smoke, I'm guessing.'

'Āe. It's not their real name—I'm not sure if they even have a real name. Some people say they're just a rabble, who've gathered together, because they can burn everything. But it's what we call them.'

'All right. And there's another lot coming down, pushing

134

them out—but there's always people coming down from the north. The Dry Way is full of them. That's what the Dry Way is all about.'

'But this is different,' Hana said. 'They're not coming in dribs and drabs, as travellers. They're coming as a group, as a force, like the People in Smoke did. They're invading south, and they want the island. They're going to take it off them. And so the People in Smoke are coming to our place. They might also try to take the Scarp, if they decide they need it. But that's not our business.'

Rau looked out there again, as if to see afresh the order that was in front of him: an island that smouldered and smoked and had looked pregnant with threat ever since it had been taken several summers back, since the Burners had set the island alight and then crossed to the beaches to torch them too, scaring the last coastal villages out. Now Hana was saying they were running from people even fiercer, even more desperate. 'But won't these other Northerners who are chasing them just come onto the mainland too, after taking the island?'

'Āe, exactly. And there could be another wave of people behind them, from those unsafe places up north. So even if we stay and fight, we'll just have to fight again when the next wave comes, and then again. So our aunties have decided that we need to find a new place. This is what Van is going to help us with.'

'Wait,' said Rau. 'Do any of these people—the Burners, or those Northerners who are chasing them—want the swamp?'

'Can I answer this?' said Van.

Hana nodded, and Van felt the strange reversal of it. He was rarely the one with news to impart, the one to explain to Rau what shape their lives were about to take.

'I asked about this. Apparently they don't, because they

135

know about the biters, and the bad water, and how hard it is to live down there. So why would they want to live there, when they can take this place and live up here instead, where it's safe.'

'But there are other places, surely. Further south.'

'That's what I said, but apparently not.' Van stopped himself, stepping back. 'Sorry. I'm not supposed to be talking. I just wanted to tell you about the swamp.'

Rau merely switched his attention to Hana. 'So it's the lake, isn't it. The good water. They want your good water, and your lake.'

Hana used the same words, the same flat tone she'd used to explain these things to Van in the night. 'They want what everyone wants. Water and high ground. And there's no room to the south, anyway. All those people who come down the Dry Way to the south and try to cross the Strait, they're ending up nowhere good. They're all crammed up on each other. Some of them don't even get across the Strait, because the boats are too expensive. This is the best place left. That's why the People in Smoke want to take it.'

Rau looked again at the view to the island and, incredulous, he laughed. He shook his head at the enormity of what he'd heard. The vast Dry Way south, the rich Whaea people and their fence, and the Scarp who preyed on them all—they'd all been certainties since before Matewai's childhood, and now it was being turned over in a single morning's talk in the middle of a teeming market of traders who didn't even seem interested. 'So when does all this fun start, then?'

'Next summer. When this hill turns red. That's the People in Smoke saying that.'

'Red means blood?'

'Pōhutukawa. When the pōhutukawa on the lower slopes turn red—when they flower—they burn us out. Then, once we're gone, they'll plant in the ash.' She pointed. 'Same as out there, on the island, except this time they'll stay for good.'

'Holy shit.'

Again Rau fell silent, and they all looked out to the island, then back across the plateau to the vast kohekohe trees that branched above them. Festooned with colours that hung and flapped, these trees all seemed so permanent, and so did the huts that stood under them. Yet it was all wood and fibre, this settlement, its forests and statue. It would go up like gorse when it burnt. *Whoosh*, like Squat had said.

Then Rau looked at Hana again, at Tuku. 'Surely there's a trade solution to this. You people are so rich in trades. Surely you can trade for this place. You can talk to the Burners. Cut a deal with them.'

'I asked that too,' said Van. 'I even offered to talk to them.' Anticipating Rau's reaction, he said, 'Why not? I've got nothing to lose from it.'

Surprised at Van once more, Rau just blinked. 'Kei a koe, I guess.'

'We tried—I mean, they tried.' Hana pointed up, to suggest the people who made decisions above her. 'But the only deal we could get is the warning. The deal is we know when the raid is coming. We know how long we've got to get out. So what we have is information. The People in Smoke have wanted us to know that. It spares them some trouble, I guess, if we know when it's coming, and we leave first.'

'So you don't want to fight them?'

Hana lifted a weary hand, as if this was the end of a long discussion, not the start of it. 'You can't fight a fire with your fists, or your weapons,' she said. 'We're so blessed with forest, but it's also our weakness, nē. We'll burn fast. And they are so many, the People in Smoke, and so desperate. You've seen what

137

they did to the coastal villages. We took in some of those people, the ones who survived and made it up this far. They were not in a good state. And the People in Smoke have apparently got worse since then. They've got harder, because they're so scared of this other lot who are coming down from the north. They've had fights before, apparently.'

'We took in a few of them too,' Rau said. 'They didn't last long.'

Hana sighed. It was the same heavy energy that had overtaken her in the night, when she had talked it over with Van.

'But you,' said Rau, turning, 'you don't agree. You don't think you guys should go.'

Tuku looked at Hana for permission to speak. Then she began in her own language and stopped, seeing that Van was struggling to keep up. 'We think we should fight for what our ancestors gave us. We should fight to keep what they worked so hard to hand down to us. And we should fight for our forest. We're trained. We're fierce. We don't need to run from this.'

Rau waited for Hana's response, but she just motioned Tuku to continue. 'You can say more, if you want. It's your right.'

Van looked outside their circle. It was strange to be having this talk in such a public place. But the others there were still too intent on their trades and praise and milling under the statue to take part.

'I don't really have anything more to say about it,' said Tuku. 'To us it's obvious. We've been trained to protect these people, and this place, and our forests. We just want to do that.'

'I get that,' said Rau. 'I definitely understand that.'

Hana put a hand on Tuku, and her voice was gentle. 'But it's not all of you, is it? Not all of the tamāhine toa think like you do.'

'A fair number of us do,' said Tuku, 'and some of our aunties have the same view as well. But we're bound by what our main rōpū of aunties tells us to do. We run under their colours. We'll obey their decision. But we don't agree with it.'

Rau again seemed persuaded by the young woman's argument. 'And what about you, Hana?'

Hana lowered her head, and Van was pained by the thought of all that she was having to deal with. 'It eats my heart to think of leaving this place. I hate it. But, like I said, we can't fight these people. We can't fight their fire with our fists. It will beat us. And even if we do, there are just going to be more waves of people coming after them, because they have nothing left up north, nowhere safe from people, and from storms and bugs. And because we have what they all want.' She put her hands towards the earth. 'This high ground. The lake we've built. They will never stop till they get it. So we are better to get our people out safely, while we can. And for me—just speaking for me, regardless of all this—I have a daughter who's near fighting age. And I have a pēpi coming. I want to keep them safe. That's what is most important to me. Keeping all our people safe. And it's what my Nan—it's what my Nan told us we should do, as well, before she passed.'

They all looked away, allowing her a moment's grief. But she wiped at her eyes, and spoke again.

'We are rich in children. That is the most important thing. So we get them out. It hurts me to say it, to say that we should leave our forest, and our statue, but that's what I think.' She lifted a hand. 'And anyway, it's what our aunties have decided, so this is all just a pointless talk, in a way, but it's important that you both, as our trading partners, hear it.' She touched Tuku's arm to show that she didn't mean to trample on her by saying this. 'And the last thing is, I've told Van it won't be easy.

Getting out of here—it will be difficult. It will be too much for some people. Some won't make it. Some of us will die. Even on this scouting trip that Van and Kahu and me and some of Tuku's crew are going to take—even that is very dangerous. Some of us might die on that trip. But we have to do it. We have to.'

Rau waited to be certain that she'd finished, and then gave Hana a final, more intense stare. 'So, to be clear, they don't want the swamp.'

Hana nodded. 'That's our information.'

'And you lot don't want it either? You don't want to come and live with us in the swamp. Where the risks are known, and where we can look after you—me and Van, and Matewai.'

'I also asked this,' said Van.

They both ignored him: Rau's eyes stayed fixed on Hana, who shook her head.

'I couldn't get that trade. The inland trade is what I could get. And, if it works, it does offer—with respect—better prospects. Safer prospects. There's a big and unworked forest in their territory, apparently. And there's a lake. And there's land where our healers could plant, and good trading links to the people who live even further inland. So there's scope for our healers and traders and trappers to work and thrive again, if we negotiate for it.' She glanced at Van, and put her hands up. 'This is just what I'm told. It's based on pretty sketchy intelligence, from scouting trips and stuff. But it's all we've got, and we're desperate, so . . .'

Again Rau waited to be sure that she'd said all she wanted to. Her face was down; she couldn't speak anymore. Van took her hand and squeezed it. It probably wasn't right that the contact should arouse him a little, at such a moment, but it did.

Rau turned to Tuku. 'E hine, I respect your position. I

140

understand it. But Hana's right. I'd rather live down in the swamp, or run further inland, than get my arse burnt off by the Burners. Especially if I had kids.'

Tuku's face was hard again, but she met Rau's eye. 'Please give my mihi to Matewai, when you see her.'

'Ka pai,' said Rau. 'I'll do that.'

'All right,' said Hana. 'We'll leave you guys alone now. Come down for a kai, please, Rau, when you're ready.'

Rau watched the women go, and for a moment Van thought he was checking out Hana from behind. But then Rau said, 'Can she travel? I thought she was hapū.'

'She told me she's all right to take the trip. She says the worst of the sick that comes with being hapū has passed. And she took a long trip when she was pregnant with Kahu, apparently, so she knows she can do it.'

Rau glanced at him, surprised by this.

'She was chasing the father, she says. He'd gone up north on trade, and Hana went up there to find him, but he died of bites.'

'Is that right?' said Rau. 'Sounds like a stupid bastard.'

Van laughed.

Rau sighed, and dropped his head, as if the last of his objections had given way. 'She must really like what you've got under your coat, Van. You're hardly an expert on the inland routes.' He paused, and indicated the island. 'And it's a hell of a fight you've walked into.'

Van scuffed at the ground, then looked over his shoulder to see if anyone was in earshot. The crowd was beginning to thin out. The boy was still there, though, still hawking his bags of liquid. 'Half-water,' he said. 'Half-water.'

'What the hell is half-water?' said Rau.

'Probably what we'd just call water,' Van said. 'Or delicious.'

Rau's lip curled as he watched the boy, as if disgusted by

the work he did or by the fact that such work existed. The boy blanched and turned away.

Rau faced again the view of the swamps and the smoking island. He coughed and hit his chest. 'Well, that's that, then.'

'To be honest, I just can't see how it can work. This whole plan Hana and her aunties have worked out. Even if we get there, even if we survive the journey, I can't see how it can work. I don't know these Inland people—these people I'm supposed to be related to—and I don't know their rites. I don't even know how our waters flow into each other. But somehow I'm supposed to just turn up and speak and . . .' He lifted his hands.

Rau took a step back. As he regarded him, Van knew Rau was trying to work out what he was really saying, what he truly wanted. 'Do you want me to come with you?'

'No,' said Van. 'You've got that trade now. You've got to take the dead one over, and get her sunk. You should concentrate on that.'

'All right then.' He hit Van on the shoulder. 'You'll be all right.'

Van looked away. His throat felt thick.

'Kia kaha, brother,' said Rau. 'You've got this.'

The boy's voice came again, further off this time. 'Half-water,' he said. 'Half-water.'

'The fire man,' said Rau, turning. 'That's what that kid was talking about. Yesterday. That kid who called you the fire man. He thought you were one of these people who's coming to burn them.'

'Huh,' said Van.

Rau grinned. He seemed happy to have worked it out when Van hadn't. 'So some of them must know already that it's coming.' He looked towards the statue back there, the dispersing mêlée of traders and praisers underneath. 'But they're all just doing their normal stuff—just doing all their business—like usual.'

'I know,' said Van. 'That's what makes it so strange. It's hard to believe that it will happen, or that they'll actually do anything about it.'

'Good luck, brother,' said Rau.

Ten

Mist moved through the trees, rubbing its damp on Van's cheekbones and hands, the only skin he'd left exposed. Its kiss was cold but fresh. Lifted far from the bogs of the swamp, it had no taste or aroma of mud. The mist also brought kākā down, their calls coming eerily through it, sometimes in fluting sounds, sometimes hoots. They swooped low through the trees and chased down the tunnel of the track and then back up, their underwings flashing red.

Unused to climbing hills this steep, Van sweated inside his freshly washed coat. It had been cleaned and patched by some Whaea worker while he slept last night, its remnant stink washed out. And now, over the top of his own coat, he wore a borrowed coat. It was made of finely sewn possum skins: fancy, high-born stuff. But it made him hot. He fell back a little, for a chance to hide his heaving breath, and to wipe off sweat.

Hana pretended not to notice. She was ahead of him, walking freely; her dark coat of possum skins blazed right down the backbone with a tan line of weasel or stoat. It was a coat to reckon with. He could only imagine what it was worth. It relieved him, though, to see that for once she was properly wrapped. As well as insect ties at wrist and neck, she was

144

cinched tight at the waist with a coloured belt, and had a scarf and wrap round her head and neck.

She stopped abruptly at a turning in the track. 'Kei te pai koe?'

He looked up beyond her. Kahu was somewhere there, far in the lead. It was safe to let her walk alone, Hana had said, until they hit the south-west fence.

'It's not far to the stores now,' said Hana. 'We just climb a bit more, then head straight over a plateau, south-west.' She eyed him. 'Are you sure you're all right?'

'I'm fine.'

She went further up the track. She wasn't even puffed. But it seemed to please her that he was struggling, that he had to put one hand on his thigh for support, while he saw her own fitness.

Kahu was still nowhere in sight. For Van it was good that Kahu got some distance from them. It would help her to walk alone, and relieve some of her tension. Last night they'd all eaten together, on the instruction of some hidden aunty. But it had been a bad idea. Over dinner the three of them were forced in on each other and Kahu retreated into quiet. She pushed her food about, until Hana lost her patience and told her to eat up, because there was a serious trip starting the next day and she would need her strength. Kahu greeted her mother's advice with a look of immeasurable contempt. She then bent her head to her food and wolfed the lot, and then sat there with her hands in her lap, her face turned away from them both.

After a time Van gestured at the remains of the food. 'Better than that soup we gave you at Matewai's camp, eh? Easier on the gut.'

She glanced up and Van recoiled, stunned by the rebuke and hurt in her face.

Hana put her hand on Kahu's wrist. 'You can go if you like. I'll come and see you in a moment.'

Kahu flicked her eyes again in Van's direction, and he sensed that she wasn't mad at him really. But before he could think of any way to respond, she'd gone through the door flap.

'Try not to worry about it,' said Hana. She's very nervous about tomorrow. And upset about Nan.'

Van nodded, and looked away. It was hard not to think of it as disastrous.

'Don't try to rush it,' Hana said.

'Like your kākā.'

She smiled. 'They're not that different. Kids and pets. You come at them slow.'

Now panting up through this mist and bush he felt something of his former confidence coming back. Surely among these trees and on this trip he could show Kahu that he was useful, or at least not a blow-arse. Perhaps they could go off and hunt something together, just the pair of them. Help her work out some of her grief, without having to talk about it. Trap a possum and stake it to a trunk. Or go after fish at night—whatever flash types of fish they had in their fresh waters. Show her how to make a barb and hook from a discarded piece of plastic, if such a thing could be found in this precious forest. It would be good to do something like that. One last thing for her and the bush before they left it—this sacred, doomed forest.

It had been a brisk farewell that morning. The oiled and wrapped body of the old nan lay in the next room, readied for transport. Hana and Kahu and a series of other groups had held their own rituals to farewell the dead one the day before, and now wider groups of aunties had gathered to farewell the body, and to see off the two parties of travellers as well. They circled in and out of the two rooms, saying prayers and karakia in both languages, hugging those who were about to go out. The air was rich with the oils they'd applied to the corpse and with the aroma of herbed candles that smoked all through the rooms.

When Rau came in, he was belted at the waist and across his chest, bags knotted in place for the trip back into the swamp. His sliced arm had been freshly bandaged and wrapped. He crossed the room to Van, and yanked him into an embrace. 'So we'll see you when you get a chance.'

'When I get back,' said Van. 'As soon as I get back.'

Rau shook his head. 'When you get a chance. You get your family safe first. Then come and see us.'

Van saw a pair of aunties stiffen. It was the first time anyone had referred to Hana and Kahu as Van's family.

Hana came through the door flap, heavily laden with bags. Kahu was directly behind, wearing a scarf and headwrap. The girl looked withdrawn, knocked into herself by grief. She shouldn't be going anywhere, Van thought. She needed rest. Or at least an easier trip. He wished again he could be in Rau's place, escorting the dead one to her resting place in the swamp, and taking Kahu and Hana there too, so the young woman could stand at the sinking place and howl out the pain she so clearly felt at her Nan's death. Then back to Matewai's camp for rest and food and a chance for Matewai to host them properly, to make a fresh start with Kahu, who was becoming her first moko. It would take her some time to show it, but Matewai would be overjoyed. A live and healthy mokopuna; a rare success. And a chance for Matewai to meet Hana too—pregnant Hana.

Rau had finished kissing cheeks with Kahu and Hana. He

147

confirmed with some of his party their travelling details—it seemed the tamāhine toa who would accompany them were waiting at the gate. Satisfied, Rau turned to Van. 'Well, that's us. If you don't come back—' He paused. 'If you don't come back alive from this trip, but your new wife does, I'll make it my duty—my solemn duty—to tell lies about you to your kids.'

Everyone laughed.

Rau's eye went over Van, his bags and straps. He couldn't help it; he was checking his readiness. His hand went towards Van's bag-strap, as if to correct the way it was tangled on itself, but then he stopped himself and punched Van on the shoulder instead. 'Kia kaha, brother.'

Van turned away. He could see in Rau's face his grief for Ava still roaming and unsettled.

'Right.' Rau hit his chest with his fist, as if that was the reason he couldn't talk. 'Hoake mātou.'

The bearers gathered round the body on its litter of stripped mānuka poles. A high thread of sound started from an aunty among them, and then a grunt came from Rau as he and the others took the weight. They hoisted the corpse and began to shuffle out, the wail going forth over their heads, covering them.

Van looked after Rau, blinking.

Seeing his distress, Hana came across the room towards him, but was intercepted by a healer. Headwrap pushed back, her face smeared with oil and work, the woman was one of those who'd been busy with the corpse since first light. Holding Hana by the elbow now, she checked the colours in Hana's headwrap, the feathers hanging from her neck and the cord round her elbow, touching each piece as she murmured a long string of talk, of Whaea thanks. At the end of this she placed a kiss on Hana's forehead, then repeated the process for Kahu.

She tied an extra plait round Kahu's wrist—for protection, Van supposed—and Kahu ducked her head, her eyes darting. Again it pierced him to see the pressure on her. She was required because of her age and family obligation to take the trip, Hana had said, but he suspected she really wanted Kahu close to keep the girl safe.

'Now you're both safe,' said the aunt. 'Go safely through the Whaea's forest. Go strongly beyond it.'

Then they all backed away, satisfied that enough had been done: the two women protected by prayer and a few coloured plaits from all that would await them on the trip to the far eastern gate. There, they would be met by a party of three tamāhine toa who would accompany them. They were proper fighters, Hana had assured him, trained in the famous tamāhine toa fighting techniques that many of the young Whaea women learnt, but still it seemed a flimsy party to Van. The whole settlement's escape route was being entrusted to a handful of kids, and to him, and to Hana and Kahu, who were surely ripe targets for kidnap—high born, rich. Three tamāhine toa would not be enough.

There was also the problem of the kākā. Hana had told him that Ru would be released at the fence, accompanying them from above to signal that they travelled in peace. That, according to Hana, was what a kākā in flight signalled. To Van, it seemed like madness. All that a kākā screeching above would say was, 'Here is someone rich. Attack them.' Yet Hana had assured him it was safe; an old way of communicating with Valley folk that worked.

Now Van searched for a sign the aunties and healers opposite him shared any of his doubts. But they all just looked back pacifically, as if wiped of fear by the morning's rites. In the next room a different sound rose in farewell to the dead, more like a song this time. He didn't understand the words, yet it got him in his throat, and lodged something thick in it.

Hana had stopped walking by the time he caught up. Kahu was just in front, waiting for them. Before her was a clearing, which she seemed reluctant to enter without the adults. As Van came up, Hana led them into it. The clearing was strewn with branches that had come down in the storm. On its opposite side a series of huts stood on stilts, their poles lashed to wooden pegs for support. And two men were on the ground, he saw now, scrambling up and apart. They'd been lying with their arms round each other, embracing. They pulled their clothes about, brushing off leaves and dirt.

The shorter one called his apologies across. 'We didn't expect you yet.'

'But we've got all your supplies ready. We finished our work ages ago, before we took this break together.' This was the larger man. He glared at Van, as if daring him to contradict him, or to make something of it.

Van took in their worn coats, their rag boots. Both wore a single coloured plait round their elbows, but there was nothing else to indicate they were Whaea folk. Men of the flats, it seemed, the workers' places.

'Kei te pai,' said Hana. 'It's nice that you get to have a moment's rest.'

'Māmā!' Kahu turned away, disgusted by something in Hana's comment, or by the way she'd said it.

'What?' said Hana. 'I was just trying to be nice.'

The smaller man smirked. Then he pointed at the food baskets. 'Dried kūmara, chipped kūmara, spiced pumpkin flakes.' A smaller stack of baskets, brought from another pit, perhaps, or stilt house. 'Rabbits in fat. And over there, cage-fed possum in fat, possum in wraps, possum in salted strips, possum . . .' He waved a hand. 'I forget. Lots of possum, all cage-fed.'

Hana removed her bags and, even as she walked across the clearing, began to give instructions about where the food should be placed. But Kahu got there first, scurrying into place beside the men and kneeling to help.

They shooed her back.

'It's all right,' she said. 'Māku e āwhina.'

The larger man shook his head and put his arm in front, barring her from the food.

Embarrassed, Kahu stood back. Then she saw that Van was watching her, and she turned away, walking into the first fringe of the bush.

The men fell into the work, loading the bags in silence. There was so much stored food. Wraps of harakeke tied with plait, gourds with grease all over their stoppered tops. Not a single mention of slopfish amongst it. Van had to look away from all this expense that was being lavished on their trip. It obligated him. He would have preferred to trap his own meat for Hana and Kahu, or spear or net some kind of fish from the river they were going to follow inland.

Hana instructed the men to fill first the spare bags she'd brought, then Kahu's. Then she pointed to the bag Van had kept on his back. 'Is there any room in this?'

'Do we have to use it?' He indicated the bags at her feet. 'I mean, there's so much already. Surely that's enough?'

'It's koha, most of this. For people we might come across. Valley people we've pissed off in the past.' She grinned. 'That's why we need a lot.'

'Plus there's the Inland people. We need a koha for them, I guess.'

'Yes, that's what that one's for.' Then she indicated his own bag again. 'Are you sure you don't have any room in this? If we can take as much of the best meat as possible, it will help.'

'Do you mind if I say no? I'd prefer not to store food in it.'

She stared, then rushed to apologise. 'Of course, of course.'

'Sorry,' he said. 'It's just that I normally wouldn't put food in a bag like this.'

'He tika tāu,' she said, her hands going up. 'It's your personal stuff. I don't know what I was thinking.' Flustered, she looked over the bags that had already been filled by the men. 'How much water have you prepared for us? My aunt said we'll need ten bags of treated water for drinking, and four for washing. For the first part of the trip anyway. Aunty says there's a place we can replenish our water closer to the Inland place.'

The smaller man nodded. 'We can easily supply that. We've prepped a lot more.'

'Ka pai. Ngā mihi.' As if she was still rattled by having offended Van, and now searching for something she could control, she called to Kahu.

Kahu was almost out of earshot, picking at the bark of a tree. Van sensed she was still smarting from the larger man's rebuff. 'What?'

'Just—' It was clear Hana had no real need to call her. 'Just don't go too far off.'

Rolling her eyes, Kahu turned a shoulder on them both.

Then it was time to load up. Van found he had an allotment of two bags. First was a vast and bulging kete of wrapped meat. The larger storeman hoisted it, his face contorting with the effort. Van put his arm through the strap and grunted as the weight descended.

'Is it too much?' said Hana. She already had two extra bags

152

stacked on her back, the straps of the second knotted to the first to keep them balanced.

Van was stunned by the downward force of the weight on his back, but he shook his head.

The two men came with the second bag. It was full of water in greased bags that gurgled and slopped. Together they lifted it into place. Van braced his feet. The weight came down and he overbalanced. Hana lifted her hands to steady him, and he laughed, amazed at the weight. He took a half-step, and the bags slid again and he staggered. Seeing the problem, the taller man went round behind Van, pushing the bags into better alignment. Then he brought plait and knotted the bags together.

'So much water.' Van's voice was not much more than a grunt. 'Won't it crush the meat?'

The man didn't respond. Instead he just plaited the top bag to the first. He had to protect secrets, Van supposed, techniques of Whaea travel that were not to be explained to any lowlife from the swamp.

The two men now stood among the many baskets of food that Hana had rejected. The shorter man lifted an open basket to Hana. 'Kai o te rā nui.'

'Taihoa.' Without warning she gripped Van by the wrist and took him across the clearing to the trees. The weight on his back sloshed and pushed, forcing him to take careful steps over roots and stumps.

At last they were in bush again, and she turned. 'I just to want to check. Your bags—are we both happy with your bags?'

'There's so much meat. I understand the water. But do we really need all this meat?'

She waved. 'I didn't mean that. Engari, āe, we can look at it again once we make the south gate.'

153

He looked towards the storemen. They were listening to Kahu, nodding at whatever she was saying. The girl lifted her arm to point and they followed it up—the mist was lifting out of the trees. Van saw the shorter man nod at whatever her insight was; it seemed he was exhibiting politeness for the sake of her rank and youth, and knowing that soon she'd be gone and he could be in the company of his friend again.

'I meant in your own bag. Are you carrying something I should know about? Something secret?' When he flinched, she shot a careful glance towards the storemen. 'We shouldn't have any secrets on a trip like this. It could compromise us if things get difficult.'

'I brought some oils from Matewai.'

'Oh, that's all right.'

'And some precious pieces. They're in my bag in a wrap.' He hurried on. 'It's my best work. I couldn't just leave it at my camp. Anyone could steal it while I was away.'

'It's plastic? These precious things—they're plastic?'

'Of course. That's why I wanted to keep the food separate.'

She looked into the trees. With great care she moved her tongue along her lower lip.

'They're wrapped up separately and tied with plait. They're quite safe. I can show you if you want.'

She shook her head. 'I don't want to see it.'

'It's my best work. It's worth heaps. We could trade with it, if we get into difficulties.'

'It's not safe travelling with that,' she said, still not looking at him. 'Especially not when I have a pēpi inside. And not when Kahu's with us.'

'This is not paru plastic,' said Van. 'It's clean. I wash and purify all my best work.'

'But you can't clean off the plastic. You can't—' With an

154

effort Hana stopped herself, and breathed in deep.

'It's not paru plastic, though. That's my point. It's precious—pure, reinforced. It's worth heaps. If you would just look at it, instead of—instead of—' He stopped. 'Look, if you want me to leave it somewhere, or bury it for later, just tell me a safe place.'

She shook her head. There was nowhere safe: that's what she was thinking. Nowhere in the Whaea forests was safe for plastic.

'This is my job. Everyone knows that. I work with plastic. It's not like I kept it a secret.'

'It's not that. I'm not saying anything about your work. It's just—' She exhaled, and put her hands up. 'Of course it's natural you'd have it with you. Of course you would.'

Beyond her Van could see Kahu watching them. The storemen too. They were all silent, with their hands clasped, waiting politely for the end of the argument.

'Just keep it away from the food,' Hana said at last. 'Keep it wrapped and keep it separate.'

That's exactly what I was asking for in the first place, he wanted to say, and didn't. But then she walked away from him into the clearing, so clearly unsettled by the dirtiness of the subject. 'They've saved her life already, you know. My pieces—they've already got her out of the shit.'

'Who? Got who out of the shit?'

He pointed at Kahu. 'On the Dry Way. We got held up by Scarp runners. They weren't going to honour the gap, so we had to buy them off. I traded, like, *many* summers' worth of work. A small fortune. That's how we got her across.'

There was a strange look on Hana's face. 'This is what Rau meant when he said you ran into Squat.'

He nodded.

'So the Scarp didn't honour the gap.'

155

'Not really. We were too late.'

'They shouldn't have done that—impoverished you. We'll have words with them about that.'

'You speak with them?'

'Not to Squat. Not me—not like that.' With sudden urgency, she pulled him close.

At the same moment Kahu hissed across the clearing, beckoning them with furious swipes. Her patience worn out at last.

'Thank you for protecting Kahu, Van,' said Hana. 'I'm in your debt. And I do value your work—your work with . . . your precious pieces. I'm sure it's good. It's just that I'm still getting used to it.'

He stood woodenly in the embrace, partly because the weight of his bags made any movement difficult.

Rushing now, Hana hurried Kahu towards the onward track. Then she remembered the two storemen, and called to them. 'Thank you for all your work to prepare us. We're very well stocked, thanks to both of you. Ngā mihi ki a kōrua.'

They stood strangely, as if surprised by her farewell, its elaborateness.

'Safe journey,' said the shorter one. 'The Whaea's hand on all of us.'

At these words, they all turned to Van—Hana, the two storemen and Kahu—as if remembering he was different, not from the Whaea.

'That's right,' said Hana. 'All of us.'

At first it was just a fringe of yellowed pines, their branches and tops eaten away by sickness, with native trees colonising the gaps left by this disease. Then healthier pines took over, mighty and aromatic and lofted. Their number and size, the needles they dropped underfoot, made Van marvel up at them. He'd heard stories of the pine forests in the Whaea territories but never actually seen more than a few pine trees together. They hadn't survived well in the swamps. It wasn't so much that they couldn't grow as well there, but that their wood was so precious, and the trees grew fast and straight. He'd heard that back when the coastal villages existed, more than one fight had developed over the ownership of pines that had managed to grow to more than a man's height.

But there was no change in Hana's pace as they entered these trees. Her back was straight and tight. She was much quieter than before, not turning to tease Van about his slow progress.

Then they came on a zigzag of upward track, and Hana and Van passed each other, working their way up. 'How are those bags?'

'I won't lie,' he said. 'They're bloody heavy. I'm not used to this.'

'We'll stop to rest at the back fence. Unless you'd like to stop now?'

He stood still. A drip of sweat ran from beneath his headwrap to the tip of his nose and fell off. 'How much further is it?'

She pointed up the track, then down away to the right. 'Once we turn off, it's not far across the hill face to the gate.'

'All right. I can last.'

They walked on, threading up through a series of trunks that had fallen in a storm, their snapped branches oozing sap that had hardened into lumps.

'Can I ask you a question?' she said.

His eye was taken by a trap in a crook of branch just off the track. A possum dangled there, its head and neck crunched between the spikes. Further on a second and third dangled, one hanging by its foot, bloated. There seemed to be a higher concentration of traps where native trees filled these storm-fallen gaps in the pines. 'Can I ask one first?' he said. 'Who goes round these traps?'

She looked up there and shrugged. 'Whoever's rostered to the traps, I guess. But I know they work from the east fence back. These probably won't get done till after lunch.'

He pictured those workers moving through the misted trunks, their scarred hands reaching down to prise the spikes of traps apart. The dull thud of a club as it rose once or twice to finish a possum that had been inadequately trapped by the foot or neck.

'Oh, shit,' said Hana. 'Hang on. We have to have a kōrero about something.'

'Really? Now?'

'Āe, now. About your waters. We're supposed to do it before we leave the fence, in case we get separated. I nearly forgot.' She looked up the track. 'Kahu needs to hear this.' She cupped her hand and sent out a cooee of Kahu's name, high and twice repeated. Then she turned back to Van. 'It's important we do this. Besides, it'll give us something to talk about. Something to practise as we walk. Better than just trudging along, getting nervous.'

'So you do get nervous,' he said. 'That's a relief.'

'I'm taking my daughter and my unborn pēpi outside the fence. What do you think, Van?' She went a few more paces, watching for Kahu. As she walked her feet crushed pine needles, and a medicinal aroma came up. 'I'm not naive. I know it's going to be awful out there, once we leave the fence. I know it better than you, in fact.'

He eased his bags, then braced his feet as the water bag moved him again.

'But you've got to have faith, Van.' She looked meaningfully up the track in Kahu's direction. 'Even if you're not feeling it, you've got to pretend you've got faith. For all our sakes.'

He bit his next sentence back. He'd been about to protest that he hadn't thought she was naive, that he'd never said that, but it wasn't true. As they'd left that morning he'd felt precisely that. She'd seemed far too naive. All of them had: Hana and Bel and Rerū and all those aunties who'd entrusted this trip to a pregnant woman and some tamāhine toa kids and a stray trader from the swamp, not to mention a kākā that would fly above them and screech to all-comers their whereabouts.

Kahu looked wary as she came down the track. 'He aha te raru?'

'Ah, noho nei, Bub.' Hana signalled her to sit down. 'We're going to have a kōrero. A quick wānanga about Van's tūpuna.'

Kahu stood looking at the place Hana had chosen.

Hana fluttered a hand again. 'Find somewhere to rest, Bub. We're just going to wānanga quickly on Van's waters, and how they join with these Inland folk.'

'Right now?'

'Āe.'

'But am I allowed to be here for this? Shouldn't it be just Van who hears this stuff?'

'Kāo. You're going to need to know it. We're all relying on this knowledge now. For this trip, at least.' She broke a small stick of tree-wood and made an experimental scratch in the dirt. 'Whakapiri mai. We should get on with it.'

Van eased down next to Hana, his right knee cracking as he crouched.

Hana made a horizontal pool shape in the dirt. 'So here's the main tupuna of these folk.'

'Māmā.'

Both Hana and Van looked up.

Kahu hissed at her mother, and made a sign that Van couldn't interpret.

'Shit, sorry, Bub,' said Hana. 'I forgot. Rushing too much.' She scratched out the line in the dirt and brought her hands loosely together, and then she and Kahu sent up a long string of karakia that he hadn't heard before and couldn't follow, many of the words completely unknown to him. Crouching with his head bent, he looked at the dirt and thought of Matewai, who was always recalled to him by complex karakia, the words she repeated from what seemed distant times and places, which sometimes even Rau couldn't grapple with. And then his own parents—they came to him too at moments like this, his few memories of their sickness and death, his broken wandering after that.

Suddenly it was over, and Hana and Kahu said the Whaea's name, and then Van joined in to say 'Āmine', and Hana redrew her first pool in the dirt.

'So, here's Donovan. Remember him. He's the one who took them back to the place where they live now.'

'Donovan,' said Van. 'Back from where?'

'Not sure. From the Way, perhaps, or the Valley. Anyway, his wahine was Mary. She was Pākehā, but it seems she was often called Mere. Certainly that's what Rerū calls her, most of the time.'

'Right.'

'So Donovan met Mary, and ka puta'—she drew a line down, and then across—'these ones, but Artie is the only one out of these you have to remember. And he met Annie, so you've got Donovan and Mere, then Artie and Annie.'

'Right.'

'Actually—' She corrected herself, going back with her stick.

160

'Jacky Donovan is the name of this first guy, but Donovan's the name that comes down—the second name. That's how these particular Pākehā do it, Aunty says. These Inland people.' She retraced the lines and pools in the dirt and went again over the names.

Van tried to pay attention, knowing he was going to forget at least some of this river of ancestors and partners and kids. Something about it made his mind go blank. Perhaps it was just because it was new and so important.

'Now, here's where it gets difficult. If I remember it right, from this pair it comes down to Maggs, but she's a whāngai from outside their place, and she's sometimes known as Meg— Meg Donovan, that is.'

'A whāngai,' said Van. 'That's good.'

Hana looked up, then saw in his face why it was important. 'Āe.' She adjusted her headwrap, which had been sliding into her eye. 'There are whāngai everywhere, Van. In all sorts of families.'

'I know, but it's still good.'

'Okay. Āe, it's good.'

'So it doesn't matter to them, whāngai lines, and all that?'

Hana looked at the downward river of waters she'd scraped in the dirt. 'Apparently not.'

'Right.' He began to recite the names from the top.

'Kāo,' said Kahu.

They both turned, and Kahu pointed at the top pool of waters, the source of all of the names. 'Jacky Donovan and Mere, not Artie Donovan and Mere.'

'Damn it,' said Van. 'Jacky Donovan and Mary—Mere—and then to these two, and then to Meg.'

'Āe,' said Hana, 'and Maggs is part of how we know about these waters, by the way. Because someone who married into

161

our side, in our settlement, flows in, way back in her own waters, to an uncle of an uncle who was a friend of Meg's.'

'Right.'

'But don't try to remember that right now. I reckon you just try to remember this line from Jacky Donovan down to these people, and then to Meg and then her daughter, whose name was Tip.'

'So who did Meg make a pēpi with, to make Tip?'

'Not sure. Tip might even be a whāngai. We don't know.'

'Oh, another whāngai. Good. So Meg didn't have—didn't have—kāore ōna hoa rangatira?'

'Āe, she did have one, but we don't know who it was. We don't know their sex, or their name, or anything like that. Just don't know. Rerū thinks they were a stray of some sort, or they were no good, maybe. But that was the person who took Meg out of the settlement. They took her and Tip north, for whatever reason, and moved them about. And that's where Tip got lost somewhere, and then she met someone else, who we also don't know about. And it was either someone else, or that first person, who helped bring about Tip's kids. But it was bad, Tip's life. Rerū said that. She didn't have a good life, up north.'

'How does Rerū know about that? If Tip went up north?'

'Traders, apparently. Coming south. They had connections to Tip's kids, so they told the aunties this story and tried to bargain their way through our fence, because they wanted to carry on towards the Inland settlement.'

Seeing Van's look, she went on.

'Apparently the aunties let them through, but they didn't make it far. Dead from disease, not far from the cliff track. They'd been bitten up north or on the Dry Way, and were already sick by the time they traded their way through our place.'

A shiver went over him.

'Ka aroha hoki,' said Hana. 'I know it's hard to learn about this stuff.'

'Kei te pai. It's just that's how my parents died.'

'I know. You told me.'

He nodded. 'Haere tonu.'

She made three further vertical lines in the dirt, leading down from Tip, and then more pool shapes. 'So from Tip then it gets to these kids of hers, and one of them is called Robbie, and Robbie is—'

'My father.'

'Āe. And Robbie meets your Māmā, and'—she scored a last, triumphant pool in the dirt—'ka puta . . . this guy here. You.'

She leaned back to survey the flow of scratch marks she'd made. It covered all of the part of the track she had cleared, so the marks to record Van's parents and his own birth were scored in a widening flow of pools joined by vertical marks, like a river viewed from above. He closed his eyes and for a moment was again standing before his parents' bivvy down a bank from the Dry Way, shielding his face from the flames that rushed and flapped over it, the pair of them lying inside and already dead. Burnt by Van as his Pa had instructed, a tactic he only later knew to be designed to force him from his parents' place of sick and on to the vast way south, to safer parts beyond the Straits. Not that he ever got that far.

'Kei te mārama?' said Hana.

Van shook his head to clear it. He traced again up the flow of pools, the river that bulged and narrowed and led all the way back to the original Donovan, the source of this Pākehā line. Jacky Donovan, he thought, sounding the name out in his head. Jacky Donovan and Mere, and then on down the generations to Meg, and on down to him. 'Sure,' he said. 'Well, not really.'

163

She grinned. 'We'll go over it again tonight, then again tomorrow night. We'll keep practising it. We'll have it all right by the time we meet this lot.'

His knee was hurting; he altered his crouching position. 'I won't be able to remember it on the spot, if I have to get up and speak. And I'm not a speaker eh—you know that. I haven't been trained in any of that stuff—whaikōrero stuff. If you're expecting me to stand up and speak on everyone's behalf, and to recall all of this river, you're—' He looked away. 'I'm going to struggle with that.'

'With any luck, you won't have to. They might not have that tradition where they live. And, anyway, of course you'll be able to do it. You'll be standing on your home turf—sort of—and if someone asks you to do it, you will, and you'll do it well. Because we need you to—we all do. And because you'll have faith.' She put a hand on him, and squeezed. 'And besides, it doesn't have to be perfect.'

She cast another look down at the scratched-in river of water in the forest dirt. 'We'll practise this together, you and I, and you'll memorise it, and it'll be great.'

Van eased his cramped knee, massaged it. He debated whether to say what he wanted to say next, then said it. 'You know I could just take you both, plus some others, to live at Te Repo instead. You know that, eh? There are, like, six empty huts there, up on the mound, and it's safe enough. And it's the place I know, and it's the place where I know I've got some rights, or at least Rau and Matewai have, and they'll make space for me—for us. They'd be overjoyed if we brought them kids.'

'I know that, Van, but like I told Rau, we didn't get agreement for that from my aunties. We got agreement for this.' She pointed at the river she'd drawn in the dirt, running her stick of tree-wood up to its source at the top. 'Our instructions are to find this Inland place. And, besides, we couldn't all fit into Te Repo. We couldn't fit all our people into Matewai's place, or over at your own camp. It wouldn't work. We'd get overcrowded and bitten to death and get disease and die out.'

Van was silent.

'I'm sorry,' she said. 'But this is the deal I could get. This is what my aunties instructed. If we do this successfully, then I get to keep you, and we all get to live in a safe new place. And who knows, maybe later on you and I and Kahu and our new bubs can go somewhere else—like to your place, if it's still safe by then.'

'But that's my point. We don't even know what's there, where we're going. It might not be safe. And there's a long and dangerous trip even to get there. Whereas we know what's in the swamp. We know the dangers, and we know how to live there. I do, at least.'

'But Rerū's scouts say it's all pai, where we're going. Plenty of room. And there's forest nearby—unworked forest. They've checked it out.'

'So why couldn't they do it, those scouts? Why couldn't they negotiate with the Inland people—these Donovans?'

'Because they don't have the best waters, Van.' She swivelled on her haunches, and pointed at the river in the dirt. '*You* have that connection. That's what this is all about, and it's why you have to do it. Māu anō e mahi, my love.'

They walked down a long slope through thinning pines colonised by native trees, the trunks and forest floor dotted with animals mutilated by traps. At the base of one trunk a dead stoat was spiked through the shoulder, the leaves and earth scratched up where it had fought to free itself. More

165

possums hung at head height, dangling. Finally there was a steep fringe of sick and yellowing pines, and there, rising and mammoth beyond a cleared strip of earth, was the fence.

Hana stopped so suddenly that Van almost pitched headfirst over her, the weight of his bags pushing him forward.

'You could still turn back,' she said. 'You don't have to trade into this.'

'Into what?'

She indicated the fence downslope and the scraps of grey sky beyond it. 'Our mess. The shit we've caused out there.'

He looked down towards the fence. It was just as massive here as at the North Gate, but less ornate. There was no metal dug into the ground to reinforce the lowest part, no colours flying from the top. And the gate was huge but plain, lashed by great binds of plait to its mooring post at the top, bottom and halfway up. As he surveyed it a group of young women emerged from a lean-to hut that was built into the fence. Even from this distance, they looked a serious lot, capable. Three of them broke off and came up the slope towards them, and Van supposed these were the tamāhine toa who were to accompany them and keep them safe. They stopped near Kahu, waiting for Hana's approach, and Kahu turned to her as well. Even from this distance Van could see how the other young women put Kahu on edge.

'Look,' said Van, 'I've thought about it, and I've realised I can't go back. I want to, but I don't know the way. I'd get lost.'

Hana's look was sharp.

'I'm joking,' he said.

She let out a terse laugh. One eye was still on the young women and Kahu. 'I've been thinking. We can leave some of your food with the gate guards here. It's too much, isn't it?'

'Are you sure?'

'It's far too much weight. I'm sorry, I didn't know how impractical it was until we'd walked a fair distance. We'll keep enough for our own food and water, plus feasting for other people we'll need to placate. But most of those people won't need a full feast. Just a ritual taste will be enough—the rest we can leave here.'

'Oh, thank god for that. It's bloody awful. My back can't take much more of this.'

She laughed. 'We should head down. They don't like delays at the gate. It's not safe.'

'Finally,' said Kahu, when they reached her.

Hana smiled at her, but Kahu didn't return it. Both brought their colours out, displaying them on their chests as they and Van walked towards the three tamāhine toa.

Van glanced again at the young women. 'That Tuku's coming?' he said, stopping Hana. 'I thought she was against this trip.'

'Āe. That's why we trust her. She's always honest, and she's fearless. She's one of our best. And she volunteered for it too.'

'Māmā,' said Kahu. 'Come on.'

As they came together, Tuku and her crew bent their elbows in the Whaea sign, which Hana and Kahu returned. Tuku nodded briskly at Van but focused her attention on Hana as the other two were introduced to Van. They greeted him by stepping forward with their forearms up, then pulling him close. It was like being embraced by the Whaea sign.

Van tried not to scrutinise the three of them too obviously. They weren't big but did look tough—hardened by work and training, he supposed. If they carried weapons, they were hidden beneath their belted coats.

Hana gave them a series of instructions in their language, and they ran ahead to the gate.

Once Van reached the gate more guards came out and signalled him to kneel so they could unstrap and remove his bags. There was a blessed moment while he was completely unburdened and parcel after parcel of meat was ferried to the lean-to against the fence. When he was loaded up again his shoulders still chafed, but the bags didn't push down with that same buckling force.

Hana thanked the gate guards, then faced Tuku's crew. 'Me haere.' She nodded to Van, and put a hand on Kahu. 'This is it, whānau. Kia māia.'

Kahu didn't respond, facing the ground and murmuring to it. Prayer again. It came to Van that she was more devout, at least in these outward signs, than her mother.

At last Hana nudged Kahu forward, and the gate guards got to work, loosening plaits and looking out its peephole at the dangers beyond. The gate scraped loudly over rock. Van felt fresh breeze on his face. After a moment, a guard at the peephole gave an all-clear and signalled them through.

Hana went first, her hand clamped round Kahu's wrist, then Van stepped into the gap.

'Not too fast,' said the guard. 'There's a drop.'

He found himself on a ledge of rock and swirling upwind. A vast fall yawned in front of him, and he reared back, sick rushing up into his throat. He tried to edge further back, but the first of the tamāhine toa came through behind him and he had to shuffle along the ledge to make space.

Soon all six of them were lined up along the narrow ledge. Van felt the drop pulling at him, wanting him to fall into it. He sensed more than he saw the river that was far, far down at the bottom of it. Somewhere at the side of the ledge, beyond Hana, was a track that would take them down this cliff. He didn't want to look that way yet.

Hana pointed straight out, not down to the river but out over the valley and south. It was wide and flanked on both sides by bush. Smoke rose from the valley floor where the scrub had been cleared and a cluster of huts hunched on the banks of the river that snaked thinly, sometimes in bush and sometimes exposed, all the way back. This was the river—more a creek here, really—that came all the way down and pooled on itself in the Whaeas' lake and then dribbled finally from their dam into the ponds of bog and seep from other streams and the sea that made up the swamps.

Hana pointed to the furthest place, where the valley stopped and the river jutted to the left and up, heading inland into high slopes of bush.

'That's where we're going, Van,' she said. 'The Inland place. That's where your waters lead us.'

Eleven

Van slipped, and dislodged stones that bounced down the cliff. Swearing, he scrabbled for grip on the rock face. His hand found a tiny plant that had somehow rooted there. He clung to it, leaning into the cliff, closing his eyes against a wave of sick.

'Oh my god,' he said. 'Fuck this.'

Hana and Kahu and the young women were all further down the track. He was trapped on his own, clinging to his plant handhold while the drop clawed at his back. He closed his eyes and swore again. It got bad enough that he had to utter a karakia, one he'd learnt from Rau many summers back.

Someone was coming back up. He opened his eyes and saw Kahu. She moved so easily, as if picking a path through her own things on the floor of her hut. She stopped a short distance from him and watched, not offering him a hand for balance or to help. Her only concession was to speak simply, not going too fast for him in her language. 'Kei te mataku koe. You're scared of heights.'

'Seems like it. I didn't know until now. There aren't any high tracks like this in the swamp.'

Her face didn't change as she looked off the path and into the drop. 'I was scared the first time I walked this track.'

Still clinging to the plant, he risked a look down the path

beyond her. There were about ten or eleven paces till the next turning. Then more turnings, on and on down the cliff. 'Is Hana at the bottom yet?'

'Āe. She's gone to check there's no ambush in the creek.'

'Is that wise?'

'Probably not. But she's got the tamāhine toa with her.' She looked at his hands: the one that gripped the plant, choking it, and the other that clawed at a handhold on the rock face. 'It might . . .'

'Just give me your advice, please. I won't take offence. I just want to get off this cliff. I'll take any advice you've got.'

'Just put your feet in my footsteps. Watch where my feet go, and put your feet in the same place.'

He looked sickly at her boots. They were small and neatly made, the possum skins sewn tight round her soles and ankles. She looked incapable of any sort of slip.

'And just imagine it's on the flat. We're on a track in the bush, walking through ferns.'

'Is that what you do?'

'It's what they taught us to do at training. Ferns on either side, like this.' She used her hands to suggest the fronds that brushed on either side. 'He māmā, nē? It's easy really, and you won't slip. No one's fallen off this track, in all the stories of us. Even people who've been loaded up with lots more bags and packs than us, and travelling in storms, and all that, they still haven't fallen off.'

Now that she was on this familiar ground of her training, she seemed more confident. It comforted Van to know the Whaea people had stories about this cliff, its gut-twisting walk. But his face must have still shown doubt.

'Honestly,' she said. 'You won't fall. Ka tiakina koe e te Whaea. She'll watch over you and keep you safe. Just step in my

171

footsteps.' She looked in the direction her mother had taken; as she did so a tūī chattered up from the creek down there, spooked by something. Kahu pursed her lips.

Despite himself, Van smiled. Her mother had spooked the bird and alerted people; she was doing it all wrong again. He breathed out, less shakily than before. 'Okay. Let's do it.'

Kahu turned to face the front.

'Āta haere, please,' he said. 'Go slow.'

'Āe. Whāia mai, e matua.'

He felt a small surge of gratitude at the term she'd used. A sort of uncle—she'd used it that way, he thought. She trusted him enough to call him a sort of uncle.

She took a few slow steps, and he let go of the plant. Faced his foot down the track and probed it forwards.

'Just try to walk normally, remember. Just a walk through ferns in the bush.'

He took a further step. Then another. His guts felt loose. He took a few more steps and then was at the next turning of the track.

'Kei te pai?'

He held on to the rock again, looking back up the section of track he'd beaten. 'I'm glad we left half that food at the gate.'

She smiled and then, when he was ready, indicated the next piece of track. Slowly they negotiated it, Van following in the girl's footsteps. At the next turning, Kahu looked up as a half-dozen birds flew above the cliff, and fluted and squawked. Kākā.

Careful to lean towards the rock face, Van looked up there. 'Is one of them Hana's pet?'

'Ru,' said Kahu. 'Maybe. The guards said they'd seen him.'

After the next turning the track was blocked by a slip of rocks brought down in some storm. Without hesitating, Kahu switched her position and walked sideways over the scree on hands and feet, spider-like.

Watching her, Van shook his head. Surely she didn't want him to emulate that. But then Kahu was on the other side and waiting, so he turned himself side-on. Put his arms and legs apart to mimic her spider shape, and focused on the footmarks she'd made.

He put a first foot and hand on the rubble, and slipped. 'Fuck.' He breathed in deep, then secured again his foot, and shifted his weight up onto the rocks. Took another step, then another, fought an impulse to scramble faster, and then took two more sideways scrambling steps, and was across.

'Ka pai.' Kahu indicated the next part of the downward path. 'It's not so steep after this. Only a few switchbacks left, then it evens out a lot.'

They went down three more turnings slowly, then the slope eased and Kahu moved away from him a little, giving him space. The kākā screeched and fluted above again, and they both looked up, Van putting his hand against the rock for balance.

'Maybe I can ask you,' he said. 'Do you think it's a good idea, bringing Ru on this trip? Surely he'll let everyone know where we are.'

'Āe. He's a peace sign. He tells people we're on a peaceful trade. Plus he gets restless when Māmā leaves the settlement.'

Van eyed her, but there was nothing in her face, no sign that she thought bringing such a blazing signal of her own and her mother's whereabouts was anything but a wise and established routine.

'So we've got these tamāhine toa, and they're constantly looking out for risks and ambush, but we also send a bird up—a bright and noisy bird—and he tells everyone everything about us and where we are. I don't get it.'

173

Kahu dropped her eyes, and toed aside a jagged stone on the path.

'Perhaps it would be better if I asked Hana about this.'

She looked up, her relief showing all over her face. 'We should get off this cliff.'

Hana was crouched on the bank of the creek.

'How did you like the cliff?' she said.

'Easy. I had to help Kahu though, of course. She was terrified.'

Hana grinned. 'Everyone gets spooked the first time.' Her eye followed Kahu, who had gone further upstream and was checking the banks of the creek on both sides.

Van found himself watching the tumble of water at his feet. This must be the river they would be following inland. Or perhaps it was part of it, a tributary that branched in. It seemed too weak to have come all that way, and too small to become the main source of the Whaea lake. He could step right over it here. 'This creek is safe, I take it.'

'It should be fine, as long as we treat it with herbs. But we'll drink our own water, I think, the stuff we brought.'

'I meant safe from ambush.'

'Oh, āe, āe.' She motioned with her head upstream. 'I checked upstream already, and the tamāhine toa are sweeping out for risks right now. Not that Kahu trusts us—or me, more like. She's checking on my work.'

'But you're confident?'

'It's quite safe. No one from the valley wants to live this close to our fence. And if they do try to settle, our tamāhine toa encourage them out.'

'What does that mean?'

Hana shrugged. 'Kick them out, I guess.'

Van knelt to the creek and scooped water to his face. It was so cold on his forehead and throat, the sweat-dampened fringes of his headwrap. Rubbing his face, he was surprised afresh by the shortness of his beard, still not recovered from his grooming efforts back at the Whaea huts.

Kahu came back down the bank, scanning the bush on either side as she walked.

'Kei te pai, Bub?' Anticipating her daughter's question, Hana said, 'I told our tamāhine we'd wait here till they come back.'

Kahu nodded, and glanced at Van. He opened his bags and brought out oil. Smearing it on his face and neck and hands, he offered it to them both. The canister was much lighter by the time Kahu handed it back. He put it by his ear and shook it. Almost empty. It was one of five canisters of Matewai's oil he'd brought with him; he'd have to be more careful with the rest.

The three tamāhine toa came out of the bush. Hana signalled them over and they all set off. Two of the tamāhine toa were in front, Hana was ahead of Kahu, and Van was behind with a further guard at his back.

The aroma of repellant from Hana and Kahu took Van's mind away to Matewai and her sharp-smelling hut. Right now she'd be cooking up, even as grief still clouded over her hut and the settlement at Te Repo, such was the importance of her trade to the survival of all those who lived there. How surprising they'd find this, he thought; how strange it would seem to the Te Repo people that he walked with this Whaea group, with its four young people grown almost to full height and health and fighting strength. Scarcely any bite marks on them, or traces of disease. What luck these people had. And a further prospect in Hana, who was growing a second pēpi inside, Van's pēpi. It shocked him again, that bolt of good fortune.

It also focused him, and gave urgency to his walk. He scanned the scrub as they went through it, keeping watch.

Van hadn't seen the kākā before it shrieked, then swooped low over his head.

'Shit,' he said.

The bird made a fluting sound and spread its wings wide, then settled in a tall mānuka. Ignoring the humans who'd stopped there, the bird shook his feathers and preened, digging along his wing and back as if troubled by nits.

Hana stood from her bags and went across. 'Tēnā koe, e Ru.'

The old bird just eyed her coldly, then turned again to preen on his back.

Hana laughed. 'He's hōhā because he's had to actually do something. Like fly somewhere.'

'I'll sort out our bags,' said Van.

'There are some shelter things in my big one.' She barely paused in her attentions to the bird to say this, knuckling the feathers on the side of Ru's head.

'Māmā,' Kahu hissed, holding up a washing bag, along with a bag of medicines that Hana had brought, some of which they would take each night as precautions. 'Are you coming?'

'I thought you were going on your own?'

Van looked away, focusing on his own bags, as Kahu was clearly embarrassed to protest in front of him. Hana had said it was safe enough to wash alone in the scrub. They were still too close to the fence for most Valley people to risk an ambush. And the tamāhine toa were setting up their camp nearby, their skin shelters already taking shape just a short way up the slope.

But Kahu was clearly on edge, and Van saw many dangers.

176

The campsite was just a clearing in scrub and felt too exposed; he would have preferred an elevated site against a cliff, reducing their vulnerable flanks from four down to one or two. The promise of a patrol by Tuku and her crew—who looked capable of violence of supreme efficiency, when needed—gave him some comfort but didn't entirely dispel his fear. It was Hana; really it was Hana who worried him. She seemed too cavalier. She'd trusted too quickly in this campsite. And earlier she'd forgotten to apply oil until Van suggested it. And she'd brought this bird, which shrieked non-stop and gave away their whereabouts. And yet she'd told him, inside the fence, that she wasn't naive. Perhaps this was part of that faith she'd urged on him, pretending to a slapdash confidence for the sake of her daughter's spirits, or her own.

'Māmā,' said Kahu. 'Kia tere!'

'All right, all right.' Hana chucked the bird one more time on the back of the head. Then she and Kahu went through the scrub, their heads bent in mutual scolding.

Van surveyed the bags at his feet. If he made a solid shelter, it would be a good start. He went to the largest of Hana's bags and untied its harakeke straps. Inside he found an armload of possum skins, rolled into a bundle and tied with plait. Unfurled and laid flat, it came to a dozen skins across. It was double-sewn to form a thick sheet, with the treated skins facing out into the weather. A three-person shelter, at least. There were also three coils of plait and a bundle of greased wooden pegs, a harakeke mat at least three paces long and two wide, and last of all a fine blanket of furs. By the time the bag was empty, the equipment lay all around him. He remembered his protest back at the food stores. No wonder Hana had given him so much to carry, and even tried to fill his personal bag, not knowing it already carried plastics. Her own bags had been over-stuffed with shelter stuff.

Now she and Kahu came back, talking to each other in a different tone, less irritated than before. Seeing him and the pile of equipment, Hana gave Kahu some quick instructions in her own language, too fast and low for Van to catch. Then she went back to the kākā, and began to break up a half-rotten branch she'd found.

Kahu came across. 'Are you putting the door here?'

He followed the movements of her hands. 'I hadn't got that far, to be honest.'

'I'll put my shelter along here then.'

'You're not sleeping in with us? Is that safe?'

Kahu wouldn't meet his eye. 'Sometimes I'll be in with you guys. When it's not safe. But here it's all right.'

He looked at the places they would pitch, working the angles out.

'It's fine,' said Kahu. 'I normally sleep in my own shelter. I'm old enough.'

'Oh, āe, I'm fine with that. Sorry, I was thinking about something else.'

She looked away to Hana, who was making a considerable show of breaking open the branch for the bird and peeling back its bark. Van realised that she was leaving it to him and Kahu to work out their camping arrangements.

He switched to Kahu's own language, hoping it would make her more honest. 'Hey, kei te pai tēnei wāhi ki a koe?'

'Āe. Kei korā ngā tamāhine toa, nē. Tino tata rātou.'

'Ka pai. Mehemea ka . . . ka . . . if you think it's safe, then it's all right with me.'

She nodded, then went to her own bags. Soon she'd lifted free her own shelter, and rolled it out into shape.

Van returned to the problem of his own shelter. The vast skin sheet was thick and would keep out rain, but it was a simple

178

rectangle, with no triangle sewn into the ends to form the front and back walls. He'd have to string it between two poles, then cover the ends with something else. He glanced over to see how Kahu had dealt with this problem, but she'd paused to drink, and in fact seemed to be waiting for him to stake out his shelter first, perhaps needing the outer wall to know where she could pitch. He stood up and, affecting confidence, studied the mānuka trunks at the edge of the clearing, selected two and lined them up. Then with a doubled-over plait he walked between them, stringing a beam-line for the roof between the trunks, knotting them tight. With the heavy sheet of skins in his arms, he walked towards the beam-line and heaved it over. Immediately the plait sagged halfway to the ground, not tight enough to take the weight of the skins.

Kahu had her head down, pretending not to notice. Beyond her, Hana had left Ru, and was digging foodwraps out of bags and dividing them up. Tuku was with her, talking over the rations, Van supposed, that she and her crew would need.

Van lifted a further length of plait and slid under the sagging roof. He tied it to the first trunk, then crawled to the opposite trunk and tied it there, the skin sheet weighing on his back as he moved. Then he pulled both plaits tight, heaving the roof up. There was still a sag in the middle, but it was better. If he'd been preparing the shelter for himself he would have put up a centre post. But he wasn't alone; he didn't want to put a post in the centre of Hana's shelter. He tried not to let his mind leap ahead to how they would be together tonight, with Kahu nearby and the tamāhine toa also in earshot. They would have to whisper if they wanted to talk.

He stole another glance at Kahu, who was now tying her own beam-line to a tree. He was relieved to see her using the same technique he had. He went around the edge of his shelter and tied and knocked in the pegs. He pulled everything tight, then stood back. The shelter itself was now taut and strong, but still open at both ends. Breeze would come in on his and Hana's heads and feet. There must be some routine solution to this, he thought, some extra piece of skin sheet he hadn't seen in the bags. He searched again but found nothing. He took another look at Kahu's shelter, but hers seemed to have both ends sewn into it, as one piece. He gave up, not wanting the women to see his problem, and took off his outer coat instead, tying it over the end where their heads would be. It didn't cover the gap entirely, but he could fix it later, with a spare blanket perhaps. He spread the harakeke groundsheet on the shelter floor, then the skin mat and finally the blanket. He laid bags along the inside walls as a further breeze block. Then he stood at the end and surveyed it.

Seeing he'd finished, Hana stood up, the foodwraps arrayed around her. 'Oh, look at that. Ātaahua.'

He winced. She'd drawn Tuku's attention and, even worse, Kahu's. 'It's not that great. I'm not used to your gear. Even though it's better than my own shelter stuff.'

Hana was loading Tuku up. She sent her away, the young woman's arms loaded with foodwraps. Then she came down to him. 'I couldn't have made a shelter this nice. Seriously. I would have just lain down with it all on top of me. I'm so out of practice.' She dropped her voice. 'You could offer to help Kahu. She'd like that.'

But Kahu was already knocking in her last pegs. Frowning with concentration, she poked her tongue out as she worked. He smiled—he'd seen Hana poke her tongue out in that same unconscious way back at the Whaea settlement, when she'd stacked up bowls from their midnight snack in the bed. A moment's drowsy contentment went through him as he remembered it. He was still tired from that night. In fact, he'd not slept properly since Ava's death.

Something flapped and stirred at the edge of his vision and he only half-registered it, his mind still on the nights to come and the ones that had been. Then the kākā squawked up and out of its tree and he remembered the presence of Hana's pet. Great, he thought. Give away our camp again, just when we've settled in for the night. But something shifted again where the bird had been and Van, coming out of his trance, looked into the scrub.

Another movement in there.

A shape.

He looked closer. A man—there was the shape of a man in the scrub.

Van leapt forward, one hand going for his plastic bar, the other out to guard Hana. 'Hands up! Get your hands up.'

The man was hidden to his waist in undergrowth. His hands were behind his back. He was hiding some weapon there. Van saw another figure, strangely obscured further back in the bush. It knelt, sideways on, so only the hump of its back showed.

'Get your fucking hands up.' Van swung the bar and scanned for others in the scrub. It was impossible to see if there were more intruders. It was still light, but dusk wasn't too far off. They were badly caught.

Overhead the disturbed kākā circled and shrieked.

The man didn't move, didn't show his weapons.

'I'll bash you if you don't get your hands up,' said Van. 'Get your fucking hands up.'

The man came closer, but without leaving the waist-high cover of undergrowth. For a time he watched Van's swinging bar, then sneered. 'Fuck you, swamp.' He lifted his voice and shouted into the night. 'Rich bitches here! Whaea bitches! Come and get them!'

Van sprang at him, aiming his bar at the man's forehead. The man danced back, lifting a hand to protect himself. Van swung the bar and felt it hit bone. It was the bone of the man's upheld wrist. Immediately, the man shrieked.

Taken on by the momentum of his swing, Van fell forward and through undergrowth. Kawakawa kissed his face; he hit the dirt.

Still the man shrieked.

'Shut up,' said Van, scrambling up. 'Stop shouting.'

Ignoring him, the man inspected his left wrist, holding it like a broken bird. 'You broke my wrist, you fucker.' He'd dropped his weapon somewhere. It was hidden by his feet. His friend still hadn't moved, crouching in that same strange pose in the scrub.

'Give me your weapon,' said Van.

'Fuck you.' The man lifted his face to shout again. 'Rich bitches. Come and get some rich bitches.'

Van came at him once more, swinging.

Snarling, the man danced back, still holding his wrist.

Then Van was ripped backwards. Hana choked him at the neck and waist, and with shocking strength marched him back, hissing at him as she walked. 'Stop this, Van. Stop it.'

'You bastard,' said the man. 'You broke my wrist, you cunt.'

Van tried to lunge at him again, but Hana's chokehold on his neck tightened, and she hauled him further off. 'Stop it, Van. Kāti. Stop.'

There was a skittering sound as the tamāhine toa dashed into the campsite, their bodies low in fighting positions, crouching at either flank. Tuku shot questions at Hana, who ignored them.

'Van, are you calm now? Van?'

He made to speak and couldn't, her arm too tight round his throat. Even once she'd released it a little, he had to croak his reply out. 'Yes. Let me go.'

'Don't fight. Promise.'

'All right.'

Still she held him. 'Because we've got the tamāhine toa for that,' she said. 'They can break his neck for us, if that's what we want. That's their job; they're the best at it.'

Van tried to nod. At last she let him go, and he coughed and massaged his throat.

'Kahu,' said Hana. 'Kei te pai koe?'

'Āe. I've got the back.'

'Is there anyone else?'

'Kāo. There's no one else here yet.' There was a tremor in her voice, but it strengthened Van to hear her, the competent guard at the back.

The man still hadn't moved, hadn't produced his weapon or ordered the other intruder out of that strange hunch. Holding his bad forearm up, he scowled at Van and Hana and the crouching tamāhine toa, his eye flicking over them all. Calculating. For the first time Van registered that the man's āhua was Pākehā, or looked like it. A dirty headwrap over his skull. His coat ragged and held together with plait. Scars round his eyes from old bites that had got infected and burst.

Overhead the kākā circled and screamed. As one, the tamāhine toa tensed, bracing for further attack.

When none came, Tuku turned to Hana. 'Me patu, nē?'

'Kāo,' said Hana. 'Wait.'

Still scowling, the man eyed them.

'It's all right,' said Hana. 'You don't need to fear us.'

Van saw the man take in her fine things: her twist of distinguished feathers, her long and unpatched coat. 'You're in the shit, miss.'

'Why? Who's with you?'

The man said nothing.

Hana repeated the question.

When he didn't answer, Tuku turned to Hana and whipped her arm about, speaking fast in her own language and with her hand to indicate the actions her crew could take. Van heard only a part of what she said, but it seemed the same as what she'd said before. They should destroy this man, and then they should leave.

'Kāo.' Hana put her hands out flat to hold everyone in their places. 'Everybody wait. There's no need to fight.'

Tuku, clearly unhappy, snapped her eyes at Hana. Then she barked a string of orders at her crew, again too fast for Van to catch, and they went to the perimeter to guard it from further attack.

'I know you,' said Hana.

'You don't know shit.' He scowled at them all, but his eye lingered most on Van. It seemed it wasn't just the broken wrist he resented him for; there was also Van's newly trimmed beard and washed headwrap, the clean clothes he was dressed in. The good fortune that saw him travelling with such a well-appointed force.

'You're Gray,' said Hana. 'And that's your daughter, and she's sick. You live up the creek we crossed.'

'Pah!'

'You have no wife or husband, no whānau to speak of. No one to call for help.'

Gray just gave her that same baleful look.

'No trade to speak of either, except for this sort of scavenging stuff. No riches, no fresh water source. No offence, but that's the truth of it.'

'You don't know shit. How would you know all this?'

'Surveillance.'

The immediacy of her answer hit him.

'Gray,' said Hana, 'what's it going to take to make this work?'

'Make what work? What do you think is happening here?'

'Trade.' Hana indicated the bags at her side, the wraps of food. 'I'm making a trade with you to keep you safe. To stop our tamāhine toa from breaking your other wrist, or your neck.'

Gray laughed softly. He shook his head at Hana, and at them all. 'You lot are in such deep shit.'

'I don't think so,' said Van. 'I think you're in trouble now. Outnumbered. Trained fighters against you. Broken wrist.'

Again Gray shook his head. 'You're in such deep shit.' Repeating himself seemed to lift his energy. 'Such deep, deep shit—all of you.'

'Why would that be, then?'

'Because the Burners have come for you lot. They're up by the fence.'

'They are not,' said Hana.

He smiled. 'Think what you like. They're right by your fence. Heaps of them.'

Hana turned to Tuku, who shook her head.

'We would've heard reports,' said Tuku. She lifted her chin at Gray. 'Tokohia?'

'Tokomaha. Toru tekau pea—whā tekau.' His reo was quick; Van was still catching up as he carried on in Pākehā. 'And another lot on the north side, they said. Then another lot coming up to your gate.'

Hana shot a look at Van, her certainty beginning to erode. 'Are you serious? Don't joke now.'

185

Again Gray gave that quiet laugh. 'I'm not joking. They're definitely not a joke. They're quite a force.'

'You talked to them?'

'Āe. I kōrero mātou.' He watched Van as he spoke. He'd seen Van's struggle in Hana's language. 'He pai te kōrero.'

'But we had an agreement. We made a trade.'

Gray shrugged. 'Seems like they changed their mind.'

'When the pōhutukawa turns red,' said Hana. 'That's what they said. We had to get out before the pōhutukawa turns red. That's not till Summer's Day. We've got all winter left.'

Gray said nothing, just watched Hana's increasingly panicked turning to Van, to Tuku, and back to him.

'This can't be right,' she said. 'We're doing exactly what they wanted—right now. That's the point. We're scouting out to find a new place.' She looked round them all, at the shape that crouched behind Gray, searching for someone who could make sense of it.

'It was the dry storm, Māmā. He tohu tērā, nē. It was a tohu for them.'

The voice had come from behind. It was a moment before Van recognised it as Kahu's.

Hana turned. 'How do you know that?

'Come on, Māmā, it's obvious.'

'Don't talk to me like that. For goodness' sake.'

Gray snorted.

'But it's obvious. The storm didn't dampen the forest. It dried it out more instead. So he tohu tērā, nē. Time to burn us out, before winter comes and while everything's still dry.'

Hana shook her head, as if amazed not just by this logic but by her daughter's attitude at such a time. 'Is this true, Gray? Tuku? Can anyone tell me if this is true?'

'It's true, lady. You're in the shit. You've got a day, I reckon, two days maybe, before they burn your big fancy place to shit—completely to shit.'

'Oh my god.' Hana turned to Van. 'This can't be right. It can't be right.'

Van put a hand on her shoulder. He wanted to say it would be all right, but there was no proof of that.

'I don't understand,' she said. 'We made a trade with them. We're doing it.'

He gripped her shoulder more firmly. 'Hey. It'll be all right. We'll sort this out.'

'We're doing exactly what they want.'

'Hana.'

She shook her head again, and Van saw her face change. She'd been vibrating with anger and upset, but now the enormity of it seemed to hit her. 'I knew it wouldn't work. Of course it wouldn't. Stupid.'

Van brought her in; held her against his chest. Over her shoulder, he saw the tamāhine toa watching. They'd abandoned their work and were no longer guarding the perimeter, instead watching the bent shape of Hana's back and head where she was curled into Van. Their faces showed blank confusion, fright. Kahu turned too and saw her mother.

Van caught Tuku's attention, and jerked his head towards the edge of their camp. She came to, barking orders at her crew; they went back to their posts.

Looking over Hana's head, Van said, 'So what do you want out of this, Gray?'

'I want my wrist back, you arsehole.'

'Yeah, well, tough shit. You're lucky I didn't do much worse. My bar could make a nice mess of your face.'

'Fuck you,' said Gray. 'I'm not trading with you.'

Hearing this, Hana moved out of Van's embrace. She wiped

her face, and blew out snot from her nose. 'What's it going to take, Gray?'

'Well, it depends how much you want what we've got.'

'Yeah,' said Van, 'and you've got nothing.'

Gray tried to lift his hand to tick off each point, but his wrist was broken and he scowled with pain instead. Holding it awkwardly, he said, 'We've got this information we've told you, about the Burners. We've got more information about them, where they are. And we've got the ability to *not* tell them where you are right now.'

Hana sighed. 'You don't have any more information, Gray. We can all see that.'

'Where's your treasures?' said Gray. 'Give us your treasures.'

'We don't have any treasures,' said Hana. 'We never travel with treasures.'

'As if I believe that.'

Hana indicated the bags on the ground. 'We have wraps of food, best water, and blankets. You can take any of that.'

'I'll take some best water,' said Gray, scowling. 'Just to piss in it.'

'Don't make a mistake here, Gray,' said Van.

'Fuck up, swamp.' He barely looked at Van as he dismissed him. 'Where's your treasures?'

'I told you,' said Hana. 'We don't have treasures.'

'Manny,' said Gray. 'Stand up. Time to sort these bitches out.'

The figure at the back moved. Slowly it uncurled and stood. Van peered. It was a young woman, taller than Kahu. Her head was covered with a wrap but, even from this distance, he could see the swollen and engorged bites on her forehead, and a further blotch of inflamed bites that ringed under her ears and showed on her throat.

188

Without looking at her, still nursing his bad wrist, Gray gave his orders. 'Go back to that spot by the Burners' camp. If I'm not there in good time, tell them we found some Whaea bitches. Posh ones they'll want. And tell them where we found them.'

She stood without vigour. Her face had a greyish cast. She seemed to sway as these instructions reached her.

'Now,' said Gray.

She seemed far too sick; she couldn't possibly carry it out. But then she stepped back and the kawakawa shifted and she was gone. It shocked Van how fast she became lost in the scrub and its gathering dusk. Perhaps her sickness had been faked. Yet there'd been bite marks on her—bad bite marks.

'Right, fuckers,' said Gray. 'Put up your treasures. Manny won't take long to reach them. She's quick.'

'We don't have treasures. We have food and water from our lake. You can take some of that.'

'All right, let me be straight with you. You're not among mates. You have no friends within a day's march. There's plenty of Valley folk out here who want to fuck you up, you Whaeas. Lots of old scores to even up. And that's not to mention the Burners that Manny's gone to alert, who might just decide to burn your settlement tonight, for the fun of it, and no warning to your people. All burnt to a posh-arse fucking crisp.'

Hana made to speak again, but faltered. Van heard her voice crack and die in her throat.

'Treasures, bitches,' said Gray. 'Make this worth it, or you know how this is going to end up.'

Van stepped forward. 'Look, Gray, here's how it is. You take what I'm about to offer you, and you fuck off, with all your hands still attached.' He brought his blade out and, still with the bar in his right, he sliced across the air. Then he backed towards the shelter. Kahu was still covering the rear and her eyes darted towards him as he passed her. He hooked his bag with the blunt side of his knife. He thought for a moment of trading his own plastic pieces, but that would mean all the best of his work would have been wasted in a few days on people who didn't deserve it—first Squat, and then this Gray. He would trade Matewai's medicines instead. It was a high-value trade—perhaps too much to pay—but it wouldn't leave them defenceless. Hana was carrying Whaea medicines that they could all use, should anyone fall sick, and he would still have Matewai's repellents for keeping the bugs off. 'You know who Matewai is, right? You've heard of her. You know her healing oils and drinks.'

Gray glanced at the bag in Van's hand. Sensing what he was about to bring out, he looked away, affecting indifference.

'Your daughter's sick, and she needs medicine, and these are the best healing oils you can get. You won't get anything better without going inside the Whaea fence, which I don't think you'll ever be able to do, especially after this little stunt. It's the best, and you know your daughter needs it.'

'I don't know what that crap is. I don't need it. And anyway their settlement's about to get fucked up, so why would I go there?' He tried to indicate all the land round them, but it just hurt his bad wrist, curling his face more. 'All this place is going up in smoke.'

Van dangled the plaited-together canisters of healing oils. 'Without this your daughter is going to get sicker and die from all those bites. We've all seen it lots of times, Gray. You know what's coming, mate.'

Gray looked further off, pretending to study the clouds above the Scarp, their purpling under-light. His hand went unconsciously to his wrist, then pulled away.

'Fix your daughter, Gray. There's enough here to heal her properly. Or you can trade it on to some else, if you want to do that.'

'What else have you got? Give us something else.'

'Food and water, like we said.'

Gray looked directly at Van then, and again that sullen expression flared into anger, as something in Van annoyed him—his height, perhaps, or the stroke of good fortune that saw him flanked by these people from inside the fence.

'But you don't have to, of course,' said Van. 'You could just sell us out to the Burners or some Valley people, or whatever you're planning to do, in which case you get no medicines and your daughter gets sicker, and then by the time the next storm comes she'll be dead, and you'll have to burn her or sink her, or whatever your tradition is.'

'She won't die like that,' said Gray. 'She's tougher than this lot.'

'All right, then,' said Van. He lifted the ugly plastic bar in his left hand and regarded it, shifting it so it caught the light. 'In that case, I'll just persuade you with my bar instead, 'cause I'm running out of patience. And I'll get these tamāhine toa to give me some help, because they need the practice.'

Gray's eyes darted to the bar. He was holding his wrist non-stop now.

Hana was back by the shelter now too, alongside Van. She bent down by her bags and held up wraps so Gray could see them. 'Four wraps of smoked meat. Fresh water. Plus the oils that Van has offered. In exchange, you call off Manny and tell us where the People in Smoke are, so we can avoid them.'

Gray growled, and shook his head like a possum that had been inadequately bashed in the head and wasn't dead yet.

'This is a good trade,' said Hana. 'You should take it now.'

191

The Valley man surveyed Hana and the string of canisters that dangled from Van's hand. He seemed to gather it all together: the canisters and the wraps and Van's bar and blade, the tamāhine toa at the side in fighting pose, and Kahu patrolling at the back. Then he dropped his face and, in a breath, all fight seemed to leave him.

'We'll leave the food and oils here,' said Van. 'Come back when we're gone from this site. We'll camp elsewhere tonight. Collect them then.'

'Where are you headed?'

Van laughed softly. 'I don't think so, mate.'

Gray sighed. Then he bent to the ground behind him and reached for something, and Van tensed—but then Gray lifted a simple stick, and threw it further into the undergrowth.

'Oh, for fuck's sake,' said Van. The weapon Gray had been concealing when he'd first appeared was no more than a stick.

But at his cursing, Gray looked at Van. 'Who are your people. Your waters?'

'Ha. I'm not telling you that.'

'Come on. You broke my wrist.'

Van eyed Gray, his impoverished look, and considered how much he should share. 'Swamp folk—the Ngaheres, to be precise. I was whāngaied by them, by Matewai.'

'No. Before they took you in,' said Gray. 'Before that.'

'There is no before that.'

Gray studied him closely, and would not stop his scrutiny, even when Van looked away and then back and still found him staring, and even when Van flared at him and twirled the plastic bar in the direction of his broken wrist.

'No, I don't believe that.' Gray indicated Hana. 'I don't believe she'd settle for that.'

Twelve

It wasn't safe to stay where they'd been discovered, and where there'd been noise of fighting, so once Gray was gone they broke camp and headed up the valley flank. They'd been travelling only a short time before Hana called along the line to stop. Van saw her bend to Kahu, the two of them quickly into an earnest talk. The tamāhine toa crowded in, sensing a strategic discussion, but Hana shooed them back. He'd noticed that Kahu tended to freeze up in their presence, and he supposed this was the reason Hana warned them away.

'Haere mai, Van,' said Hana.

Kahu's eyes were wide as he came up.

'Tell him, please, Bub.' Hana's voice was gentle, speaking in Pākehā for Van's benefit.

'Do you think he was right about the People in Smoke?' Kahu's bright focus on him was unnerving. 'He tricked us about the weapon he had at the start—that was just a trick— but do you think he was lying about them too? Do you think they're really that close?'

Van thought for a moment. 'I don't think he was lying about it.'

'I don't think he was either,' said Kahu.

'What do you think we should do?'

Tuku made to speak, but Hana hushed her with a hand.

Kahu breathed in deep. She forced herself to say it. 'I think we should find them, and ask to talk to them, and try to find out what they're planning.'

'I agree,' said Van. 'We can't camp safely if we know they're close but don't know their plans.'

'Āe,' said Tuku, 'that was all I was trying to say in the first place.'

'I *really* don't want to,' said Kahu, 'but I think we have to find them and talk.'

'But we've done that,' said Hana. 'We've talked to them before, and made an agreement. And they've broken it, if Gray was telling the truth and if they're really here. So we can't trust them again. It's not safe.'

'So what should we do instead?' said Van.

Hana looked at him, and thought for a moment, and then shrugged. Her face showed her surprise that she didn't have an answer.

'Tuku,' said Van, 'if they're close by, is there a way you can signal them, but say that we want to talk peacefully, trade-style, and not to fight?'

Tuku's eye went to Hana, seeking permission, perhaps, or simply wary of her response. 'Āe. Of course.'

'So if we find out where they are, could one of you guys signal them and get them to come out to talk with us?'

'It would have to be done before dark, and dark's not very far off.'

'Right, so we'd better be quick.'

'I don't see the point of this, Van. We know what they're like.' Hana gestured towards the coast. 'We know what they did to the island. The coastal villages. They're not nice.'

'But you made a deal with them. You must have thought

they could keep a promise.'

'I wasn't there when that deal was made. I didn't trade directly with them. I don't know any of these people. And anyway, they've broken their promise. We shouldn't trust them.'

'But something's changed. That's obvious. And we don't know what it is. Maybe they're not here to burn you out. They might be heading further inland, like us, in which case I'd like to know where they're going, because it could endanger our journey. And if they're not travelling somewhere, if they're really here to burn you out, we need to know how long you've got, so we can warn your people.'

Hana looked not at Tuku and her tamāhine toa, but at Kahu. 'What do you think?'

Kahu moved her tongue along her lip. 'I don't want to do it,' she said. 'But I think we have to talk to them. We have to know what they want.'

Van looked around for height, a viewing point. 'I'll climb something and have a look.'

Immediately, Hana shook her head. 'Kāo. That's what our tamāhine toa are for. They're better at it.'

She sent a rapid string of talk to Tuku, who then directed instructions towards the other two. Evidently one of them was better at climbing and the other would help her to get started. They ran off, and Hana spoke again with Tuku. Van got the impression it would be Tuku herself who would be hailing the Burners.

Van caught Kahu's eye, and murmured, 'I thought only older women could do that job.'

Kahu paused, her eyes fixed on his face, as if she was searching for a way to explain it. 'Fight calling is different. All of us are trained for it.'

'But it's not a fighting thing, right? She's going to say we *don't* want to fight. It's a call to a talk, not to a fight.'

Kahu shook her head, frustrated. 'That's not really what we call it. I just don't know the Pākehā word for it, so I said it was "fight calling", but that's not what it really is.' Her eye went beyond him, as if to put an end to his questions, but then he saw she was tracing the climb of the other pair of fighters.

They'd circled round and were now behind them, and the smaller one was already climbing with surprising speed up the tallest of the trees they'd passed. She grasped a branch and swung up, grasped another branch and looped further up. She was halfway to the top before Van lost sight of her behind the trunk. Beyond her the sky was darkening fast, the last tinges of red showing above the back slopes of the Scarp. Looking up there reminded him he hadn't seen Ru since the confrontation with Gray, when the kākā had shrieked into the air above them and away. Van wasn't unhappy about it; part of him hoped the bird would now be gone for good.

'He ahi. I see their camp.' She was quickly down, and the pair of them came running back. 'There's a camp a short run to the north-west. The number of fires seems about right, for what that Pākehā said. Whā tekau—' She shook her head, remembering to stay in Van's language. 'A camp for forty people, perhaps.'

'Are they fighters? Scouts?'

'I couldn't see that. But I suppose some of them are.'

'Why didn't we know about this?' said Hana. 'How can forty people get round our south-west gate without anyone noticing?'

'Kāore au i te mōhio.' A similar bafflement in Tuku's voice. 'Their stealth must be good.' She gave Hana a careful glance. 'Can you run all right? We should run to get there before dark.'

196

Hana nodded, and pulled her belts tight. 'Kei te pai, Bub?'

Kahu nodded, her tongue going along her lip. It was her nervous habit, Van realised, when truly scared. He'd seen it first when she'd entered Matewai's camp.

Hana motioned her and Van to come close. 'Stay with us. We'll be in the back, until it's our time to talk. Then Van and I will speak. You stay right in here by me, Bub.'

They were still not in sight of the camp when Tuku stopped.

'We're running out of time,' she said. 'Me tuku au.'

Noiselessly the other tamāhine toa fanned out on Tuku's left and right. Without any preamble Van could see, Tuku sent her voice ringing out through the stillness of the bush. It was unlike any kind of call Van had heard before. But as with all the other types of calls he'd been present for, he couldn't understand or even really hear many of the words. He caught a phrase that mentioned their Whaea roots, but not much else.

Afterwards there was a long silence of nothing in the trees but birds chattering down for dusk, and then Tuku's own voice again ringing out. With her hands, even as she sent her voice out, she ushered her group forward. It seemed the Burners hadn't heard her, and now Tuku was urging her own party closer to ensure they were heard, and to try to summon a response.

Then a man's voice came back. It was more of a chanted shout than a call in the style Tuku had delivered. It was uncertain, though, wavering, and it repeated simple kupu that even Van could catch. 'Ko wai tē-nā, ko wai, ko wai? Ko wai tē-nā?'

This time Tuku's call was easier for Van to understand. She adjusted its difficulty, telling the distant man who they were. She told him they came under the guiding hand of the Whaea; they came in peace.

Instead of a response Van heard voices in the trees ahead. Then a man's voice came, but this time in a single shout. 'Tāria!'

They stood still, and the junior tamāhine toa readied themselves, their blades out.

A pair of lights showed through the bush and became larger. Soon they became more well defined, and Van saw they were fire-torches, held by a pair of advancing men who also held wooden clubs. Both men looked ragged, but the younger man was in a worse state than the old one. Illuminated by his torch, he looked half-starving, his cheeks hollowed and his headwrap ripped and greasy with dirt. From a distance of ten paces the men surveyed the group.

'What do you want?' It was the young man who spoke. His āhua looked to Van to be Pākehā, but he couldn't be sure.

Van looked at Hana to see if this was the moment they should speak, but Hana shook her head sharply.

'We want to enter your camp to safely talk,' said Tuku. 'A peaceful talk. Trade-style.'

The young man's eye went from Tuku to Van, and rested on him. He looked to be puzzled that it was Tuku doing the talking, not Van. 'Were you the one who karanga'd us?'

'Well, it wasn't . . . Anyway, yes, it was me who called you.'

'That gave us the total shits,' the man said. 'I nearly shat myself.'

Van snorted, and the young man's eyes came to rest on him again, then searched beyond into the darkening trees. 'Just one dude with you,' he said. 'No one else?'

Tuku's voice was different this time. 'I told you in my call that we're a peaceful group. Engari, ehara—' She stopped, and searched for an adequate way to say it in Pākehā. 'But that doesn't mean we're defenceless.'

'Well, maybe we'll see about that.' The man's lips worked on each other while he eyed them all again. 'Youse are all Whaeas, right?'

Tuku sighed. 'I told you that as well. In the call.'

'Yeah, most of us couldn't understand that, lady. It just put the shits up us. Calling to us like that, almost at dark.'

It seemed strange to Van that the younger man did the talking, not the older one, and now Hana lost patience with it. She stepped forward and addressed the silent older man. 'Look, can we come safely into your camp to talk, or are we just going to have a picnic out here, or what?'

'Hey, taihoa, lady.'

But the older man cut across him. 'Whākina mai ō koutou—' Running out of language, he used his hands to show what he meant. 'Your blades and weapons and shit.'

Hana was the first to move, bringing from inside her coat a blade that Van hadn't seen yet. It was a square chopper of considerable depth, like Rau's but not so old.

'Ki te papa,' the man said, indicating the ground in front of Tuku. As if unsure again of what he'd said, he added, 'On the ground.'

'We've got no choice,' Hana said. 'Do as he says.'

They all put their weapons down, Van withdrawing his from inside his coat. His plastic-handled blade and the brutal plastic bar stood out amongst the metal finery of the Whaea women, but the man didn't separate it or try not to touch it. Instead he took his own coat from round his shoulders and laid all the weapons in it and scooped them all up.

'All right,' he said. 'Whāia mai.'

The younger man came in round the back of the group, and Van saw Hana and the young women casting looks back there, uncertain of his intent, his clear interest in the fact that all but one of the group were female.

199

Fires began to show through the trees as they walked on, then a clearing opened out. Van heard a child crying somewhere and a man hushing it; a pair of boys, barely clothed and no more than seven or eight summers, chased each other in the further reaches of firelight. These people had been blessed, it seemed, with at least some children.

'Anei,' said the older guard. Then, as if translating for his own group, he added, 'Got them. Just six.'

An older man stood from the fire, then a woman and another man. Elsewhere people swivelled to watch. There were some temporary shelters of fern and nīkau leaning against tree trunks, but overall it was a rude camp. And the people were not the fighters Van had expected. There were a number of grey heads, and a gaunt look in most of the faces. A lot of Pākehā-looking people amongst them, perhaps half, all of them smeared with camp dirt. There was a mound of what looked like water and supply bags stacked well beyond the fire, a trio of the younger adults guarding it.

The woman was the first to speak. 'Tēnā koutou e ngā wāhine o te Whaea. Kei te ohorere mātou ki te kite.'

Hana took Van's hand and pulled him forward. 'Mā māua te kōrero e tuku.'

The two women eyed each other.

Hana continued in her own language for a time, and Van wondered how long she would keep it up. Perhaps she wanted to pretend that her knowledge of Pākehā wasn't good enough for trading speech.

But then the older man at the left of the group flapped an impatient hand. 'So what do you people want? We haven't got all night.'

Van felt the pressure of Hana's hand. She wanted him to speak.

'We came here to ask you the same thing,' he said.

'Well, what does it look like, mate? We're having a camp. We were just getting ready for sleep when you called us.'

'But what are you doing here? This is a long way from your island.'

The old man looked from Van to Hana, and back again. His hand went between them. 'Are you one of these Whaeas? Or are you this swamp guy we've been hearing about?'

Van tried not to flinch. 'Nō Te Repo au. Ko Matewai Ngahere tōku whaea.'

The man looked at the woman beside him, who nodded.

'Right, so you're the guy from the swamp. I'm Max. Congratulations on the kid.'

'Oh my god,' said Van.

'Don't react, Van,' said Hana. 'He's trying to fuck with your head.'

Van breathed out slowly, and smoothed a hand over his headwrap. 'So can you tell us why you're here?'

'Sure thing,' said Max. 'We're burning you out—well, the Whaeas. We're burning them out.'

'Now?' said Van. 'Right now?'

'Yes. Well, as soon as we get the signal.. There's camps like this all round the Whaeas' fence. But the others have more fighters in them.' He eyed the tamāhine toa who flanked the group. 'But don't get any ideas. There's plenty of nasty fuckers in here to keep us safe.'

Van looked around the camp.

'Anyway, to answer your question, mate,' said Max, 'yes, we're burning the Whaeas out now, or as close to now as makes no difference.'

Now Hana reacted. She sent a stream of her own language at the woman, fast and fierce. The other woman stood there, weathering Hana's blast. Round the campfire Van saw people turn. A pair of men stood up and came closer. Having got no reaction from the woman, and not noticing the new pair's approach, Hana turned on Max and continued her tirade in Pākehā. 'We had a trade. You promised us—you *promised* us it would be next summer. When the pōhutukawa turns red, you said. But they haven't turned red, and it's *not* summer yet.'

By now the largest of the two new men had come right round the campfire. He took his place beside Max, dwarfing him. His face was smooth, his hair pulled back from his forehead and secured under a headwrap. 'What's this noise about? I'm trying to get my kids to sleep.'

'Kua whati,' said Hana. 'Kua whati te whakaaetanga.' She continued her tirade in her own language, the big man just watching it.

Finally he cut in. 'Yeah, I don't want to talk to you, lady.' He pointed at Van. 'That fella. I want to talk to that fella.'

Van tried not to, but he quailed. It was the way the big man pointed, shoving from the shoulder, not just his fingertip.

'I'm Bolt,' said the man. 'I'm the big fucker round here. So you need to talk to me. You need to tell me what this is all about.'

Behind Bolt someone threw wood on the fire to illuminate the talk.

Van gripped Hana, imploring her silently to shut up, even as he gave an appeasing smile to Bolt. 'We came peacefully,' he said. 'We came peacefully to ask why you're here and what you want. You said you would come in summer—next summer— and it's definitely not summer yet. It's barely autumn, but here you are.'

'So why didn't she just say that?'

Van felt both Hana and Tuku bristle but he again stayed Hana with his hand. 'With respect,' he said, 'I think she did.

I think that's exactly what she's been saying, in her language.'

'So what? So you people can speak flasher than us? Is that supposed to frighten me?'

Van swallowed. 'It's just the language she speaks.'

Bolt glared at him, at Hana.

'Can you please tell us why you're here?' said Van. 'That's all we want. It's all we came for.'

'Why should we tell you fuckers anything? We don't have to.'

Now Max cut a hand at Bolt, losing patience. 'Just tell them straight, Bolt. Stop fucking about. I want to get to bed tonight.'

But Bolt gave no sign of having heard this. His eyes fixed on Van. 'Things change, bro. The sun moves, and the world changes. It goes like this.' He said nothing more to explain, making only a side-to-side motion with his hand. Van supposed it was meant to suggest the movements of the sun, or of change.

'But why kick these people out now? They're leaving already—planning it at least. That's what we're doing right now. We're scouting out a route they can take when they leave their territories in the summer. Which is good for you, right? If they all leave before summer, and then you arrive when the pōhutukawa turns red, like the trade said you would, and there's no one there, it will be so much easier for you to move in, right? No resistance.'

'I told you, mate. Things change.'

'But there are other places you can go to. Why don't you want those? Why do you need the Whaeas' place?'

'Well, that's above me, bro. It's not me who makes that call. You'd have to ask somebody else. But it's what we've decided— and it's an old decision. I think you know that.' He indicated Hana and her troupe. 'We need their place, so they gotta get out. They already know that, 'cause we told them.'

203

'Yes, but you're two seasons early. You haven't given them a chance to get out. That's my point.'

Bolt shrugged. 'Like I said, things change.'

'So you're running from them, aren't you? You're running from the people who're coming south, who are pushing you out of the island. They've come early, haven't they? They've come earlier than you planned. That must be it. Otherwise why would you rush? Why break a good trade and risk a fight with the Whaeas by coming early?'

Bolt said nothing.

'Thought so,' said Van. 'So who are they? Word is, they're pretty fierce.'

Bolt eyed him. 'You don't wanna know, mate.'

Van looked along the line of people opposite him, and a question came. 'So do you want the swamp? Actually, do *they* want the swamp—these people you're running from? Since they're the ones calling the shots here.'

Bolt eyed him, as if intrigued by this change of topic and sensing a vulnerability. 'The swamp. Maybe. Maybe we *do* want it. It could be useful to us. Could be useless, though. Might be worth burning a few people out, just to check.'

'Whatever,' said Van. 'You don't want it, I can tell. It's diseased, and you know that. The water's no good. That's an old decision too. I know your people have already decided against that.'

Bolt shook his head, pretending to more certainty now. 'We think it's worth a raid.'

'Tēnā rūkahu tēnā,' said Hana.

'She says you're a bullshitter,' said the woman beside Max. Her translation was immediate, her stare blazing at Hana.

Even though it wasn't directed at him, Van foundered against her hostility. There was such fierceness here. On the

204

surface, this camp looked little more than a huddling place for kids and old folk and parents. They seemed the scrag end of an evicted settlement, not a gang of fighters. Yet there was something hard there too, not just in the talk of people like Bolt, but running underneath. Van knew they were capable of backing up their intensity with force.

'Can't we trade?' he said. 'Isn't there a trade solution to all this? Because you know these people are rich in trades.'

But Bolt was glaring at Hana. 'You think I'm bullshitting?'

'Hana, don't answer that,' said Van.

But he was too late. Bolt had already turned with instructions to the older guard, who now sent his voice into the darker reaches of the camp. 'Homai te ahi.'

From a lean-to of fronds deep in the camp another two figures emerged, scrawny and rushing about. At the mound of guarded bags, one of them loaded up the other and led him, limping badly at one side, towards Bolt.

Desperate to stop this, whatever was coming, Van spoke fast. 'I thought you wanted your kids to sleep. Why don't you let them sleep, and just talk with us quietly about trade? We can talk about what these Whaea people can give you.'

'Fuck up, mate,' said Bolt. 'You're too late for all that shit, anyway. All that talking's done, so fuck up with that.'

As the new pair came into the firelight it was clear both faces had been disfigured, the laden man the worst. He put the bags down and stood crookedly. To look at the intruders he had to peer out the good side of his face. From his eyebrow and down to his throat the right side was puckered and pulled tight by a wound that seemed to have melted the flesh and re-formed it. The other man had the same cut down the right side, but he was not bent in the same way towards it, and his scar didn't have the same horrid melted look.

205

'These are two of our best burners,' said Bolt. 'Pike here used to be our richest man in kids. He had three healthy ones, two of them higher than half-height. Not anymore, though. Pike, show us your guts.'

Without hesitation the crooked man pulled his coat over his head. The melted wound tightened his whole right side. From his shoulder it scored over the place where his nipple should have sat naturally but was now mutilated, and on down his guts to his groin. The man opened his mouth and a gargled, choking sound came from the throat; in the firelight Van couldn't see exactly what was wrong, but it seemed the man's tongue had been cut.

Kahu moaned and turned away.

'They had metal,' said Bolt. 'They used a hook. They did the same thing to his kids.'

Bolt let the visitors stare at the disfigured man and listen to his attempts to speak.

'Out of all of us,' said Bolt, 'Pike was the loudest opposing them. He said we should stay, and he said it wasn't right. So when they came they pushed his huts down, and then they staked him out with pegs and plait. Methodical, like. And then they got the hook. They cut his best side, his working side and working arm, right down his arm and guts, like you can see. And then they used hot water on each side of the cut, to be sure it would always hurt him to work. And then they did the same thing to his kids.'

'Stop,' said Hana. 'That's enough.'

'And then, 'cause he kept on screaming and protesting about it, they used the hook on his mouth.'

As if to correct an aspect of what Bolt had said, the man tried to say something, but only that choked gargle came from his throat.

Van felt an acid sick rise in his own throat. He turned away from Pike, and from Bolt's voice.

'His kids didn't survive it, of course.' Bolt paused, waiting until Van was facing him again. 'So if you think we're going to hang around and wait for those people to come down here and do that same thing to the rest of our kids, then you're fucking stupid. And I'm not even telling you what they did to my old man. I'm just not going to.'

Now Bolt motioned at Pike. 'Throw fire.'

The two men dropped to the bags at their feet. The first they opened released a sharp reek. Pike lowered his own dirty coat, the same one he'd removed to show his guts, and submerged it in the liquid. Then he stood and hobbled with it a few paces, and stopped just beneath a mānuka branch. The other man went to the pile of fuel beside the fire and lifted a length of dead and dry foliage. He dunked the rest of the liquid on the dead foliage and gave the branch to Pike to hold. Then he parted the group at the fire and withdrew a burning branch. Ready beneath the mānuka tree, Pike handed the soaked branch to the other man, who set it alight. Then Pike threw his soaked and stinking coat into the mānuka, and at the same moment the man threw the burning branch up. Light leapt and flashed as flames caught and snaked up the tree and carried on burning after the first flash. Flames licked into the inter-twigs and small foliage, and soon the whole tree was burning properly.

'All right.' Again, Max sounded exasperated. 'Kill it off.'

Immediately the younger man reached behind his neck and withdrew a long and heavy blade that must have been strapped to his back beneath his clothes. Heedless of the heat from the tree and its falling fire scraps, he went to the trunk and hacked at it with ferocious energy. Chips flew back from the wound that he opened in the wood, and soon the tree waved, losing its own balance but still flaming. Pike hobbled in then, and reached up with his good side and pulled the tree towards him while the other man kept chopping at the base again—then the entire tree fell and both men leapt back as it hit the ground and bounced off sparks and coals, and then, barely pausing, the men turned their attack on the fire itself, thrashing it with the long blade and stomping the flames with their rag boots. Even as they attacked it they screamed at the fire, cursing its heat and pain.

'Oh, oh,' said Hana, over and over as the attack continued.

Van felt sick. It was the frenzy of their attack, their disregard for the tree they were mutilating and the flames and even their own safety that made it so shocking. They kept stomping and soon the entire charred tree, once as high as two men, was just a blackened and broken mess of charred trunk and soot at their feet.

The men then went to the same pile of bags they'd come from in the further reaches of the firelight, and doused each other's rag boots and legs with water.

Everyone was quiet, sickened by what they'd seen.

But then without warning Bolt shouted. 'So ya see, we're not fucking around. And if you ever say that to me again—if you ever call me a bullshitter again, or if you laugh at what I'm saying to you—I swear, I will get your daughter there, and I will burn her, and I'll burn all these fucking *kids* you've got with you too.' His eyes huge, he spat at Hana's feet. 'Get out of my sight, you spoilt bitch. You don't know anything—fucking *anything*.'

'All right, Bolt,' said Max. 'All right.'

'You don't even know our names,' said Bolt. 'You call us Burners, the People in Smoke—all kinds of shit. You don't even ask our real names. You have no respect.'

'So what are your names?' said Van. 'What should we call you?'

Bolt spat. 'As if I'm telling you. No fucking respect.'

'That's enough, Bolt,' said Max.

Bolt threw his arm again, and Max reared back, then took him gingerly, and turned him, ushering him away from the discussion. He went a short way, murmuring to the big man and calming him. Then he came back, wiping his hands, and surveyed the visitors in front of him.

'So we've got eight of these fire-throwers in our camp, and there's another fifteen with the main group who are near your front fence right now, and there are more in the other groups. So you're pretty well fucked, 'cause I know you can't fight a fire like that. You just can't.' He looked along the line of distraught Whaea people in front of him. 'Hey, at least we don't kill you, normally. If it goes all right, and if you know how to run from a fire, then you don't get killed.' He wiped his mouth. 'Not like that lot Bolt's been talking about. Apparently, because they haven't found a safe place to live yet, we've all gotta pay for it. Every single person in their way. We've all gotta die for it.'

His eyes had moved to the ground as he said this, but now he lifted them again. He looked from Hana to Van, and back again, as if still unsure who was the pre-eminent boss. 'But I can assure you ladies, there's no place left for you in that settlement. You've got to get out.'

Hana's voice came at last. 'You people are just shit from stoats. You're just—'

'You ladies really need to find a new place to live.'

Van gripped Hana's arm, silencing her. 'How long have we got?'

'Well, your forest is dry. We're just waiting for the signal from the front. We'll be burning any day now, any night.' He shook his head. 'I tell you, you've got to get out quick.'

For a time the only sound was the campfire as it crackled

and gave warmth.

Van cleared his throat. 'Can't you give us another five nights? In five nights we can reach the new settling place, and negotiate—our party can and the people who are still in the settlement can also get out of there. They can evacuate.'

Max shook his head. 'Your forest is dry, and we're getting chased out. The island is finished for us. Like Bolt said, we're not going to hang around and harirū with the next lot—with these friends of Pike here—let me tell you.' He shook his head at Hana, at her daughter and fighters. 'I hope your Whaea-God-Lady . . .' He twirled his fingers above his head, to suggest something supposedly divine and airy-fairy that he didn't understand but knew was important. 'I hope your Aunty-God-Person's got your back. Because you're going to need it.'

Van felt the heaviness in his group. They could be overwhelmed right now without putting up a moment's fight. 'Tuku,' he said. 'Is there anything you want to ask him for? Anything I haven't said.'

The young woman stared at him, too shaken to respond. Then she nodded, and searched the ground, as if struggling to think of what she could ask. 'Can you let us run back, at least? Let us run back tonight and warn the people. Let us give them a chance to get out. If we warn them, they can run from the fire.'

'All right,' said Max. 'I doubt it will happen tonight in any case.' He waved a hand at the people sitting, giving some instruction. 'Someone give these visitors back their weapons. And now you Whaeas run home to your leaders, and I'll send a message round to the front.' Having learnt who to focus on at last, he looked straight at Tuku. 'Get your people out of there, girl. Be quick about it.'

Thirteen

Against the arguments of Tuku and Van, Hana sent all the tamāhine toa back in the night.

'We should keep one of them at least,' Van said. They were no longer in sight of the Burners' camp, but had travelled only a short distance down the valley flank. The moonlight was just beginning to filter down through the bush.

'We can cope without them,' said Hana. 'We've got you, and both Kahu and I can fight, if we need to.'

'I don't like it,' said Tuku. 'Me tiaki mātou i a koutou—me te pēpi hoki. That's our job.'

'Kāo. You've got to warn the people, and help them. The heke out of home—' She stopped. 'The heke out of home will be very difficult. They'll need all the help they can get.'

'We should fight,' said Tuku. 'We have to fight.'

Hana shook her head, choking back her distress. Then, seeing the strengthened moonlight, she looked up. 'Ah, kei te tīaho mai. She's helping us.' She cleared her throat. 'There's no point in trying to fight those people, Tuku. They're here to burn us. We can't fight their fire with our fists. We can't fight it with our blades. It won't work. And, anyway, those aren't our instructions. You all heard Rerū and Bel and them.

211

Our instructions are to go inland and find this new place.' She indicated Tuku and her two companions. 'You lot go straight back to Bel. Give her your report. Tell her what those People in Smoke said about the forest, how dry it is. Then tell them what you saw, how you saw their skills with it, and how—' She shuddered. 'How horrible they are with it. Then you help our aunties with whatever they decide to do.' She cleared her throat again. 'And tell them I think they should all heke mai, just like we planned. Only sooner—right now. Ināianei.'

Hearing something in this that he didn't, all three tamāhine toa looked at Van. He saw their serious faces silvered by the moonlight. Then he flinched—it was Hana, putting a hand on his arm. He felt a tremor through it. She was shaking with shock—shock at the impact of what they'd seen in the camp, and what Bolt had said—but working hard to keep that fear out of her voice. Only he knew she was shaking like this.

'All right,' said Van. 'Let's separate. You three go back, and we'll set up camp.'

Immediately, Kahu looked up, as if Van's voice had released her to speak. But it was to her mother that she spoke. 'Me hoki au. Me āwhina.'

'No. You stay with us.' He'd said it before he even thought about it. 'We stick together, us three. That's our task.'

Kahu was silent. He wanted to put an arm across her shoulders, to pull her into a hug. But he was not letting her go back.

'Ka pai,' said Hana, her voice quieter. 'So all of you go back now. Trust us to look after ourselves. We're trained for it, don't forget. Now, you toa—' She paused. 'You three just be strong for your aunties. Kia kaha. Kia—' But again her voice cracked.

Tuku sighed, exasperated. She didn't want to run from the invaders. She wanted to fight them and their fires, and keep

212

fighting them until they were all turned back. She would get on well with Rau, Van thought, if they ever met again. The thought took him across the Dry Way to those empty huts at the mound camp, to Matewai and the others sleeping there, unaware of the fire that would soon come boiling up at their inland flank. But they would be all right, he told himself. They were protected by the vast surrounds of bog and swamp water that began at the Runalong Ponds and then linked and spread and pooled everywhere across those vast stretches towards the coast. The fire would barely get across the Dry Way; it would never reach their camp. And Rau would be back from his burial duty by the next night; he would tell them what he'd learnt.

The tamāhine toa tightened their belts and bags, Tuku giving rapid instructions about their route back.

'Taihoa,' said Hana. 'Me inoi tātou.'

'Māku e tuku?' said Tuku.

'Āe.'

They bent their heads and Tuku sent out the karakia, her tone firm and quick over the repeated bits. To Van it sounded more of an instruction to the Whaea than a request for help.

'Ka pai,' said Hana. The Whaea's hand on all of us.' She looked to the moon again as she said this. There must be some connection between their forest-statue goddess and the moon, Van realised, some link he hadn't been told about yet.

After they'd set up camp by the moonlight, Van took the first watch. There was the odd night noise from the scattered huts further down the valley flank, the far-off sound of a woman calling into the night and a man shouting back. Then nothing but a possum rasping, and then later the crunch and shriek of some animal spiked in a trap. Then the noise died down, and Van spent the rest of his watch trying to remember and recite the Inland waters he'd been taught, the river of ancestors that ran down from Jacky Donovan to Artie to Meg and Tip, all the way to himself. It wasn't easy. He dreaded the moment he'd have to recall them all under pressure, to roll them out with no mistakes. It seemed unlikely he'd ever be able to do it. 'Aroha mai,' he'd have to say. 'I can't remember all of this kōrero. I've only just learnt it.'

In the morning Van pushed up through the undergrowth and out of the camp to shit. Blearily, he scanned the bush for dangers. At last he found a safe place with a view over the valley. He plucked a handful of wide and velvety leaves and unbelted his clothes and crouched, his eye still roving out.

When he got back Kahu was moving around her shelter, banging the skins with her hand to shake the dew off. Seeing him, she straightened her headwrap and shot him a guarded look. She'd been shaken by the night's events, knocked into herself again. The poor kid hadn't even had a chance to get over her Nan's death yet.

'I pēhea tō moe?' he said, pitching his voice to be gentle.

'He pai. Well, not that great, really.'

He looked along the skyline; there were no storm clouds up there. 'But we're going to make good progress today. I'm sure of it.'

She ducked her head and went back to her work, pulling up the stakes at the base of her shelter.

Hana stirred, rubbing her back. In the rush of setting up camp a second time the night before, and with only the moonlight to help him, Van had pitched the shelter over an exposed tree-root. It had been an uncomfortable night. While he slept he'd crowded Hana to the uncomfortable part, and now her back was hurting because of it. She'd insisted on taking a full turn at guard as well, which probably hadn't helped.

Now her hand moved to her middle, and he watched as she stroked it. It stunned him how he could forget she was hapū for quite long stretches at times, only for the knowledge to come back with a stronger and deeper force.

'How is it out there?'

'Just some clouds high up, over the coast,' he said. 'No storms coming, I don't think.'

'Māmā,' said Kahu, from outside. 'Aren't you up yet? Kia tere. It's getting late.'

Hana rolled her eyes at Van. 'Mōrena, Bub,' she said, calling across. 'Pēhea tō moe? He pai?'

When Kahu didn't respond, Hana put her question to Van. 'Is she all right?'

'I think so, considering. But she looks pretty shaken.'

Hana nodded, then hoisted herself up in the bed.

'Does it change your mind about anything? What those Burners said?'

'Kāo. It just makes it more important. We *have* to find this new place, Van. We have to make it work. They're relying on us now.'

'All right. We should get going then.'

She closed her eyes and squirmed her lips tight against something unpleasant. With an effort, she swallowed, and said, 'Āe.'

He wondered what she felt inside, what the baby was doing in there. She'd said her morning squeamishness was over, but perhaps that was just so he didn't fret or interfere.

'I'm worried we won't make it in time,' he said. 'If your aunties decide to evacuate your settlement right away, they might have caught up with us even before we get to talk to these Inland people.'

'Let them take care of that, Van. We've just got to get there—that's our only job.'

'Ka pai.'

'I don't think that'll happen, anyway.' She pulled her hair into position. Securing a headwrap over it, she visibly firmed up her thoughts, her resolve. 'They'll take longer, because they'll have all sorts of people with them, all sorts of things. Bags of trades. Water and food, and old folk. Besides, it's not our job to worry about that. Our job is just to reach your Inland people, and trade with them.'

It seemed she'd conquered whatever nausea she'd been feeling. 'We've got to get there for Kahu, and for the pēpi, and for the others. There's no future anymore at our settlement. Those People in Smoke are too desperate. There's no other way than this way, Van. Haere tonu.'

'All right,' he said. 'Let's go.'

They pushed on for the rest of the morning, keeping to a high track on the eastern flank of the valley. The track was overgrown in parts and blocked by storm-fallen trees, but in other places had been maintained, Hana said, by Valley folk who used it to travel north and south to hunt and trap and for trade trips. The prospect of meeting them made Van nervous, but so far the only sign of them was a single trap up high on a branch, the bark fresh with blood but the possum gone, its owner already come to retrieve it.

They stopped only once for water and a handful of dried food in wraps. Both Hana and Kahu took their food without enthusiasm, their faces distant.

Van didn't try to lift their mood with banter or light talk. From his experience of Rau's long agony during Ava's time of sickness and then death, he'd learnt not to do that. Instead he passed them food, packed it away again, made sure they were watered, and led them back onto the track, pushing branches away. There was still no sign of Ru; he'd not been seen since the meeting with Gray, but neither of the women had remarked on it, and Van wasn't about to.

High on the valley flank they walked on, keeping well above the river that snaked down the valley below. The people who scratched out their lives in the huts down there wouldn't hesitate to rob a party like this: so comparatively rich, so laden with supplies from inside the Whaea fence. Van walked with his blade and bar both drawn, to make it easy to cut back the bush where it came too thick across the track, but also to be ready when an attack came.

The path led higher to a more open stretch and he walked more freely, the women quiet behind him. They were deep in their own thoughts, their shock at the news of the night. It pushed him to recite the names inwardly again, the speech he would have to make. When he thought of that talk now his mind seemed to freeze; he could picture only standing in front of a faceless group, his mouth opening but no words coming from it, his heart hammering loud in his chest.

Suddenly he became aware of a deeper silence behind, and turned to check.

They weren't there.

He ran back, crashed against a tree, and bashed a branch away with his bar. Ran on.

'Hana!'

Another branch hit him, its leaves fluttering cool against his face. He stumbled down tree roots and fell, colliding with the floor of the bush, his bags slamming on top. Stood up and ran further, and saw them.

They were in the track and crouching. Hana's hand was on Kahu's back. At his racket she looked up.

'Not so loud, Van.'

He looked wildly at them, at the bush all round. 'I lost you,' he said, panting. 'I thought you'd been attacked.'

Hana just shook her head, and returned her attention to Kahu. One hand was on her shoulder, the other round the back of her head.

Kahu was slumped, her face away from him. Crying silently. 'What is it?' he said.

Hana didn't answer, just moved her hand on Kahu's shoulder, and murmured to her so soft and low he could barely hear the words, let alone understand them. Her own face immeasurably sad.

He stood in the track uselessly, his weapons still in both hands. He tried to think of something to say, something of comfort. But there was nothing that could help, nothing that would speak to what was hurting Kahu. *I'm sorry about those people, that Bolt. I'm sorry for your settlement. I'm sorry you can't just grieve for your Nan.*

By now even Hana offered little more than her own repeated nickname for Kahu, a long murmur of phrases and questions all ending with the same word: 'eh, Bub; nē, Bub.'

'I'll keep watch,' said Van.

It was mid-afternoon before they stopped next. This time Kahu was in the lead, by her own request. She wanted to keep their lookout and cut bush. It seemed to help her, walking out in front with Hana. For some time Van heard their voices coming back, the girl talking to Hana about things related to the track, then again falling to silence as the bush closed and she had to

218

bash it back.

Then they started a descent to a gully, and a cry came from the front.

Van ran to find them again, his bags crashing. His blade was high as he approached.

Both Hana and Kahu had stopped and were looking up. 'What is it?'

Kahu bent to her mother and said something quiet, gesturing at the canopy above them. Hana laughed and pushed her back, mock-scolding her. It surprised Van to see Kahu give a small smile, then duck her eyes away.

'It's all right, Van. You can put your knife away. I was taken by surprise by these mamaku. They're special for us.'

He followed her eyes up to the fronds' bright greens and blacks. 'I thought it was nīkau that were sacred.'

There was a strange bashfulness in Hana's face. 'These are special for a different reason.'

Kahu groaned. 'Oh, āe, Māmā. A "special" reason.'

Hana laughed, her hand at her mouth.

'Ugh, Māmā. You're so gross sometimes.' But her voice wasn't harsh. Her eyes were still red, and she had that knocked-in look of grief, but Kahu was enjoying, too, the chance to mock her mother.

'What's the deal with mamaku?' he said. 'They're just ferns, where I come from. Or food, if we're short. And I think Matewai uses part of it for medicine sometimes.'

'There's a place of mamaku where our sweethearts go,' said Hana. 'For picnics and things like that.'

'Oh, āe,' said Kahu again. 'Funny kind of picnic.' She shoved Hana. 'You're so moony, Māmā.'

Hana laughed again and Van could only watch them, shut out of the deeper meaning of it. It was good, though, to watch

Kahu tease her mother, and push her once more, mocking scandal at Hana's private delight.

There was still no attack as they reached the gut of the gully. Van had been dogged by a sense of being watched, of a shadow that ducked behind a trunk or some far reach of the track. But there was nothing substantial there, ever, and as they reached the next creek they decided to stop for food and rest, breaking upstream for a safer place.

The creek was cold, a tributary to the river below, and it came steeply over great rocks that were hard to climb up, sometimes forcing them back into bush that Van had to cut. A particularly hard scramble up over a bank of rocks brought them to a pool where a family of ducks circled frantically before bobbing over the downstream fall, the youngest cheeping as it disappeared over the drop.

Grazed and bruised on his knuckles and knees from the climb, wet to the wrist and shin, Van looked his question at Hana.

'This is good.' She wiped creek mist from her face. 'It's clean water—Rerū said all these awa along this valley are clean. And you shouldn't worry too much about ambush here. We're in Raka's rohe now. He controls this southern part. His workers and scouts will see us, I'd say, but they shouldn't cause us any trouble. Not on this side of the valley.'

Van frowned. It still puzzled him, this trading relationship. The Whaeas and the Scarp in a kind of agreement. It had seemed the opposite from his own, other side of the Scarp— the swamp side.

But then Hana asked him to help remove their bags. Van took his own to a sitting spot where he could see easily downstream and up, and into the bush opposite. He brought out oil and dosed himself with it, and was relieved to see Hana and Kahu had already done the same. He hadn't seen Hana apply oil as regularly as he did; perhaps those things took place when he wasn't watching, when she and Kahu went away to wash and go wharepaku in the mornings, sometimes together and sometimes separately.

Kahu collected washing water from the creek. Then to Van's surprise she asked if she could swim.

He eyed the water's eddying surface. 'You want to swim in that? It's freezing.'

She snorted. 'I'm not scared.'

'I don't know if we have time.'

Hana was laying out food. She glanced at the water and Kahu crouching next to it. 'As long as you don't stay in forever. It's certainly safe enough here, in Raka's territory, and we'll both keep watch.'

While Kahu began to unbelt and remove her coat, Hana murmured to Van, 'It helps her to relax if she can swim. It's a good sign, actually, if she's not too upset to have a little kauhoe. I think you're helping with that.'

'Really? I don't think I'm doing much.'

'Just by being here,' said Hana. 'It helps her to be less tense.'

'Huh.' He looked at the water, at Kahu, the shadowed bush beyond. 'All the same, I don't think we can take too long here. It doesn't feel very safe.'

Hana nodded, then said a quick karakia kai for the food, and put a handful of dried stuff in her mouth. She offered meat to Van, and kūmara. A further wrap of possum.

'It's safer for us, too, if we all wash.' She grinned at him. 'You could try it too. I'm not saying you stink, but . . .'

He smiled vaguely, still unsure how he felt about the safety

221

of this. To someone from the swamp, submerging in water was seldom safe. The dangers were too numerous down there: attacks from the biters that hovered above, ambush, and poisoning from the water itself, that black and stinking juice of brack and salt and sunken junk.

But this water was different. Kahu, a long and fine undercoat falling to her knees, was toeing it now. Van knew how cold the stream was from their scramble up it, yet she seemed unfazed by the temperature. But the rocks were jagged underfoot, and she lurched with her arms out for balance.

'E kai, Van,' Hana said. 'We'll go faster after this, if we eat and have a proper rest.'

He took some of the kūmara strips and chewed. Kahu was thigh deep in the water now, her fingertips trailing in it. She took a breath and lunged towards the deepest part. Paddling there, she gasped at the cold, then dived under and emerged at the pool's far side.

'Pēhea?' said Hana. 'Maka-chilly?'

'Āe! He tio!'

But then she lifted her arms and dived under once more, the water eddying after her. It disturbed an insect with a long body that flitted and hovered, flitted and hovered, as if keeping watch on the water's surface.

'Where did she learn to swim like that?'

'Our lake,' said Hana. 'It's incredible, isn't it. I can swim a bit, but not like that. They train our tamāhine for it, as part of their toa training.'

Kahu burst from the water and smoothed her hair back. She blinked and looked at them. It seemed to please her that both were watching.

'Oh, tino pai,' said Van. 'I'd be drowning by now.'

She smiled, then blew her nose clear of water. 'Do you want

to see something?'

'Āe, of course.'

She bobbed on the spot, thumb and forefinger on her nose. Then she dived forward and under, her legs coming up after her. A moment later she was up again, wiping hair from her face.

Van was so surprised that he laughed. She'd done a flip underwater. 'That's amazing. I've never seen anyone do that.'

She looked across the pool to where it hissed and fell off the rock, and it seemed she was searching for the Pākehā term for the move. 'Do you dare me to do a double one? A double flip?'

He laughed again. The water had relieved her of her weight of grief, for a moment at least. 'Absolutely.'

She did the same bobbing motion up and down. Then she dived forward, rolling once and then a second time, before exploding up from the surface. It took longer to clear her face this time, smoothing back her hair and blinking water. She looked for Van's response again, and smiled, and he felt a great surging up inside that made him want to shield that small and wet head with his hands, to protect her from any more hurts. 'So great,' he said. 'You're so great at swimming.'

'Come out now, please,' said Hana. 'Have a kai. We shouldn't be much longer.'

It made Van's mind return to the journey ahead. One more camp before the break inland, then the uphill trek to the saddle camp, where they should meet their first Donovans. According to Rerū's intelligence, the saddle was a kind of perimeter camp, guarding the highest border of the Inlanders' settlement.

But instead of coming out of the water, Kahu sought out Van's attention again. 'Van,' she said. 'Vannie, watch this.' She was on the far side of the pool now, with her back to him, but she watched over her shoulder until she was sure of his attention.

223

Then she bobbed on the spot, held her nose, and ducked backwards into the pool, rolling the opposite way, coming up to stand in shoulder-depth water with her back to him again.

'Did you see it?'

'I did,' he said. 'That was amazing.'

She smiled. 'Do you dare me to do another one?'

'Āe! I can't believe you can do it.'

She got in position and ducked backwards again. Just before she emerged, Van caught Hana watching him.

'What?' he said.

She shook her head. 'Nothing.' She'd hidden her face, as if focused on the food in front of her, but he could see that she was smiling.

Kahu came up from the water. 'E Van, did you see it?'

'I did,' he said. 'It was brilliant.'

The valley narrowed and their track came to a fork beneath bluffs. They were near the most southern point of the valley, and were faced with a choice. They could either head up alongside the bluff and then further up the steep flank, or continue down-valley till it got narrower and ended completely at the steep slopes that marked the end of the Scarp's territories. Van again had the sense of being watched, and convinced Hana to take the detour uphill, at least to scan out for risks.

He went up first, Hana and Kahu talking as they came along behind. It seemed those creek waters or her growing fatigue had brought Kahu's grief and fear back. Walking ahead of them, Van could hear it in her voice. But Hana's reassurance went back in another tone. Almost without stopping to let Kahu talk, she spoke of their lately dead Nan and that old woman's faith in them all, how she'd known that telling Hana to fetch Van and take him on this trip would be fruitful, and how that old woman had also known that Kahu herself would be brave when it came to the test, just like all the people of the settlement would be, trusting in the thorough heke plans they'd all made for just such an emergency as this. Her Nan and all those wise ones had thought of all this and prepared for it, so the younger ones didn't have to. 'Me haere tonu,' she said. 'That's all we have to do. Just keep going.'

It wasn't clear to Van how Hana did it. How she summoned from somewhere this enormous faith, or the appearance of it at least. For his own part, he still roved the track ahead, searching its points of safety and ambush, all the while going over that river of ancestors' names he needed to remember. It was the coming pēpi, he supposed, that made her that way. And the presence of Kahu herself. Hana had such faith that their journey would be successful, because it simply had to be. It was the only option left.

Cresting the bluff first, he looked out, and again caught a movement of shadow in the bush, a flutter of kawakawa leaves that went still under his focus.

'Have you seen any sign?' said Van. 'Anyone following us?'

'Kāo,' said Hana.

Kahu's eye darted to the trees, and immediately he regretted it. She was always more alert to risk than Hana, on the surface at least, and he shouldn't have added to her tension.

'Me neither. I'm just checking.'

Hana put her hand on the girl's arm. 'It's all right. We're safer here. Raka's camp's just opposite.' She indicated the valley's opposite flank, where Van had seen only fists of kohekohe forest. But then he began to make out huts amongst those trees, and a pathway leading down from the ridge and into the canopy. That camp was the home place of the Scarp,

225

Raka's people who preyed on all who travelled on the Dry Way or worked in its shadow. Yet now it looked to Van like the settlement of a different people. A people who revered trees above all else, who wouldn't cut them down even to make space for their own huts. They looked fat with wealth, those trees, protected by the possum-killing work that the Scarpers' trade on the Dry Way paid for. These were the fecund back-slopes of the Scarp that Way-travellers and people of the swamp never saw.

'Why haven't they confronted us, at least?' he said. 'Raka's people. If we're in their wider territory, why don't they approach us?'

'I don't think they will,' said Hana. 'We have our own purpose of trade. That's obvious—they will have seen that, and they'll know they can leave us alone.'

Kahu looked at her mother. It seemed she was learning this at the same time as Van.

'And they won't let anyone else attack us either. Not in their place.'

'So we're actually safer here than before?' said Van.

'Āe.'

He tried not to show it, but he still couldn't get this alignment of the Whaeas and the Scarp to sit right in his head. It was a blurring of a relationship that, from the swamp, had seemed so stark, so hostile. 'So if you have trade with the Scarpers, and connections and all that, why was Squat so horrible to both of us?' He indicated Kahu and himself. 'When we came across the Way?'

Hana rubbed Kahu's arm once more, as if to soothe her in a trauma that had already passed. 'Because the Way is a different matter. That's where they make their trade and wealth. There are no friends on the Way. And I've heard they put their most feral people out there. It freaks the travellers, and ensures they pay.' She lifted her shoulders. 'And that's the system, I guess. The world we live in.'

'Huh,' he said, acknowledging the complicit tone. He couldn't claim to be above it, that trade in Wayside misery, its brutal taxing of travellers and their starving families on foot, all of them plodding south and sustained only by a hope of sanctuary at last, somewhere beyond the Straits in the south.

A lone blackbacked gull came over the escarpment, drifting inland on some unknown purpose. It sparked a further question, which Van couldn't stop this time—although he paused to formulate it in their language. He'd been trying to use their words when he could. 'Kei hea a Ru?'

Instinctively, both Hana and Kahu looked up, tracing the sky for their pet, and he regretted asking. It visibly troubled Kahu to look towards the sky above the Whaeas' place, right now under threat of burning. Then she faced the ground and pulled at a plait that secured one of her bags.

'Kia kaha, Bub,' said Hana. 'One step at a time.'

She nodded, still pulling at the plait-strap on her bag. He'd noticed it worked loose when she walked. Often she hitched the bag off her hip and pulled the strap tight, and sometimes simply walked with the loosened strap clamped in place in her fist. It was annoying for her, but would be easy for him to repair. He should fix it tonight with one of the plastic needles he'd brought, and stitch the strap in place with a length of plait or even, if she'd let him, a strip of knotting plastic. It would be a chance to show her the value of his work and the plastic the Whaea people apparently all distrusted.

'Ru's gone,' said Hana.

'Where?'

'That man you fought with.'

227

'Gray.'

'Āe. Gray. He spooked Ru. When you two had your fight, and there was all that shouting, it scared him, so he flew back home. He always does it, when that sort of thing happens.'

'So will he find us again?'

'Kāo.'

Van wasn't disappointed, but this was another thing that didn't make sense. 'But if he's supposed to be our peace signal, how does that work? If he just flies straight home as soon as he's scared.'

'Well, they always get spooked at some point, and then they fly back.' She waved. 'Don't try to understand it, Van. It's just how our kākā system works. It might not make sense to you, but it does to us.'

Van saw Kahu glance away, her increasing heaviness, and he decided to leave it.

'So we could break inland here, right?' He searched the broken bush above the bluff. It didn't look promising. 'Actually, maybe we'll find a better trail further south. How about we go back downhill and head south for a time and then camp for the night, and then go inland from there tomorrow. And if it turns out we can't find a better route inland, we can easily come back here and follow this one.'

They both looked at Kahu.

She lifted her head, and nodded.

Hana pulled her in against her. 'Kia māia, Bub. At least we'll have Raka's eye tonight, watching us. Scarp protection. We can relax a bit.'

Kahu looked across there. The thought of the Scarp's attentions didn't seem to offer her much comfort.

Van decided to try to appear decisive. He hitched his bags and went straight towards the downhill track. 'I'll take the front again.'

After a time, he let Hana come alongside, so he could talk to her with less risk of being overheard. 'So if you have this agreement with Raka and the Scarp, won't they help you—help us—with this problem you're having with the Burners? Can't they shelter you, if Bolt and them really do burn your settlement?'

Hana motioned him to keep moving, to keep their momentum up. 'I don't think they'll want to be seen to help. Some people say they've made a trade with the People in Smoke. I don't know this for sure—it's only a rumour—but apparently they've agreed to let the People in Smoke take our place and lake, and in return the People in Smoke will allow them to keep control of the Dry Way, and that whole trade.'

'So they've sold you out.'

They came to a steeper downslope, and Kahu caught up with them.

'That's what I've heard,' said Hana. 'But I don't know it for certain. I don't talk to the Scarp. That trade happens much higher up than anything I'm involved with. But the talk is that they made a trade like that.'

'But *we* had a trade,' said Kahu. 'We traded with the People in Smoke. And they fucked us, just the same.'

'Hey!'

'Well, come on, Māmā. It's true. You said it yourself. They can't be trusted, and there's no guarantee they won't fuck over the Scarp too, even if they've traded with them.'

'Āe, that's true. But I still don't like you talking like that.'

Kahu's laugh was derisive. It seemed she'd seen through all the bullshit, not just the betrayal of the people from the island.

'But if you're right, Bub, and if it turns out that the People in Smoke do the same thing to the Scarp—if they break that agreement too—then that will be the Scarpers' own bad luck, won't it.'

'But then the Scarpers will just come inland too. They'll follow us, and kick us out of our new place. That's obvious.'

'I don't think so, Bub, to be honest. They don't have the waters. Not like Van has. And Raka's proud too, don't forget. If they break his agreement, then he'll get angry, and he'll fight. You know what the Scarp are like. They'll fight till their riches are all gone, till their kids plead with them to stop.'

Kahu said nothing to this.

'And then, even if the People in Smoke do win that fight, and if they burn Raka out successfully, there's no guarantee the Scarp will come to our new place inland. There are other places to go to. But if they do, we'll face that problem then. We'll make a new trade, because we'll be strong again by then. Because we take the forest with us, in our hearts, and it will be growing up again in our new place, rushing up.'

Van went down a knotty fall of track, tangled with tree roots. He turned to see if either of them wanted a hand for balance.

Hana grunted as she came down but didn't take his hand. Even with her footing so insecure, she spoke over her shoulder to Kahu instead. 'And you'll have a new sister or brother by then. The new pēpi we're bringing with us. Think of that.'

It hit Van differently every time, that thought, but always with force. The new child, the family taking shape around him.

'Can you imagine, Kahu?' said Hana. 'I bet this pēpi will be a right tangiweto, just like her pāpā here. I bet she'll cry so loud that no one will ever come to visit us because of the noise. We'll be safe from visits because of her crying, and from attacks too, for, like, three summers in a row.' She grinned at Van. 'All thanks to you, Mr Swamp.'

Kahu didn't laugh, but Hana chattered on, sometimes in

her own language and sometimes in Van's. Sending it along their line again, her faith in them, in what they'd find ahead propelling them all forward.

Fourteen

Their luck held. None of them was sick; none of the bites they'd suffered had flared up. They'd reached the valley's southernmost point without being confronted, although Van was still dogged by the sense of being watched, and at one point was convinced he'd seen a human shape ducking into undergrowth. He crashed off the track and swiped at the plants, where he was sure the spy had hidden themselves, determined to uncover them at last. But all he got for his efforts was a mash of leaf juice on his blade, and a glare of rebuke from Hana for spooking Kahu.

The river curled inland and went up. Immediately there was a change of atmosphere, cooler and more damp as the bush thickened and the gully closed the sun off. Then the upward hike levelled and they came into another stand of mamaku.

'This is a good camping place,' said Hana.

Van hesitated. Something felt wrong about it. The fronds formed a good cover overhead, but it was a lightweight place to shelter. If a storm blew up they'd be in trouble. And still Van felt they were being watched. 'I'd feel safer if there was a bank at least, or some proper trunks. Thicker bush.'

'Kahu,' said Hana. 'Me noho nei tātou?'

Kahu had gone further up. She looked back down at them

both, as if trying to gauge from Hana her level of commitment to this place. 'We're still in Raka's rohe, right?'

'Āe. Which makes it safe. Plus we'll keep watch.'

Kahu didn't reply. She went up a little further and scouted to the left. After a moment, she came back and pointed. 'There's a better spot up here.'

A giant tree had come down in a storm. The roots torn up by its fall had left a crater with dirt walls that would be good to camp against. Van went down into it and surveyed the ambush points. He still felt exposed, but less so. He dithered a moment more, looking for the best position, but then saw how Kahu's shoulders sagged. She needed her bags off, food in front of her and a skin shelter over her head.

'He pai tēnei wāhi,' he said. 'Good work. Let's set up.' Coming up out of the crater, he went to Hana and turned her, pointing up the gully and inland, through the gap in the canopy the tree had made when it fell. Up there was the saddle, where the Inland people—the Donovans—had a sentry camp. If Rerū's scouts were right, a heavy guard protected this border. 'Why haven't they hailed us yet? The Inland folk. I thought they'd have scouts. We're getting pretty close.'

'Maybe they've seen us and are keeping their distance. Just making their reports for now, since we probably look harmless enough.'

Van frowned. Perhaps it was these people—his whanaunga—who'd been trailing him and Hana and Kahu, always ducking just out of sight when he sensed their presence.

'Kahu.' Hana made that same signal, which Van could still barely detect, for karakia. 'Tukua te karakia, Bub.'

Wordlessly Kahu went back uphill in search of a suitable tree trunk. It pierced Van to watch her kneel before it, her elbow bent in the Whaea salute. She was deeply tired but still devout.

233

'Van, don't watch her, please,' said Hana. 'She still gets a bit whakamā about it.'

'Aroha mai.'

He went down into the crater of their camp and rolled out the shelter. Laid the skins and plaits in place. Knocked in the pegs. As he focused on these simple tasks his mind filled again with the ancestral names he was trying to get to stick. He said them under his breath as he worked, and got right to the end without a mistake. He ran through it again without stopping, still under his breath. Thrilled at his success, he understood why they called it a river of names, when it came out in a stream like that. But then he ran down the names again and forgot one, and had to trace back, and lost the easy rhythm he needed to remember it.

He pulled out a plait and staked it till the skins of the shelter shuddered and came tight. He'd have to add some other names into these waters. Not only his whāngai waters and their joining with the Ngaheres', as far as he'd been taught those, but also Kahu's. And the unborn pēpi's, perhaps, his own new flow into the Whaea people, into their famous trades in clothes and skins, traps and meat, and the all-around richness that was said to make them more successful at having kids and raising them to full height.

'Anei,' he would tell those Inland people in his speech. He'd indicate Kahu, who in his imagining was sitting close by. Perhaps he'd even gesture towards the coming pēpi inside Hana, if it seemed safe to do that. 'You should make this trade,' he would say. 'It will bring you numbers. It will bring you this happiness.'

A still night without breath. The only sound a late bird that ghosted the trees, making some territorial point. The head of their shelter was against the base of the fallen tree, the twined bank of roots and dirt forming the wall on Hana's side. Kahu had again insisted on sleeping in her own shelter, pitching it up and out of the crater and ten paces directly down the slope, protected by an intact branch of the same tree.

It worried Van that she would be camping so separately, but over their kai he'd decided not to protest. Kahu was too tired even to eat much. She hunched over it, her mind somewhere else.

They all took turns with the washing water, Van walking well downhill before he partly stripped and washed his returning beard and armpits and crotch. He wondered if sex might be a possibility that night, and looked about with absurd worry someone might have heard that thought. Then he gave his crotch an extra sluice with water just in case.

Now he lay back on the blankets. Given they were in safer territory, they'd decided he could rest a short time before taking the first watch. It felt very good to lie flat on his back.

'Ngā mihi,' said Hana. 'For all your help today.' She was fussing with her bags, rolling things up and repacking them, pulling other things out.

'Will Kahu be all right down there?'

'I don't think so, to be honest,' she said. 'I think she'll end up with us tonight at some point, or I'll end up in her shelter.'

'Huh.' He looked into the gathering dark. The moon hadn't come up yet. That was one thing that had helped them, on this trip—the autumn moon, always so miraculously bright. If it came up strong again it would make his watch easier tonight. Autumn always brought the last decent moon before the calm weather ran out and the awful times started. He prayed their journey would be finished before the winter storms hit in earnest. The season of shrieking winds and downpours and floods, of water sluicing through the roof, Van reaching up to lash and re-lash the thatch of his battered hut and, each morning, building up the mini-dam round his fresh water source to guard it against rising seep, sometimes barely finding time to dry his patching-fire fuel, let alone tackle any plastics work. Strange to think that this time he probably wouldn't be there for that. He felt sleep pulling at him, and fought up from it. 'I should go to keep watch.'

Abruptly Hana kissed him. Her hand went round his neck, pulling him further in.

'Is this a good idea?' he said. 'Won't Kahu be coming back soon?'

'Kāo.'

He eased back from her. 'But you just said she wouldn't sleep.'

'She'll sleep for a bit,' Hana said, 'because she's exhausted. Then she'll wake up, and if she's going to have trouble tonight, that'll be when it happens. She'll try not to need us, because her training tells her she's got to tough it out, but she won't be able to get back to sleep, and we'll have to give her a hug at least.' She rubbed her face. 'I'm not being mean; that's just how it always happens for Kahu. She's always done that, when she's upset. Poor little Bub.'

'I see.'

'So that's why we've got to use this little time while we've got it.'

'Right.'

'Trust me, Van. You have to learn to take your chances to be private.'

It wasn't an absolute guarantee that Kahu wouldn't hear them, but for Van it was enough. He was pleased to stop thinking about it. He pulled Hana close again and they kissed with more intent. She had sweetened her mouth with some herb or flower water, and he savoured it. Then he pulled her hair by mistake, his hand catching in one of the colours she still had worked into it. There was so much hair—in the small space there seemed far more of it than before, and when he pushed her back down he had to smooth it away from his own face.

He turned over and hit the roof of the skin shelter and winced at the noise that juddered through it. Then Hana's elbow also struck the earth wall beside her, dislodging clods.

'Sorry,' he said. 'I should have put the shelter somewhere else.'

'No, it's great. It will make for a good story for the aunties, won't it, when we tell them.' Sensing his shock, she shoved him. 'It's a joke.'

He moved from kissing her mouth to her cheekbone and neck and shoulder, then the base of her throat and down the line of body painting, just visible by the leaking moonlight, that went down between her breasts. Kissed her breasts as well. She made a sound and twitched.

Then he worked lower until he hesitated, and abruptly she turned him onto his back. Went straight to his gut and kissed across to his hip bone, its hard rising ridge. A shiver went over his whole body as her hair tickled his gut.

Then she lifted her head. 'I can hear your heart. It's loud.'

He tried to laugh, but his throat was thick.

She kissed again along his gut, making it buckle and go taut. Her lips went lower on him. She kissed along his erection, and then she took it in her mouth. He gasped. It had been a long time since anyone had done this to him. It made him shiver, and shudder all over, at how good it felt.

He was still a long way from leaving their shelter for his watch when he heard something outside, and froze. The noise came again, and he reached across the bed for his blade.

But Hana put a hand on him. 'Shh.'

He heard the sound again, right outside.

Hana waited another moment, then propped up from the blankets. 'Bub?'

'Māmā.'

Van searched for his coat, pulling it round himself.

'He aha te raru, Bub?'

When Kahu's voice came again, it sounded terribly young. 'Where do you think Ru is?'

Hana sighed. 'Kei te ngahere, Bub. Kua hoki ia.'

There was another silence. 'I feel horrible.'

Van wrenched his coat back into place; tried to make himself look less sexed-up. Then he crawled down the shelter and pulled away the blanket he'd hung as a door flap. Lit by the moon behind her, Kahu was a silhouette.

'Kuhu mai,' he said.

The girl just knelt there. She seemed unwilling to come in, but also unable to go back to her own shelter. 'Māmā.'

Hana sat up, holding the covers over her chest.

'There are possums out here. It's horrible. I can't sleep.'

'Kuhu mai,' said Van again, waving her in. 'Come in here with Hana. I've got to go out for the watch, anyway.'

If Kahu had noticed that Hana's clothes were missing, or if she'd sensed the after-atmosphere of sex, she didn't say anything. Another of her tactful silences, Van thought. The poor kid had been forced into a few of those lately.

Hana had her coat on at last. She eased across and patted a space beside her. 'You can probably wait a bit, Van, before you go out,' she said. 'How about you just wait until Kahu and I have

238

gone to sleep. That would make us both feel better, eh, Bub?'

Van hovered still, unsure, but then Kahu went straight to her mother's side and lay down, curling towards Hana's shape.

He lay back down, and worked himself right up against the wall of the shelter to give them room. His back was exposed to the breeze now, but both Kahu and Hana were quiet, and soon there was the sound of Kahu sleeping, with the occasional twitch and whimper as something disturbed her. Out there in the night the possum that must have disturbed Kahu, but he—too preoccupied with sex—hadn't heard, renewed its rasp and cough. He would make a temporary trap for it when he went out for his watch, and have it gone before dawn, before anyone of the area noticed a new trap and took offence.

Hana's breathing lengthened into sleep. Just a little while longer, he thought, still lying there. Then Hana jerked violently, thrown from sleep by something.

'Māmā,' said Kahu, barely waking up to protest.

'Aroha mai, Bub.' She rolled over and reached an arm right across Kahu to Van, gripping his shoulder. 'Pōmārie, whānau.'

They settled back into rest and Van lay there, listening to them both. He worked the blanket over his back and got warm and felt himself slip towards sleep and fought it. Staring into the dark, he was grateful for whatever it was that had protected them so far. If tonight it was the presence of the Scarp that allowed them to camp safely, he was glad to be drawing help from that source for once. Drowsy, he listened to the sounds of his family's slumber, and to the possum and ruru that continued to call out there, still sounding the night for mates or dangers.

Fifteen

There should have been scouts, surely. A guard at least. Someone must have seen them by now. They should have been challenged—Van, Hana and Kahu, crouching in undergrowth, within shouting distance of the front fence of the saddle camp. Yet no one had called out to them, or come down with weapons drawn.

It made him uneasy, this lack of security.

As they'd walked up to this camp, Van had felt that same haunting sense of being trailed. But the only human sign all morning had been a taint of smoke on the air, its source untraceable, perhaps the ghost of a cooking fire drifting up from down in the valley.

Now only fifteen paces of uphill rock separated them from the fence. It would be a hard scramble up that rock and stone, and they would be very exposed to attack. Maybe it was this gauntlet that made the Inlanders complacent. Anyone attacking the saddle camp would have to run up this hill of rock, and would be easy to cut down.

Hana was beside him, under cover of taupata. Kahu was further along, scanning the slope and the fence.

'What do you make of it?'

'I can't work it out. That gate's open.'

He followed her eyes along the fence of trunks and lashed branches. The gate was ajar and plaits trailed from it, the gap just wide enough for one person to flit through.

'A trap,' he said.

Kahu came towards them, crawling to keep under cover. 'I don't like this. I could scout round the back. I could see if anyone's waiting there, for ambush.'

'Kāo,' said Van. 'I don't want you splitting off from us.'

Kahu frowned, but then he saw she was looking beyond him. She'd caught it too, that same taint of smoke—a more substantial scrap of brown this time, high away to the north and drifting.

He focused again on the fence and the strange quiet of the camp behind it. The only sound the cicadas that sawed in the trunks, then a pair of tūī that swooped overhead and scolded. The camp itself was perfectly sited for sentry work. It straddled the saddle and commanded a view back towards the north, and of the back slopes of the Scarp opposite, yet it had been difficult to detect from below.

'Right,' said Van. 'I think we're just going to have to risk it.' He started taking his bags off. 'I'll run straight up there. If it turns out to be an ambush, here's the plan: I shout as loud as I can while I fight them, and you both run like shit.'

'We should go together,' said Hana.

'No,' said Van. 'The pēpi. And if I get taken, you and Kahu can help each other. This is best.'

Hana eyed the camp once more, as if giving the people in there a last chance to call out a welcome. 'All right.'

Van brought out his blade and readied himself, then squeezed Hana's hand. He crept right to the edge of the cover. He paused there for a few more breaths, getting ready for the assault. Then he darted out. Ran a few steps and hit the steeper

241

part. Fell to his knee and cursed, and got up and climbed again. For what felt like a long moment, he was exposed on the uphill scramble of rock. At last he reached the lashed poles and trunks of the fence, and crouched, getting his breath back. Tried to see Hana and Kahu back down the slope, and was pleased to see he couldn't; they were obscured in the taupata's gloss.

He crept along the fence to the gate's edge. After a pause, he poked his head around. Inside, no one showed. A dead campfire in the middle of the camp; a hut at the rear, its window-flaps down.

He pulled his head back, listening for sounds on the other side of the fence: the creep of feet, the shing of a blade being drawn.

Nothing.

He counted five more breaths. Then he stood and sprinted through the gate. Wheeled around with his blade out for fighters. There were none yet. Two buildings were visible: a small hut at ground level and a building up high on stilts, wide and facing the valley. He ran to the hut on the ground and punched the flap open with his free hand, then lunged after it with his blade poised. He blinked, circling on the spot while his eyes adjusted. Empty.

He ran back out and to the foot of the building on stilts. There was someone up there, or something; he felt it. 'Hey,' he said, squinting up. 'Traders down here. Show yourself.'

No voice up there, no movement.

'He whanaunga tēnei. Family. Show your face.'

Nothing.

He put a hand on the ladder's first rung. He'd gone up five of the lashed timber rungs when the queasy sick came in his guts. His fear of heights. He swayed a moment, holding on to the ladder. Then he swallowed his nausea and forced himself upwards, even surer now that a rag boot would come down on his head when he reached the top. Absurdly, he found himself repeating the river of names—Jacky Donovan, Mere, Artie—as if he would shout them as he entered the high hut and was then beaten and thrown back out by whoever was hiding there.

His foot slipped a short way, and he retched and put a hand on his mouth, forcing it down. Clinging one-handed to the ladder, he felt the drop pull at his back. There were only two rungs left.

'Hey,' he said, to whoever was in the hut. 'I'm coming up now. Be peaceful.'

No reply.

He breathed deep and climbed the remaining steps, and hauled himself in by the elbows. Again he was wrapped in dark. But no foot crashed down on him. The room was empty. A wide bench spanned the far wall beneath two windows. He strode across to it and felt underneath for hiding people, for weapons. Then he pulled up a corner of the window flap. Sunlight blared in and he blinked but could see for sure now that no one was hiding. Stools sat before the bench, positioned for people to look out the window. The bench-wood was greasy, as if many elbows had been supported there. A watching place. He found the dangling plaits of the window flap and yanked them up. A wide windowsill, angled to cast rainwater outside. Two rough branches bisected the empty window. Once he'd rolled up the flap he knotted the plaits tight.

'Oh, fuck.'

The window looked out onto the whole valley. From this elevation he could see the Whaea territory. There was smoke there. Not at the settlement but at its perimeter. Five points of fire showed at the front fence, pushing smoke high, plus more around the sides and a larger, more voluminous pouring of smoke at the rear. He dashed to the other flap and rolled it, his hands clumsy with rushing. The flap flopped free of his grip and he shoved it up, and knotted the plait on itself. The pouring smoke seemed to have grown in size even in that short time. It bunched and boiled, dominating the sky.

The Whaeas were under attack.

They were burning.

A clatter of stones came from below. He went to the door and peered down. Hana was at the campfire, toeing the dead stones. She'd not followed the plan to wait for his all-clear. Not that it mattered now. He saw at once that she hadn't seen the attack, the smoke.

'Hana,' he said.

She squinted up. 'This cooking fire's been dead for ages,' she said. 'They've abandoned this camp, I think.'

His voice stuck in his throat.

Kahu called from the gate. 'Clear back here.' She had her metal blade out, the one she'd shown him on the first night of the fetch. 'I've run the fence. There's no sign of fresh track. The gate at the back is open as well. It looks like they've retreated for some reason.' Her small face looked up towards him, expecting his report from the high hut.

'Please guard the gate,' he said.

She stared. 'I've been round already. I just told you that.'

'Hana,' he said. 'Up here.'

'Is there someone there?' said Hana.

'Just come up.' Unable to face them, he turned back inside.

The logs of the hut creaked as Hana came up, still talking. She put her elbows into the room, and pulled herself in.

'I'm sorry,' he said.

She stood up and looked through the window. Her mouth fell open. She went towards the window with her hand out, as if to understand it that way, or to stop it from happening. The smoke had thickened further, and the whole Whaea hill and much of the back territories were obscured by it. He couldn't see the lake. He pictured people running to that vast pool, dragging their children and old ones in, submerging them to their nostrils.

One hand was over her mouth. She put her other hand on the bench to support her. She made a sick-sounding groan. He got a stool and brought it behind her. She slumped, and he stood uselessly beside her. Laid a hand on her shoulder.

'Tīkina a Kahu,' she said.

He poked his head out the door. Kahu was down at the gate, still guarding it well. 'Kahurangi. Come up here, please.'

She squinted up. 'What's wrong?'

A heaviness crushed down on him. He couldn't protect her from what she was about to find out. He couldn't take it away.

'Van, what's wrong?'

'Just come up here, please.'

She ran to the ladder. As she climbed she said, 'Is it Māmā? Is Māmā okay?'

'Just come up here.'

She was up it quickly, clambering in without his help.

He stood aside.

She stopped. She looked at the window, then at Hana, and at Van.

'I'm sorry,' he said.

She cried out. She went to Hana, and sank beside her.

He turned away, unable to bear it. From the door he looked at the empty sentry camp below him. There were no people down there. The Inlanders—the Donovans. His so-called people. They'd all gone. There would be no help here.

He went back down the ladder and gathered their bags and water. Dumped them at the base of the ladder. Started up again, taking a water bag so that Hana and Kahu could drink. He barely noticed the twisting in his gut this time as he went up.

Hana and Kahu were alongside each other, both supported by the bench. At the sound of his footsteps, Hana turned. Her face was wet with tears and snot.

'I'm so sorry,' he said.

'It's one thing to hear them say what they're going to do, but it's another to . . .' She shook her head, and turned away from him.

Kahu was still facing it. Hana put her arm over her.

Van put the water bag on the bench. He thought of the workers' huts that he and Rau had walked through on the flats of the Whaea forest, with the rows of drying harakeke and skins out the front. The roofs of dried thatch. How fast the fire would rip through them, leaping from roof to roof. He couldn't imagine how the people could get away in time. He was on the brink of suggesting they should go back. They could help the lucky ones who'd got out. They could guide them to their first escape camp, and down that horrid cliff and to the creek where he'd smashed Gray's wrist. But Hana wouldn't want him to suggest that, he was sure. Even now, she'd be against going back.

Hana still held her daughter tight against her side. At last she lifted her head and sat up. Cleared her nose of snot. 'They've already left, don't forget. They've had two nights. It's two nights and almost two days since Tuku took our message back. They've had time to get out.'

Kahu tried to sit up on her own. She wiped her face.

'Eh, Van?' Hana's voice was still thick and wet. 'They'll be safe by now. They'll be safely out.'

He tried to speak but couldn't bear to look at Kahu. Instead he grabbed a stool and sat beside her. Pulled her in. She buried her face in his shoulder. His hand was on her headwrap; he felt her shaking. There was so little he could do to help her. He didn't really believe what Hana had said, but he pretended to.

'They'll be safe by now. Tuku took that message home. They'll be out already.' He kept Kahu's head buried against him, so she didn't have to see the smoke pouring up. He kept on talking. 'Like Hana says, the aunties have planned for an emergency like this. They have their heke plans, and they had plenty of warning to get out. They will have calmly followed their plans.' He kept talking like this, making it up as he went. At length he felt her shaking stop.

Then she pulled away. 'What about Ru? Māmā? What about Ru?'

Van could see that Hana wasn't able to answer. It was the childishness of her question, her out-of-proportion concern for the pet.

'He'll be fine,' said Van. 'He can fly away from fire. It's easier for him, with his wings and everything, eh. So kei te ora tonu ia.'

Perhaps convinced by this, perhaps just moving from the first part of her shock, Kahu nodded. She turned from the window and stared into the room.

Van offered water to her and then to Hana. Neither of them took it.

'We should go back,' said Kahu. 'Help them.'

Van looked at Hana, who just shook her head.

'I think we have to keep going, Kahu,' he said. 'Your aunties—your people have their heke plans. We have to trust them to follow those plans.'

Kahu said nothing.

'We can help them best by following our instructions. We have to find them a new place. Somewhere safe to come to.' He searched for the word. He'd learnt Hana's own word for sanctuary during their first night back in her room, that night of sex and laughter and late-night trade that now seemed so distant. 'He kāinga haumaru. We have to find them a kāinga haumaru. That's how we can help them best.'

For a long time there was only the sound of late morning outside, the background clatter of cicadas. He could smell smoke more strongly now; through the window behind Kahu it billowed hugely, dominating the sky. He saw too the shapes of birds that were in flight down the valley and out to the coast, fleeing the fire.

'Can we go, then, please,' said Kahu. 'I hate this place.'

Sixteen

Beyond the saddle camp was a broad path of trampled mud. It had been often walked by whoever guarded the camp going back to whatever home place lay beyond. The saddle camp itself had turned out to be a blind; there was a further saddle that had been hidden by the camp's rear fence. They'd have to drop down through trees and come up again, cresting a tight notch between peaks. Both Hana and Kahu were quiet, and Van took Kahu's usual place in the front, working to keep them all to a decent pace. He gave no thought to why the Inland people had gone; he focused only on moving his own group further along the track. He'd get Hana and Kahu to a safe camp that night, restore them with some rest, and decide from there.

He wasn't hungry himself, but before long he made them stop for food and a drink. 'We've got to keep our strength up,' he said.

Both looked blankly at him.

Without bringing her off the track, without sitting her down, Van dug into Hana's bags. He drew out wraps of dried meat and vegetables, his search through her bags shoving her about. Not protesting, she simply swayed with the movements.

'We can eat it standing up, to save time,' he said. 'But we've got to eat.'

Hana nodded but didn't speak.

Kahu also looked dazed. She took her food without interest, chewing as if barely aware of it.

Van swilled water and passed it round, then stowed it once more in Hana's bags. Again she was jerked about by his work but didn't resist it. 'All right,' he said. 'Haere tonu.'

They nodded but didn't otherwise move.

'Hey,' he said, still with his voice quiet. 'Perhaps we should say a karakia first. For the people, and for us.'

'He karakia?' said Hana, roused at last.

'Āe. For your folks.'

'Māu e tuku?'

'Kāo,' he said. 'I don't know your karakia yet.'

'Oh. Kei te pai.' Still dazed, she took his hand, and Kahu's in her left. When Kahu made to lift her spare hand in the Whaea sign, Hana shook her head and made her join hands with Van instead.

'E te Whaea,' said Hana.

Van's head was bowed, but a blackbird chattered in fright about something and he looked up. There might have been a movement there, the shadow of a man slipping through trunks. But he saw Kahu's face come up, following his gaze into the bush, so he dropped his eyes again.

'Manaakitia mai ō mātou whānau . . .'

It was a long karakia. Careful not to disturb Kahu, he eyed the trees as Hana's voice went on. This time he saw no moving shapes.

At last she finished and they all brought their heads up. Hana spoke to Kahu in her language, and rubbed her arm for comfort. Kahu didn't reply but nodded with more vigour, and hitched unconsciously at her bag. The movement made her look to Van; she'd forgotten he'd fixed it before they broke camp that morning, and she no longer needed to pull the loose strap tight.

'Ka pai,' he said. He hoisted his own bags, and led them back out into the track.

They crested the rear saddle at last and saw it. Before them was a long valley with steep sides and several clutches of huts with gardens and, along one side, a lake. Bordered with huts, the lake took up half of the valley's flat space. The Donovans' camp.

They watched it for a long time before anyone spoke.

'Karekau ngā tāngata,' said Kahu. 'Kei hea rātou?'

She was right. There was perhaps half the afternoon left, and there was no wind or rain or particular cold, yet no one was moving down there. No human shape took bowls or tools between huts. No one worked in the gardens that stretched from the flats into terraces on the left-hand slope.

'This isn't right,' said Kahu.

Van's eye followed the fence. It went high on both sides of the valley, running along a strip of cleared bush above the lake and right up to the ridge on the left. It came round low and out of sight beneath them.

'Māmā,' said Kahu. 'Are they dead?'

Van looked further inland, beyond the furthest reach of the settlement and its lake. There were long stretches of bush back there, more territories beyond the border of this fence. Many more places these people could have gone to. 'Kāo,' he said. 'I think they've retreated further inland.'

'How do you know that?'

He shrugged. 'That's just what it looks like.'

'I don't like it,' said Kahu. Her face was still streaked from

251

her grief at the saddle camp.

Hana's hand was on her belly, her expression uncertain too.

Van looked down there, into the valley, and tried not to feel desperate. Why couldn't this one thing have turned out right? Why couldn't his whanaunga be there; why couldn't they greet them and help? Both Hana and Kahu needed rest. They needed a safe place to give in to their fatigue and shock. And they had to know that the people who were following behind them, a few days back—burnt-out, evicted—would have somewhere to come to, and to camp.

He brought out his canister. It was his last bug oil, but he spread it liberally on his neck and wrists and face. The aroma of Matewai and her camp gave him back some strength.

'Come on,' he said. 'We're going to find out.'

The first huts they came to had their window mats rolled up. Van walked towards the nearest building, his hands open and weaponless, calling to it. 'Traders. Your whanaunga, coming in peace.'

Even as he drew close, the window-spaces of the hut remained dark, shadowed in the afternoon sunlight. Mānuka logs had been bound and stacked to make the walls; the roof was thatched. It was just like Van's own building back in the swamp, except for that low roof—when they'd built his hut, Van and Rau had deliberately searched out tall corner poles to accommodate the sudden height that had come on Van when nobody expected it, thanks to the boost in Dry Way traffic that saw Matewai's trade multiply, meaning that for a short time better meat and medicine plants had came into her camp, until the Scarp simply stepped up their Way-taxing work to match the increased traffic.

Now Van hailed the hut again. 'Anyone?'

He came to the window and peered in. A mud floor that had once been covered, the mats now taken away. A bare table of bound logs against the wall. No canisters or food scraps or signs of ongoing life.

Through the open door at the far side he could see the mud path beyond. There was a mound of waste there. He saw a pair of rats; as he watched, one of them put a pink paw up on a little hill of bones. He pulled back from the window and signalled Hana and Kahu to wait, then went round the front. There were further piles of food scraps outside other huts. The people must have thrown them out as they left. Vegetable skins and scraps, and bones that looked like possum and rabbit.

'Anyone?' he said. 'We're family. Your whanaunga.'

He went down one line of huts, then up another, weaving among waste heaped on the mud. One pathway had a stand of high ake ake growing right in the middle of it, as if to provide a supply of hardwood right inside the settlement. It suggested good weapons, a fighting group.

He scanned the fence and skyline once more, then went back to where Hana and Kahu waited. He waved at them to come forward. 'They've gone,' he said. 'There are rats.'

They stopped.

'In the huts?' said Hana.

'In the pathways. They've left scraps of food outside. They don't trap, it seems, and now they've left the camp and thrown scraps out, which has made it worse.'

Hana made a face.

'What's happened to the people?' said Kahu. 'Is it safe to be here? Māmā?'

Hana just looked to Van.

He scanned round the upper slopes. There were still no

253

human shapes up there. It wasn't an ambush. 'It looks like it's not been long since they left this place, but they've definitely cleared out. I think they've gone to some other camp.'

'Why would they do that?' said Kahu.

Van looked to Hana. 'Did Rerū say anything about another camp further inland?'

Hana just shrugged. She looked entirely defeated by this latest problem, and gazed vaguely about the huts, as if unable to give it any more thought.

Van's mind raced ahead, running through possibilities. Maybe it was to do with the Burners. Maybe the Donovans had been given warning about the burning attack on the Whaea settlement. Maybe they'd made some trade, like the Scarpers, and agreed to fall back from this camp to some other place inland, in return for something else. Maybe the Burners were coming here too. But he didn't speculate aloud. It wouldn't help. Hana looked too fatigued to walk back out of the camp, even though the mess disgusted her.

'We need to camp,' he said. 'Let's see if there's somewhere we can rest for the night.'

They walked the remainder of the settlement, skirting the lines of food waste and checking buildings. In the corner of one hut Van found a heap of old and shredded harakeke bags; when he toed it with his boot, a rat ran out and collided with the wall. Unable to burrow through, it turned and ran straight for the door, its underside flashing white.

Van shuddered. Then his eye caught on something as he turned to go out. The door pole. It had notches cut into it. A family: these were the height marks of a family who'd lived here. There were two marks up high for the parents, and two down very low, no higher than waist height. They'd been blessed with children.

254

But then he looked again. None of those notches advanced up the door post. They didn't progress above waist height. He looked again over the hut. There was only one place where the floor-mud was greased in a rectangle shape, suggesting a sleeping space. These people hadn't been blessed. They'd lost two children, at least.

He saw Hana through the window and went towards her. She walked with care through the piles of scraps, her mouth set in a tight line of distaste.

'How long since they left, do you think?' she said. 'It's disgusting, this mess.'

'I don't know,' he said. 'But Kahu's scouting further down. She thinks there might be a better spot—a cleaner spot—in that other clump of huts.'

She looked down there, doubt showing on her face.

'We should get more washing water from the lake,' he said. 'So we can have a good wash when we camp, and make it nice.' The place wasn't perfect, he told himself; anyone could see that. But they could make it work for the night.

They started towards the lake, but they'd gone only a few steps when Hana groaned. Her hand went to her face; she looked ill.

'What is it? Are you sick?'

She pointed beyond him. A rat nosed up from a pile of scraps. With a lump of gristle in its mouth, it ran straight into the nearest hut.

'Who lives like this?' said Hana.

Van sighed. 'I don't think they lived like this. I think they left it this way.'

'But why? Why would you make your own place all paru? I don't understand it.'

'Maybe so nobody else would take it.' As soon as he'd said

this, Van felt a new heaviness. This was surely the reason. Nothing else made sense. These people had dirtied their own camp in a bid to keep others out. 'We can leave again if you want to,' he said. 'But I think if Kahu finds somewhere good, we should stop here. Surely they won't mind us staying for one night, with everything that's going on, and especially if we're family and we're trying to find them anyway.'

Hana looked back towards the gate they'd come through, way back by the forest. He saw how distant it looked to her. She seemed defeated by her disgust of this place, but also exhausted by the idea of having to find somewhere else to camp.

'Come on,' he said, turning her. 'Let's just get some water, and set up a temporary camp. Somewhere nicer, but close. You guys need to rest.'

The shoreline next to the lake was muddy. It seemed many people used to wade into the water here. There was a wooden structure that went out into the lake. Its timbers were dark with the grease of many hands. It was made of cut-off trunks that had been pushed into the lakebed, each pole lashed across with branches that interlocked. The people must have walked into the lake on either side of this structure, he supposed, holding on to its timbers for balance when they washed or collected water to drink.

Hana knelt and uncorked a washing bag.

Further down, Van saw Kahu coming along the shoreline, finished with her scouting.

He looked across the lake's dark surface, the harakeke that lined the opposite shore. Across there, a lone pūkeko picked along the water's edge. Perhaps it was just the late afternoon light, but the water had a strange look to it. 'Where are their latrines?' he said. 'Have you seen their tūtae pits?'

Hana looked up. She'd been about to fill the washing bag. 'I saw a few latrine bowls in those huts, but I haven't seen their pits.'

He looked over the water again. 'Perhaps we should just use our own water,' he said. 'Until we know theirs is safe.'

Hana stood up. She held the water bag away from her, even though she hadn't submerged it. Only the very tip had got wet, that part of the possum hide darker brown than the rest.

Kahu was within earshot now. She held up a pair of ancient pots. They were metal, and looked as battered and patched as the most aged in Matewai's camp. 'I found these in a better hut. A cleaner one. It's separate from the rest. We could camp there.'

Hana, her face twisted with disgust, thrust the water bag at Van's chest. Then she hurried towards Kahu. When she reached her, she turned her away from the suspect lake.

Van sighed, scanning again over the empty huts, the gardens above.

It could still work, he told himself. They still had enough bags of safe water: several in his own bag, and a couple in Hana's. They had some food left. They could camp safely tonight, and rest up, and in the morning they could start again.

Seventeen

It was after dinner that Hana said she felt sick. Sitting against the wall among her blankets, she held a hand against her mouth.

'You don't look too good,' said Van.

She looked doubtfully towards the fire he'd built, the pots he'd hung up to heat.

'Is it the pēpi?'

She shook her head. 'My puku's just a bit upset, I think. If you could please hurry up your work on that wai māori, I think that would help. A drink might settle it. I'll have some medicine too.'

Van pushed a further log onto the fire, and adjusted the pot above it. They'd decided to boil their drinking and washing water for the night, given Hana's doubts about the lake and camp and any remnant sick that might live in this hut. He looked up to check the smoke was mostly going up the battered metal chute that was wired into the roof, directing the smoke out a well-guarded hole in the thatch.

'Shouldn't be long now,' he said.

Hana was digging in her bags for the medicines she'd talked about. Kahu was quiet, lying on her own bed in the corner of the hut. Her eyes were on the fire but unfocused, the events of the day catching up with her.

'We'll all feel better for a drink of safe water,' he said. 'And a good sleep. An indoor sleep.'

Earlier, with both Kahu and Hana unhappy and worn out by the day, Van had taken charge of setting up their camp. First, he'd campaigned hard for them to camp in the better hut that Kahu had found, rather than outside in their own skin shelters. He'd checked inside for rats, and shown Hana how much cleaner it was than the huts they'd seen further back in the camp. No hills of waste or food scraps outside it—abandoned earlier than those other buildings, perhaps. Then he'd asked Hana to tuku karakia to make the hut safe and to make her more willing to enter and sleep in it. He'd built the fire up, and set the two pots to boiling, nominating one as the washing pot. He then had success in finding wooden mugs in a nearby hut, and sank them in the washing pot to boil clean. Then he rolled out all their shelter skins as sleeping mats, and laid their bed-things over top. In his mind as he worked was a hope that if Hana and Kahu could sleep just one night, they'd all regather some faith. In the morning they would find the inhabitants of this place, wherever they'd gone to, and make the trade perhaps the day after that.

Now the water began to bubble. With a length of stick he brought the drinking pot from the fire, and fished the mugs from the washing water and filled them with boiling drinking water.

Hana blew on her drink, winced, and set it beside her bed. 'It will probably be best if I just go to sleep.'

'I'll bank the fire for the night,' he said.

'Kua rite koe, e Bub? E moe.'

Van took another turn outside, checking for threats and signs of ambush. In this hut they would be obvious to anyone watching from the slopes. The fire he'd lit inside surely made

259

it worse, and Hana and Kahu weren't at all in a good state to repel an attack. But he felt ready, himself. He wouldn't mind a fight, in fact. Some kind of confrontation, at least. He was emboldened by his success in setting up in the hut, and part of him hoped his glaring camp would provoke them, flush out the Donovans from wherever they were. Surely at least a scout must have remained behind to watch their settlement. He wanted to talk to them, or deal with their attack. Learn the status of this place, and their chances of safely sharing some of it. Tomorrow, he thought. Tomorrow he would find those people.

Back inside, both Hana and Kahu were nearly asleep. He hung his coat across the door as a flap, and took up a sitting position against the wall opposite it.

'I'll take the first watch,' he said.

Hana murmured something indistinct.

'Pōmārie, whānau,' he said.

Hana's vomiting woke him up. By the firelight that remained he saw her turned away, leaning out of the bed towards the far wall. She lurched again, and the guttural noise of puke came out.

He went to her, into the sharp reek.

'Māmā?'

Van felt an immediate need to calm Kahu, to pretend nothing had happened. 'It's all right. Hana's just a bit sick. Go back to sleep.'

But Kahu stayed up on one elbow, and they both watched as Hana leaned to the wall again and was sick. She groaned and wiped her mouth, spat a few times, and finally flopped back.

'Māmā?'

Hana moaned.

'It's all right,' said Van. 'I'll just clean this up. You go back to sleep.'

Instead of lying back, Kahu sat up more, rubbing her face.

He went to the fire and lifted the washing pot to the side of the shelter skins that made her bed. The vomit ran in a riverbed shape down the wall and onto the bed's edge. He saw flecks of pumpkin skin in it. Hana was lying barely two handspans from it, curled away with her hands over her stomach.

'Hana, can you get up, just for a moment? I need to clean this.'

'Kāo.'

He knelt there and considered.

'Van, do you need help?' said Kahu.

'No, it's all right.' He knelt by the side of the bed. 'Hana, I'm going to pull the whole bed away from the wall so I can clean up.'

Hana just groaned.

He gripped the edge of the bed and pulled. It moved only a little.

Hana protested at the movement.

'Hang on.' He gripped the bed harder, and heaved. He got it well clear of the wall. He brought the washing pot close. He looked at the mess, and realised he needed something to wipe it with. He went to his coat where it hung over the door and sliced a section off with his blade. He dunked it in the water and began washing the puke off the wall. He rinsed it out and soon found the water was rank. He would boil more after the first wash. He wrung the rag out again and felt a fleck of something from Hana's sick glue to his forefinger; he wiped it on the hardened floor mud.

He had finished with the wall and bed, and was sponging the worst mess from the floor mud when Hana spoke.

'I have to go outside.' She lumbered up to an elbow.

Van put an arm round her back and under her armpit. She managed to stand up. They hobbled to the door and out. He went with her a few paces and then she pushed him off and, in a rush, got down to a squat.

'Don't look, Van. Go back.'

He turned away but heard first the blurting sound of her guts coming out.

He went back inside and to the water bags. There were three drinking bags, and three for washing. He placed the two piles far apart. He would keep these two piles separate. He wouldn't panic. He refilled his washing pot, built the fire up and set the pot to boil. Then he went to the door and, with his head turned away, spoke loud enough that Hana would hear it.

'Do you need help to get back?'

There was no sound from outside. Something made him look towards Kahu's bed. She was lying still with her eyes open, the blanket pulled right up to her chin. 'She'll be all right,' he said.

He stood up and went out. Hana was upright, one arm out for balance. Below the waist, part of her coat was ripped away.

'Don't look—please don't look.'

He turned away, but not before he saw the dull shape of torn-away coat she'd left on the ground beyond. He caught a whiff of watery shit, unhealthy shit.

'Get washing water,' she said.

'It's not boiled yet.'

'It doesn't matter. I can't wait.'

Hana had only just come back in and Van had again refilled the washing pot to boil and cut more rags from his coat when she needed to go outside again, he didn't know whether to puke or shit. He brought washing water to the door and left it there, busying himself with cleaning up inside.

After she was finished Hana called him outside. She was standing ten paces off, her hands over her guts. 'There's a koromiko mix in my bags. The smallest canister. Can you get it out?'

He went back inside the sick-smelling hut and dug in her medicine bag. While he worked there he was aware of Kahu's attention. She was wide awake and frightened; he knew that. He would get the koromiko mix to Hana and then he would look after her.

But then Kahu made a sound and he looked towards her. She was sitting up, her blanket around herself.

'What is it?'

'Is Māmā all right?'

'Yes. Go back to sleep.' Then, more gently, he said, 'Can you try to go back to sleep?'

'I can't,' she said. 'My puku hurts.'

There was still some time to pass before morning and already he'd used two of the remaining bags of water and dispensed many drops of the koromiko mix. Kahu had been sick and then Hana had been sick again, retching up very little but an acrid juice, and then Kahu had been sick and then she'd needed to go outside to shit. She had managed to not soil herself, partly because by now she was dressed only in a blanket and cast this aside while Van looked the other way, but afterwards she'd needed to wash her hands and herself, and he'd left the pot outside, and that was the last of another bag of water.

Once Kahu was back in bed and Hana also lying still, he went out and got firewood and built the fire up and thought about how he could ration the water. He had two bags left and both the pots had become washing pots—earlier in the night he'd made a mistake, rinsing a rag in the washing pot, so now neither could be used for drinking water, which in a way was all right because Hana and Kahu could bear only the smallest sip of water or brush of his finger with koromiko mix, enough to wet the lips and tongue and not much more, before they'd groan again and retch up a palmful of foul-smelling liquid, and then a fingerful, and then nothing but spit.

He would have to keep the last bag of drinking water separate, he decided. He would have to trust it was safe without boiling it, because there was nothing safe to boil it in. He would have to trust in those Whaea men at the stores, who Hana said had treated the water. He had some koromiko mix left, and some bug oil, but no other medicines. He'd given Matewai's to Gray in that trade that now seemed very stupid.

He decided to rest a moment and slumped against the door post and closed his eyes and drifted and heard Kahu's voice calling out. She called again, and he jerked awake.

'Māmā.'

Hana groaned.

Van wiped his mouth and creaked upright. 'Are you going to be sick?'

There was a long silence, as if Kahu was summoning the strength to speak. Perhaps, though, she was unwilling to say whatever it was to him. 'Māmā?'

'Not now, Bub, please. Talk to Van.'

Kahu sighed and lay back. After a time he began to think she had returned to sleep, but then she lifted her head. 'Do you think she is still up? The Whaea?'

Hana didn't answer.

Van went over to her bed and pitched his voice to be quiet. 'The Whaea? What about her?'

'Do you think she's still up?'

It was a moment before he understood what she meant. The statue. She was worried that it was no longer standing after that fire had raced over the forest and flats, reducing the trees and trades and huts and hanging colours to ash. He thought a moment more, deciding how he should answer. 'Āe. I think she is.'

'He aha ai? How can she be?'

'Because there are no trees around her. There's a good fifteen paces between her and those big kohekohe trees round the plateau. The fire can't have reached her.'

'But she is mostly wood, and tāna hoa is wood too.'

'Tāna hoa?'

'The tower round her, the ladders the fixers use. That's her husband. And he's made of wood.'

He pictured that latticework, the mêlée of shouting traders and pilgrims and singers that thronged beneath it, and Rau standing out at the edge, looking over the swamp. He saw Kahu's relatives huddling there from the flames, or climbing the statue to get away from the ferocity of that heat. But he told himself not to think like that. He had to think the right thoughts, the thoughts that would calm Kahu. Those people would have gone calmly down the correct evacuation route, which according to Hana led down to the bottom of the lake and then on round its far shore. Once there, the lake would have protected them from the fire and contained it.

Kahu was silent another long time, and then she said, 'She is burnt. You know it.'

Again, he thought carefully how to answer. 'Maybe. But remember the Whaea is not just in the statue. That's what I've learnt from Hana, and from you. The Whaea is in the forest too.'

265

Kahu said nothing.

'The Whaea is in the forest, and she is the forest, and the forest regrows. She regrows with it.'

There was a long silence after this, and again he thought she must be drifting noiselessly, breathlessly, off to sleep. But then he heard her guts work, a bubbling and bad sound, and she put her hands over it, and he realised she was pausing between each sentence to gauge the level of emergency in her guts. 'Do you believe in her?'

'Huh?'

'What you just said. Do you believe in it?'

Again he thought carefully before answering. 'My life has been different from yours. My people believe different—Matewai, Rau.'

'I know, but do you believe in her?'

'I know *you* do,' he said. 'You and Hana. I believe in your belief in her. And I believe in Rau's belief in his gods, and in Matewai's. I honour it.'

She was quiet.

'Does that make sense?'

She murmured something he couldn't catch.

'Anō?'

'Where do you think they all are? All our whānau. Our settlement.'

'I think they're all at that camp Hana talked about,' he said. 'At the river, the one we came to after that horrible track down the cliff you helped me walk down. But they will have taken a different route to get there. Not down the cliff but along the side of the lake. That's in their plan, isn't it, for their journey out of there.'

She seemed about to say something about that, but then her guts worked again. With great care she eased up on an elbow. 'I need to go to the wharepaku.'

He helped her towards the door. Her blanket began to work loose and she stood very still so he could re-secure it for her. Then he helped her on, and she made it outside before the worst of it.

In the morning they still hadn't come out of it. Surely, Van thought, Hana would have nothing left to vomit up, but still she retched and spat out a brownish taint. But despite this she pleaded with him to keep the pēpi wet, keep the pēpi wet, which meant he had to help her drink. So each time he washed his hands as best he could and brought her some tiny amount of water and she would swallow it, and then some time after convulse with a fresh bout of sick.

Kahu, meanwhile, had the shits. Three times in the night she'd been outside with that same clenched haste, and then once again when it was light. After the second trip Van took his blade and dug her a hole five paces from the hut, then returned with two sticks of firewood and dug them vertically into the mud with his coat tied between as a screen. He wanted to give her some privacy from whoever was up there on the slopes and watching and so cruelly not coming down to help. Not that Kahu cared; she went mutely forward and back, smelling of watery waste and looking in the daylight so shadowed and weak.

He had half a bag of drinking water left. He had run to the lake for washing water, and boiled it, and used it for cleaning up mess, without telling the others where it was from. But he would need fresh drinking water before long. He prayed the Inland people would come soon, so he could plead or fight for water with whoever arrived.

He'd burnt all the firewood he'd assembled, and then a pile of shredded mats from a nearby hut, and the straw and sticks that had once made a rats' nest inside it, and now that was all gone. Bleared with fatigue he trekked back to the main cluster of huts. The wind blew at him, and he was aware of the slopes about and he wanted to shout at the people up there, the tormentors he was certain were there but didn't help, who just watched what was happening instead. In the larger settlement there were only a few sticks here and there, no dedicated stacks. Most firewood had been taken with the departing residents, it seemed, or burnt up by them in readiness, perhaps knowing in advance the date when they were to evacuate the settlement. His mind rested on that thought for a time—the uncanny timing of the attack on the Whaea people and the recent abandonment of this camp; the fact they must have taken place at almost the same time—but he was too worn to think or care about it much.

Still seeking firewood, he turned his attention to the hut nearest theirs. He felt scraped raw with fatigue and cloaked in the smell of sick, and he lost his focus and spent a long time staring at the wall logs of the hut and the plaits that lashed it in place. Someone had taken care with those fixings. They'd greased the plaits and knotted them tight, then burnt the ends black so they wouldn't wick rain and bring moisture inside.

But they'd also fouled this camp. They hadn't trapped their pests, and their latrine pits weren't obvious and their lake was poisoned, and they'd abandoned their huts and not come to help, and somehow they'd made two faultless people sick. They'd brought so much risk—so much risk that he couldn't bear to think of it—to the pēpi that was supposed to be sleeping safe inside Hana. He lifted his face again to the high fence and the ridge and felt sure that somehow they saw him and knew what he suffered and yet didn't care if his family died, if they all died.

So he took out his big blade and sliced the plaits, from the lowest wall log all the way up to the thatch. When they were all cut, he took out his plastic bar and circled its vast ugliness and then aimed a great swipe at the hut. He bashed at the door post once, twice. It jarred his hand so he adjusted the way he hit the post, and then switched to kicking instead. On the third kick it cracked, took on extra weight, and then the whole hut sank towards him. He took fresh aim with his bar. Slow at first and then with gathering rage, he bashed the hut, then kicked it and bashed it again until it was all blown apart, this home of the people who'd been here, these people who'd been his own but were gone, who'd let this damage happen to his family and then so slyly left him all alone to deal with it.

Swearing at them, he took great swipes with his rag boot and bar.

At last the hut was all kicked and struck apart and his hot rage was the only thing left standing in it.

He was damp with sweat and panting. His foot hurt.

He bent to the firewood he'd made, and gathered an armload. Then he went slowly back, laden down with these bits of the hut he'd kicked to pieces.

As the day wore on and wind blew outside the hut and there was no sign of improvement, he tried not to give way to panic. He tried not to cry out, tried not to scare Kahu, but he couldn't help it, because it was too much. *Please. Help.* He blocked the sound with his hand, forcing the panic back down his throat, and returned then to his tasks of washing and dispensing drops of Hana's medicines, and helping Hana and Kahu to take

269

some water in tiny amounts, and keeping watch. He held to this routine for so long he lost track of what part of the day or night it was and sometimes even where he worked, murmuring aloud to himself in scraps of disconnected talk that made no sense.

Then Hana called him.

Automatically he got her mug and went to her, thinking he would have to wet the pēpi again with a further sip.

But she was still lying down. She faced the wall. When he tried to bring the water to her lip, she shook her head.

He had to bring his ear down close to her mouth to hear what she said.

'Kahu?' she said, switching to Van's language. 'How's Kahu?'

He looked across there, and tried to think of a way of answering her. Kahu had begun to shiver, her blanket rustling and moving like a mouse in the walls of a hut.

'It is very violent,' said Hana. 'This bug.'

Again he couldn't think of any response. He tried to swallow down his upset.

'You still haven't got it.'

It was a moment before he understood what she meant. He hadn't fallen sick.

'You can't get it.' Too weak to speak long, Hana had to pause between sentences. 'Because you've had it already. It's a bad-water sickness. It comes from bad water, which you're used to. So you're resistant.'

Van thought on this for a moment, but found no comfort in it. 'But it's so much worse than what we get. You can't drink. You should be able to drink by now, more than just a sip.'

There was a long pause.

At last Hana said, 'Is there any sign of them?'

'Who?'

'Their people—the Donovans. Or our people. Anyone.'

'Kāo.'

Hana was quiet again and it seemed she was sleeping, and he eased from his crouch to the wall and rested there and drifted in sleep and his head fell forward and he woke.

Hana was buckling against another tightening of her gut, and she tried to spit, but couldn't get it further out than the corner of her mouth. With a weak hand she made to wipe it off, but missed and flopped back on the bed.

Van crawled to her and held her head up in his palm, and with his sleeve he dried her face. As he lowered her again he saw that her eyes were wet. He put a finger to her cheekbone and she blinked and her eyes leaked faster. It went onto her temples and down over his hand. He knelt there and wiped her face.

'I'm scared for them, Van.' Her voice was choked with tears and snot, but she didn't try to sniff it back. 'I'm scared for both our kids.'

He couldn't say anything. He couldn't think of any bright thought.

'You can't get sick like this,' she said. 'When you have a pēpi inside, you can't get sick like this. It kills the . . . it doesn't . . . she can't.'

He couldn't stop the thought anymore. All the time he'd been washing and bringing water and cleaning up, he had pushed away this thought: the thought of the pēpi falling too sick, too far into the dark to bring back. But now he couldn't push it away. The baby's light would go out. And he couldn't push away either the flash of remembered standing that came, standing that time his parents fell into the dark, and he'd stood before their hut, burning them down as a boy, burning away their sick. Now he couldn't keep those thoughts out.

He sagged back and it all came at him. His eyes filled up.

'I'm so sorry,' he said. 'I can't make it stop. I've tried

everything and I can't make it stop.'

Hana didn't speak, or couldn't.

Kahu's shiver-sound clawed at him from the far corner of the hut.

'Van,' said Hana, at last. 'He karakia. Tukua.'

She moved her hand towards her buckled gut. With an effort she straightened out and lay back, and put both hands over her belly.

He wiped his nose, his eyes. 'I don't know any of yours.'

Her fingers moved on one hand. She was dismissing this. 'Anything.'

He closed his eyes. He put his hands over hers and tried to summon strength. He had nothing left. But he had to do something. He had to start. 'E te Whaea.'

He coughed, and wiped his eyes and his snot. With Hana's pained form under him, it was supremely hard to speak.

He tried again. 'E te Whaea.' He used the words of Hana's language that he could gather and could speak. He used what he'd heard. He spoke to the statue, and to the forest. He asked for her help. He ran out of things to say and went to one of Matewai's karakia instead, and gave part of a day-starting one that he remembered. Then he attempted again a kind of Whaea thing that was a patched and sorry piece of phrases he'd heard Kahu and Tuku and Hana put out.

'And, āe, tō tātou Whaea,' he said, 'please—please—bring down your help.'

He heard Hana's lips crack as she attempted to answer it.

Feeling her again beneath his hand, and her hooped-over shape, and thinking of the high fence outside, he was renewed with anger and spoke to the Whaea again in his own language. He pleaded and shouted. He told her to fucking hurry up, and to come down and help these two breathing survivors and the

272

tiny unharming baby in its human house. He also called on all his newly known ancestors for their help, and in his snot-drowning voice he gave those Donovan names he'd been taught by Hana and had practised and half-remembered, a river of names that came out.

When he was finally finished with this, the hut filled again with silence, except for the shiver-sound of Kahu in her corner.

Then Hana spoke. 'Ka pai,' she said. 'Tīkina he wai.'

He went for the water—they would try another sip—and then he saw that Kahu was standing. It seemed she'd wanted to go outside again to shit, but had got halfway and stopped. The blanket sagged from her body; her face looked strange, confused.

'Bub?' he said. 'Are you all right?'

She murmured, and went two more halting paces towards the door. Then she seemed to hear him and looked his way. Then the look of confusion slid off her face and she went blank.

Falling.

He leapt up as she pitched towards the door. He caught Kahu just before her head hit the door post. She lolled in his arms, and he swore, holding her dead weight.

He called her name, touching her face to bring her back.

Her eyes rolled.

'Kahu,' he said. 'Bub.'

Suddenly she returned. Her eyes came to focus, her legs took some of her own weight. She muttered something that didn't make sense, then drifted and seemed about to fall again, then she made another effort and pulled up. Her sight seemed to fix on him.

'Uh,' she said.

He was entirely holding her up. He thought it was important to smile. 'Steady now,' he said. 'You're all right.'

273

Roiled in her own bed, Hana was struggling to get herself upright.

'Hana, stay there,' he said.

Kahu's eyes followed the movements of his mouth. She looked very lost.

'Let's get you back to bed.' He turned her slowly, still holding her up.

He saw her gaze over there towards her bed. For her, it seemed, it was an impossibly long way off.

'Back to bed,' he said.

'Make medicine.'

'What?'

Kahu's voice had a strange sound to it, way off. 'Like Matewai's. From the bush. To fix us.'

He stared at her.

'Mahia,' she said. 'Ours don't work—our medicines.'

He hadn't thought of this. The mixes from Hana's medicine bag that he'd been giving Hana and Kahu hadn't worked, but perhaps the Whaea medicines weren't the right ones to fight this sickness with. It was a bad-water sickness. Something different was needed. Something like Matewai's, made by someone who lived in a bad-water place and was used to fighting it. Something like the oils he'd stupidly traded away to Gray. Still holding Kahu up, his mind raced. He could get ingredients. He could run to the bush.

'But I don't know the mixtures. I don't know how to cook up. I could poison you.'

The girl's head lolled again, and jerked. 'Uh,' she said.

Then Hana spoke. She'd dragged herself to the wall, and was lying back against it. She looked smashed by fatigue and sick. 'It can't be worse than this.'

He looked towards the fire, the place where he would have

274

to cook up. He wished he knew more about it, knew anything substantial of what Matewai did in her hut. If Ava had been with him, even Rau, he would have a better chance. His mind went to their Te Repo camp, to the crops that rustled around it. Kawakawa was there. It was important. Perhaps it was kawakawa leaves or root they needed, plus something else. He'd chewed kawakawa leaf at Te Repo, when Rau had first dragged him up from the orphan bog and taken him to Matewai's hut. He could fetch it for this new family of his. They could chew the leaves while he somehow worked out what else was needed in the mix. Maybe he could steep the root faster than usual. Perhaps he could boil it, if that was safe. If he got back quickly, Hana could help him with ideas from her bed. He'd have to return while she could still speak.

He took Kahu towards Hana's bed. They could huddle together, he decided. They would be safer that way. The girl's legs were a little stronger as he lowered her down by Hana, able to take more of her own weight.

He fetched some water. Kahu let him put the mug to her lip, but then shook her head. Hana took a small amount.

'I'm going to the gate—the bush by the gate. I saw kawakawa there when we came in. And maybe I'll also find something else there as well, some other plant that will help. Horopito, maybe?'

Neither answered. Both were lying on the bed. Hana was curled against Kahu, who'd started again to shiver.

He fetched his blade and was about to go to the door when he stopped. He came back to the pair and put a hard hand on them, and he spoke again but this time very fast. Into them he sent prayer, but this time it was the rough favourite of Rau's, a terse karakia that he and Van said with bowed but watchful heads in the moments before trade or running fights.

'I'll find something,' he said. 'I'll fix this.'

Eighteen

He couldn't run as fast as he wanted to. It was dark, so he'd made a torch, wrapping a broken door post with remnants of rags and mats from the hut, to aid his search of the bush for medicines. Doused with a mix of oils from Hana's bags and plaited tight, the torch fluttered and flamed as he ran, and he had to both shield it from the wind and keep the flames clear of his face. So in a running and half-sideways hunch he went down the path that led past the bulk of the settlement's huts. As he ran he pictured himself as he'd be seen—as surely he must be seen—from the skyline fence or beyond the lake, or wherever the spies of the Donovan people were watching from: an orangey blazon flickering through the settlement towards its exit. Come out, you Inland fuckers, he thought. Come down from your hiding places and fight us at last, or help.

He closed on the gate and went through it and up the track. Bush closed round him on all sides, and he slowed to allow the torch to halo out. The flames threw maniac shapes. He saw five-finger, taupata. None of the plants he needed. There was a crash behind him, and he swung the torch and a creature was lit up, a possum that bounded across the track, showing its tan underside in the light.

He swung the torch low again. No kawakawa. He went

further up the slope, swearing. How could there be none. It was everywhere else—fucking everywhere. Every day since the swamp he'd seen kawakawa in undergrowth. Each time he'd gone into the bush for a piss he'd landed it on kawakawa, and now he couldn't find any of the stupid stuff.

He went further up the path and still found none. He checked for anyone following him, and when he was sure it was safe he stepped off the track and into the undergrowth. Something shone, and he swung the torch. From a low branch a ruru's eyes stared roundly back.

'Fuck,' he said. 'You scared me.'

The owl whirled and without noise flew up out of sight.

He shuddered.

He pressed on through low bushes and vines, and something cold palmed his hand and he flinched and reared back, and then when he was sure it was not some frightful night creature he shone the light on it. A kawakawa tree of chest height, and another behind it.

A jittery laugh came out. He'd been spooked by the very medicine he sought.

He held the torch to the leaves to check them. They'd been holed by grubs. That meant they were good, and safe. He said the quick karakia of Rau's, and plucked leaves from the plant. He ripped a length of his coat free and laid it flat and filled it with the leaves. As he worked he felt the vast and uncaring dark come down on him from above. But he shut it out. He had these medicine leaves now, and he would give them to Kahu and Hana to chew, and he would source more safe water from somewhere, and somehow he would steep the root, and then he'd find more medicine plants too, better ones, and he'd make the right mix, and then Kahu and Hana and the pēpi would drink it, and they would all be restored.

Careful with the torch, he knotted the leaves inside his wrap, and secured it beneath his clothes and his blade in its rag scabbard. He began to surge back through the bush to the track, and then remembered he had to get kawakawa root. He turned and found the smaller kawakawa that was friend to the larger one he had plucked.

'I'm sorry but I have to pull you up by the roots,' he said.

It was not even knee height but the small tree had a resolute look. It stood behind the larger plant and merged with it, as if they were joined.

'E te rākau,' he said. 'I'm sorry, but I really need you to bring the life back to my family. I need your leaves and roots.'

He held the torch away from himself and lowered his right hand round the base of the trunk and pulled up. The tree swayed towards him, sucked at the earth, and clung fast.

'Come on,' he said. 'I need your roots.'

He couldn't pull it up while still holding the torch. He looked for a safe place to put it. It was burning lower now; only plait and wood were still left. Even as he looked at it the plait separated and fell towards his wrist, a small section breaking off. Immediately he stomped the fallen and burning piece underfoot to kill the flames. Then he found a sturdy piece of exposed root that stood from the forest floor. He angled the torch against the root, and commanded it with a hand. 'Don't burn the forest.'

He went back to the kawakawa. 'Help me, please,' he said. He wrapped both hands round the base of the trunk and yanked back with all his force, throwing his weight against it. The tree sprang free and he toppled back, his arse hitting the ground. Earth and leaf mould showered up and hit his face. But he had it—the tree was uprooted in his hands. He stood and shook it free of soil, and turned it upside down. He had plenty of root there. It would do. He could run with this medicine tree. He'd work out what to do with it.

He lifted the remnant of the torch and angled it down to get it to burn more strongly. He went towards the track with the tree and his wrap of secreted leaves. As he pushed through the undergrowth his mind went to the problem of water, to where on their trail since the saddle camp he'd seen fresh water. He needed to refresh their supply back at the hut. There must have been some mossy pool in the bush or moistened rock. Preoccupied with trying to remember, he tripped and fell forward. As he fell, the torch flashed across his face and he was blinded.

He froze.

In the blast of light from the torch, he'd seen something.

Two figures on the track.

'Stay where you are,' said one of them. A male voice.

He kept his head lowered, blinking to get his sight back. He was at a disadvantage. There were two of them and they had the benefit of height. They were standing above him on the path. He had an uprooted tree in one hand and the torch in the other. To go for his blade would take time, and it would be obvious. His plastic bar wasn't even with him, was still where he'd laid it down in the hut.

'Are you Donovans?' said Van.

'Kāo.'

'All right then.' Van hulked his shoulders to appear bigger than he was. 'Get off the track.'

'No.'

He felt fear grab in his groin and his throat. But he had to go through them. He had to get back. 'I won't ask you again. I'm in a rush. Get off the track.'

'We will not.'

He looked up there. The torch no longer threw enough light. It didn't show their faces, their weapons. But he saw that one of those dim shapes was smaller than the other. He could go through that one, at least. With enough fury he could get through them both. And as he thought on it he felt rage come up, a hot outrage at what had happened to his family in the last days and nights.

'Well,' he said, 'I have warned you.'

He surged up to the track, roaring.

The man shouted something at him but Van didn't hear it. He barged up and onto the path. Once he was there, he went straight for them, swinging out with the torch and the kawakawa tree itself. They held their ground at first but then danced back, and as Van swung the torch and tree in a great arc of light and whooshing leaf-sound, they danced further off. Shouting, he pursued them, giving in at last to the hot feel of furious attack.

The pair retreated further down the track, the man saying, 'Whoa, whoa,' and 'Kāti, kāti,' with one hand out to calm his attacker, the other held gingerly against himself.

Van swung at the man again and connected with nothing, and the torch sputtered up and flamed and threw light. He saw there was no weapon in the hand the man held forward. He saw the strange way the man held his arm.

He ceased his shouting and stood still in the track, panting. 'Kia tau!' said the man. 'Calm down.'

Van held the torch downwards to bring the flame up the remaining wood. He went for a better look.

This time the pair stood still. He moved the flame towards the smaller figure to see. A young woman, her features hidden in headwrap and shadow. He brought the torch across to the man, who held his good hand forward in a wary but useless defence, and something was dawning on Van. The man said, 'Easy, easy,' and Van brought the torch right up close and peered in the face it illuminated. Rag-scarf and headwrap, bites along the brow.

Van dropped the torch, and stepped back. 'Gray,' he said.

Gray paused, and when it was clear Van would not attack him again, he lowered his good hand to support the other. Van saw the arm had two sticks knotted on either side of it. A splint for his smashed wrist.

'We mean you no harm,' said Gray.

Van sagged. Defeat drained him. 'You've followed us. You've been the one following, and watching.'

'Āe.'

Still they hadn't come. The Inlanders. The Donovans. They hadn't come to hear his request and consider it, or even to cut him or cast him out and send them all away. Instead there was only this man, who would simply make things difficult. He would make absurd demands and delay him from getting back to Hana and Kahu. Yet Van had no energy left to fight him or wait it out.

'Please,' he said. 'I have to get back.'

'We've come to trade,' said Gray.

'What for?' said Van. 'What with? I have nothing. I've got nothing left. And this trade's come to nothing. They won't come out, won't trade. The Inlanders. Surely you've seen that. They've only made my family sick.'

'For safety. A safe place.'

'You've got a home, though.'

'No, we haven't,' said Gray. 'Well, we might have had a hut, but it's not safe anymore. If it's not burning already, it's too dangerous. We can't live that close to the Burners.'

Van looked at Gray, putting it together, this new

configuration. Thinking it through, though, was difficult. He faced the earth and felt its seductive pull. For a short time he was washed with such fatigue that it seemed he might pitch onto the track, unconscious.

'We're trading to come with you,' said Gray. 'We want to settle where you settle. When you get the Inlanders' approval, we want it too. That's our trade request.'

'I don't have anyone to trade with, though,' said Van. 'They've gone. They don't care.'

'You've found their settlement,' said Gray. 'We've seen you occupy one of their huts.'

Van's torch sputtered and went out, and the dark rushed for his face, but he barely noticed it. He barely cared. 'So help yourself,' he said. 'It's all poisoned, but help yourself. Grab a handful of poisoned land and poisoned lake. The sick will finish off your kid.'

'You don't know the lake is poisoned,' said Gray. 'I know your family is sick, but that could be anything. It could be shock for their burning home place. It could be from any of your food. It could be from that river your daughter swam in, by the rocks.'

'You watched all that.'

Gray hesitated. 'You broke my wrist.'

'You watched all our private stuff. You sneaky little arsehole.'

'You broke my wrist,' said Gray, louder. 'You broke my wrist, and just when I needed my strength.'

'Get out of my way,' said Van. 'I'm going back to them.'

'We need a home.'

Van's eyes had adjusted now to the lack of torchlight. He was able to see Gray's outline better, the track leading to the gate and the unshaded places beyond. It seemed that dawn wasn't far off. He gripped the dead torch as he would his plastic bar. Dropping the tree to the track, he brought his blade out as well. 'Get out of my way. I'm going through you.'

Gray eased his stance, his rag boots shushing on the track. Manny was somewhere out at the right.

'Gray, it's urgent, and this is a big, dirty, fuck-off knife. Get out of my way.'

'We have medicine.'

He stopped. 'What medicine?'

'Oils. From Matewai. Those oils we traded, back by the fence.'

'Okay then,' said Van, advancing. 'Give me it.'

'It fixed Manny,' said Gray, shuffling backwards. 'She's better now—much better—and it will fix your family. It will fix your daughter, and your new pēpi.' He was talking fast, retreating down the track while Van advanced.

'Where is it?'

Gray put his hand beneath his coat and drew out the plaited-together canisters, and held them up at his side. 'Trade for them, man. Trade for our safe place.'

Van lunged for the plait. 'Give me that.'

But Gray jerked it away, and danced further down the track. 'Trade.'

'Gimme that fucking stuff.'

Van lunged hard this time and was knocked sideways with sudden, stunning force. A hard blow to the neck, followed rapidly with two blows, one to his ear and the other to the hand he held up. He fell sideways off the track, crashing to the ground. He got to his knee and tried to stand but his attacker jumped from the path and kicked him in the throat, blasting him backwards. He landed on his back and gasped, both hands at his chopped throat. Then his attacker knelt on his shoulder and crushed him flat.

'Stop this.'

He gasped, pinned flat on the forest floor.

'Kāti.' It was the young woman. Manny. 'Stop.'

He coughed for air and kicked, and she wouldn't get off him. She gripped his coat and shoved him against the earth, her knuckles grinding in his choking throat.

'Trade.' She shook him with such violence that his head hit the ground, branches, leaves, and then she pushed him flat again. 'Trade,' she said. 'Trade for it.'

He couldn't answer, his choking too urgent.

She released her grip a tiny amount. 'Make a promise. Make a trade.'

With an effort, he nodded.

He felt her weight adjust as she moved her knee. 'You'll trade for a new home for us, on our behalf. You'll barter for a new home with your people, and you'll make sure that we get one.'

Still he choked and coughed.

She shook him again, but with less force this time.

'Okay,' he managed. 'I promise.'

'You're trading for that?'

'Yes. All right. Please get off.'

'You heard him,' she said.

Gray's voice came down from the track. 'I heard him.'

She released him, took her weight off.

For a long time Van lay on his back, coughing and trying to massage the violence from his throat. At last he was able to get to an elbow.

Manny put her hand down to him—he flinched, but it seemed she wanted to help him up. But once she'd gripped him again she held him in place, reminding him of her force. 'Are you calm now?'

'Yes,' he said.

'If I give back your blade, you won't fight?'

'Where is it?' he said. 'I also had a tree of medicine, and a wrap of kawakawa leaves.'

Manny pulled him upright and then went quickly up onto the track. She bent over to search for his things, and shortly had them all. But she didn't hand them down yet.

Van was still off the track, the pair of them above, once more with the advantage.

'We'll come with you to the gate,' said Gray. 'We'll give you two canisters of Matewai's oil there. We're not going through the gate till we are sure we have rights, until you've got them for us. So we'll give you two canisters at the gate and then, when you've traded with the owners and everything is tika, we'll come in and give you the rest of the canisters.'

Van stood still, getting his balance back. His throat felt brutally chopped. The back of his head hurt from where it had been shaken against the earth and branches and tree roots. 'You're a bastard to deal with, Gray.'

'Just keep to your deal, and we'll keep to ours, and both our families will survive this. Now come with us to the gate.'

By the entrance to the Inlanders' camp, where the early dawn began to spill its cold light, Van was able to reorder his coat, restow his blade, and then open his palm for the plait of canisters. All the while Manny loomed in potent readiness at the right.

Gray held up the coil of medicines, pulled four canisters from it, and handed them to Manny. She took her bag off and secreted the canisters deep inside it. Then Gray held the remaining two towards Van, but still didn't let him take them.

Exhausted, Van waited for Gray's next demand. He smelt the blast of Matewai's oils. He hoped Gray wasn't giving him empty canisters, used already by Manny to fight her own sick.

'Remember our trade,' said Gray. 'Remember that you and your two Whaea women are no match for Manny when it comes to a fight.'

Van nodded, cowed on that point. He indicated the gate. 'Can't you come through with me and give me some help? Give me a hand to get some fresh water, at least.'

Gray looked through there, into the Inlanders' camp, and shook his head.

'You don't think we should have gone into the settlement. That's it, isn't it?'

Gray shrugged. 'Kei a koutou, I guess. But I wouldn't have just blundered straight in there.'

Van's mind went back to the empty saddle camp, their hike down, and their first view over the settlement, its gardens and pathways vacant. 'We were desperate. Kahu and Hana were in shock, and exhausted. We had no choice.'

Gray shrugged again. 'I wouldn't have just blundered in, all the same.'

The dawn was spilling its colours now and the way back was well lit, but his return was pained. His throat, legs, the back of his head all hurt from Manny's assault. The upended tree was unwieldy at his side, and it caught wind and blew about. In his fatigue Van's feet didn't coordinate, and just as he passed the main huts he tripped and fell. Splattered on the earth, face down, with his tree and blade around him, he groaned. He lay there, the wind going over.

'Get up,' he said, out loud. 'Take the medicine to them.'

He'd gone only twenty more paces when he passed the hut he'd bashed apart. The rubble of snapped logs and thatch looked bad in the greater light. Demolished. It would be uncomfortable explaining that to the owners of this settlement. But he also took a grim satisfaction from the destruction he'd wrought. They'd hurt his family. He'd hurt them back.

His walk became very slow. He was so sore.

The wind bossed him from the side. It tangled the tree in his legs.

He closed on his family's hut. Purple light was falling on it. No hint of what agonies were taking place inside it.

'Hana,' he said.

He rounded the corner of the building, and stopped.

Four people were standing there. At his arrival they looked up. Two women and two men. Some of them seemed Pākehā and some didn't. The largest of them was a massive man who went to the door of the hut and blocked it.

Van swayed on the spot, stumped by this last obstacle. In his hand was the trunk, roots up. His blade also. The canisters of Matewai's oils were in his belt, along with the wrap of kawakawa leaves.

The visitors eyed him.

Uncut, their faces. High scarves and headwraps. Their coats plain, belted with plait. One of the women had a vast metal chopper at her side, the blade as deep as two handspans.

They all turned towards the woman who seemed to be their leader. She was walking among the mess that Hana and Kahu had made over the last two nights. Her face was twisted with disgust. Walking delicately, she picked her way through Hana's scraps of coat where they lay ripped and discarded, and the sprays of sick and shit.

Van looked wearily to the door. It was blocked by the guard. No expression on the enormous man's face.

The lead woman turned, her lips still pursed. 'So. You are the man who has occupied this house.'

He tried to speak. He tried to shout to the hut—'Hana! Kahu!'—but it came out as little more than a croak.

'What's that you say?'

He massaged his throat, and tried again. 'What have you done to my family?'

'They're fine. They're just as you left them.'

He heard Hana's voice; something indistinct.

'Let me in. I have medicines. They need medicine.'

She surveyed the upended kawakawa in his hand, its roots and dirt. She didn't look convinced by it. 'That can wait. This won't take long.'

'Why can't I fix them first? What can you want that's so urgent?'

'Well, this is our building, so I'll ask the questions, thank you. And if there's to be any more fighting, we'll be doing it.'

He made to swallow, but it was difficult. His throat was still chopped and bruised from Manny's attack.

'Actually, I don't have any questions,' the woman said. 'I know you're anxious for your wife and your child, so I'll go straight to the point.' As if unable to stop herself, she looked again to the mess behind her, her face moving with distaste. *These are dirty people*, she was thinking, Van could see it. *Look at their mess.* And yet these Inlanders had left their entire settlement piled with waste. It didn't make sense. 'We've seen you,' she said. 'We've seen your trespass. We've seen the mess you've made. I'm now going to tell you what will happen from this point.'

'We're related.'

'Oh,' she said. 'How?'

'From the Donovans,' he said. 'I'm descended from the Donovans.'

There was a flicker of recognition, but then it was replaced

288

with her hard, trading face. 'Oh, that line. I'm sorry, I don't know it very well. We are, most of us'—she indicated the group—'from a different line. But we know of it.'

He searched the other faces, but there was no change in them, no sign of new warmth or recognition.

'I'm a Todham, myself,' she said. 'You should call me that, in any discussions you have, from now on.'

'So there's no connection between you and the Donovans,' Van said. 'You are the Inland people, right?'

'We're the people you've been seeking. This is our camp you're defiling.'

'That's a bit strong.'

'Pardon?'

'Well, it's already covered in rubbish. All that mess you left.'

'And why do you think that is, eh? Why do you think we left our waste out?'

He stared at her.

'To keep intruders away, of course. I would have thought that was obvious.' She watched him with her head on one side, as if expecting his reaction to be one of embarrassment. But then she waved the whole subject away. 'Our message is this. You are clearly desperate. You bring sick people. But you can't just barge in here. This is not your home, or your latrine, as you seem to think. You have to ask for entry, and you have to trade, like everybody does.'

'I wanted to,' he said. 'But you weren't here.'

'So you just came in? Helped yourself, I suppose.'

'I'm sorry about that. But my family was exhausted, and shocked. Their home was destroyed yesterday. And my wife got sick.' It was the term Todham had used for Hana; he used it again. 'My wife got poisoned by something here. By your lake, probably.'

'Our lake is not poisoned.'

'So why have you abandoned this camp?'

'We haven't abandoned it. We are very much present. We are in full ownership. I just told you that.'

'So where have you been? Why haven't you helped? I wanted to ask your permission to enter, but I couldn't find you. Not at your saddle camp, not anywhere. And then my wife got upset—got deeply shocked by something—and my daughter too, and I had to find them a place to rest. And I thought that if we camped here you might help us, since we're family. And it was just for one night anyway. And then they both got sick, and I had to keep them alive, and stay with them.' He looked despairingly to the hut. 'And could you please let me in? Let me check on them, and then we can do this properly. We can trade then.'

'You ask why we're not here. Well, we're not here, right now, because we have trade neutrality.' Todham's voice was clipped, as if she was now explaining more than she had planned to, and wanted to be careful how much she revealed. 'We're trade-neutral, so we have retired from this camp. We're aware of movements outside of our borders, and we're aware of the Burners' intentions, and we wish to maintain our security and neutrality. It is strategic, and it is a delicate balance, and we are still in full ownership, and you are not free to barge in here and start shitting and farting in any hut that you like.'

'I was desperate. I needed your help, and I hoped that when you came, we could talk.'

'You were not entitled to this hut. You should never have entered our settlement.'

Van groaned. 'But there's a whole *settlement* coming,' he said. 'A whole settlement of people. The Whaea people. They're all burnt out. You're going to have them all here in two nights, possibly three.'

'And whose fault is that?'

'The Burners. They've burnt them out.'

'I don't think it's their fault. We have no fight with the Burners. We hope to trade with them.'

'Are you serious?'

'And there is this other man too,' said Todham. 'Gray. And his daughter. You brought him with you.'

'Gray isn't with us. He's not with me.'

'He said you would speak for him. He told us you would be his voice.'

'Oh my god. Whatever.' He lifted his hand. 'Look, I don't know what to say to you. I'm sorry. But my family was in terrible shock and I needed shelter for them. And I understand that you're upset, but I don't think you know what's coming behind us. I don't think you've seen what the Burners are like, how desperate they are. If you knew what they're like, you wouldn't be like this. You would be making connections to help you, like this connection with us that we're offering.'

Todham eyed him, the mess of sickness behind her. 'What I know is this,' she said. 'You have to come to us properly. You have to bring them all—your sick and other ones.' She indicated the hut, the ridge above the fence where Gray and Manny must, he supposed, have been camped. 'You have to come to our place and ask us properly, with everyone there, in the open. Like trading people. Like normal people.'

'When?' said Van. 'Now? While they're still sick?'

'Of course not,' said Todham. 'We're not inhuman.'

Van just shook his head. 'Whatever. Can I help my family now?'

Todham seemed about to acquiesce. Then she held a finger

up. 'First, let me be clear. Right now, your family links are one of the few things saving you and those women in there from punishment. Serious punishment—the type that sees you cut at the ankle and groin and neck with blades, and left to bleed, and permanently put to rest. But if you're telling the truth about your ancestors, and you can prove it, then you have a right to stand and trade with us.' She moved a hand, taking in the soiled camp again. 'But if you don't come to see us, and if you continue to occupy our places without seeking proper trade, we will cut you, and we will evict you from this place.'

'Right, I get it—very serious. Now can I get inside?'

Todham pointed to his tree of kawakawa. 'That won't help. You need the bark of young kohekohe for the sick they've got. There's a mix you make—' She mimed water going in, then a stirring motion.

'Can I have some?'

'We didn't bring any.'

'Can you make me some? Or show me how, please?'

She shook her head. 'We weren't mandated to help you in that way.'

He stared. Each one of the Inland people just returned his look, their faces expressionless. 'All right then. So can I at least see my family now?'

Todham gave a sign, and the large man stepped away from the door.

The medicine tree and its leaves scraped on the door poles as Van entered. In the sudden dark he heard Hana's voice before he saw her.

'Vannie,' she said.

He blinked, and made out her figure against the wall. She barely seemed to care he'd been gone so long. She barely seemed to notice that those four strangers were still outside the hut, swapping instructions. She made a great effort to sit up straighter. 'I feel a bit better, Van.'

The tree dropped from his hand. He sagged.

Van looked towards Kahu's corner. Her turned-away shape was still.

'She's sleeping, but she's a bit better too. She drank two mouthfuls of water, and she hasn't sicked it up.' Hana gave a washed-out smile. 'She kept it down, and now she's sleeping.'

The uprooted kawakawa was all over the floor; now that it was inside, the tree seemed larger than it had in the bush. He took out the canisters of oils from inside his coat. 'I've got oils from Gray. They're Matewai medicines. Like Kahu said. They'll fix you up.'

Again Hana barely seemed to notice this. 'It's going away, Van. You've beaten it. You've brought us through.' She gave that same weak smile. 'Nā tō karakia, nē. It saved us—your karakia. Nā tō karakia māua i whakaora.'

His voice choked. 'And the pēpi?'

She put her hands over her middle. 'I'm sure she's still in here. I'm sure she's all right. I can feel her, even though I know she's still too small for that, really. Somehow, I can feel her. You protected her.'

He smiled. His fatigue drained through him, leaking down his legs to his feet and into the ground. 'So she's going to survive.'

'Āe,' said Hana. 'Just like Kahu.'

Nineteen

The work went faster now that they had good tools. The second latrine pit was already waist deep. Working down in the hole with his digging tool, Van was pleased with their progress. In a day's time, the surviving Whaeas would have somewhere to shit safely. Bel and the others would relax a bit then. Water and waste, they kept saying, those aunties—water and waste. If they protected their fresh water source, and separated their tūtae in proper waste pits, then they'd all have better prospects. Better chances against disease. And less risk of enraging the Inlanders while they waited outside their outer fence, huddled in skin shelters and shacks, for permission to enter the vacant camp that Van and Hana and Kahu had blundered into, before Todham and her crew ordered them out.

The first pit Van had attempted, several days ago now, had been a painful rooting in the earth. Using their own hand-blades, and some wooden stakes they'd managed to sharpen, he and Kahu and the tamāhine toa had finished the day with raw knuckles and their faces grimy, and only a pitiful trench under trees to show for their work. Since then Van had traded for better gear. Escorted by Tuku's crew he'd journeyed back to the saddle camp, then down into the valley itself. There he'd found a pinch-faced Valley family who were prepared to barter.

Every single one of his remaining precious pieces, those fine plastic treasures he'd brought all the way from the swamp, had disappeared into that trade. It was massively unfair, but the trade earned him two digging tools with reworked metal blades that could cut through earth and roots, plus a wide tray, also metal, that could be loaded with earth.

And because he'd secured these tools, Van had considerable say over who used them. So now he worked beside Kahu at the face of the new latrine pit, slicing into the earth and flinging it onto the tray to be removed. Kahu was still too weak from her sickness to work like this, really, but every morning she was fierce in her entreaties to be allowed to do her share of the mahi. So Hana and Bel and the others had relented, letting her join Van each morning, where she worked ferociously until she was near collapse and he had to make her stop.

Now as Van dug alongside her, a shape came into his eyeline. He straightened. 'Ata mārie.'

It was Bel, walking down towards the pit. She'd been injured on the journey south, clubbed on the side of the knee in a Valley attack, and Van could see how much it pained her to walk. But she did her best to hide it, disguising her limp with a very slow pace, as if she was always deep in thought, her lips pressed tight together.

She paused now at the pit's entrance. 'He pai tō koutou mahi.'

They looked together over the walls and corners of the pit, now braced with wooden stakes. Then Bel's eye went beyond, to where Kahu still worked.

'Have a rest, Bub,' said Van.

But she didn't stop; if anything, her attack on the pit's depths increased in ferocity.

'Hey, Kahu—kāti!'

Kahu turned, panting. Then she saw Bel. 'Oh, tēnā koe, Whaea. Aroha mai. I didn't see you.'

'Ka pai, he wahine pukumahi koe. But don't exhaust yourself, Kahu. We need you to be strong for the trip.'

Kahu frowned.

Van knew how impatient this sort of talk made her. He indicated the corner where she'd been working. 'We just want to cut that corner out, Whaea, and then all the digging will be finished. Then we'll stop for a kai.'

Bel looked over the rest of the freshly dug pit, and the workers who stood beyond Van and Kahu, piling up dirt and the chopped-off bits of tree roots and ferrying them away. It was Bel herself who'd pushed for these sanitation works. While they camped in this holding place, their shelters and shacks straggling along the edge of the Inlanders' fence, the Whaea survivors were all at great risk of falling sick. Only relentless attention to their fresh water supply and the disposal of their waste and shit, Bel said, would keep them safe. And so Van led the crews digging at the latrine pits each day, and the surviving tamāhine toa ran along a supply chain from the fence camp to the saddle and into the valley, fetching back trusted water under guard, fighting off Valley folk when they were ambushed.

'Ka pai. Good work you two.' She waited for Kahu to return to her digging, then drew Van aside. 'Keep an eye on her, please. We need her well for the trip. And can you please tell her that she doesn't have to make up for anything, just because she was away when the fire came and couldn't help us in the time of our heke. She was māuiui then. We all know that. She doesn't have to prove anything to us.'

He sighed. 'I've told her that, Whaea. Many times. She's just—'

Bel put a hand out. 'I know you'll look after her. It's just that

296

she's so precious, and we nearly lost her.' She gestured at the other workers. 'They all are, of course—they're all precious.'

Van said nothing.

'I'll come past again after kai. See how you're getting on.'

'You don't have to.' He indicated her leg. 'You should give that a rest.'

Bel's face hardened, and she turned, moving slowly up and out of the pit entrance.

'Tuku atu āku mihi ki ngā . . . ngā . . . water workers, please.'

Bel lifted a hand in assent, not bothered by his jumbling of languages. It happened a lot now that he had more of Hana's reo; he'd often start off in her tongue and run out of words or names for things, finishing in his own.

Taking his place at the pit face again, Van swung the overpriced digging tool, cutting the corner out with Kahu. He tried not to be annoyed by what Bel had said. Unspoken in so much of their concern about Kahu—her sickness and recovery, and her still-fragile state—was a rebuke for Van and his role in causing it. *We nearly lost her—because of you. Because you took her straight through that fence into that unsafe camp.* The tool arched up and down, flinging dirt back. Yes, Kahu had fallen sick, but she was alive now, wasn't she? He'd kept her from death, and Hana too. He'd kept them both alive when no one else had been there to help him. He'd kept the pēpi wet.

Not that Hana was fully recovered yet. Each morning she was the focus of much attention by the Whaea healers. Even as Van left for his latrine work in the mornings, they started to come. Already exhausted from their efforts amongst the survivors, they took on a new energy in Hana's shelter. It was the pēpi inside her, Van supposed, that drove them— the miracle of its survival. They said prayers over Hana and rubbed oils into her belly and back. They brought medicines at mealtimes, including the infusion of kohekohe bark that Van had suggested, and applied body paintings in curling designs that told sometimes of her sickness and recovery and sometimes of the further journey that would come as soon as she was well enough. Sometimes this went on well into the night, and Van stayed outside by the cooking fires, helping the ringawera with their tasks, or just staring into the flames beside Kahu, not talking much.

'Van—Van.'

Kahu's voice came to him from a distance.

'Kua mutu,' she said, pointing. 'We've finished.'

He creaked upright, pushing his headwrap back. 'Sorry Bub, I got a bit caught up in it. Time for a kai, eh?'

'I called you, like, five times,' she said. 'I couldn't get you to stop.'

He laughed, then turned to the others. 'All right. Have a kai, everybody.'

Hoisting their tools, too precious to leave at the site, Van and Kahu cleaned them of dirt and came up out of the pit. Threading through the bush, they were soon among the lower trees near the main camp. As he walked, Van felt the shadow of his bad mood with Bel lingering on him. Kahu was in front now, weary from the morning's work but strong in the way she stepped along the track—like Bel, he realised. Determined to send out the right message. Van saw her signal the first group they came to, a loose knot of adults hunched around a shack of branches and fronds. No gesture of the Whaea was returned, no words of greeting. Instead a low thread of prayer came from the oldest of the women, muttering on and on. Someone was dying in there, it seemed, some victim of the fire or the long march that came after.

Kahu and Van went on into the most desperate fringe of the

298

camp, where the late-comers had pitched their shacks. They lived under sticks and fronds here, and whatever else they'd been able to scavenge. Some lucky ones had a torn and grimy coat hung as shelter too. Van even saw a couple of skins draped over one angled roof. The people must have grabbed those from the curing lines before the fires came, and somehow smuggled them all the way down the valley, evading theft. It had been rare, that kind of luck.

Not watching properly, Van almost tripped over the feet of an old woman.

'Ah!' he said. 'Nōku te hē.'

But the old woman didn't look up. Nor did she lift her head when Kahu spoke, sending her the Whaea's love. Supporting herself on one hand, she stared at the blackened arch of her own foot. It was coated with soot and grime from the fire. She'd refused to wash, it seemed. Perhaps she felt that to clean the fire-grime off her legs and feet would dishonour those who'd been lost to the smoke or the horrid journey south.

It was in the first days after Hana and Kahu's sickness had eased—when Van had been able, at last, to follow Todham's instructions and relocate his family outside the fence of the lake camp—that the first survivors arrived. They'd been the luckiest of the Whaea people, those leaders and fighters who got there first. But still their flight from the fire had been so streaked with violence and fear that when they reached the fence of the Inland camp at last and saw Van and Kahu and Hana camped by its entrance, they'd fallen in the dirt and made sounds of grief, cutting their own arms and calling out. Unnumbered others hadn't made it. Mothers and children and old ones lay along the myriad tracks back at their settlement. Trapped by the racing fires, they'd suffocated in the smoke, and been turned to ash.

And even for those who escaped, the evacuation was almost worse. As they'd entered the valley itself, and the scale and shattered nature of the heke became plain to the Valley folk, the fleeing Whaea people were attacked in revenge raids that soon became brazen. Whole Valley families darted at them, slicing and grabbing with hungry faces. Whatever trades, treasures or bits of shelter the Whaeas had been able to rescue were ripped away then. It was in one of these fights that Bel's leg had been bashed by a man so demented with rage that he seemed not to notice her grey and uncovered hair, or to see that she had no possessions left at all.

Now Van and Kahu approached what was always the worst part of their trip back from the latrine pit. Only ten paces from Van's own shelter, Gray had pitched camp with Manny. Van was sure he'd done it purely to remind him of the debt he owed.

But it wasn't Gray who was worst. It was his neighbour, an old Whaea man with a ruined leg. It was burnt in many places, and for some reason the healers had wrapped only parts of it in flax. Perhaps the extent of the damage was too extreme. Open to the dirt and air, the exposed parts of his wound bubbled with swelling and pus. Each day more grits and camp muck adhered to the wound's sticky yellow bits. The man's eyes were also bad. How he'd made it all the way down the valley was too hard for Van to think about. Now, as he always did, the old man bent outside his tiny shelter of taupata branches. The hovel was barely big enough to cover him when he slept in it, but its entrance mud was always swept. He was brushing the dirt now, his hand passing again and again with a handful of raupō reeds over the earth.

'Tēnā koe,' said Kahu.

The man peered up. It was obvious that Kahu was no more than a shape above him. But he reached to her, wanting some sort of contact.

Van looked away, only to see Gray lifting his chin at him. 'How's the shitter going? Will you need me today?'

'All the digging's done. Just the sitting sticks left now, and some more reinforcements. I'll come and get you when you're needed.'

Gray lifted his hand, as if to acknowledge this news of progress, but really to display again the splints on his damaged wrist. 'Ka pai. I'll be ready.'

Van stood before his own shelter, and slumped. He couldn't face it. A gauntlet of healers would be in there, bending over his wife.

'Kahu. Could you—' He made a face. 'I just can't, today.'

But before she could come across, a healer stepped out of the shelter. Then another.

Then Hana stepped up and out. Blinking in the daylight, she looked at Van, then Kahu.

'I'm ready,' she said.

'Are you sure?'

She put a forearm up to shield her eyes. 'So bright! It's a while since I've been out here.' She looked at them both again, and grinned. 'But I'm ready. They've said I'm ready to make the trip. My healers.' Following Van's eye, she put a hand over her belly. 'The pēpi too. She's well, they've said.'

Van nodded. 'It's really happening, then. Tomorrow.'

'Āe. That's all right with you, nē?'

'Of course. I still don't think Bel should come, though.'

'Me neither. But I don't think anyone will be able to stop her.'

Van looked away. It was an unhappy place for the Whaea people, this camp along the lake camp fence, but it had been good for him to work here. He'd been able to lose whole days while digging the pits and helping Kahu. Being useful. Pretending that the trading trip, further inland, and his own speaking role in it, wasn't really going to happen. 'Have we got any of that koha stuff left—from the stores? Not the best water, but the food. The ritual taste we were supposed to give them.'

She shook her head. 'We've got nothing. There's pretty much nothing we can take.'

Once more Van wished he hadn't had to trade away his precious pieces. They would have made a fine present for the Inland people, and proof of how he could work.

'It's going to be all right, though, Van. I can feel it. You're going to do well. You're going to trade us to safety.'

He looked up, and forced a smile. 'You've got faith.'

'Āe. Lots of it.'

'You *are* feeling better, then. That proves it.'

It was a full day and a half of hard walking upriver. The route led up a gully of rocks and bush that closed tight on either side. Shaded by trees, the water they crossed and recrossed startled Van with its cold. How the Inland people had evacuated their entire lake settlement up this track, complete with their belongings and old ones, was unclear. Perhaps they'd made several trips, staging the evacuation over the whole season. Or, more likely, they'd followed some other route, which they'd kept secret in the directions they'd given to Van all those days ago.

He was in the lead with Kahu, but barely spoke to her, his mind preoccupied with the people who waited somewhere upriver. They would be difficult. There'd been so little hint of welcome when he met them, when they set out their demands in front of the hut. He saw again Todham's tight face as she surveyed the mess of sick that Hana and Kahu had made on the ground. *These are dirty people. Disgusting.*

It couldn't have helped that since then the long straggle of Whaea people had arrived at the lake settlement's fence and camped there. But at least they'd stayed outside. They hadn't made Van's mistake of coming inside the camp without permission. *You have to trade*, Todham had said. *You can't just help yourself.*

'But I didn't just barge in,' Van said now. 'I had distraught people. A wife and daughter in shock. I wanted your shelter. I wanted your help.'

'Van,' said Kahu. 'Kei te pai koe?'

He stopped. They were on a flatter stretch of easier walking. It must have lulled him deeper into his own thoughts.

'You haven't said anything for ages,' said Kahu. 'And now you're talking to yourself.'

'Sorry. Just thinking about this trade tomorrow. Are you all right?' He looked down the river, searching for the others. 'We should wait a bit, I suppose.'

'Kāo. I just checked on them. Māmā said to carry on for a while. It hurts Bel to start again once she has stopped, so she'd rather keep going.' She watched him, tracing something in his face. 'You didn't even notice I was gone.'

'Oh god,' he said. 'I'm sorry.' He looked upriver, into the steepening hills. They still had to climb through a low saddle and then further up. The main settlement, they'd been told, was on a plateau hidden beyond the saddle, where the river had its source in the hills.

Kahu eyed him again, wary.

'What is it, Bub?'

'Can I suggest something?'

'Anything that can help me, I'll take it.'

She looked up the river, its endless roiling down rocks and eddies into pools. 'You're worried about your trading speech, aren't you?'

'Āe. Very.'

'It might help to practise out loud. That's what we do.'

'You've had to do this kind of thing before?'

'Just for training. But I've done it, yeah.'

'So you could do this talking job? Instead of me.'

Still looking at the water's movements, she shrugged. 'We're all trained for it. Māmā too.'

'So you should do it then, one of you. It makes no sense to have someone like me try to do it, and muck it up completely, when all you trained people are going to be there and just listening. Instead you guys could do the talking, and do it properly.'

'We haven't been asked, though, have we? You've been asked. It's your job, nē.'

Her face betrayed no subtlety on the matter, no deeper intention. For her it was simple. He'd been asked, so he would be talking. The fact that he was not the most skilled speaker made no difference.

She looked away, uncomfortable under his scrutiny. But she said it again. 'It's just your job, eh. You've just got to do it. Then it's over.'

'Sure,' he said. 'Sure. So we should go through it then.'

They set off again. Hana and Bel and Rerū were still some distance behind, but Kahu shooed him forward.

'Don't let Whaea Bel see that you're checking on her. She hates people fussing about it.'

'I know. But her leg is very bad.'

Kahu lifted her hands. 'Believe me, I know. Don't talk to her about it, though.'

304

He laughed. 'Okay, so let's try this again. First, there's Jacky Donovan and Mary, or Mere, who was his wife.' He hoisted himself up onto a wet rock, and slipped. Arms swinging out, he searched for balance, and failed. Both feet plunged into the cold, and river water invaded his rag boots again. 'Damn it,' he said. 'How many times?'

Light-footed beside him, Kahu leapt onto the rock he'd slipped from, then beyond to the next one. 'Haere tonu,' she said. 'Keep the names going.'

'Mate, I'm in the water.'

'I know. You have to keep the names going, though. That's how you remember.'

'Let me guess,' he said. 'Your training. That's what they told you at your training.'

Her look was sharp.

'I'm joking,' he said.

She just moved her hand. 'Haere tonu.'

'Okay. So it's Jacky Donovan and Mary, and then it goes Artie and Meg, who is the whāngai.'

'Kāo,' said Kahu. 'Auē, you always get that one wrong.'

'Which one?'

'Artie and Annie. You always say Artie and Meg, when it's not that. It goes Jacky Donovan and Mere, then Artie and Annie, and then Maggs, or Meg.'

He watched her stand so easily on the rocks while she explained this tumble of names, her hands making a falling river in the air.

'Yeah, I did get that wrong, didn't I.'

She laughed. 'You always do.'

It was such a good sound, her laughter. It had been so rare. He wondered how much she used to laugh before all this happened, before he'd met her.

'So it goes Artie and Annie,' he said. 'And then Meg, and then Tip, and then Robbie.'

'Āe,' she said. 'See?'

He considered making the same mistake a second time, deliberately, just to make her laugh again. But he thought better of it. He'd learnt not to push it too far. He knew, too, how it weighed on her, the camp they'd left behind back there, those sprawling and unhappy shelters along the fence. It haunted around her mood every day. It frightened him too, and Bel—he knew that. She'd been adamant that no tamāhine toa would travel with their trading party up this river. The need for them was more urgent in camp, Bel said. It was more important for them to continue to fetch water and treat it and dig fresh latrine pits in the bush and fill over the old ones. Water and waste, water and waste. She refused to divert workers from that effort. Only she and Rerū, and the newly recovered Hana and Kahu, plus Van and a single healer, and Manny and Gray, were spared for this journey.

Now Hana and Bel came into view, and Rerū was just visible beyond. Hana was bent towards Bel in listening or a tentative offering of help. Van felt for her. It wouldn't be easy being Bel's travel-mate.

He saw Gray and Manny come up too. All day they'd kept their place at the back, often falling well out of sight. But he had no fears for them. Anyone who felt like targeting that young woman would be trading for a serious fight.

'Have you talked to Manny much?' he said.

Kahu shrugged. 'A bit.'

Hearing her tone, he didn't pursue it. Walking on, he returned to the river of names, reciting them all in his head. He got past his usual stopping place, his pool of error.

'Hey, I had a thought,' he said, still walking. 'If I could find somewhere they'd let me do it, after all this, would you like me to teach you how to work a patching fire?'

'We've already done that,' she said. 'I've learnt it.'

'Really? Plastics?'

'Oh, kāo. We did metals.'

'What sort of work?'

'Lots of stuff. Honing weapons, and—what's that word?' She looked up, searching for it. 'Tempering them.'

'Right,' he said.

'Āe, we've done all that.'

He turned right round. 'Oh yeah? Can you make a kawakawa leaf so fine that people mistake it for the real thing? Holes in the leaf and everything? Veins on the bottom side?'

'Nah. Is that plastic, though, what you're talking about?'

'Āe. Of course.'

'Well,' she said, making a face, her voice going sing-song. *'That's not safe.* Plastics aren't safe, tamariki mā.'

He laughed. 'I'll show you how to do it safely. It's worth it, you know. One kawakawa leaf on good plait is worth, like, heaps in a trade. You could trade some seriously good stuff, when life gets back to normal.'

'Māmā would kill you if she heard you saying that.'

'Nah, I don't reckon she would. Not really.' All the same he looked back there, checking the others weren't in earshot. 'Besides, it's a changing world these days, isn't it. The whole world is new. We've all got to adapt.'

'Oh, I hate that,' said Kahu. 'They keep on saying it. Even Māmā. She says it every day. We've got to adapt. I can't get her to stop saying it.'

Van sat in the long hut, wreathed with nerves. The speaking was due to start any moment, but he had little idea of what the Inland people expected from him. One of the home people had given speaking guidance to Bel, but it had been very simple. Two traders would speak on each side. Van would be first. Bel would be second. The hosts had given no other guidance on what form his trading speech should take, how long he should stand for, or what language to speak in. And none of his own party had been able to help him with extra information. Bel hadn't visited before, and Rerū's intelligence from the tamāhine toa hadn't stretched to these traditions. Perhaps it was a tactic of the Inlanders' trade: it would help them if the first Whaea speaker didn't know what was expected of them, and what was coming next.

'Just mimic what they do,' Hana had said.

'But if I'm first, how can I mimic anything?'

She put a hand on him. 'Just trust that it will be all right. We'll be right there with you.'

'And that doesn't make sense either,' he said. 'If you're there, and you know better how to do this, I just don't see why you shouldn't do it instead of me. They've already said, back at the lake, that they don't give much weight to my family connection, my waters.'

'But Todham said it gave you a right to speak.'

'Yeah, but did you hear the rest of what she said? She wasn't exactly welcoming.'

'But that was just Todham, and she was already upset at us for coming straight in to her camp. I bet some of them will think those hononga are really important.' Hana made a firmer contact on his forearm. 'And stop saying this. Stop fighting it. Just concentrate on the important stuff. Focus on doing what we've asked you to do—what *I've* asked you to do. And concentrate on trusting that you'll do it well. On making this trade successfully for us.'

The long meeting hut was up on stilts, as were many of the other buildings in this settlement. Now Van's heart began to hammer as the Inland people came up the ladder and into the hut. Mostly silent, they lowered to the floor on the opposite side of the room. Ranged along the visitors' wall, Van sat next to Hana, with Kahu right alongside her. Bel and Rerū were on his other flank, and Gray and Manny further down.

Opposite were Todham and what seemed to be her crew: the imposing and dour trio who'd confronted Van at the lake camp. Then a man of about Van's age, and a group of older women and men who sat on mats. They were dressed in coats that were no different from the others: plain and dark with simple belts. But Van judged from the way the latecomers ducked their heads towards them, then found sitting places far from them, that these were the leaders he would have to address and persuade.

At last everyone was seated, and silence gathered along the room. He noticed that there were only three children in the whole group. The quiet stretched on, and his heartbeat throbbed in his face and hands and throat. It made it hard to think about anything, to remember any of the words he wanted to say.

He closed his eyes, and searched for calm. An image came to him of Matewai, the older woman crushing Kahu in her hug all those days ago at her camp.

He opened his eyes to find the people opposite watching him, and flared with fresh panic. Surely they didn't want him to start the whole thing? But then a tūī burst into song in a glossy and rich trill of notes, and a satisfied sigh went through the room. The man of Van's age stood up and brought his hands together. They'd been waiting for this, Van realised, the

309

birdsong outside to start the ceremony.

'Welcome, everyone. A big welcome to all of us—' The man brought his arms apart to encompass the home people on his side of the room, and then Van's group. 'And to our visitors. Nau mai.' He caught Van's eye, and Bel's, and nodded at them both, and seemed satisfied with this. 'Now I'm going to go quickly through some of our process, or at least the parts of it you need to know.'

Van felt awkward under the attention of everyone in the room, but he didn't look away. He nodded firmly to show he understood.

'First, ki te hiahia koutou ki te kōrero i tō koutou ake reo, ka wātea. Ka wātea.' He indicated some of the younger people who sat near him. 'Some of us have an understanding, and at the moment you turn to your language for something serious, and not just in greeting or acknowledgements, they will simply take over the trade.' Then he turned to the other ones, the older ones. 'But I should warn you that we'll trade harder if you do that, because the understanding of some of our elders will not be so good. It's your choice to invite that, you see. It's in your hands.' He turned then to his own people. He put his hands out towards them, facing almost entirely away from the visitors. 'It's a hard trade we make today. A serious trade. But we will trade as we always have. To our advantage.'

He turned to Van's group again. 'Ko Jack tōku ingoa. I'm from the Donovans. Nō reira, kei te mihi atu au ki a koe, e te whanaunga. Tēnā koe.' He lifted his palm at Van. 'Kei a koe te rākau kōrero.'

Van stared. It was over already, Jack's part. He hadn't acknowledged their old ones, their dead. He hadn't addressed the river of ancestors. He hadn't told him anything, really. He'd just sketched out their trading position, and not much else.

But now it was Van's turn, it seemed. All their eyes rested on him.

He got to his feet, his heart blasting harder than before. For a long time, no words came, no phrases. There was just a blank whirling in his mind. He closed his eyes again, searching for calm. Jack had warned him not to use too much of Hana's language, of Rau's. But now with his mind so deafened, the only words that would come were the words that had come from Rau, so many summers ago, when they'd first run together on trades or fights or trapping trips along that swamp-side coast of the Dry Way. Even though some of them might be misremembered, they were the words that had helped him when Hana had nearly died, and they were the words that would help him now.

'E ngā atua,' he said.

'Whakapakaritia te hinengaro

'Whakakahangia ōku ringa

'Hāpaingia te wairua

'Kia tū mārō te tangata nei

'Kia rere tōtika tōku reo

'Kia ora ai te whānau

'Mō ake tonu atu.'

It calmed him to finish this patched-together prayer, but when he looked up the faces opposite him were forbidding, and Todham's was worst of all. He tried not to be spooked. He pushed on.

He hadn't heard any mention of gods on their side, nothing in Jack's talk. But the plain formality of their clothes suggested they honoured something above themselves. 'I acknowledge your gods,' he said. 'I bow my head to them.'

There was no reaction to this.

'I acknowledge your many dead and honoured ones, and I

311

acknowledge our own. I honour them, and we remember them and tangi for them, but I ask them to go. Go to your resting places, old ones, go.'

This part felt purely stolen, stolen from what he'd heard from Hana and her people, and from Matewai and her older ones when he'd been small and they'd been talking or trading in high voices and strangers had sat opposite them at Te Repo at times of great gravity. But there was no other way he knew how to say it. There was no other way that felt right to talk to Ava, who hung about him now, and to Kahu about her Nan, who also hovered with her, and to Hana and Rerū and Bel about the people who hadn't survived their wrenching hīkoi. This was the only polite way to say it, and it was more truly polite to say such things in their own language, even though it wasn't his own, so he did switch to Hana and Kahu's language then, and said it all over in sentences that were similar but weren't the same.

And as he did this his eye caught on an older man who sat next to Todham and supported himself with a stick, even as he sat, holding his head on one side. He seemed to glare at Van as he listened, and to be newly furious with each sentence he heard. But then Todham leaned to murmur something to him, and he glared with equal fury at her, and Van thought it might just have been the effort of listening, that expression. It was just his listening face.

Further along Van saw movement from a young boy who'd come in earlier and been the centre of much fussing. The boy was paying no attention to Van's talking. He was focused on his own game. With great concentration he walked his fingers along the floor log in front of him, and then walked another pair of fingers from the other direction. Having caused them to meet, he set them to a whispered conversation, his mouth moving in exaggerated shapes of words. His head went side to side as he mimicked their talking. Van grinned, buoyed by the boy's lack of attention. 'Now I dive into my family's waters,' he said. 'Let me swim in them briefly. I can swim in them only in the way taught to me by my wife and her whānau. So I may tell you some of this story in her language, and some in my own. That's just how I've remembered it; it's the only way I can do it. So I ask you to bear with me, and to my own whānau I ask you to kindly forgive any hapa I may tuku atu now.'

There was a shift in the room. It seemed he'd taken a wrong turn. But no one stood up. No one shouted him down.

Along the room the boy had been hoisted away from his game and now looked thoroughly bored, trapped there on his father's knee and staring at the wall opposite, no longer mouthing words. This helped Van too. The kid didn't care what Van said or didn't say. Van's eye kept going to the boy as he spoke out loud the river of names, sometimes in his own language and sometimes in the words Hana would say, until the boy's father became awkward with it and Van looked out the wide window instead, where slow smoke rose from the cooking fires among the gardens and stilted huts on the slope opposite, giving up a smell of kai. Even as he talked he hoped those cooking fires were for some kind of after-trade feast. It would be good to eat after this, and to find out what food these Inland whanaunga did well.

'This is the river I have come from,' he said. 'It's the river I've been asked to follow. It's the river that has led me here.'

Jack got to his feet. It seemed he was receiving a signal from further down the room. But it was Van, still standing, whom he addressed. 'We have a tradition that listening traders can interrupt the speaking trader to dispute or correct them.'

'Oh,' said Van. 'Okay.'

'But don't sit down,' said Jack. 'You've got to keep standing.'

Van looked along the people opposite. It was a while before an older woman stood, not from the group that Van had thought were the main traders, but far down the room, beyond the boy. She stood up with difficulty, and once up there motioned some other woman, much younger, to take her arm and stand beside her. It was difficult for Van to see what relation she might have to anyone, or whether she was Pākehā in a way that he was, or how much so. These people looked as joined up and mixed as any other he'd seen, really. They could have swapped places with some of the Whaea people, and no one would have known, except by the clothes and colours they wore, and by what came out of their mouths when they opened them.

She watched Van for a time, altering her stance as she did so, easing some form of pain. 'You've talked about some of our early ones,' she said. 'Liz and them, and all those old ones, and old Mr Donovan, our first one.' She moved a hand to suggest other ancestors as well. 'All them ones.' With the same hand she indicated the people sitting along from her, including the boy and his father and those around him. 'We have a different version of that line, of how it comes down through those names.' She eyed Van again, and moved her hand to show the names coming in a down-flowing river in the air. 'I won't say them all right now; I'll just say that we have a different version.'

'Shit,' said a voice behind Van. It was a moment before he realised it was Gray. 'So he's not whānau with them, after all.'

Van stood there, his face burning. It wasn't clear whether he'd been taught the wrong names or made a mistake in reciting them. He looked at Jack, at Todham, for what the implications might be, but none of them was paying attention to him. They all craned towards the older woman, waiting for what she might say next.

314

She eased her weight again, shoving slightly the woman who supported her. 'So that's our story. That's the way of things, isn't it. Some of you ones might say—' She beckoned at Van down the room, at the women sitting behind and along from him. 'You might say that could be a difference between us, even a raru, maybe. But I don't think it is, really. 'Cause the waters are often like that, nē? And they go back so far that who knows for sure—who knows. Here in this camp, in our place, we're not experts at the waters and names, not like some of your ones are.' She gestured in Bel's direction again, in Rerū's. 'I don't know all the details, probably. But what I do know is that you're a Donovan, boy. I saw it as soon as you walked in here. It's as clear to me as when the birds wake up to bring in the day, and then the day comes.' She lifted a hand. 'So tēnā koe, e tama. Like the boy Jack says, I greet you, cousin. Welcome. Your waters give you the right to stand here, and to trade.'

Van looked along the line of people once more and saw no sign in their faces that this had changed anything. They were listening only to the old woman.

'Course that doesn't mean you'll be good at trade,' she said. 'You might be shit at trading, eh.' She moved this aside with her hand, as if sweeping it to those who took care of such things.

'Now, this is what I wanted to say. My dear old ma knew that Meg one, that Maggs that you mention. She knew Maggs, before she went away.' She moved her hand in that same motion, a gesture to summon up something or to help the story. 'She was a whāngai of course, like you say.' She paused to adjust her weight. 'A hard worker. He ihu oneone, they used to say—the people who lived here first, and who welcomed us when we first came to this place here. We worked together a lot then, our groups and theirs, before we all got our big ideas, and before we crowded them out. But that's another story, which we all know about, eh, whānau.'

She looked over the people near her, and then grinned down the room at Van. 'I'm always on about these old things, eh. They get bored of them, these ones.' She rose and fell, moving on her pain. 'Anyway, those old ones back then, they knew Meg and how she worked, and they called her that—he ihu oneone. A hard worker in the gardens, eh. And Ma said they worked together all the time, her and Meg. And she told me there was this one time they were making kai together. She was only young then, although Maggs was a bit older, as I say.' She indicated the window. 'It would have been just out here, you know. Past where the gardens are now, beyond that big tawa there. They've been moved now, of course, and they haven't been there for a long time now, the gardens.'

Van looked out there where she pointed, and he nodded so everyone could see he was paying attention.

'And Ma, she told me there was this one time they were scraping potatoes together. Maggs and her—you know.' She brought her hands together to suggest this work, jostling the younger woman at her side. 'And she said they had only enough potatoes, that day, for half a potato for all the ones in the family. 'Cause the spuds had started to fail, you see. And this is where the stories in our families take a different turn sometimes. Because I always say it was because we'd got too big with our ideas, and made some mistakes with our planting too, and because we forgot to mind our Ps and Qs, as Ma and them ones used to say.' She smiled at the old expression, repeating it a few times quietly. Then she resumed. 'Anyway the spuds were a real shit, that year, like I said before. And so on this one night I'm talking about the old people came and said there's only half a potato each tonight but scrape them anyway. And so Ma and Maggs did that—they scraped the potatoes. And they ate them too, that night, the people. Half a spud for each person in the family. And then the next day the old ones came and told Ma she didn't need to scrape the potatoes that day, because there weren't any to eat. The spuds had all run out and failed, you see.' She motioned down the hut, suggesting the places beyond where this must have happened. 'They'd put the potatoes in the same plots for too many seasons in a row. They'd made that mistake, you know.'

She looked down the hut at Van, as if to check that he understood, at least, this basic rule. Satisfied somehow by him, by his baffled standing, she nodded to herself. 'Plus that thing about their Ps and Qs. They just forgot their Ps and Qs right across the way. That's what I keep telling these young ones here, and I told my silly husband too, before he passed, and may he rest now. Not that he was much of a one for the gardens.' She moved her pain about, and sank back into the same lopsided stand. 'And so that's the thing I heard about Meg from my ma. She went away, of course, sometime after—Meg, I mean, Maggs. There was no food left, eh, so she went away and we lost that line.'

She leaned a moment longer on her young support, looking into the middle distance, as if remembering all of what she'd been told and had now told others, and then she nodded to herself and got back down.

Van looked to Jack and Todham and the fierce-faced man and his fellow elders to see if there was something in her rambling story that they'd understood that he hadn't. But if there was, they gave no sign of it. They just turned and gazed at him once more, their faces inscrutable.

Jack motioned to Van to continue.

'Do I answer now,' said Van, 'or do I go on?'

'Kei a koe,' said Jack. 'The trade is in your hands.'

His mind a whirl, Van searched for what he could say. 'In that case, tēnā koe e Whaea. Ngā mihi ki a koe. I acknowledge your recognition of me, and your mihi to our shared waters. And I acknowledge that in your whānau, in your story of that river of people—that line, as you call it, from those early ones—there is a difference there. I can only say that this is the river that has been taught to me. It's the story that's been entrusted to me. I've given it as honestly as I can.' He stood there and waited, satisfied at least that he'd found some way to respond.

But no one stood up. No one said anything. The only movement opposite was the shifting of people for better comfort on the logs. He wondered whether this had been a long meeting for them, compared with their normal hui and speechmaking. It couldn't have been comfortable to sit on that floor of wooden logs so long.

'I'll go straight to the trade now,' he said. 'We ask for a place to stay. We ask for a refuge. We want to settle in the camp you have abandoned, even though it is paru with waste right now, and even though it made some of us sick. We want to seek sanctuary there and make it well, because we have nowhere else to go. At this stage we recognise that we can have no other claim to land and waters than those that are paru.' He paced along the logs. 'It is a large request, I know, but it's a good one, for you. You must make this trade. Not only is it upon you. Not only are there people camped right now at your gate, needing help. People I am joined to, that we are all joined to.'

There were a few grumbles along the line opposite him. More people shifted in their places.

But he didn't let himself feel fear. He pushed on. 'That's not a reason for trade, you might say. That's not'—he indicated Jack, then Todham—'something that turns this trade to your advantage. And perhaps it endangers whatever trades you've

318

already made with others. Perhaps this "delicate trade" that Todham told us about is an agreement with the Burners.' He turned to indicate his family, and Bel, and the others. 'The same Burners who burnt out these people. Who evicted them, and caused the deaths of many families. These may be the people you've traded with. Perhaps this is the alliance you've made. Or maybe you just don't want to jeopardise your trade "neutrality" by helping us.' He opened his hands wide, acknowledging the possibility. 'Sure, that's a risk. But let me tell you, whānau, this trade is to your advantage. It is a trade with people who are rich. They're rich in trapping work, in clothing made with thick and double-sewn skins that keep out cold and biters and disease, and that's not to mention their finer coats of muka and possum felt and—I don't know exactly how they make them, but I know they're finer than what anyone can get outside their fence back home. And they're rich in growing forest too, which is also why they're famous across the motu for medicines and healing, because their oils come from within the forest that they protect and grow.'

Todham stood up fast, and addressed her own people. 'This man talks about things that they've *had*. He lists things that have all been burnt now. Burnt things that are no longer any use to us.'

'The people aren't burnt, though,' said Van. 'Their trades might be—their goods—but not the traders and the knowledge they use to make their trades. They still have those skills. That's my point. That's what this trade offers. It offers a connection with traders who can make many things for you, and who can teach you how to make them. And their trading links—up and down the coast and swamp, and into the Scarp as well—they come with them too.'

Todham was undaunted. 'And they camp at our gate with

319

nothing, dirty and without asking,' she said. 'They came right in our gate, in his case, and they sickened our huts and our soils.' Van noticed that she didn't address the elders on their mat but the family of the boy, and the families of the other two children, and the people around them. Perhaps she didn't have the full support of the older ones, or perhaps the whānau with children were the most important to persuade. 'These are not rich people, and they do not show respect.'

It had a strangely calming effect, her attack. It gave Van something to counter with his own talking.

'There's another group I haven't mentioned,' said Van. 'Among the people who are camped *outside* your gate at the lake camp right now are the famous tamāhine toa, whose fighting skills I bet you've all heard about. They are fearless in the defence of their people, and they are highly trained, and there are many of them. And if our waters join more closely than they already are joined, then these fighters will be aligned on your side. They will defend your waters and lands. And shortly another will join their ranks, and she is among the hardest fighters I've known.' He turned to show Manny, who was sitting beside Gray, her arms wrapped tight round her knees. 'I can vouch for her ferocity. I can show you the bruises from my fight with her, if they will persuade you.'

There was a snort behind him from Gray, and a ripple of laughter went through the others too. 'Good one, girl,' said someone, and 'I'd whack him too,' which got a further laugh, and Van lifted a hand to show he didn't mind.

'And you're forgetting the very richest aspect, Todham. Anei.' He turned to indicate Manny again, but this time showed Kahu as well, and then Hana. 'Children. These people are rich in children. They're rich in raising them. They've raised this whole force I just spoke of—this whole force of young women who've grown to full height. The tamāhine toa. And because their forest is so good, and their oils and healers are so powerful, they're rich in pēpi. There is one right here in our group right now, unborn yet, but on her way. A real, live pēpi. This is our joy, in this family, and it could be in yours too, if you join our waters now. Join in with people who are rich in children, who are rich in making them. You all know there is no greater joy than pēpi, than children who grow.'

Now Todham watched him more closely. Her mouth moved as if chewing on something. Then she stood again. 'They also sicken easily, these people.'

Van blinked, surprised. She'd spoken directly at him this time, not in the direction of her own community. 'It's true that my wife and daughter got sick, but that sickness was not normal. It was born of shock and grief and . . . unfamiliar water and surroundings.'

'I know your position is that our lake is sick,' said Todham, 'and that our lake somehow sickened them. But that is proof of nothing. It's proof only that you entered our camp and got sick. You might have brought that sick with you. It might have been from the burning, or from this pēpi you boast about.' She glanced at Jack. He'd leaned to the old man with the furious listening face, and now he nodded as the old man said something to him. It seemed the ground was shifting under Todham. 'And if your position is that our lake is sick, then it's your responsibility to fix it.'

'Eh? What now?'

Todham just glared.

'Anō? Can you say that last part again? I don't think I understood you.'

'Well, I just said that it's not sick, but *you* say it is, and if you say it's sick, then it's your job to fix it. We know it's not sick—we know there's no proof of that—so we're not going to fix it.'

Van stared at her still—he couldn't help it. 'In that case,' he said, 'where are the latrine pits of that camp? Where do they lead to? Don't they lead to your lake? I bet they do. And why were the paths filled with so much crap when you left, and with rats?'

'I told you why. I told you that was to keep you out, boy. It was to keep out intruders. And you ignored it completely.'

'And I accept that that was wrong,' said Van. 'I know we shouldn't have done that.'

But Todham continued to argue with him anyway, as if he hadn't said anything. 'The state of the lake is not up for discussion. It's not up for trade. It will be your responsibility to fix any problem with the lake that you believe you identify.'

'Unbelievable,' said Van. Then he lifted his hands. 'Okay, whatever. But you've reminded me of something.' He pitched his voice to carry beyond Todham to the other people. 'You heard me talk of Matewai in my river story. You know that I come from the swamp originally. And you may know that down there, in the swamp where Matewai and Rau and I and the others live, we have bad water. We have swamp seep, and salt, and we have a river that isn't well, because of a dam that was put across it.' He didn't look behind him, didn't care how this was taken by Hana's group. 'My point is that Matewai knows how to find the best waters, even in a place like that. And she treats those best waters and helps make them safe to drink. In the seasons to come I'd like to bring her to your territories, if we are allowed to remain here, to help in this work. Or perhaps take some of the whānau to be trained by her in those important skills. And that is another connection you are making, of course—direct to Matewai.'

Todham's face didn't change, but both the older man and

Jack had stopped their conversation, their eyes fixing on him.

'I fear that she may be too unwell to travel. They haven't been overly blessed, her Te Repo people, with children and with good health. But I'll bring some of them, at some time. And Matewai's son, Raureti Matewai, will come with his trade and with his kaha. And that is another water you are joining. Another trade. And Rau's trade, and Matewai's trade, I am sure, you will have heard of.'

He stopped. The room was quiet again, and he could think of nothing to fill the silence with, but he didn't panic. His heartbeat was calm now. His mind was blank but not because he was overcome; it was because he couldn't think of anything else he wanted to say. A pīwaiwaka chirped outside, its own oblivious chatter going up and down, and it made him aware that he'd been standing up for a very long time.

Someone coughed, and in a rush he remembered one last point, the final thing he'd planned, on that long walk up the slippery riverbed with Kahu and the others, to say.

But Hana stood before he could continue. Putting a hand on his arm, she began with great kaha to sing. It was a long and dirgeful sound, the like of which he hadn't heard since he was a boy at Te Repo. Rerū stood up beside Hana and helped her sing, and then Bel and Kahu did too.

Standing with them, Van didn't understand all of the song. In fact he caught only a few of those words that sounded so melancholy. For long parts of it he wasn't even listening, and instead was simply grateful that he could stand there without talking or anyone focusing on him. But he recognised, all the same, some of the tūpuna names, and he heard the Whaea's various identities threading in and out.

Rerū sang with a distant fierceness. By the time it was halfway done, tears were running straight down her face. But she didn't pause to wipe them. She just let them course down her cheeks and off her chin, the drips making circles of dark on the logs at her feet. He heard Kahu's voice cracking too as it went above and into the other voices.

Then the song ended and Van was still standing.

He looked along the faces opposite, the boy who'd now turned into his father's chest and was held tight in a hug.

'Make this trade,' he said. 'Make this trade for the land and lake that we can repair, with the skills that we have and the skills we will share with you, and let us bring our riches to it, and to you—to us—to the waters and the whānau that we're all part of.'

'Nō reira—' said Hana, prompting him, because he'd paused to swallow a sudden lump in his throat, and because he'd talked for long enough now anyway.

'Nō reira, e te whānau, ko tēnei tāku mihi ki a koutou—' And he finished in the way that he thought would be acceptable to Hana and Bel, and in their language, because his talk had been for them, because he'd given it on their behalf, and because it seemed many in this room would understand him anyway.

He sat down.

In the quiet that descended he couldn't gauge the success of what he'd done. Clearly he'd taken too long, but apart from that he didn't know. Hana took his hand and squeezed it hard, but that was just because she loved him. She would have squeezed his hand even if he'd made a disaster of the whole thing, even if he'd inflamed these people to fight him.

Todham didn't seem to be in conference with the others. She stood up without seeking counsel from them. But the people looked up at her with care. They fixed on what she had to say. 'We don't see it as abandoned,' she said. 'That land you occupied. The lake camp is not abandoned. I told you that, and

I make that point of clarification again. But hei aha.'

She walked a few paces, then faced him again. 'I've heard your trade. I've heard the advantages you lay down—the advantages you claim will come to us. I've made my objections clear to the people here. But I've also heard the mood of this room, and I've heard the talk of my aunty there. I'm satisfied with what she has told us, and I'm satisfied with what's been said, and I'm satisfied that I've heard what I needed to. And I should greet you as a cousin, too. Tēnā koe.'

Saying nothing more, she sat.

Stunned, Van stared at her.

But Todham gave no sign of cunning or tactics in what she'd done, or in the speed and turning of her position. She gave no sign it was even unusual. She simply looked straight back at him. It was very strange. But perhaps, Van thought, it was just Todham who was unusual. Perhaps she wasn't representative of these people in terms of her personality, despite the speaking rights she seemed to have.

Bel didn't seem so troubled. It made her groan to stand up, but she brushed away the hand that Hana offered to help her stand. She stood by propping on her good knee, and walked a pace or two.

'I'll spare you my kōrero about my waters,' she said. 'I gather you're not too eager to hear that. I've worked out that you're not too keen to hear long speeches.'

A few faces looked Van's way.

He shrugged. He wasn't bothered. He'd done his job, in the way they'd told him to do. His only job now was to sit and listen, and to watch Bel. As she took another step, wincing with pain, he let his mind go to other things, and started to plan for how, at the end of this trading visit, he would get Bel safely back down that river they'd climbed to reach this second camp.

Perhaps he could ask these home people to look after her for a time. Or perhaps they'd give him information about some other travelling route that would be easier.

'And I'll spare you my whole kōrero, in fact,' said Bel.

Van jerked to attention again. Surely Bel wouldn't throw it back to him. Surely he wouldn't have to speak a second time.

But Bel smiled. She turned so she faced the people down the far end of the hall, where the children were. 'I was told to be our second trader. I acknowledge that. But I'm not the right person to do this. Not anymore. My world has gone. My world was the Whaea forest and statue back home in our hills. None of that is there anymore. It's been burnt. Right now, the People in Smoke are moving over the remains of my world. They're planting in its ash. They're planting their settlement on top of our burnt one. They're patrolling our fence, if it still stands, or putting up their own fence, or burning perimeter fires, or whatever their tradition might be.'

She looked towards the long room's end, then up towards the thatch that sheltered them.

'That's a sad kōrero, but it's a real one. It's happened. It's like the river we walked up to get here. I didn't want to walk uphill to reach you, not with this bloody knackered knee. I didn't want that hard climb. But I couldn't turn your river round and make it flow the other way. You can't push water uphill. At least not yet—not now. For the meantime, we can only go where it takes us, nē. Like Van says, this river has brought us here. We've come here in the hope that you'll trade with us for a refuge, a kāinga haumaru, like he says. But it's not good trading sense for me to make this trade. It's not good trading sense for *you* to trade with me. Because I won't be here for long, and you won't be able to hold me to it. I'll be gone by the time anything comes of it. Because, before long, ka hoki au, nē. Ka hoki au ki te ngahere.

I'll be bones. I'll be back in the forest. So you shouldn't trade with me. You should trade with Hana. She is our second trader.'

This time it was Hana who stared. Her whole face a question about this. But Bel simply turned on her bad knee and motioned Hana up. Then she made a series of painful shuffles, easing down to sit on the logs again.

Beside Bel, Rerū wiped her eyes with the same ferocity she had when she sang.

Hana breathed out, shaky at first. Then she put a hand on Kahu's shoulder and another on Van's, and gave them both a strengthening squeeze as she stood. She removed her own coat and held it over her belly and lap and legs, right down to her knees. 'I'll keep this brief. Like Bel, I've seen that you like things to be a little shorter than we're used to. Kei te pai. That's your tikanga, nē.'

She paced a little, still holding her coat over her front.

'Look, we've made mistakes. We've made many mistakes. We've got a history of this. Van knows about it, although he was too kind to dwell on it for long. And I'm ashamed to say that, as you've said, Todham, we've made fresh mistakes. Fresh hurts. We made those mistakes in the pain of our journey here, in the great dark of that fire that we saw at our settlement, that we saw boiling up from your sentry camp at the saddle. We'd come there to your saddle camp to find you and seek permission to enter your territories, but we found no one, and then we saw the smoke and fires, and in the pain and shock of all that we came straight through the gate of your main settlement, seeking rest and sanctuary. Van and I did, and our daughter. We came straight through your main gate, because we had no minds to think with at that point. Our minds were just full of smoke and hurt. And so we came straight in, when we shouldn't have. We should have waited, and asked, but we were seeking you out, because we hadn't found you. We were seeking sanctuary for all the people we knew would follow, and we were searching for some help and some aroha, as well.'

Again she gave that same backwards movement of her hand, a gesture that gathered up Van and Kahu, this time not to absolve but to implicate them. 'Nō mātou te hē. We accept we shouldn't have done that.'

Then she took several steps into the room, closing the distance between her and her listeners. 'But we all heard my tāne. We all heard how well he spoke just now.' She looked along the row of people. 'But he would speak well, wouldn't he? Because there's a pēpi coming, in here, in me, and he has a family here'—with a moving hand behind, she gathered them up again—'and he's in love. He's in love with us, and with me, and with this new pēpi who is sleeping in here right now. This powers him. You can see this. It's what stands him up, and makes him big and strong-speaking, and persuasive when he speaks to you.'

She didn't face Van as she said this, or her own family. Instead she stayed focused on those other people, the families who returned her attention with renewed concentration, their faces and bodies leaning to her, listening. 'We've had other people like him, of course, just as you do now. All healthy and strong places do. There were many like him in our settlement back home. But we had to run from that place, as you know. All my cousins and families, they've all had to run from—' She moved her hands up to suggest the vast and up-flowing pours of smoke. It made something catch in her throat, and for a moment she said nothing more, letting her eyes fill up and spill until she could go on again.

After a time, the listening people murmured words of tautoko and sympathy.

Hana wiped her face, and smiled at them all. 'Well, won't you look at me. I said I would be brief, and here I am rattling on. I'm going on like the worst of us, like old river-mouth here.'

She turned to Van, her wet smile shining at him, and there was more laughter this time.

He grinned too, happy to take it. It had become the joke they could all be included in, and anyway it was so good to see her smile, even this way, and it was good to watch her kōrero. Just like Bel had, but through different methods that were all her own, she was turning them. She was speaking straight to them, tōtika ki te ngākau.

'So that's all we're asking for, really. We're asking for this great thing, this power that Van feels, to be allowed to grow up inside us all again. This thing that Van has inside him now. We're asking for our people to have it again, to feel it unfurling inside them once more. If we get that again, there is no limit to the ways we can help you in return. When we're strong, the energy and skills of my families will amaze you. They'll help you and lift you. And all we need for that to happen is a place to shelter and then stand, and to let our kids run around, and to plant a bit of forest and some vegetables in the whenua we all share.'

'Oh, bugger you, girl,' said Rerū. 'Bugger you.' She was wiping at her eyes. She'd sworn because she was pissed off about having to cry again.

But Hana didn't stop. 'Like Van said, this is our real trade. It's about growing up our forest. It's about joining our waters with yours, and growing our families and our children, and making us all big again.'

She made a motion like the old woman had, her hands moving down the air to show a river coming down and growing fat.

'That's the way we can all get big again, eh. Big like a river gets, when it's in good health. Big with water, and with all the waters that are joined in it. Big with aroha.' She looked along the rows of sitting people, and then she looked into the distance, and Van knew she was searching for the right word in his language. 'Limitless, nē. That's it. Kāore e ārikarika. Not just big with aroha. Limitless with it—because of it. Like a river. Let's be like that again.'

She turned to Kahu and beckoned her up. They stood together and gave out a short song. It made Van's throat choke up to see them standing together in front of him, Hana's arm over the girl's small shoulders.

Then they were finished and they sat down, and Hana took Van's hand again. With his other hand Van wiped at his eyes.

There was a long silence in the room.

It seemed that no one knew how to respond, or wasn't quite ready to.

Then down the end the boy complained to his father. At first his words weren't clear, but the message in them was. He was just so bored.

'Shhh, boy,' said his father.

Then the boy sparked with an idea, and turned right round, but saw the people watching and spoke his question in the kind of kids' whisper that isn't a whisper at all. 'Dad.'

'Shh, boy.'

The father saw them all watching, and tried to smile it away. But the boy pulled at his arm and said, 'Dad, Dad,' and the father saw that everybody wanted to hear what the child had to say. 'Okay, what is it, wee man?'

Again the boy spoke in his loud whisper. 'Can you do your fart sound?'

The laugh erupted first from the boy's own part of the room, and then it went all round. Even the old man with the fierce listening face, who hadn't heard the whisper properly, broke into smiles once he had been told. Even Todham did.

Jack was particularly affected. He bent over, his body shaking with laughter and his hand at his eyes. It was the release of tension that did it. Everyone knew the speeches were over now, or nearly, and the hardest edge of their opposition was gone too. It would be left to the trading leaders from this point; they would go away and sort out, at some later time, all the details.

A chatter started up, and Jack stood and put out a restraining hand. 'So apart from the tama there,' he said, 'does anyone else wish to speak?' He turned to Van. 'Not you, cousin—please no. You've had your say.'

Van joined in the laugh that went along the room.

'Last chance,' said Jack. 'Because otherwise, if no one else speaks up, I think that's us, eh. I think that, like Todham says, we've got a clear mood from the room. So if you don't agree with what's been said, you should say so now.'

It was all impatience now in the people. They got to their knees and gathered coats and their children and old ones.

'Knock it on the head, Jack,' said the old woman. 'The wee boy here needs to go outside and play.'

Immediately, all of the home people stood. Some of their number—Jack and Todham and some of the older ones—offered up their voices in a song. The others simply started to talk to their neighbours and to shake out limbs that had become achy from sitting on wood. The song was quickly lost in their noise.

Then even the song was finished, and Jack came across the room. He went to Kahu first, and then to Manny. Then he went to Hana and Van and Gray, and then to all of them. He shook

331

all of their hands, and passed them on to the elders, who had to fight their way towards the visitors. Showing little of the wary respect they had before the speechmaking, the workers and families simply streamed past on both sides, impatient to get to the ladder and down. They had jobs to do, Van supposed, serving kai or helping old ones.

'Come and have a feed,' said Jack, when all the greetings were done. 'You must be starving.'

Van let the older ones go first, and then he went down the ladder behind Kahu. He didn't rush or panic. Instead he let his feet and hands go slowly from rung to rung, making sure of his grip on each step before going further down. And he wasn't overcome with his fear at any point; he didn't get stuck halfway. Back on solid ground, he found Hana and took her hand. Abruptly she turned and kissed him.

'Oh no,' said Kahu. 'Really, Māmā?'

Jack waited, his face formal again. 'This way.'

They walked towards the hut where they would be eating. It wasn't high on stilts but lifted from the ground by a few steps of bound logs. In twos and threes and with a lot of noise the Inland people were pouring in. It seemed to Van that many more were coming to this feast than had been present in that high room.

'Looks like it's going to be a huge feed,' he said to Hana.

She smiled. Her eyes were still red from what she'd had to say upstairs. 'We should all fill up our bellies,' she said. 'It's going to be a long walk back to camp.'

'That's a good thought.' He watched her closely, wary of her tone.

But then she gripped his hand, and her eyes shone. 'No need to be polite this time, Van. Not like the last feast we had together, back home.'

He laughed. They were in the crowd of people now, pressing

to get to the steps and inside. A song was coming from there, welcoming them in. The words were in his own language, and the names of his new ancestors were among them—Donovan and Jack and Artie, and a string of names he didn't know. And then it went into Hana's language too, and the Whaea was mentioned, followed by names he'd never heard before. It must have been an old song, or one they'd only just made to remember the new and ancient joinings. He tried to see through the crowd to the singers, but the people in front of him were too many.

He was about to cross under the hut's roof pole when his eye caught on the trees above the building and the sky beyond. Clouds had begun to gather there. Weather was crowding along the hills and thickening along the coastline. There'd be rain tomorrow probably, maybe a storm. The survivors at the lake fence would be exposed. But not, he told himself, for much longer. They'd be under thatch in two nights, maybe more. They'd be moving into the huts at the lake camp just as soon as he could finish the details of the trade and return to help get the clean-up underway.

The song was coming stronger now. He heard the run of Donovan names again.

Hana was jostled against him, and he gripped her hand more firmly. Kahu was lost somewhere up ahead in the swarm of people. He and Hana squeezed through the door. They went into the smell of food and bodies, into the song of the people welcoming them and remembering.

Acknowledgements

The Burning River has been many years in the writing. I'm grateful to the people who helped it come together.

I was honoured to work in a collaboration with Aaron Randall on te reo Māori and related content. E hoa, kāore āku kupu. Ka wani kē āu mahi. Thank you for all you did to make the altered, 'patchwork' world of this book deeper and richer.

Ko te reo te taikura o te whakaaro mārama. During the time it took to write this book, my writing was profoundly changed by the effort to learn te reo tuatahi o te whenua, and by the kaiako and ākonga who kindly shared so much with me. Ka rere atu āku mihi ki a koutou katoa. Ngā mihi nui ki a koutou ko Danny Makamaka, ko Rīpeka Ellison, ko Te Hiko Akuhata, ko Purere Winterburn, ko Hine Potae, ko Hōri Mike, ko Alice Patrick. I hope this book reflects some of your influence, even as it suggests the continuing learning journey.

A huge thank you to the team at Victoria University Press: Fergus Barrowman for your encouragement and patience, and for your assistance in funding Aaron Randall's work; Kirsten McDougall; Ashleigh Young; and Craig Gamble. I'm particularly grateful to Jane Parkin for your improvements to the book as editor.

The Burning River was written with the assistance of the Todd New Writer's Bursary, and I'm grateful to the Todd Corporation and Creative New Zealand for that support. Thank you to the Michael King Writers' Centre, where I worked on an emerging writers' residency, and to the Randell Cottage Writers' Trust, who allowed me to use the writing studio while my partner was the resident writer.

Huge thanks to those who provided vital guidance on various drafts: Tina Makereti, Dougal McNeill, Pip Adam, Sarah Bainbridge, Sarah Jane Barnett, Alison Glenny, Lynn Jenner, Bill Nelson, John Summers, and Brian and Robyn Patchett. Again I'm grateful for the example and inspiration of Joao Lung, Gavin MacGibbon, and Laurence Fearnley. Thank you to Rowan Clemerson for the conversations. Breton Dukes, thank you mate, for helping to bring this book through the winter.

Thank you to my friends from the Hansard Office, and especially John Greenlees, Lynlee Earles, and Maria Samuela. He mihi maioha to my friends, as well, the wonderful whānau of the Waitangi Tribunal Unit and Māori Land Court.

Thank you to my parents, Brian and Robyn, and my family, for your continued support.

I'm deeply grateful to my daughters, Kōtuku and Aquila, whose influence is everywhere in this book, but even extended to important advice on character names, birds and animals, and lame elements to avoid. He mihi aroha ki a kōrua, e āku tamāhine.

Finally, to Tina Makereti, this book exists because of you. Without you, it would never have got started, and without your feedback, interventions, and akiaki sessions, it would have disappeared into the dark. Thank you for believing in it, and for believing in me.

Some publications were particularly helpful to me in the writing of *The Burning River*. I'm grateful to their authors.

Crowe, Andrew. *A Field Guide to the Native Edible Plants of New Zealand*. 1st ed. 1981 (Auckland: Penguin, 2014).

Emmott, Stephen. *Ten Billion*. (London: Penguin, 2013). Kindle Edition.

Freinkel, Susan. *Plastic: A Toxic Love Story*. (Melbourne: Text, 2011). Kindle Edition.

McGowan, Rob. *Rongoa Māori: A practical introduction to traditional Māori medicine*. (Rob McGowan: Tauranga, 2009).

Weisman, Alan. *The World Without Us*. 1st ed. 2008 (Great Britain: Random House eBooks, Version 1.0). Kindle Edition.

Williams, PME. *Te Rongoa Māori: Māori Medicine*. 1st ed. 1996 (Auckland: Penguin, 2008).

Excerpts from *The Burning River* have appeared previously in *Sport* and *Overland*. I'm grateful to their editors.